NORTHERN ROULETTE

B BASKERVILLE

HYEM BOOKS

DURHAM COUNTY COUNCIL LIBRARIES,LEARNING & CULTURE	
C0 1 76 84291 78	
Askews & Holts	

- CHAPTER 1 -

LIKE MOST THINGS, THE gym was better after dark. With the television unplugged, the music switched off, and the guests safely tucked up in bed, the gym became a different entity. He preferred it that way: quiet. Not that the guests used the gym all that much. Most of them came here to attend snooty, exclusive weddings or to hike up to the fairy pools, returning in the evening to bathe before feasting on venison and wild Scottish salmon.

Quiet, save for the rhythmic sounds of his feet hitting the rubber belt of the treadmill and the cadence of his breath increasing until he couldn't take another step.

He hit the red button marked *stop*, and the belt slowed to a crawl. Though management called it a gym, it was smaller than most of the guest rooms. Windowless, the room was usually illuminated by harsh fluorescent lighting that bounced off the mirrored wall and stacks of chrome-coated dumbbells. Tonight, he worked out using only the lights from the machines and the green glow of an emergency exit sign that hung above the door. Someone had the bright idea of squeezing a treadmill, a cross-trainer and a rowing machine into the limited space. Anyone wanting to dismount from the cross-trainer had to step on the treadmill, though it hardly mattered; the cross-trainer hadn't worked in months.

A water cooler in the corner bubbled next to a pile of cone-shaped paper cups. Management had watched one too many episodes of Blue Planet and had, bit-by-bit, started a war on plastic. Paper cups? Had you ever heard of anything as useless? Chocolate fireguard, anyone? No more taking a sip here and there between sets. Now you had to drink before the cup blooming disintegrated.

The treadmill came to a stop and he hunched over the control panel, taking deep gulps of cold air. Sweat chilled his skin almost as soon as he stopped running, and he had to slap his hands against his arms to stay warm.

In front of a mirrored wall, two stacks of weights reminded him of miniature metal Christmas trees. The girlie one started with dumbbells that weighed less than a kilogram – utterly pointless. He'd caught rats that weighed more than those. Each set below increased in weight, with the bottom pair tipping the scales at five kilos. Still pretty pathetic now he thought about it.

He'd long since stopped using the girlie weights. He used to be a scrawny little shit, all chicken legs and arms like cotton buds. They used to call him

Twiggy, like that model in the sixties. The one with the long lashes and short hair. It was insulting having the same nickname as a lass. And a skinny one at that. Not that he could do anything about it back then. What was he going to do? Tell them not to call him that? That would only make it worse. Fight them? He didn't think so. He'd been the smallest one by far. Underfed and underdeveloped.

Not now.

He ran a hand over the sets of dumbbells, feeling the smooth surface of each one in turn. He made his selection, choosing a hefty pair polished to a mirror finish, and stepped back onto some rubber matting. He completed his reps and lowered the set of heavy weights to the floor, embracing the thudding sound as metal hit rubber. Sixteen kilos each. Thirty-two kilos a pair. Most people couldn't curl that weight. He could. He'd worked up to it day by day since he started here. Since the day he decided he wanted to start afresh. New job, new town, new friends, new body.

New life.

He removed his sweat-soaked t-shirt and admired his torso in the mirror. He'd grown so much. His arms were firm, swollen from the effort of his last repetitions. Veins protruded out of his biceps, and sweat pooled in the crooks of his elbows. He straightened his arm and watched droplets of salty liquid trickle down thick forearms before dripping from his fingertips. His pectorals glistened under the eerie green light; the patch of dark hair between them only served to make them look bigger.

Twiggy was no more.

3

He was twice the man he used to be, and while he savoured looking at his reflection and acknowledging the fruits of his labour, he never used the mirror to look at his face.

He couldn't look himself in the eye.

Not yet.

A few more sets and his workout would be finished for the day. Running and arms today; rowing and legs tomorrow. A mesh-patterned grip helped stop the dumbbells from slipping, but it didn't feel rough against his skin. He'd lifted so much over the years that his palms had callused over; he was as proud of the calluses as he was his muscles. It was all part of the same transformation.

Grunt followed curl as he lifted the weight from his thighs to his shoulders. Again. And again.

He returned the weights to the rack of heavier weights and used his t-shirt to wipe down the bench. He'd clean it properly in the morning, disinfect it with Dettol and freshly-laundered cloths. The clock on the wall told him it was close to midnight. He could get five hours of sleep if he showered quickly and went straight to bed. He had to be back here to clean and open up by six. Then he had groundskeeping work to crack on with before more guests checked in at noon. He was usually the one tasked with helping them carry their luggage to their rooms. He massaged his arms where the bicep tendons attached to the radii and hoped tomorrow's visitors hadn't over-packed.

Leaving the gym, he glanced at a rack of newspapers. Reading sometimes helped him sleep, but he wasn't into novels. Romance was for bored housewives, and horror was for weirdos who liked vampires and crap like that. A tatty copy of the Guardian topped the pile, but he wasn't one for the broadsheets; they were poncey and elitist, and if he was honest, he couldn't understand half of it.

Telegraph? Nah.

Financial Times? He'd rather read the back of a shampoo bottle.

That'll do, he thought, picking up yesterday's Daily Mail. He didn't always agree with their politics, but the articles were short and punchy. He liked that.

Showered, teeth brushed, and bladder emptied, he clambered wearily into bed. His room was bare. It was better that way – less dusting. He didn't need photos of loved ones, trinkets, pointless ornaments, or wooden letters that spelled out *home* or *peace*. What was the point of those? To trick yourself into feeling at home or feeling more at peace? Read it enough times and you might believe it? He didn't think so.

He flicked the switches by the bed, turning the ceiling light off and the bedside light on. A headline in thick black letters said something about the Queen's Birthday Honours List. The perfect mix of celebrities who thought they were social champions and Joe-publics who'd done this, that or the other for some cause that only mattered to them. It was bound to put him to sleep.

Giles Crouch for services to the NHS... Alba Kavanagh – *hmm, she's a looker* – for services to the community... Glenn Kennedy for services to business and the economy. *Boring.*

His eyes became heavy as the paper lulled him to sleep. After that workout, he'd sleep well, wake up famished and enjoy bacon, eggs and black pudding for breakfast before starting his shift. The thought of one of Stacey's breakfasts warmed him, and he was about to drift off to dreams of golden yolks and crispy bacon when something made his eyes pop wide. He sat up, pushing the paper under the bedside lamp, feeling his heart hammer against in chest like it had when he ran on the treadmill.

Like it had earlier in his life.

He wasn't a big strong man anymore. He was a little boy with sticks for legs and no one to turn to. He was scared.

His eyes fixated on a name. One he hadn't been reminded of in a long time. One he'd hoped would never pollute his mind again.

For services to...

He swallowed his fear and, in a moment of frenetic madness, tore the paper to shreds. Like a terrier that had hold of a rat, he shook and ripped at it until newspaper confetti rained down upon his bed.

No. This would not do.

It would not do at all.

- CHAPTER 2 -

Three weeks later.

DETECTIVE SERGEANT JACK "TENNESSEE" Daniel made his way to the stage. Sweat made his curly hair claggy with salt, and his thighs burned with lactic acid. He and his colleagues – DCI Erica Cooper and DS Paula Keaton – had just finished a charity relay triathlon: Northumbria Police versus Tyne and Wear Fire and Rescue. Cooper went first, completing the open water swim, followed by Tennessee, who tackled the cycling leg from Tynemouth to neighbouring Whitley Bay and back. He handed over to Keaton, the true athlete of the team, who sprinted the final section along Longsands beach. He and Cooper kept the team in contention; Keaton powered them into second place.

It was a bright, beautiful day, and barefoot families enjoying a day at the coast had packed the award-winning stretch of sand. Now that the race was over, children went back to their ice creams and admired the entries in the sandcastle competition.

Tennessee pulled at the hem on the left leg of his cycling shorts, levelling it with the right. A group of yummy mummies had gathered by the stage and had just finished eyeing up the team of firefighters who'd come third. As soon as they clocked Tennessee, their eyebrows began wiggling. The bright pink lycra had seemed like a good idea at the time, and while it was a sunny day in North Tyneside, it was still chilly. The lycra left nothing, and he meant *nothing*, to the imagination.

Hashtag Me Too, Tennessee thought to himself as he jumped up and shook hands with Commissioner Begum and Chief Fire Officer Spence. He'd looked forward to this event for weeks. The idea of competing for a good cause had fuelled him and Keaton through an arduous double murder investigation. When they'd convinced Cooper to join their team, he felt like he'd hit the jackpot; it wouldn't have been right having anyone else from the squad, and he knew she needed the distraction.

The news about Cooper's father's heart attack had come at the tail end of the investigation. Her flight may have been booked for tomorrow morning, but the look on his chief's face when she'd been handed a phone told him everything he needed to know: Ben Cooper had died before she'd been able to say goodbye.

It was with a heavy heart that Tennessee accepted the large silver trophy. He'd swap it for Ben Cooper's life in a heartbeat. As the mummies nudged each other and a boy mercilessly kicked over the entries in the sandcastle competition, Tennessee could hear the desperate sobs of his grieving boss and her daughter.

"Erm... Yeah... I'd like to thank everyone for coming out to... erm, support this event," he said, taking the mic. Unaccustomed to public speaking, Tennessee's words were peppered with stutters and hesitation. "Thanks to Superintendent Nixon for asking me to enter a team on behalf of CID. And... yeah, thanks to Hayley, Pat and Alfie," he added, naming his wife, mother-in-law and young son. This wasn't exactly the motivating and rousing speech he'd come up with while powering his bike along the A193 – known locally as The Links. Not that it mattered, no one was listening to the young DS. Not when they could earwig on Cooper crying to her bereaved mother over the phone.

"Yeah... Cheers and erm, congratulations to the winners."

Tennessee jumped back off the stage, landing softly with knees bent. The trophy felt heavy in his hand, and he didn't quite know what to do with it. Cooper wouldn't want it. It would forever be a reminder of Ben Cooper's death – he'd give it to Keaton. The former full-back probably had a trophy cabinet at home. Heck, she probably had a trophy room. Grabbing the trophy by one of its silver handles, Tennessee let out a long sigh. He was a fixer. He shouldered family pressures, made sacrifices for those he cared for, and tried to do right by the team at CID, but he didn't know how to fix this. What could he say to Cooper? *I'm sorry for your loss?* Five words he'd had to say too many times since he started working for the police. Cooper didn't deserve the same five words he gave to everyone else.

Tennessee didn't have time to think of something more personalised. As he took two steps towards his team and family, a scream reverberated down Longsands. It was a panicked shriek that came in short sharp bursts before releasing into an almighty squeal of fear and horror.

The young boy who'd been kicking over sandcastles staggered backwards, his arm outstretched and pointing to what had been a sand sculpture of a giant snake. He continued screaming until a woman raced to hold him. She, in turn, began to shriek when she saw what had frightened him.

Tennessee's training meant he didn't jump to conclusions; he didn't trust anything until he'd thoroughly examined it. Still, there were certain things Tennessee knew instantly. Certain sights, sounds or smells that didn't leave a trace of doubt.

Poking out of the sandy tumulus was something pale, bloated and mottled with hypostasis. Tennessee was looking at a human arm.

- CHAPTER 3 -

MURDER VICTIMS WEREN'T USUALLY found this way. Typically, they were found in the early hours by dog walkers. The only demographic to be out twice a day, every day, regardless of the weather. Dog walkers frequent hedgerows, woodlands, and secluded country lanes. They know the land and know when something is out of place. Their furry companions have a sense of smell forty times greater than that of their owners, and because of neophilia – an attraction to new sensations – the dogs are drawn to different scents in the undergrowth. If something is decaying in a shallow grave, the beloved pet who licks their master's face, shares their bed, and steals their favourite biscuits is the one who'll sniff it out.

Not on this day.

This body wasn't found by a lone gentleman and an enthusiastic spaniel. It wasn't found in the early hours, in the dark shadows, with no one else around. This poor soul was discovered on a busy beach, to the sounds of a steel band playing calypso tunes and spectators cheering on runners as they crossed the finish line.

"What's going on?" Copper asked.

Hayley Daniel passed her young son to her mother and wrapped an arm around Cooper as she escorted her off the beach. Behind her, Cooper's teenage daughter was comforted by her boyfriend. Josh moved to kiss Tina on the head, but she pulled away. In times of stress, she hated physical contact. Sometimes she could be the polar opposite of Cooper, who could be made to feel better with a simple hug or touch of a hand.

The Daniels' people carrier was parked on a steep incline that carved a route down to the beach. Hayley pulled a key fob from her pocket and opened the car remotely. Pat, her mother, wasted no time in securing baby Alfie into his car seat. She soothed his restless cries with cooing noises, then ushered Cooper and Tina into the back seat.

Josh's face clouded when he realised there was no room for him in the car. "I'll see you back at yours, T. I'll bring... I don't know... I'll bring something."

The poor lad was trying, thought Cooper. That was all any of them could do. Still, she was distracted from her own pain by scenes of utter chaos.

"Seriously, what's going on? she asked again. "I heard screaming."

"Don't worry about that," Hayley said in a baby voice because she was patting Alfie on the belly with one hand while starting the engine and checking her seatbelt with the other.

As she turned the key in the ignition, the radio switched on, tuning in to a local station. A jingle advertising a funeral director began to play at full volume. Hayley's hand flew to the off button with lightning speed.

"Sorry," she said, looking at Cooper in the rearview mirror. "Look, we'll get you two back to your place, get the kettle on and help you with anything you need." She turned to look over her shoulder. "I'm so sorry, Erica."

Cooper didn't want a cup of tea, and she definitely didn't want company; she wanted to be with her grieving mother. She looked at the mobile phone she clutched in her hand and realised her fingernails were blue with cold. Cooper pulled her thick dressing gown tighter around her. Only minutes before the news of her father's death, she'd been swimming in the unforgiving North Sea. Other than the dressing gown, she wore only her swimsuit. Cold water dripped down her goosebump-covered legs and dampened the car mats beneath her feet.

As Hayley forced a reluctant gearstick into reverse and began to edge out of the parking space, Cooper looked past Tina to the expanse of golden sand that ran through Tynemouth. There were tens, possibly hundreds of people crowded around one of the sandcastles. People ran across the sand for a closer look; others jostled their way through the human wall to get the centre. Amid the madness, a streak of pink lycra that Cooper presumed to be Tennessee was pointing in all directions to a smaller group gathered around him.

Northumbria Police and Tyne and Wear Fire and Rescue were suddenly in a joint effort to clear the immediate area. Tennessee's first concern was to preserve the scene, which meant escorting the rubberneckers from the vicinity. He gathered the nearest members of the emergency services and began to dish out instructions.

"Get everyone back," he called. "Don't let anyone touch anything." Though, as he said it, it seemed like an impossible task. The beach was heaving with all manner of folk. While some were getting out of there as fast as they could, others clearly revelled in the bedlam. Clearing the area was going to be like herding cats.

Still exhausted from the triathlon, the competitors were quickly renewed with adrenaline and a sense of purpose; their training kicked in despite the unusual circumstances.

"Get them off the beach," he said over the commotion. "I want names, as many as you can. Find a way to record who's here. We'll need as many witnesses as we can."

As well as patrol officers and firefighters, Tennessee had gathered a group that included the drug squad, the K9 unit, and armed response. All of them suddenly thrust back into the line of duty after an enjoyable morning doing their bit for a local charity. Despite the volume of emergency services at his disposal, Tennessee was well aware only two teams in the race had included members of CID. Now that DCI Cooper has been taken home, that left he and Paula Keaton – a fellow DS – as the likely candidates to take the lead. He caught her eye, and they exchanged a look they both knew and understood.

Looks like we're in charge.

The mother of the naughty boy who'd discovered the body ran up to DC Elliot Whyte and grabbed him by the lapels of his navy dressing gown. Like Cooper, Whyte had taken on the swimming leg of the triathlon, and as the woman grabbed him, his dressing gown came loose, exposing a chest of dark wiry hair.

"Phone the police," she gasped. "Someone phone the police!"

Whyte freed himself and fastened the towelling fabric back around him. "Ma'am, I am the police. You're surrounded by police." He turned his eyes to Tennessee. "Where do you want me, Jack?"

"Take her and her son to the café." He nodded towards Crusoe's, a castaway themed eatery at the southern end of the beach. "They're bound to have a pad of paper you can use. Start taking her statement."

Whyte signalled his assent and guided the mother and son towards a roped-off deck. Under different circumstances, Tennessee, Keaton and Cooper would have been sat on the deck, drinking refreshing pints in celebration by now.

"You. Sorry, what's your name?" Tennessee asked a young female police officer. "PC Gibson? I know you're tired, but can you run up to the Grand Hotel? We'll need stationery. As much as you can get your hands on. Give them a heads up that we'll be needing their CCTV as well."

The PC didn't hesitate. She jogged uphill, calling another officer to follow her to her stately Victorian building. Keaton had managed to form a perimeter around the snake-shaped sandcastle. She'd gathered cones and tape that had been used to mark the start and finish lines of the three elements to the triathlon to create a cordon. It would do until someone arrived with official blue and white tape marked *police line do not cross*.

A man moved closer to take a photo with his mobile. Keaton folded her arms over her broad chest and strode towards him, clearly unimpressed with his lack of respect for the deceased. The man took one look at Keaton's stern face and formidable build, tucked his phone away and left the scene.

Minutes ago, Superintendent Howard Nixon had handed out trophies to the teams in bronze, silver and gold positions. He was now apoplectic as he growled down his phone, demanding as much manpower as they could spare to process all the witnesses. When he was done, a nervous Tennessee asked to borrow Nixon's phone. His own mobile was in Hayley's handbag as his lycra outfit lacked pockets.

Dialling Byker Police Station, Tennessee asked to be put through to Rebecca Hogg's team. "Becky, did you hear? Yeah, crazy. Listen, do me a favour and set up a website where the public can submit photos and video footage they've taken today. We might catch something suspicious. Cheers, Becky."

Experience had taught Tennessee that killers often wanted to witness the aftermath of their crimes, to revel in the pain and confusion that followed. Hanging up, he knew there was a significant chance that the person or persons responsible would be in one of the photos. Heck, they could still be on the beach right now. A shiver ran down his spine. With a feeling that he was being watched, he looked about the scene. Was anyone staring back at him? Was anyone showing an unnatural fascination with what was going on? The back of his neck prickled. He shook the feeling away by turning his attention to Oliver Martin and Saffron Boyd, young detectives who'd worked with him during the Blackburn case.

"Martin, Boyd, good work clearing the masses. We're going to need those cars moved from the bank." He pointed up towards where Hayley had been parked. "The pathologist and SOCO will be here any minute. They'll need access."

"Consider it done," said Martin. He was still out of breath from the cycle ride to Whitley Bay and back.

Boyd led the way but not before Tennessee had clocked the look on her face. This had caught her off guard; she looked shaken. He couldn't blame her.

Howard Nixon checked his watch. He'd made the call over five minutes ago; the help he'd ordered should be here in thirty seconds. He angled his head away from the gentle waves of the North Sea and strained for the sound of sirens. His hearing wasn't what it was. He'd likely see the flashing blue before he heard the warning tone.

He wasn't supposed to have favourites, and yet he somehow had a soft spot for Cooper. She stood her ground with him and wasn't afraid to call him out when he used terms the youngsters considered offensive. Terms he regarded as harmless fun. Truth be told, she could be a right pain in the arse. Still, he didn't like seeing her in so much pain.

Nixon had approved the DCI's leave. He knew her father had taken ill rather quickly, and he didn't need to call on his many years of police training to put two and two together. She'd missed her chance to say goodbye, just as he'd been too late to say goodbye to his dear wife. He felt saddened by the memory, then put it aside.

From his elevated position on the stage, Nixon had a decent view of everything around him. It was chaos, but it was organised chaos. Young Jack Daniel and that Keaton woman – who for some reason put the fear of God into him – had taken command. It was admirable. They had taken units from all walks of the services and formed them into a cohesive unit: a team of teams. Perhaps Cooper's trusted detective sergeants were ready to move up the ladder.

-CHAPTER 4-

"CAN'T A GIRL HAVE a Saturday off once in a while?"

Margot Swanson was the sort of older woman who ate impressionable young men for breakfast. She was a curvy-bodied, curly-haired unapologetic flirt, and she was one of the best pathologists in the north. Tennessee made a point of never being left alone in a room with her.

Uniformed officers had arrived ten minutes before Margot. They closed the beach and set up inner and outer cordons. A male officer in his thirties was appointed scene manager. Tennessee had already made a note of all the police and fire officers who were present using the stationery they borrowed from the hotel. The scene manager took the list and began transferring their names to the official logbook. Margot showed him her ID, pulled on a forensic suit and tied her wild hair back into a chignon. Next, she unfolded the legs of a pop-up table and rolled out some plastic sheeting. She muttered to herself that any efforts to keep sand off the body while she worked would be like shutting the stable door after the horse had bolted.

Tennessee spotted the van used by the scene of crime officers as it forced its way through traffic on Grand Parade. They were admitted through the outer cordon and parked on the ramp leading down to the beach. Justin Atkinson and the other scene of crime officers exited the vehicle, signed in and began laying boards and erecting tents. Once the sandcastle and the body that lay within were hidden behind white plastic, the crowds gathered on Grande Parade began to thin. A crime scene hidden by a tent was far less interesting than a crime scene out in the open.

Tennessee took long strides as he went to greet Atkinson. He was a tall man, as tall as Tennessee, but he was thinner, and his wisdom showed through peppery hair and lines around his eyes. Despite the wrinkles, his eyes sparkled behind rimless glasses. They shook hands, then Atkinson pulled on nitrile gloves.

"Don't feel pressured to watch," Atkinson told Tennessee.

Tennessee didn't have an iron stomach, so he stepped back and let his eyes wander around the roof of the tent while Atkinson sifted away the top layers of sand. So far, he'd only seen the arm, and Tennessee wondered if they were only dealing with a severed limb. Of course, if they moved all the sand and only found an arm, it would raise a whole host of new questions. *Where was the rest of him? Or her?*

He glanced.

A shoulder, a chest, a head. It was a full body.

Atkinson, his assistant – Hong Evanstad – and Margot carefully lifted the deceased onto plastic sheeting to take a closer look.

Margot confirmed death, then swept the victim's hair from her face. "Female. Mid-to-late sixties would be my first estimate."

Atkinson straightened up and rubbed his back. He took a look around, paused, then scanned again.

"Isn't Erica here? I thought she was competing today."

"She was," Tennessee said. He tipped his head towards the doorway to the tent, and Atkinson followed him out into the sunshine.

"Cooper got some bad news after her swim."

His face saddened. "Her father?"

Tennessee nodded. "There were complications during surgery; they triggered another heart attack. He didn't make it."

Atkinson pulled off his gloves and brought a hand to his face. "Poor woman's been through so much."

"If you need to go," Tennessee started.

The tall man shook his head. "No. My duty's here. But Erica's not alone, is she? What about Tina?"

"My wife's with them. My mother-in-law too."

Atkinson's Adam's apple bounced as he swallowed. They had history – Atkinson and Cooper – Tennessee didn't know where they currently stood with each other, but the pair were close. Always had been. He sighed deeply before speaking. "I've started. I'll finish."

A mentality shared between SOCO, CID and Magnus Magnusson.

Back in the sweltering heat of the tent, Tennessee heard Hong say, "She's fresh."

He and Atkinson readied themselves to return to work with an emptiness in their chests.

"I agree." Margot tilted her head and made some notes. "I'd say the time of death was twelve to sixteen hours ago. I'll know more when I can examine her properly." She removed her gloves, picked up her phone and dialled the morgue. "Peter, dear. Who or what is scheduled for tomorrow morning ?... Okay, move that to Monday; Frida won't mind... Yes, I'll be in early tomorrow to take a look at this one. Eight a.m. sharp. Oh, and a coffee – black, one sugar – wouldn't go amiss."

Margot put her phone away and looked down at the unfortunate woman lying on the plastic. She had a full figure and warm brown hair with white roots. Though the blood had drained from her face, it was clear she had a tan. Red polish adorned her fingernails and a loose-fitting black dress, now damp from the wet sand that had been formed around her, clung to her torso.

Turning her large eyes towards Tennessee, Margot formed her lips into a pout. "A Sunday morning post-mortem? Just what every girl dreams of. Tony and I were supposed to be heading to the lakes for a romantic night away. In fact, I got the call just I was lifting my overnight bag into the boot of his car." She placed a hand on Tennessee's shoulder and slowly looked the lycra-clad detective up and down. "You owe me a dirty weekend, Detective Daniel."

- CHAPTER 5 -

ELLIOTT WHYTE AND SAFFRON Boyd were the first to return to HQ. They set up an incident room and typed the first entries into HOLMES2. Next on the agenda was to liaise with Missing Persons to see if anyone matching the victim's description had been reported missing. *Who was she?* Only one person matched the basic description Tennessee had sent through to them: Clara Rosewood, missing for three years. Whyte printed a photograph of the missing woman and handed it to Tennessee.

"No," he said, handing the picture back to Whyte. "It's not her."

The door to the incident room squeaked as Paula Keaton entered. "Right, gather round, peeps," she announced. "Granted, we all know we should be in the pub right about now, but we're not, so let's get on with it. First thing's first, has anyone heard from Coop?"

Tennessee waved a blue ballpoint in the air. "Hayley messaged me. They're all at Cooper's house. She's not good," he said.

"I'll swing by when we're done here," said Keaton.

"*If* we're done here. Where are we with the list of witnesses?"

Keaton sat on the edge of a table and rolled her eyes. "So far, I have over five hundred names on my list. And that's just the people who were on the beach at the time the body was discovered."

"Bloody hell. It's going to take forever to get statements from all of them."

"We've made a start," Keaton assured him. "And uniforms will pick up where we left off first thing tomorrow."

Tennessee started chewing the end of the ballpoint. He stopped when he felt the plastic crunch under his teeth. "During the race – while I was peddling – I was thinking—"

"Did it hurt?"

"Shut up. I thought to myself, some of those sand sculptures must have taken hours, the intricate ones especially. They must have started in the wee hours or even in the middle of the night. I want to know if anyone saw the snake being built and if anyone has a description of the artist."

Elliot Whyte cleared his throat and raked his fingers through his thick black hair. "From what's been processed so far, no one recalls seeing the sandcastle being built yet. But as Keaton says, there's a lot of people we still have to talk to."

"Ah." Saffron Boyd lifted up a piece of paper. "Erm, I have a report from someone saying it was already built when they went running at five a.m."

"Who goes running at five a.m.?" asked Oliver Martin. The young detective constable was standing in the corner of the room, leaning against the wall and toeing one shoe against the other.

"The same weirdos who go to bed at half-eight," said Tennessee. "Cameras?"

"Magic Seaweed have a surf-cam. The hotel and the café both have security cameras, and there are plenty of houses along Percy Park and other nearby streets with doorbell cameras," Martin replied.

"Whyte, can you crack on with the business cameras? Let the local residents get some rest; we can pester them in the morning."

"Has Becky the Techie set that website up yet?" Keaton asked.

"I'll check." Boyd sat down at a computer, entered her credentials and logged in. She slid the mouse smoothly from right to left then double-clicked. "Oh."

"What's up?" Tennessee leant over her for a closer look.

"It's live. People have already started submitting photos and video from today."

"That's good. Isn't it?"

"There's already thirteen hours worth of footage."

Tennessee sighed, then spat the bit of plastic he'd bitten off the pen into the nearest bin. "Keep updating HOMES2 and process every statement that comes in. You'll act as our statement reader,

Saffron. Keaton, can you nip to M&S and get us some microwavable popcorn?"

She raised a brow.

"We've got a lot of footage to sift through. We're in for a long night."

- CHAPTER 6 -

COOPER GLANCED OUT THE taxi's window as they drove past farmland on the way to Newcastle airport early the next morning. She barely acknowledged the driver as he greeted them and loaded their cases into the boot of his Mercedes. Tina, who wasn't one for interacting with strangers, was forced to fill the gap in small talk. When the driver asked where they were off to, she answered Lanzarote. When he asked if it was business or pleasure, she said neither.

Check-in was equally dreamlike, as if Cooper weren't really there. Tina had to nudge her to get her passport from her handbag and was the one to answer the usual questions about packing their own bags. Passing through security to move from landside to airside was never a problem at Newcastle; the airport had won awards for positive passenger experience. Queues were short, and the staff were friendly. It was a good thing too, because both Cooper women had to pass through the metal detectors twice. Cooper, because she left her keys in her pocket, and Tina, because she tried to walk through while reading something on her phone.

"Do you want something to eat?" Tina asked as they wandered through duty-free. The store was an assault on the senses. Between lighting designed to make everything sparkle, joyful music to inspire the holiday spirit and customers testing every brand of perfume and aftershave, Cooper was surprised Tina hadn't made a run for it.

Cooper shook her head and took a seat in the departure lounge near the bureau de change.

Tina was about to sit next to her when an affectionate, white-haired couple shuffled towards them. The shorter man used a cane, and Tina nodded towards the seats to indicate he and his partner could take the only remaining seats in the area. She stood awkwardly in front of Cooper and clutched the shoulder strap of her bag to her chest. "Bagel, then? Or a Danish? They have giant Toblerones in the gift shop."

"No, I'm fine, but here's my card. If you want a giant Toblerone, go get a giant Toblerone."

Tina huffed and checked her phone. "I don't want a giant Toblerone; I want you to eat something."

"I have."

"You're such a liar." The two men glanced in their direction. "You didn't eat last night, and you didn't eat this morning."

"Tina..." Cooper's eyes narrowed on a television as the latest headlines scrolled across the bottom of the screen. Isle of Wight given UNESCO biosphere reserve status. Body hidden in sandcastle confirmed as female. Met Office records hottest June temperatures in forty years.

"Don't *Tina* me like I'm being some sort of pest. Do you think, in all honesty, I didn't notice how skinny you got when you had cancer? Do you think I didn't notice how you lost weight after you were held by that madman? Not eating is what you do."

The men shuffled, suddenly becoming fascinated by something on the floor.

Tina was right; she usually was. Little smart arse. Cooper acknowledged she was being selfish with her grief. Yes, she had lost a father, but her daughter had lost a grandfather. She shouldn't have to worry about her mother on top of everything else. Still, Cooper was in a dire slump, one she had no idea how to escape. She knew she should have booked an earlier flight and handed the Blackburn case to another senior detective. But she didn't. Her stubbornness at wanting to wrap up the double murder had meant sticking around in the northeast. She should have been on the first flight after she heard her father was having chest pains. That was what a good daughter would have done.

It was sunny outside the terminal. Light beams filtered through floor-to-ceiling windows, offering travellers an unobstructed view of the runway. Around her, happy families were excited about their summer holidays. Children pulled miniature suitcases designed to look like pets. Adults packed into the bar for a pre-flight drink despite the early hour and inflated prices. Cooper knew she should already be in the Canaries, and yet, she was ashamed to acknowledge that part of her wanted to be back in CID.

They'll be fine without you; your daughter and mother might not be.

Tina's phone beeped. She glanced at it and a tiny smile formed on her lips. She quickly buried the phone back in her shoulder bag and pushed a mop of untamed hair from her face.

"A coffee then?" Tina asked with raised eyebrows and no joy in her voice.

Cooper barely heard her. "No."

"Tea?"

"No, thank you."

"Wine? Beer?"

She shook her head, her mind already two thousand miles away in the Canaries.

"Absinth? MDMA?"

"No— No, wait. How do you know what MDMA is?"

"I'm fifteen. I might be an awkward weirdo who can count her friends on her left hand and still have a finger spare, but that doesn't mean I live under a fucking rock."

Cooper clenched her jaw and shot a warning look at a tweed-clad man who tutted as he passed. "Please don't swear at me, Tina. I'm struggling here."

Tina's phone beeped again. She stole a sneaky look, her cheeks flushing slightly. "We both are," she said, "but in case you hadn't noticed, only one of us is being present, and it's the one who's predisposed to living in her own head. So, I'll stop swearing when you start fucking eating."

- CHAPTER 7 -

FORENSIC PATHOLOGIST, MARGOT SWANSON, should have been in the Lake District. She should be waking up in Tony's youthful arms and enjoying a morning quickie before room service delivered their breakfast. She should be filling a flask with coffee and donning her hiking boots for a trip up Fleetwith Pike, an imposing hill that towered over the Buttermere Valley. Instead, she was securing a plastic apron over her scrubs and preparing to examine the latest Jane Doe to be referred by the coroner.

Tennessee remained behind the viewing window. He looked the same shade of green that he usually did during these situations. What was it about men that made them so much more squeamish than women? Yes, they were bigger on average, stronger on average, saw more war and went into more dangerous professions, but cut your head open or dare to mention the menstrual cycle, and the delicate things fell apart. She unzipped the body bag, checked the serial number on the toe tag and looked across at the viewing window. When she blew a kiss at the striking DS, he looked at the floor and ran a hand over the back of his neck. She really should stop playing with the poor boy.

The corpse was in relatively good condition, considering it was, well, a corpse. Taking fingerprints was simply a matter of rolling ink over the tips of the fingers and pressing them onto the specialised piece of card. In more gruesome cases, Margot had to remove the skin from the hand and place it over her own glove to perform the same task. Now that was something worth becoming peaky over.

As she walked around the table to repeat the same task on the deceased's other hand, she waved an arm towards the viewing window.

"You might want to come in here. She has something in her hand."

Tennessee pulled a face like he'd rather step into the bowels of hell. "Come on, sweetheart," she said, addressing the body rather than Tennessee. "Let me see what you have there."

Her fingers were stiff with rigor mortis and had to be prised open, confirming Margot's suspicions that she hadn't been dead all that long.

"Rigor mortis disappears between twenty-four and thirty-six hours after death depending on how fast the actin-myosin complex starts disintegrating."

Tennessee hovered by the door and nodded as if he understood what she had just said.

"It's a piece of material," she said, extracting it from the woman's grip with a pair of tweezers. She held it to the light and peered at the wee scrap of synthetic fabric. It was patterned yellow and green and was very thin, the light shining through it easily.

"Was that taken from the attacker?" Tennessee asked.

"How would I know?"

"Of course," he faltered. "Sorry."

"Relax, Jack. It might well have been." She bent over and examined the woman's fingernails, using the tweezers to remove a single strand of green fibre. "It does look like she's ripped this from a larger piece. It might well have been her assailant's attire. But I'd say finding out falls into your remit."

Margot placed the scrap of fabric and the fibre into evidence bags and labelled them. Next, she carefully removed the women's clothing so she could begin the external examination.

"Extensive bruising to the ribs. Appendectomy scar. Bruising to both wrists. Treble clef tattoo on left hip." Slowly, she turned the body so she could view the posterior. "Widespread abrasions on the backs of the heels and both calves. Potentially road rash, and would suggest she was dragged with her feet trailing. Livor mortis matches the position the body was found in: lying on the back with legs raised. Discolouration obscures bruising to the lower back. Significant impact to the back of the head, one centimetre above the occipital bone."

"Cause of death?"

Margot stepped back from the table. "Well, it's not suicide or misadventure, Jack. As a rule, people don't bury their own bodies."

He ignored her sarcasm. "Homicide by blunt force trauma?"

"Hold your horses." Margot turned the Jane Doe so she was face-up again. "I know you're keen to get out of here, but I'm just getting started."

TENNESSEE TRIED NOT TO watch as Margot went about her business. Behind Margot, several posters were fixed to the wall. Most of them were about sanitation and preventing cross-contamination; one poster was of Harry Styles – Topless Harry Styles. Tennessee read all the posters that didn't concern *One Direction* twice. Meanwhile, Margot took urine, blood and bile samples. When she removed the woman's heart and weighed it on a set of scales that looked suspiciously similar to the ones in his kitchen, Tennessee distracted himself by examining the piece of cloth in the evidence bag. It seemed familiar somehow.

"Hmm." Margot was frowning. She removed the lungs and placed them on a clean, polished surface. With surgical precision, she opened them up to reveal the bronchi and bronchioles. She took some samples to send to histology but took another thin sliver to place on a glass slide. She put the slide on a microscope's stage and switched to a high powered lens before peering through the eyepiece. She turned a dial to bring the image into focus. "I had a hunch."

Tennessee put the evidence bag down so he could focus on Margot. She seemed concerned.

"Cause of death is homicide due to suffocation as a result of occlusion of the respiratory tract by sand."

Tennessee squinted at her. "In English?"

Margot's face creased with disgust. "Jack, she's aspirated sand particles deep into her air passages. I'm afraid to say this woman was buried alive."

- CHAPTER 8 -

THE FLIGHT WAS FULLY booked. Cooper could tell just by looking about the gate. Once those requiring assistance and those with priority boarding had descended the steps from the terminal to the tarmac, it was time for passengers travelling with young children. A couple, whose child was taller than Cooper, approached but were told to sit back down. *Nice try.* Finally, it was time for the masses to queue, show their boarding cards and dither over whether they should take the stairs to the front of the plane or the ones to the rear. Cooper wondered why everyone looked so grouchy. They can't all be in mourning. But airports, even ones that run as smoothly as Newcastle, had a habit of making people tetchy. Perhaps it was the pre-breakfast alcohol.

They took the stairs at the plane's rear and had to jostle to get past people fighting for space in the overhead luggage containers. A burly man in a leather jacket was already being threatened with disembarkation after giving a flight attendant some backchat. Others darted back and forth across the aisle, swapping seats and passing hard-boiled sweets.

Cooper took her seat. An older lady and her word search book had the window seat, Cooper took the middle one, and Tina plonked herself next to the aisle. Though entirely at ease in a mosh pit, Cooper felt uncomfortably claustrophobic. Her daughter, who was never good in large crowds, was probably finding it excruciating. However, Cooper and Tina were still frosty with each other after her earlier swearing. People cope with grief and guilt in different ways, and whilst Cooper wished she and her daughter could hug it out all the way to Lanzarote, it appeared they would be spending the flight in polite but awkward silence.

Tina pulled a heavy-looking textbook from her bag. It was a good job the airline hadn't weighed their hand luggage because Cooper suspected that the chemistry book weighed in the region of three kilos alone. Who knew how many other books she had packed. Tina turned to a page she had marked with pink Post-it note, pulled her uncombed hair into a top knot and busied herself in the nitration reaction of phenyl to produce paracetamol.

Cooper hardly gave any regard to the air steward as he read out the pre-flight safety information over the tannoy. A few rows in front, another steward relished having the attention of most of the plane on him as he demonstrated how to put on a life vest and use a whistle. Cooper's eyes turned away so she could gaze past her neighbour out of the window. She thought of a happier time, not that the expression on her face would ever reveal that.

She remembered being thirteen years old, on a trip to New York with her parents. She had almost fallen asleep – in fact, she had fallen asleep – during the off-broadway show her parents had taken her to. They loved the long monologues and a script that felt like the author had swallowed a thesaurus. But afterwards, when they'd gone to the Hard Rock Café, Cooper had been absolutely enthralled by the memorabilia belonging to some of her favourite bands and artists. Some handwritten Jimi Hendrix lyrics caused her to drool more than she had over the humongous ice cream sundae she'd ordered. Despite a sign asking her not to, she reached out and stroked a green Motto Guzzi motorbike once owned by Billy Joel. She'd whispered how one day she would have a motorbike, only to have to listen to her mother perform a twenty-minute monologue of her own about how no self-respecting person would be seen on one. *Those monstrosities are for men having a midlife crisis or those with a death wish.* Cooper was in her thirties, approaching mid-thirties to be precise; a midlife crisis was still a long way off.

They hadn't been in the air forty minutes when turbulence struck. This wasn't the slightly annoying sort of turbulence that made plastic glasses of wine judder on the fold-down tables. This was the sort of turbulence that meant passengers were confined to their seats while nervous-looking crew members staggered up and down the aisle catching luggage as it fell out of the overhead compartments. While Tina's main concern was not vomiting everywhere, Cooper's concern was that the flight would be diverted and she would be further delayed from being with her bereaved mother. Tina brought a hand to her mouth, unbuckled her seat belt and stood to go to the bathroom. Her backside was only a few inches from the seat when she stumbled and fell back into it, half landing on her mother.

"Please stay in your seat, ma'am," called a flight attendant with a wonky nose.

Tina, who always complied with authority and never wanted to cause a fuss, did as she was told. Cooper, who never had much of a problem challenging authority, and who couldn't stand to see her daughter suffering from motion sickness, was about to lay into the man when Tina's first bout of sickness exploded from her mouth.

Some of it went on the back of the seat in front of her. Most of it went on the air steward.

Cooper pulled a sick bag from the net and handed it to Tina.

"It's okay, T."

"My book."

"Don't worry about your book. It'll wipe clean. I promise." She rubbed Tina's back, feeling it shudder as a fresh wave of sickness overcame her.

Around them, people covered their noses at the acrid smell of stomach acid. Hopefully, no one else was going to vomit. Still, if they did, Cooper hoped they'd follow Tina's example and puke on anyone who got between them and the toilet bowl.

- CHAPTER 9 -

IT MAY HAVE BEEN Sunday lunchtime, but Tennessee
was back in CID. If murderers couldn't stick to a
nine to five, Monday to Friday schedule, neither
could the police. He checked the time; Cooper's
flight wouldn't have landed yet.

It was a clear and blustery day, and Tennessee's
family had ventured out for some fresh air without
him. Understandably, they wanted to stay away
from the beaches after the events of yesterday.
They were heading south of the Tyne for a stroll
around Thornley Woods and a walk along the
riverbank. A family man, Tennessee, longed to be
with them. He knew how vital nature and fresh air
were to his wife since her diagnosis with postpar-
tum depression. It was important for all of them.
Since moving in with him and Hayley, Pat – Hayley's mum – had been more active, helping with
the baby and coming out on family walks. As a
result, she'd lost weight, and the arthritis in her

knees had improved. Even baby Alfie was reaping the benefits of time outdoors. He always slept better after a big day out.

Meanwhile, Tennessee was confined to fluorescent lighting, linoleum flooring and cheap plastic chairs. He was about to text Hayley and ask her to take some photos of Alfie while they were in the woods when a voice barked behind him.

"Daniel." It was the authoritative tone of Chief Superintendent Howard Nixon. "A word."

Tennessee shuddered. *Here we go*, he thought. He was too young; he was too inexperienced. The case was going to be handed over to someone else. With head bowed, he entered Nixon's office and waited for permission to sit down. Permission never came.

"Congratulations on your performance yesterday, DS Daniel."

Jack stood up a little taller. "Thank you, sir. Though full credit should go to my teammates, DCI Cooper and DS Keaton. It was DCI Cooper who had the tough job of the open water swim. She got us off to such as great start, and as for DS Keaton, we all know how seriously she takes her fitness training, sir. I don't think some of the blokes from Fire and Rescue appreciated being overtaken—"

"I appreciate your modesty DS Daniel, but I was referring to your work after the triathlon."

"Oh." *Could it be?* A compliment from the man himself? Stranger things had happened.

"Your quick thinking, decisiveness, and leadership did not go unnoticed, Daniel. During DCI Cooper's absence, you will be acting SIO."

He could hardly believe it. This was what he wanted. This was what he had trained for. But, now that the time had come, the thought of doing it without Cooper filled him with dread.

"I won't let you down, sir. "

Nixon took a sip of coffee that looked like creosote and looked up at Tennessee. "That being said, I will be watching you like a hawk. Every move you make. Every HOLMES2 update. Every action, every interview, every time you stop to take a shit. If I get the slightest whiff this is too much for you, I will hand the reins over to someone more senior."

NIXON SMILED TO HIMSELF once Tennessee left the room. His super had given him almost the same speech when he had his first SIO gig on a murder case. Of course, back then, it was HOLMES, not HOLMES2. Nixon was one of only a few people left in the department who remembered life before the new and improved system. The thought of using a computer back then had him snorting with frustration. Damn things would crash right when you needed them the most, and he had the sort of finger dexterity that meant it took him an age to type a simple report. He had always been old before his time and never enjoyed using a keyboard when a pen and paper would do. He didn't think about it too much these days. He knew forces had come to rely on HOLMES2, especially as it overcame the difficulties associated with the original version – that it could actually function across police force boundaries.

TENNESSEE RETURNED TO THE incident room. He found Keaton, Martin, Whyte and Boyd deep in conversation. He took a gingersnap from an almost empty packet and dipped it into Keaton's mug of tea. He savoured the taste of crumbly, gingery goodness because he might not eat again for hours.

Keaton yawned and reclined in her seat. "So, is it true? Is our beloved Tennessee the new guv?"

"Acting guv. Yes. But only as long as Nixon thinks I'm up to it. So unless we want some outsider coming in to tell us how to do our jobs. We'll be burning the candle at both ends to show we can do this. And to honour Cooper," he added. "If we do a good job, it's down to her leadership and the example she's set to all of us."

"Damn straight," Keaton said.

"Agreed." Martin dipped his head. "Let's do it for Coop."

Whyte gestured towards the front of the room." The floor is yours, guv."

Tennessee approached the murder board and pointed to the photo of the victim. "IC1 female between the approximate ages of fifty-five and sixty-five. As of yet, she is unknown. No one has come forward saying they know the victim or that they are missing a wife, a mother, grandmother or sister. Prints taken at the post mortem have been run through the system – no match. Whoever this woman is, she suffered a terrible death."

He sucked his lips into his mouth as he thought back to the autopsy. "Margot found evidence that she sustained multiple impacts, possibly from kicks and punches. She suffered trauma to the back of the head, and her legs looked as if she'd been dragged some distance." He gulped and gathered himself before adding the final detail. "She was beaten, dragged to the beach and buried alive."

His last two words visibly upset the four people in front of him: Keaton coughed; Boyd's mouth fell open and her eyes filled with sorrow; Whyte adjusted his weight and scratched the back of his head; Martin wrapped his arms around himself in a self-soothing gesture.

"That's awful," said Saffron. She looked shaken.

"It really is," Tennessee said. "She suffocated. Margot found sand particles deep inside her lungs. One of our first jobs is to find out who this poor woman was. Only when we have a name can we start looking at the people in her life."

Martin suggested releasing a description of the victim to the press. Tennessee agreed. "But check Mispers once more first. Check for treble clef tattoos and appendectomy scars."

He pinned a photograph of the fabric found in the victim's hand to the board. "Yellow and green polyester. In an ideal world, we would ID this lady, speak to her significant other and find him wearing the matching top with a hole in it."

Keaton snorted. "But this isn't an ideal world."

"Because in an ideal world, women aren't buried alive on award-winning beaches."

He thought of his wife, his mother, his mother-in-law. He thought of the boy who'd kicked a hole in the sandcastle, revealing the woman's arm. Sure, he'd been acting like a naughty little swine, but that didn't mean he deserved to be scarred for life.

"Whyte," Tennessee said, "where are we with the cameras?"

"Not a damn thing. The external cameras at Crusoe's are working just fine, but they don't cover that far along the beach. Besides, they would have only picked something up in the dark if it happened within a couple of metres of the camera. The hotel cameras cover the road outside. I've taken a look, and there are plenty of cars going past at all sorts of hours. Mainly taxis. A couple of drunk people wandering back home. But no one dragging anyone down onto the beach – at least, not directly outside the hotel. "

"Take a closer look at the drunks, see if any are a fit for the victim. What about the surf-cam? Magic Seaweed?"

"Way too dark to pick anything up."

"Okay. Well, it's a good job uniforms started knocking on doors this morning. Let's see if anyone saw or heard anything in the middle of the night. Anything of interest so far, Boyd?"

She shook her head. "Not yet."

"Unless she lived extremely close to the beach, our perp needed to transport the victim. I want to know if anyone heard cars pulling up in the early hours."

"You don't think she could have just been in the wrong place at the wrong time?" asked Martin with a shrug. He pulled his mug of tea towards him and cupped both hands around it. "Maybe she went for an early morning walk and bumped into the latest psychopath to walk the streets."

"Not a chance," Keaton said. "Stranger killings are rare. Besides, you'd have to be more than just a psychopath to bury someone alive and then spend hours building a giant sandcastle around them for no bloody reason. You'd have to be a completely cocoa-bananas, crack-addict, goat-banging flat-earther."

- CHAPTER 10 -

BENJI'S BAR WAS A few streets inland from the Old Town Harbour. Being slightly off the main tourist trail in Puerto del Carmen, the bar catered mainly to ex-pats working in the tourism industry or those who had retired to the sunshine. Still, they got a reasonable amount of tourist custom from the sort of Englishman who craved a small dose of familiarity. An English pub with an English name and good ol' pub grub on the menu. The outside terrace had been tiled with tiny squares of dark blue, and diners often commented on how it was like sitting at the bottom of a swimming pool. They found it relaxing.

The early afternoon sun flooded the terrace in warm light. It would stay that way until half seven when the sun would start to dip behind the villas on the other side of the street. On a sofa made from pallet boxes and pale blue cushions, Julie Cooper held court. She was dressed in a knee-length black cotton dress, black sandals and oversized sunglasses. Three couples sat with her. On the table was a large cafetière and a bottle of whiskey. It may have been too early to start on the wine, but it was clearly never too early for an Irish coffee.

Cooper and Tina watched from a distance. The street was quiet, the sun worshippers would be at the beach, and it was at least two hours until happy hour. The drive from Aeropuerto de Lanzarote was markedly different from the drive to Newcastle Airport. At home, they'd driven past fields of green and bright yellow rapeseed. Here the land looked more barren at first glance. Scorched reddish-brown soil was punctuated with the occasional cactus reaching to the sky like green fingers. The North Sea was dark and blueish grey; the Atlantic, a more inviting shade of cerulean.

Julie made grand gestures, regaling her support network with tales about Ben Cooper. She tipped her head back and let out a loud laugh. She was having fun, soaking up the attention. But soon, the shock would wear off and Julie would be left with emptiness and sorrow.

A couple of bare-foot tourists who had clearly drunk too much the night before staggered towards the bar and asked if they were still serving breakfast.

"Sorry, darlings. The bar's closed today," Julie told them.

They lowered their shades and looked around, glancing at the bottle of whiskey and the seven people sat around it.

"It doesn't look closed," said the female of the pair, popping her hands on her hips as if she'd never been told *no* before in her life.

Cooper wheeled her case across the road. "If she said they're closed, then they're closed."

Julie and her guests jumped to their feet. Julie pushed her shades up into her hair, revealing bloodshot eyes. "Erica!"

She padded over to her and embraced Cooper for a moment before releasing her. She brushed a hand over her head, feeling her buzzcut for the first time. "Oh, darling. I know you told me you were keeping your hair short, but honestly, I wish you'd grow it out. You used to have such beautiful hair." She turned to her granddaughter, holding her at arm's length, scrutinising the young woman she had become. "And Tina, look how you've grown! Speaking of hair, what is going on here? Haven't you heard of a hairbrush?"

Cooper pinched the bridge of her nose as she often did when stressed. "Tina doesn't like brushing her hair. And I don't like forcing her to."

Julie frowned. "You're her mother. You're supposed to make sure she follows basic hygiene. Everyone knows you have to brush your teeth, wash your face, brush your hair—"

Tina pulled away and looked at the floor, holding her elbows awkwardly. Now, it was Cooper whose eyes were turning red. "For Christ's sake, Mum. Brushing your hair has nothing to do with hygiene. Her hair is clean; it's just tangled. She has..." She lowered her voice. "Sensory issues."

"Oh. Well, how was I supposed to know?"

"Because I've literally told you a hundred times. And what the hell is this? We fly out to be with you, and all you can think about is what we look like? Dad's dead; Tina's lost her grandad. My hair is the last thing I'm thinking about, but it's good to know you have your priorities in order."

And that was when the waterworks started.

The three couples shuffled towards Julie. The smallest of the women wrapped an arm over her shoulders and pulled her to her. "There, there. It's okay, Julie."

All Cooper wanted to do was find a dark, quiet room and be by herself. She could feel a migraine coming on; a white-hot ball of pain was building behind her eyes. First, she was snapping at Tina. Now she was snapping at her mother, a woman who had just lost her husband. Was *she* the problem? Was Cooper the one acting like an arsehole?

SILVERLINK AND COBALT BUSINESS Parks housed steel and glass giants: DIY warehouses, council buildings, swanky offices, and expensive car showrooms. But nestled amongst the homage to out-of-town corporate Britain was a green oasis. The Biodiversity Park was eighteen hectares of woodland, scrub and hedgerows, exposed rock habitats and wetlands. The nature reserve's fields and ponds were home to majestic roe deer, tiny blue-tailed damselflies, and everything in between.

Tennessee watched a meadow brown as it danced from flower to flower, its diminutive wings humming at an impossibly fast speed. He and Keaton had gone for a walk to clear their heads. They had been looking at footage of Longsands beach for hours. Their eyes were tired, their brains hurt, and they were no further forward. It was a beautiful Sunday, and since neither of them could be with the ones they loved, they could at least do the job they loved out in the fresh air. It beat fluorescent lights and over-enthusiastic air-con units.

"Do you think the snake's important?" asked Keaton. "I mean, he either followed her to the beach, or he attacked her elsewhere and transported her there. Either way, if he simply wanted to hide the body, he could have dug a deep hole and dumped a load of sand over her."

"But he didn't."

"No. He painstakingly decorated that thing with shells and intricate carvings. It must have taken ages."

"And what if that kid hadn't knocked a huge big hole in the side of it?" Tennessee paused while a rabbit crossed his path. "How long would the sculpture have stayed standing? It could still be there now. It was too high up the beach to be washed away by the tide. Heck, it might have even won the competition."

Keaton pushed a stray hair from her face, tucking it behind her ear. "It was good enough to win."

"Imagine if they awarded the prizes and our perp came forward to collect his winnings? It would have made our lives easier."

"What was the top prize?"

"Gift vouchers for the Metrocentre."

Keaton snorted. "Gift vouchers. Like money; only shit." The rabbit twitched its nose before disappearing into the long grass. "But why a big snake? Everyone else made ships and mermaids or actual castles of sand. But the victim was hidden in a massive coiled snake. And it's not like she was poisoned or choked."

"She sort of was," said Tennessee. "She was suffocated. And isn't that what snakes actually do? They suffocate you. Constrictors don't crush you to death; they stop you from drawing air into your lungs, and you die from asphyxiation or cardiac arrest."

"I thought they cut off the blood supply to the brain?"

He shrugged. It had been a long time since Tennessee had found the time to sit down and watch a wildlife documentary.

They turned left and followed a track up a hill at the centre of the park. It wouldn't take them long to reach the summit. Truth be told, Tennessee was grateful for the opportunity to stretch his legs; he had seized up since yesterday's cycle ride. Above them, a kestrel hovered. The bird pivoted to its right, folded in its wings and dove. It rocked backwards at the last second, presenting yellow claws that kicked up dirt as the bird hit the ground. When it returned to the sky, an unlucky mouse hung from its talons. The kestrel wasn't the only one on the hunt; Tennessee hoped his prey would be captured just as swiftly.

They reached a towering sundial that stood at the peak of the hill. A shard of white pierced the sky, its shadow telling them it was gone three o'clock. Tennessee rolled his shirt sleeves up and looked east, wondering if he could see his house from there.

He couldn't.

"Maybe it's symbolic," Keaton said. "Like the snake that tempted Eve into eating the apple."

Tennessee turned to the west. "Could well be. Do you think the vic was the temptress?"

"What did she tempt him into doing?"

"Like you said. Maybe she tempted him into taking a bite of the apple." He wiggled his eyebrows at Keaton. "And then she took the fruit away?"

"Another woman killed for turning down a man?" Keaton kicked a stone and watched it tumble down the hill. "I wouldn't be surprised. But this can't be a simple case of a man with a bruised ego. Because why go to these lengths?"

"Snakes represent other stuff. Like in medicine, the staff with a snake wrapped around it. Isn't that the logo?"

Keaton waved her phone around above her head. Once she had a signal, she googled the staff. "The Rod of Asclepius. A Greek deity associated with healing and medicine."

"Or rebirth and transformation? Snakes shed their skin. Perhaps he's shedding something through killing."

Keaton shuddered. "That's dark."

"Do you think there are any snakes here in the park? Adders or grass snakes?"

"There's one on your shoe."

Tennessee jumped a foot in the air before realising Keaton was winding him up. "Was that necessary?"

"Super necessary," she said with a grin. "If there were, they'd be hiding in the long grass. They wouldn't be sunning themselves out in the open with us here." She brought a finger to her lips and hummed for a moment. "Hmm. The snake in the grass; a hidden danger. Someone who feigns friendship only to betray you."

Tennessee sat on a wooden bench and looked up at Keaton. "Rejecting the wrong bloke's advances might get a woman killed. But betraying the wrong bloke?"

"That might get you killed in a manner meant to set an example."

- CHAPTER 11 -

IT HAD BEEN A morning of admin: registering Ben Cooper's death with the Spanish authorities, making arrangements at the chapel of rest, cancelling his passport and driving licence, speaking to the DWP and paying for a five-year lease of a niche – an above-ground crypt where Ben would be interred. Cooper stared at her phone; she was looking at the last photograph taken of Ben Cooper – a Facebook snap of him laughing and joking with friends. He looked old and vulnerable and yet not old enough to die. As far as Cooper was concerned, death had taken him far too soon. Like most in her profession, Cooper had seen more than her fair share of death, but only three times had it touched her in a personal capacity: the murder of her best friend when she was still a teenager, and Tina was a newborn; the death of her grandmother whom she and Tina lived with when her parents moved abroad; and now, her father.

Tina hadn't wanted to accompany her mother and grandmother to the funeral directors. Cooper couldn't blame her. Instead, Tina had taken a bag of textbooks, a bottle of sunscreen and a two-litre bottle of diet Coke to the beach.

Cooper sat down next to Tina, straightening out the towel to make room for herself.

"I brought you one of Benji's famous bacon butties."

Having closed the bar on Saturday and Sunday, Julie decided to leave Benji's in the capable hands of her young staff. Regardless of her personal circumstances, bills still had to be paid, and they'd already lost revenue from closing over the weekend.

Tina looked up from a mathematics workbook and lowered her shades. "Are you having one?" she asked pointedly.

Cooper reached into a brown paper bag and pulled out a second bap with a light dusting of flour.

"I am. Sorry for being a pain yesterday. I know you were just trying to help."

Tina shrugged but was too busy stuffing bacon and ketchup into her mouth to say anything.

"Have you heard from Josh?"

"Why?" Her voice was muffled but defensive.

"Just showing an interest," Cooper said cautiously. She didn't want to end up in another argument with her daughter. She thought asking if her boyfriend had been in touch would have been safe territory. Tina knew Cooper approved of Josh. They'd been inseparable for over a year now, and

Josh came over for tea at least twice a week. He was practically part of the family.

"Oh. Yeah, he text before going to school this morning. Said if there's anything we need for when we get back, just to let him know."

"That's sweet," said Cooper, taking a bite of her sandwich even though she didn't want to. She never felt hungry when she was stressed. And with tomorrow's funeral and her mother's hints that Benji's wasn't doing well financially, she was very stressed indeed.

"And if we need a lift from Newcastle airport, Josh's dad will come and get us."

"He's a good lad."

Tina gave a coy smile. "Yeah."

A seagull landed on the sand three or four metres in front of where they sat. He patted his big feet, picked up a discarded cigarette butt and took to the skies again.

Tina slammed her book closed.

"You okay?"

She gestured to the gull as it flew away. Earlier in the year, Tina had rescued a baby herring gull that had fallen from the roof of their Tynemouth home. It had become Tina's mission to raise the chick until he was ready for release. The noisy little bird was staying at Paula Keaton's while the Coopers were in Lanzarote. Cooper thought her daughter must be missing Steven; he'd been a good distraction for Tina with everything she'd been through lately.

"He can't eat that!" she exclaimed. "I don't care if people smoke. Half the people in my year smoke, and it's their own damn business, but why do the y..."

"Have to litter?" Cooper asked. "Because they're lazy or selfish? Because they think it makes them look cool? Because their mothers didn't love them, and they lack empathy? Who knows."

Tina took another bite of her bacon butty but didn't stop scowling until she'd swallowed.

"I need to go to the *registro civil* to arrange Grandpa Ben's death certificate. Will you be okay here until I get back?"

"How long will you be?"

Cooper scrunched her face up. "Your guess is as good as mine. Depends on how much *mañana attitude* they have. But if you need to get out of the sun, just head back to the bar or your grandma's house. Do you have a key for the villa?"

Tina waved her wrist; a small brass key dangled from a bracelet. She turned back to her studies and Cooper walked away. She'd almost reached the edge of the sand when she heard Tina's irritated voice call after her.

"Hey! You only had one bite of your sandwich."

TENNESSEE STOOD AWKWARDLY IN the middle of the room. His hair was a mess, but his shirt and trousers were immaculate. He'd look stylish if he could stop fidgeting for a moment. His tongue clicked against the roof of his mouth as he turned his attention from one computer screen to the next. CID now had a whole host of people helping them sieve through the footage and photographs taken from the day of the triathlon. Through her role as statement reader, Boyd deduced the sand sculpture must have been erected after twelve midnight but before four a.m. The team conducting door-to-doors in the neighbouring streets now had a narrower timeframe for speaking with residents and viewing their home security cameras. So far, they didn't have a single lead.

"Wait. Rewind twenty seconds." Tennessee approached one of the computer monitors. Though the victim was buried hours before the crowds had gathered for the charity events, they still needed to look for anyone giving the giant snake an unusual amount of attention. Someone had gone to a lot of effort to make this temporary grave. Surely they would have hung around to see the admiring glances and the chaos that ensued when the sculpture's real purpose was revealed.

"What do we have here?" A group of older teens approached the sand sculpture. A slender, barefoot female with long black hair ran her fingertips along some of the snake's coils before picking up a seashell and placing it next to some others that had been used in decoration.

The technician working the monitor leant back in his chair and folded his arms. "Aside from the boy who discovered the body, this young lady is the first person I've seen who actually touches the sculpture."

"Print off a still for me."

An ancient printer whirred and groaned until it finally vomited out the image.

"Keaton. You have a minute?" Tennessee beckoned Keaton and asked her opinion.

"The victim wasn't heavy, was she? About ten stone soaking wet."

"Sixty-one kilos, according to Margot's report."

"Close enough." Keaton held the image at arm's length. "This girl looks more like fifty kilos max. No way on God's green Earth did she drag someone heavier than herself down to the beach, beat them badly and bury them alive. No way a lone teenage girl could do that."

Tennessee agreed, but it was the only lead they had so far. Besides, they didn't know that the person responsible acted alone. "A lone teenager? No. But a gang of teenagers? Maybe." He moved to the front of the incident room to address the group as one. "I want to find out who these kids are. Especially the girl with the long black hair." Pinning the printout to the murder board, he added, "It's probably nothing, but they may have seen something of interest. TIE. Trace, interview, eliminate."

Elliot Whyte hung up a phone and called out across the incident room. "Guv. Might have something here."

When no one acknowledged him, Keaton dug her elbow into Tennessee's ribs. "He means you. You're the guv."

"Oh, shit. Of course. Sorry Whyte, what have you got?"

"Someone called about the e-fit that we released to the media: Mrs Avani Amin. Says the e-fit looks like her neighbour. She hasn't seen her for a few days. Apparently, she knocked last night and this morning, but there's been no answer."

"Where does she live?"

"Coronation Street," said Whyte. "Not the one on the telly, before you say owt."

- CHAPTER 12 -

CORONATION STREET WAS A terrace, just like its soap opera namesake. Keaton hummed a tune to herself as she turned a corner. She performed a parallel park as she pulled into a bay marked with red bricks in a herringbone pattern.

Tennessee stepped out of the car and stretched his arms above his head. "Why are you humming the Eastenders' theme tune?"

"It's the Coronation Street theme tune."

"It's not," said Tennessee.

"You sure?"

"Pat watches it religiously."

Keaton wrinkled her nose. "So, what's the Coronation Street one?"

"No idea. Come on, we have work to do. If you're lucky, I'll hum the Emmerdale theme for you on the way back."

Whether the dwellings here had always been flats, or if they had once been houses that were converted, Tennessee had no idea. He looked up and down the street. As almost all the properties had identical white doors with brass door handles and semicircular windows, he guessed the properties belonged to the local authority. They were close to the river, Smith's Dock and the ferry landing. The wind carried the scent of damp trees and earthy mud, the tang of ferry fumes and the sound of water lapping at the banks.

Tennessee adjusted his tie and knocked on the door at the end of the terrace. A woman in her early thirties with silky hair secured in a chic bun answered the door. She wore a yellow and green kurti over jeans and cradled a newborn in her arms. Tennessee smiled at both mother and newborn, then lowering his voice so he wouldn't wake the peaceful baby, he introduced himself.

"Mrs Amin? I'm DS Jack Daniel. This is DS Paula Keaton. You spoke to one of my colleagues earlier about a victim we have been trying to identify."

"Yes. There was a picture on the news. It looked a lot like my neighbour, Eve. Eve Lynch. She's a lovely lady. I hope she's okay."

"Do you know her well?"

"Better than I know anyone else in the street. She dropped off a lamb casserole for my husband and I on Thursday. She said new parents had enough to worry about out without having to cook as well. She said the less time I was in the kitchen, the more time I could spend with this one." She glanced down at the baby in her arms, her face glowing with pride. "I tried to return the casserole dish last night at about six, but there was no answer. I tried again later at, oh, I'd say maybe eight forty-five and again this morning."

"What time this morning?" Tennessee asked.

"It must have been ten to nine because my husband had not long left for work."

"Does Eve live alone?"

"Yes, for as long as we've lived here, which would be, goodness, two years now."

"I don't suppose you have a photo of Eve?"

Avani shook her head. "Sorry, no."

"Not to worry. Your neighbour didn't mention going away? Visiting family?"

"No. Nothing like that."

"And you haven't heard any arguments or raised voices?"

"I hear plenty of raised voices," said Avani, "just not from Eve's house. Over there, though." She nodded towards the house opposite. "Music playing till the early hours. Always some drama. Not Eve, though. She's a quiet, little old lady. Well, not that old, I suppose. Sometimes I heard her singing, but I never minded that; she has such a lovely voice."

"And was Thursday night the last you saw or heard from Eve?"

She nodded. Keaton approached Eve Lynch's home and peered through the windows.

"We are going to conduct a welfare check and enter Ms Lynch's house," Tennessee told her. "Thank you for calling us. We won't take up any more of your time."

Keaton knocked on the front door and waited. "If the noise from across the street is persistent, call the council and quote *the environmental protection act 1990*. Tell them to serve an abatement notice."

Avani smiled and thanked Keaton before disappearing back inside.

"No answer," said Keaton, knocking again and pressing her ear to the door to listen for sounds from the interior. She pushed the letterbox and called through in a loud voice. "Ms Lynch? My name's Paula Keaton. I'm a detective sergeant with Northumbria Police. Can you open the door, please? We just want to check you're okay."

When there was still no answer, Keaton straightened up and looked at Tennessee. "Foot through the door or hand through the window?"

"Your choice."

"Well, in that case—" She lifted up her heavy-duty boot and kicked the door. It opened on the first attempt.

"Impressed?"

"Always."

"You know, they really should make these things harder to kick down."

"You're a walking big red key," he said.

In UK police slang, battering rams used in dawn raids were often called big red keys because they were big, red – and with enough force – opened any door.

"Ms Lynch? Eve?" Tennessee stepped over a water bill and a copy of that morning's paper. He looked down the hallway towards the stairs. "You take the downstairs; I'll have a look upstairs."

Eve Lynch's stairwell was adorned with a collection of art prints. All the images featured bands or singers. The style was abstract, almost as if the people were made up of triangles and squares. He thought the style was called cubism, but he wasn't sure. Art wasn't his thing. All the pictures were painted in warm tones of red and yellow. One painting of a slim woman in a long white dress with short black hair caught his eye. She was singing and waving to a crowd while two saxophonists played behind her.

Tennessee checked the bathroom; there was no sign of a struggle. In the bedroom, the bed was unmade, but the room is otherwise tidy and well presented. The second bedroom appeared to be set up as some sort of sewing room. A large sewing machine sat on a wooden desk, and piles of different coloured fabric were neatly folded. A pincushion shaped like a set of drums was placed on a book of sewing patterns. He checked the pile of fabric for anything resembling what was found in the victim's hand before returning downstairs.

"Anything?" he asked Keaton.

She was standing in the kitchen. "Nothing. Have you seen any photos? Anything to tie the occupant to the murder, other than the neighbour's testimony that she matches the description?"

"Negative. No photos; plenty of art. The occupant's clearly into music and crafts. But nothing to suggest a family: no spare bed in the second bedroom, only one dressing gown on the back of the bedroom door, only one toothbrush in the bathroom."

"What now?"

Tennessee tapped his foot while he thought. "I say we bag the toothbrush, have the lab compare fingerprints and DNA. See if we can confirm that missing Eve Lynch and the lady from Longsands are one and the same."

- CHAPTER 13 -

TENNESSEE PACED IN ONE of the upstairs corridors at Northumbria Police HQ on Tuesday morning. He hadn't had breakfast; he'd barely had time to shower. Alfie hadn't slept well, and he seemed to be living by the mantra: *if I can't sleep, no one can.* Tennessee held a file in one hand and his phone in the other. He was talking to baby Alfie, or rather, he was trying to soothe Alfie because Hayley thought the infant was getting sick of her voice. As if a baby could ever get sick of its mother's voice, especially one as soft and loving as Hayley's. She was giving herself a hard time again, trying to be the perfect mum. She was loving and caring and doted on all of Alfie's needs. She was a great mother and a wonderful wife, and he would tell her that every day until his dying breath.

"Daddy loves you," he said, knowing fine well his son didn't understand a word he said. It was all about tone. "Be a good boy for your mammy. And please, for the love of Peppa Pig, go the..." – He swore under his breath – "...to sleep."

Tennessee hung up, pulled his shoulders back and checked the half-Windsor knot in his tie.

Dad mode: Off. DS mode: on.

He marched confidently into the incident room, placed the file on a desk and with his back to the room, let his eyes scan over the murder board.

"Fingerprints are a match," he said. "Victim is Eve Lynch, fifty-four, single, never married, no children, both parents are deceased." He turned to face the room but found only one pair of eyes looked back at him. "Where the hell is everyone?"

Keaton rested her elbows on a desk and supported her chin in her hands. "Boyd's stuck in traffic; Martin slept in, but he's doing the Starbucks run; Whyte's chasing up a lead. He thinks he's identified one of the teenagers from the beach and says he'll be here as soon as he can. As for the others, I have no idea."

"Unbelievable," growled Tennessee. "They wouldn't dare be late for Cooper. I know I'm only acting SIO, but we can't be sloppy and let standards slip. This is a murder investigation for Christ's sake."

"You're preaching to the choir. Anything I can do?"

"Yes. Send a group message. Anyone not through those doors in the next ten minutes can foot the lunch bill."

WITHIN SEVEN MINUTES, SEATS were filled and eyes were firmly angled towards the murder board.

"Right, thank you for gracing me with your presence. As I was saying, Eve Lynch, fifty-four, single, never married, no children. Eve has an eclectic employment history. She spent ten years working for South Tyneside Council before jacking it in to work front of house at a swanky restaurant. At thirty-five, she changed careers again, this time to be a jazz singer. She toured the local pub and club circuit for a while before getting a job singing on cruise ships. She's been to the Caribbean, around the Baltic sea, all over the Med, Alaska, and right through Asia including a stop in North Korea."

"Wow," said Oliver Martin. "She's better travelled than the entire department put together. The most exotic place I've been was a lads' weekend in Ibiza."

"That is exotic," said Keaton. "I can't begin to imagine the strange and terrible creatures you encountered there." She put on her best David Attenborough voice. "Cocktail lounge cougars, a pride of leathery-skinned sun-worshippers, roaming packs of horny virgins, and the lesser spotted yogi-by-day-coke-head-by-night?"

Martin laughed. "Aye, that was just the first night."

Tennessee cleared his throat. "If you're quite finished... Yes, Whyte?"

"Famous jazz singer sounds interesting. Do you think she had a crazed fan or a stalker?"

"I wouldn't rule it out," said Tennessee.

Martin frowned. "Aren't crazed fans and stalkers the domain of the mega-famous?"

"Not necessarily," Boyd said in little more than a whisper. "One in five women and one in ten men experience stalking at some point. And as victims don't tend to report their fears to us until the hundredth incident, cases could actually be much higher."

"Whoa."

"And of the cases we actually get to trial and get convictions for, only nine to eleven per cent get a custodial sentence." She picked up a glass of water and took a sip. Her hand was shaking.

Tennessee wondered how Boyd knew so much about stalkers and their conviction rates. Unfortunately, he could guess the answer. He understood all too well that it wasn't only the rich and famous who could be victims of stalking. He remembered how pained, hurt and embarrassed Cooper had been when she had to phone her colleagues to report what had happened to her. He thought of the women in his family and the ones he worked closely with. He did the maths in his head.

One in five.

"Like I said, I wouldn't rule it out." A line formed between Tennessee's brows. "But as always, the most likely candidate is a lover or ex-lover."

Keaton interlaced her fingers behind her head and stretched her elbows backwards. "But Avani Amin, the neighbour, said she didn't know of Eve being in a relationship."

"You're right. We're speculating," Tennessee said. "Let's stick to what we know. On Thursday night, a fifty-four-year-old former jazz singer dropped off a casserole at her neighbour's home. She isn't seen since, and there was nothing to indicate a struggle at her home. Between eleven p.m. on Friday and four a.m. on Saturday, she was taken to Longsands beach and physically assaulted. For some reason, she had a scrap of fabric in her fist." He put his hands on his hips and closed his eyes. "Then she was buried under a pile of sand, the sand was shaped into a huge coiled snake, and she died a horrible death."

"We know her name and we know the kill site," added Keaton.

"What we don't know is motive," he replied. "Everyone, start talking to neighbours and people she worked with. I think Keaton's right about this murder being a message. Let's find out why someone wanted Eve Lynch dead."

- CHAPTER 14 -

HUSHED VOICES FOLLOWED COOPER as she walked across the terrace outside Benji's Bar. She could feel the mournful eyes of her father's friends upon her, but they weren't the only eyes that followed her. The staff were watching her closely, their lips sealing shut as soon as she was within earshot.

"They're worried about their jobs," Tina told her. She was fluent in Spanish, but as she was too shy to practice, she had to make do with listening to other people's conversations. "Apparently, the bills have been piling up, and it was Grandad Ben who was the numbers man. They think without him, the situation will only get worse. They don't want to drop Granny in it, but they're wondering if they should start looking for jobs elsewhere."

After a late lunch, Tina left to go for a walk and to call Josh. Cooper sat alone, sipping what she suspected was supermarket brand cola rather than the Pepsi she'd ordered. It was warm on the terrace, but it would have been sweltering had it not been for the ever-present breeze of the Canary Islands. A patch of painfully pink skin on the back of her thigh told Cooper she needed to do a better job applying sunscreen. She edged forward on the pallet-box sofa so her sunburn wouldn't rub against the cushions or the wooden frame. Since Tina told her about the staff's concerns, she couldn't help but notice small signs around her – like a detective hunting for clues. Cracks in the plaster hadn't been filled; the chip missing from the plate she'd just eaten from; the low-quality toilet roll in the bathroom; a patch of damp in the kitchen.

A portly man with little to no chin entered the bar and made a beeline for Cooper. She recognised him as one of her father's friends. She couldn't for the life of her remember his name, but she remembered he and Ben liked to go fishing on Sunday mornings. The man, arms wide and face pitiful, enveloped Cooper in a hug. It was a good thing Tina had taken off, she hated strangers touching her, and this particular stranger hadn't applied deodorant that morning.

"Erica, darling, it's good to see you. I just wish it weren't under such dreadful circumstances. How's your work going?"

Cooper shrugged. Was it Alec? Allen? Albert?

"Your dad was so proud of you. Always talking about his daughter, the great detective. In fact, the last time I saw him, the night before he passed, I'd been to visit, and he was telling me how you'd just solved some huge case involving the Blackburns. That's a name that takes me back. Those Blackburns were causing trouble back in the seventies, maybe even earlier."

He released Cooper from his grip, and before she could answer any of his questions, he headed to the bar. Julie, dressed in black joggers and a baggy black t-shirt, gave him a tearful hug. She poured him a pint. As he reached into his is pocket to pull out a wallet, she waved his money away. Julie took a wine glass from the rack above the bar and poured herself a considerable measure of Rioja.

So that was where some of the profits were going.

She knew her parents' friends were suffering, but if the bar was in trouble and jobs were on the line, Julie shouldn't be handing out free drinks or helping herself to the stock. Last night Julie had finally stopped talking long enough for the grief to finally hit her. She'd fallen apart with wailing sobs and loud cries that could have been heard several buildings away. She locked herself in her bathroom and cried for hours. When she emerged, her makeup was perfect once more.

"Mum, I'm heading to the *tienda*. Do you need anything else for the wake tomorrow?"

Julie shook her head and took a sip of wine. "I don't think so, dear. Everything's under control. The lads in the kitchen are going to put on some nice nibbles for everyone."

Cooper was about to leave when her mother called her back. "Before I forget, you are... you are going to wear a hat when we go to church tomorrow, aren't you?"

Cooper's mouth pinched and she chewed her tongue for a moment. God forbid Julie Cooper might look like the sort of woman who had a skinhead for a child in front of the congregation. Just because Cooper had a buzzcut, it did not mean she was a skinhead. She spent her career arresting people for hate crimes. Her choice to have short hair represented neither racism nor anarchy.

"Yes, mother," she said through clenched teeth. Cooper liked having her hair short and had done every second since she decided to opt for clippers. One set of clippers, versus hairbrushes, shampoo, conditioner, hairspray, straighteners and argan oil? Some style choices just made life that little bit easier.

Unless you had a mother like Julie Cooper.

Cooper walked away, shaking her head in disbelief. Talk about priorities. She hadn't actually packed a hat for church. When Tina and Cooper packed their suitcases, they hadn't expected to be attending a funeral. Her father had still been alive until the day before they flew out. It had only been the morning of the flight when they remembered to pack some sombre outfits. Tina had packed some black school trousers and a smart black top, while Cooper found a black dress that was neither too short to be decent or too heavy to be comfortable. The only hat she had with her was a khaki-coloured baseball cap.

The shops along the main thoroughfare sold summery dresses, sun visors and straw cowboy hats. She had to wander over a mile to find a boutique that stocked black sun hats. Cooper bought one but winced at the price; it was hideously expensive, but it was her only choice.

Cooper's feet dragged as she headed back to the bar. Instead of turning right, she decided to follow the path that led to the harbour. She sat at the end of the pier, looking out at the boats as they made their way back into port for the night. The shipping boats made her think of North Shields: the fish quay and Royal Quays Marina. A small, comforting reminder of home. She drew out her phone and selected a contact who was equally comforting.

"Erica."

"Sorry I missed your call," she said.

Justin Atkinson gave a small chuckle. "You mean, sorry you missed my twenty calls?"

"Yeah, sorry, I know you just wanted to see how I was, but I wasn't in a communicative mood. Still aren't, if I'm honest."

"How are things? Are you doing okay?"

"Things are... things are shit. I didn't get to say bye, and my mum is driving me crazy. I know that's a horrible thing to say." She pressed a hand against her clammy forehead. "I know she's grieving, she's just lost her husband, but she's doing my head in."

"Isn't that what mothers are for?"

This time Cooper chuckled, and it felt like the first time she had smiled since watching Paula Keaton cross the finish line on Saturday.

"How's Tina?"

Cooper always appreciated how good Justin was with Tina. When she and Atkinson were dating he had neither pressed Tina for a father-daughter relationship nor had he ignored her. Instead, they had grown closer as two adults who shared a love of science. Though she'd never told him, he'd been a better father to Tina in those few months that they were together than her biological father had ever been.

"She's in another world," Cooper said. "She avoids the bar like it's contaminated with something. If it's busy and loud, she just can't stand it. And Mum and Dad's friends don't help. They keep wanting to hug her, and then they look at her like she's rude for refusing and offering a handshake instead. She spends most of her time either down on the beach with her head in a book or texting with Josh."

Atkinson sighed. "She's always felt more comfortable talking to Josh. It's probably a good thing she's texting him all the time. Plus, she'll be worried about tomorrow. She hasn't been to a funeral before, has she?"

Although Tina had some experience of death – a couple of students in her year group had been killed last year – she hadn't been able to attend the funerals or the special school assembly.

"No. This will be her first. She'll probably disappear about ten minutes into the wake. Hopefully, no one will make a big deal out of it."

"Well, if they do, I'm sure you can put them in their place. Everyone deals with death differently, and if Tina prefers to be alone, then Tina should be alone. She doesn't need to be unnecessarily uncomfortable on top of losing her grandad."

"Not everyone sees it that way. I'm sure I'll overhear the words *unsociable, teenager, disrespectful.*"

"And if that's the case, you can use the words *uneducated* and *insensitive.*"

Cooper smiled but said nothing. Overhead, two clouds seemed to merge into the shape of Mickey Mouse.

"But other than driving you mad, how's your mum doing? She must be in bits?"

"She has been. She's up and down. One minute she's bawling her eyes out, and the next, she's on the karaoke machine singing Dad's favourite songs. From what I can gather, the bar's in trouble. They're in debt and the staff are ready to walk out. I'm not sure they've even been paid this month. And if the Spanish equivalent of the Food Standards Agency takes a look in the kitchen cupboards, I'm not sure they like what they find." Cooper tipped her head up in time to see one of Mickey Mouse's ears float away. "Mum and Dad love this bar; it was always their dream to move here. I want to help. Keeping Benji's afloat would be like keeping Dad's memory alive, but I can't throw money at a struggling business. I have a mortgage to pay and a daughter who will definitely be going to a top league university."

"You're an amazing woman," Atkinson said. "You've solved some of the most complex and brutal cases, but you can't solve all the world's problems. Tina will get through tomorrow like she gets through everything – with grace and intellect. If people castigate her for wanting to skip the wake, then that's their own damn problem. And as for the bar, that's not your responsibility. You have enough responsibilities of your own without taking on those of your parents. I don't think your father would want you to go into debt to save his project. His legacy will live on in your memory or in the drunken stories of his ex-pat friends."

Cooper played with the brim of her new hat, running her fingertip over the ripples in the material. Although the heat of the late afternoon sunshine warmed her skin, it was Atkinson's kind heart and thoughtful words that warmed her from the inside out.

"How's the case going? Is Jack coping?"

"Nice try," said Atkinson. "You're on compassionate leave. If you think I'm going to start talking about the case, you've got another thing coming. Besides, what did I just say about not solving the world's problems?"

Cooper looked at her watch. It was almost five o'clock, which meant it was now a socially acceptable time to start drinking. Whilst she felt guilty about spending her money in another venue, Cooper wasn't ready to go back to Benji's just yet.

If truth were told, she didn't like the white wine they served there anyway.

There was a peaceful-looking seafood restaurant behind her with a lovely deck looking out over the harbour. She would buy herself a crisp glass of sauvignon and watch the tourists come back in after a day's snorkelling.

"I miss you," Atkinson said just as Cooper hit *end call.*

"I miss you too," she said to the dial tone.

TENNESSEE WAS KEEN TO get home. Tonight was Alfie's first swim class. He and Hayley had been looking forward to this since they booked the course last month. Tennessee had bought his little one a range of swim nappies with designs varying from nautical stripes to dinosaurs. He'd even started learning the words to the various nursery rhymes and children's songs that would be sung by parents during the class. Alfie loved nursery rhymes; he always made cooing noises and wiggled his feet whenever Tennessee sang them to him.

As his car rolled to a stop and Tennessee found himself at the back of a traffic jam, his heart sank. He needed to be home within twenty minutes; otherwise, Hayley would set off without him. He'd miss out on cradling his son in the water, hearing all the babies laughing, watching him submerge for the first time. Tennessee tried to put it from his mind and focused on the radio instead; the station was having a throwback to 1988. After a bit of Kylie, a touch of Elton John, and a sprinkle of Bobby Brown, Tennessee's car had moved approximately thirty metres. He folded his arms over the steering wheel, rested his head on his forearms and groaned. He now had eight minutes to cover four miles.

The traffic started to crawl again, and when Phil Collins began to sing, Tennessee turned the radio off. He felt like he was missing something. Was it important? There was definitely something niggling at him. Eve Lynch's neighbours knew very little about her. Avani Amin probably knew her the best; she was devastated to find out Eve was dead, horrified to hear she'd been killed. He went over her words in his head to see if anything stood out. Any clues that would explain the uneasy feeling. Could it be Phil Collins? He was a drummer, singer and actor. Their victim was a singer. Was that it? Or was it the Bobby Brown track? His wife had recently bought some cosmetics from a company with the same name or what he thought was the same name. Hayley had giggled and explained it was a Bobbi with an I. It must be that. He was probably just remembering his conversation with Hayley.

Five minutes to cover three miles. Tennessee loved his job at CID, but he also loved his family. It didn't matter how many advanced driving courses he took; he had more chance of winning the lottery than getting through this traffic jam.

Hayley would be strapping Alfie into the baby seat about now.

Without Tennessee.

- CHAPTER 15 -

HE PULLED HIS THICK coat tighter around him. It may have been late June – technically summer – but the exposed north shore of Holy Island felt like a cold, winter's night. Known for the Lindisfarne Gospels, Viking invasions and foolish tourists being cut off by the tide, this place was both a holiday destination and a site of holy pilgrimage. He checked his watch. The sun was beginning to peek above the horizon; it wouldn't be long now. The man he was waiting for would show his face soon; he always did. Like clockwork. He'd been watching him on and off for weeks, ever since he'd read the news and come back home. He hunkered down and pulled his knees into his chest. Around him, the long grass of the sand dunes swayed in the wind, the tallest blades caressing his cheeks.

This part of the island was called Coves Haven. It was a quiet sandy beach away from the priory, the lime kilns and the famous castle. It had been his haven when he'd arrived in the total darkness. He sipped whiskey to stay warm while he fantasised about what the morning would bring. It would not be a haven for the man he was waiting for. This was no place of safety or refuge.

This was a place of retribution.

He stretched his legs and wiggled his toes, trying to bring warmth back to his extremities. Coffee helped. It was lukewarm now, but caffeine was caffeine. Not that he needed stimulants to be able to do what he was about to do. It would be easy. The man and his collie left their home on Marygate every morning at dawn and followed the coastal path. The tri-colour border collie was a bonny dog. Her black, white and tan fur shimmered, but the poor thing's eyes had started to cloud with age; she looked as old as the man who walked her. Both underweight and succumbing to ageing joints, to think, he'd been the skinny and scrawny one once. Not now. Not after dedicating years to building muscle and functional strength. Building his cardio and the power of his lungs. All those hours in gyms and on building sites. He wanted to change his body like he'd wanted to change his entire life. He hadn't realised all that time had been preparation. Preparing for this day. For this mission.

The smaller creatures of Holy Island were beginning to wake. A grey seal briefly poked his head above the water before disappearing back into the depths. Butterflies danced around purple northern marsh orchids. An eider duck called out to her mate. Around here, they were known as cuddy ducks due to St. Cuthbert's fondness for them. But besides the creatures that called this island home and the old man and his dog, the Holy Island of Lindisfarne was sound asleep. This side of the island was deserted, and the tourists wouldn't arrive until nine-thirty when the tea rooms opened.

He spoke to his victim yesterday. It gave him such a thrill; he didn't know if he'd be able to do it. An internal battle raged between the fragile, insignificant boy he'd been and the strong, dangerous man he'd become. Yesterday, he watched the man and the collie return from the newsagents. He watched as he dropped his paper and struggled to pick it back up. It was his chance. He'd walked over, picked up the paper and handed it to him. His hands were shaking, but the old man didn't notice. There was no look of recognition on the old man's face when he handed him the paper and stroked the dog. He thanked him and struck up an inane conversation about the weather. He had no idea.

From the dunes, he watched the old man approach. The dog zig-zagged behind him, fur billowing gracefully in the wind. Her herding instincts causing her to walk slightly crouched, head lowered and tongue lolling.

His heart fluttered as he watched the pair. They were both so blissfully unaware of what was to come.

He stood, dusted the sand from the back of his legs and walked casually towards his target. Just another early bird out for a morning stroll.

"Mornin'."

"Good morning," replied the old man. He stopped to pull a pebble from the sole of his shoe.

"Crackin' day for it."

"Aye. Clear skies forecast all day."

His heart beat faster, his head filling with questions of morality. Was this worth his soul? He would be damned to an eternity of hell for his actions. Yes, he concluded – it was worth it. Some things could not go unpunished.

"You don't recognise me, do you?"

He squinted in the dawn glow and spoke in a weak, crackly voice. "You're the young man I spoke to yesterday. You helped me with my paper."

He shook his head and laughed, though there was no humour in his tone.

"No. Think back further, much further."

The old man took a step back; his presence clearly intimidated him. Power – It was a good feeling.

The old man shook his head. "Have we met before?"

"You were quite the pillar of the community. An authority figure. A father figure even. The one they could all turn to. All except me." He tilted his head to the side and cracked his neck. "You saw the bruises, and yet you did nothing. You saw the warning signs, saw I wasn't eating, that I was withdrawn. But you chose to look the other way."

There it was: the look of recognition and familiarity. The old man's eyes swept over him in disbelief as if the man standing in front of him couldn't possibly be the boy he remembered from all those years ago.

In his hand, the sharp edges of a rock dug into his palm. He gripped it tighter, then swung with all his might.

HE SAVOURED THE MOMENT. Standing over the unconscious man, he ignored the frantic dog's barks.
He closed his eyes and took a deep, deep breath.
That felt good. He passed the rock to his other
hand, balled his fist around it, then pounded it
into the old man's face. It was a cheap shot, hitting
someone who couldn't hit back. But, he'd been on
the receiving end of many a cheap shot. He was
allowed a few in return, was he not?

Once the mist cleared, he grabbed the man by
his ankles and dragged him into the hole he'd
prepared earlier. Though the man was slim and
his body atrophied, it still took strength and determination to move the dead weight over dry
sand. The dog growled, barked and nipped his ankles. Stupid creature. She barked again, a horrible
high-pitched yelp that reminded him of nails on
a blackboard. She lunged at him, her teeth bared.
Thick canines sunk into his flesh. The pain radiat-
ed in white-hot waves across his thigh. He grabbed
the dog by its scruff and shook it violently. Though
he could do much, much worse, he reminded himself that the dog was innocent. She was just sticking
up for her owner the way no one ever stuck up
for him. He threw the dog towards the dunes. She
whimpered as she walked away.

Time was getting away from him. He grabbed his
tools and got to work, shovelling the sand, piling it
higher and higher. He sprayed the outside with wa-

ter mist, keeping it moist while he started to carve his design. It wouldn't be as intricate as his work on Longsands, but it would still be impressive. He formed the coils and moulded the head. He took his time carving scales that gradually got smaller and smaller as they approached the serpent's tail.

As he felt the cool sand under the pads of his fingers, it took him back to learning pottery as a child and the feeling of wet clay. How ironic. The only skill the old man actually taught him was the one he used to adorn his broken body right now. He always liked making things. You didn't need good spelling or sums to build something or paint it, just patience, and he had a lot of patience.

He stood and admired his work. The snake was a suitable resting place for the old man. He gathered his things, making sure not to leave anything: half-empty whiskey bottle, flask, blanket, and tools. Banging his hands together to clean them of sand, he started walking back towards the headland. The tide had receded further, forming rock pools around Coves Haven. By the time the islanders had woken and the tourists began to cross the causeway, he would be back on the mainland, ready to tick another item from his list.

- CHAPTER 16 -

ON ANOTHER ISLAND, TWO thousand miles away, where the volcanic landscape could look lunar grey one minute and Martian red the next, a small, white church was surrounded by British ex-pats. The Anglican church was square in shape, with a rectangular bell tower. The building and its surroundings were immaculate. No litter, no chips in the paintwork, no graffiti. This was somewhere the locals took pride in. A place to be respected.

"Do you want to hold hands?" Copper asked Tina, who had been silent during the drive over to Tías.

She shook her head. "Unless you want to."

Cooper wanted to hold hands. She felt weak and needed something solid to cling to. "How about linking arms?"

Tina slid her arm into the crook of her mother's elbow and gave her a supportive smile.

"Love you."

"Love you, too." Tina said it quietly but with a squeeze of her arm and enough eye contact for Cooper to know that she meant it.

Tina was the only constant in Cooper's life. Kenny, Tina's father, abandoned her before she was born. Her parents moved to the sunshine the second Cooper turned eighteen. Her grandmother, whom she had lived with for a few years after Tina's birth, had passed when Tina was still in her first year of school. The team at CID had changed many times during her career, with some leaving to have their own babies. Some, unable to cope with the stresses of the job, had quit for civilian life. Some didn't make it to a police pension for more unfortunate reasons: an RTA, a bullet wound, a noose.

Through it all, there had always been Tina.

She was fifteen and already thinking about which university to attend. She would easily get the grades for Oxford, Cambridge or Bath, but Cooper knew Tina would go wherever the best science course was. Her little brainbox would probably save the world one day. All Cooper ever wanted was for Tina to have an easier time than she had in her young adult life. Thinking about her potential caused Cooper to feel a pang of pride mixed with sadness. She would never guilt Tina into attending Newcastle or Northumbria University. She had to face facts, her one constant would be flying the nest within a couple of years, and once more, Cooper's life would change forever.

It was cooler inside the church. High vaulted ceilings allowed air to flow, causing the fine hairs on Cooper's arms to stand on end. This was an old church with dark wooden pews, once polished to perfection, now dulled with time and wear. The floor was clean and shiny, reflecting the glow of candle-shaped lightbulbs in North African style pendant lamps. The minister stood at the front in brilliant white, his robes so clean they could feature in a Persil advert. Was he a minister? Cooper wondered. She'd been introduced while they were planning the service, but she'd hardly been paying attention. She wasn't religious and had no clue if the man at the front of the church was a minister, priest or father. If pressed, she could call him *padre* and hope he took no offence.

Cooper and Tina took their seats in the front row beside Julie. On one side of her, Tina was stoic and dry-eyed. On her other side, Julie sobbed into a crumpled tissue. Cooper took her mother's hand and interlaced her fingers into her own.

The minister waited for everyone to take their seats before speaking in a clear and practised voice. "We are here today to pay tribute and respect to a man of God, our brother, Benjamin Cooper. We are here today to show our love and support for Benjamin's precious family. His loving wife, Julie, and his daughter and granddaughter, Erica and Tina."

He looked at Cooper as he spoke. "We are here today to seek comfort. As our hearts ache with loss, we trust that God will give us the strength to walk with Him. Today, we remember Benjamin Cooper. Ben spent his early years in the west end of Newcastle upon Tyne. He enjoyed playing football with his friends, camping with the Scouts, and riding his bike."

It was strange hearing the minister talk about Ben as if he knew him well, but it was also comforting. The idea of her dad riding a bike around Fenham brought warmth to her chest.

"In secondary school, Ben excelled in science and maths, and it was here where he first met Julie."

"I didn't know Grandad Ben liked science," whispered Tina.

"Where do you think you got it from? Cooper asked with a wry smile. "Me? Your dad?"

Tina suppressed a laugh and turned her eyes back to the minister. Cooper put an arm around her daughter's shoulders, pulling her closer to her.

"I remember one summer when your grandad took over the entire house with glass bottles because he decided to brew his own beer. Your granny would tell him to leave it to the brewers, but he would scoff and say it's *just basic chemistry.*"

"Was it nice?" Tina whispered.

"It was bloody awful," said Cooper, allowing herself another smile at the memory. "I was only fourteen, but I snuck downstairs in the middle of the night and opened a bottle from his finished batch. There must have been fifty bottles. I figured he wouldn't notice if one went missing."

"Did he?"

"Nope, but it gave me the squirts for the next three days."

Tina pulled a face, and Cooper didn't know if she was grimacing at the subject matter or Cooper's use of the word squirts.

The minister continued speaking about how Ben and Julie met, their marriage, and the birth of their daughter. He talked about them following their dreams, moving to warmer climes, and running their own business. This set Julie off on another wave of hyperventilating tears. He spoke of Ben being an example to everyone in life, about following your heart and living each day as if it may be your last.

That was the point when Cooper fell apart. Had she been the best daughter she could have been? No, of course not. She'd been a boisterous, energetic child who hardly gave her parents a moment's peace. As a teenager, she had caused all sorts of trouble. She stayed out past curfew, stole money from her father's wallet, and – with Kenny's help – got herself pregnant before leaving school. She played music too loud, avoided helping with the dishes, and was responsible for over ninety per cent of the phone bill. But she had matured thanks to the lessons Ben had taught her about holding her head high and being totally dogged in the pursuit of one's ambitions. She would always appreciate him for that, and she would always regret having never told him so.

- CHAPTER 17 -

"You drive like an old codger who hasn't had his eyes tested for ten years."

It took over ninety minutes to drive to Holy Island, and DS Paula Keaton was not going to hide her displeasure.

"I suppose I should be grateful we got here at all," she said with a sharp edge to her voice. She tugged at her seatbelt and squirmed as if she had a bad case of ADHD. "Given your inability to follow directions, I'm surprised we didn't end up in Carlisle."

Tennessee liked to think he was driving like the sensible new dad he was. No more speeding for this responsible father. Besides, Nixon would blow a fuse if Tennessee was flashed by a speed camera. He'd lose his SIO role faster than his wife could spend money.

"What's bugging you?" he asked as they approached the car park.

"Nowt."

"I've seen wet cats happier than you."

She scrunched her face up. The skin around her eyes folded into thick creases; she tensed her jaw and ground her teeth. "You're right," she said, letting her face relax. She shook her arms as if loosening up before a big game. "It's my dad. He's marrying some tart half his age."

"Good for him."

Anger flashed in Keaton's eyes.

"No? Wrong answer?"

"Urgh. It's a long story. And I hardly got any sleep last night because that blooming seagull was cheeping away all night." She rubbed her eyes. "Cooper must have a soundproof kitchen. Look, I know I'm about as fun as a yeast infection right now. I'll sort myself out. The fresh air will wake me up, and there's nothing quite like a murder investigation to take your mind off family drama."

Tennessee reversed into a parking bay and switched the engine off. The rugged beauty of the island never failed to take his breath away. The tower of Lindisfarne Castle rose from the land, and flowers in the wild meadows danced in time with the wind.

When the Viking raids took place on Holy Island in 793AD, Alcuin of York described a *heathen pagan race who poured out the blood of saints and trampled on their bodies in the temple of God*. For seven decades, the raids continued until a full-scale invasion of Danish Vikings headed for East Anglia under the rule of Ivar the Boneless. Soon he set his sights on the great kingdom of Northumbria and subjected Aelle, King of Northumbria, to the most brutal of Viking murders: the blood eagle. Northumbria conquered and a puppet king on the throne, Ivar's attentions turned to Mercia. But as Viking forces headed southwest, a part of them was left behind – their DNA. Many northeastern men can claim a direct ancestral link to the Viking invaders, and Danish words are used to this day in the local dialect. Bairn, the Geordie word for child, and hyem meaning home, come from the Danish *barn* and *hjem*.

The first man to greet Tennessee and Keaton as they exited their vehicle was as part Viking as they came. He had a heavy brow and piercing blue eyes, with shoulders twice as broad as Tennessee's, thick blond hair and a wild beard.

"John Raven," he said, extending a hand. "The road doesn't extend beyond my farm. I'll take you on my quad; it's quicker than walking." He patted a dirty quad bike and indicated that they could sit on the back facing rearwards.

Keaton jumped aboard as if riding a quad was a daily occurrence. Tennessee looked at the mud-covered vehicle, then glanced down at his woollen coat: it was Hugo Boss and had cost him a small fortune. He sighed and climbed up.

"Hold on tight," Raven called over his shoulder. "It's going to get a wee bit bumpy."

Raven twisted the throttle and started the quad bike. He steered it off the road and over the fields, taking a direct route to a beach on the island's north side.

Keaton jabbed her elbow into Tennessee's ribs as they bounced up and down on the back of the bike. "Now we're talking. Told you I just needed some fresh air." Her eyebrows peaked and a cheeky grin formed on her lips. "And he drives better than—"

The back wheel of the quad hit a puddle, splashing Keaton in the face with what looked like a mixture of mud and manure.

It smelled like it too.

It didn't take long for Raven's quad to reach the outer cordon. When they jumped off the back, Tennessee joked that if Keaton wanted to wear a mud mask, she should have gone to the spa and not a crime scene. This earned him the sort of stare Medusa would have been proud of. They thanked Raven, introduced themselves to the crime scene manager, showed their IDs, and added their names to the logbook.

The crime scene manager pointed to a shortish man in his fifties with cropped brown hair and a broad flat face that reminded Tennessee of a pug. "That's the sarge from Berwick. He'll fill you in with what we know so far."

They ducked under the cordon and strode towards the pug-faced man. He saw them coming and made to meet them halfway, walking uphill through the dunes. By the time he reached Tennessee, he was out of breath and had his hands on his hips, his panting making him even more dog-like.

"Detectives. A young mum found the sculpture shortly after dawn." He pointed with his head down towards a half-moon bay with off-white sand. "Her baby couldn't sleep, so they went for a morning stroll. When she saw the sandcastle, she thought it looked similar to what she'd seen on the news. It freaked her the hell out, and she was too scared to touch it."

With any typical crime scene, Tennessee would have said she did the right thing. It was always best to preserve evidence and to avoid contaminating anything with your own DNA or footprints. But there was a voice of doubt in his head. If he'd released the information about the first victim being buried alive, perhaps the woman would have got to the second victim in time.

"Luckily, the causeway was open when we got the call. It didn't take us long to get here. We arrived by quarter to six. By then, there was a large crowd gathered. Well, about thirty people, but that's like a sixth of the population."

Tennessee's mouth curled at the corner as his mind flashed back to the chaos at Longsands. If this guy thought thirty people was a large crowd, goodness knows how he would have coped at Saturday's crime scene.

"One of the residents is a doctor. He's officially confirmed the death, but we're still waiting on SOCO to arrive. You've beaten them here."

And Keaton thought I was slow...

"What time did the causeway open?" asked Tennessee.

"'bout four forty."

Whilst Tennessee had an inkling the killer may have been hiding in plain sight on Longsands beach, he didn't think they were hanging around now. Not when they'd be an extra face on an island where everyone knew everyone. The killer was likely back on the mainland by now.

"Want to take a look?" asked Detective Pug, again nodding his head in the direction of the beach rather than use his hands.

The answer was no. He did not *want* to take a look.

They followed him down the dunes, Tennessee's smart shoes sinking into impossibly soft sand. The sand from the top half of the sculpture had been moved away to expose the body. It was an older man, perhaps in his seventies or even eighties. His pale skin was smudged with blood and mottled from death. He had a mole on his right cheek, and wore a rust-coloured jumper over a white shirt, its collar speckled with wet sand. The mound of sand, though partly destroyed, was definitely once a snake. The colubrine coils tapered into a tail, and smooth indents denoted scales layered on top of one another.

What the hell did it mean?

Tennessee turned his mind back to the conversation he'd had with Keaton. Did the perpetrator see himself as a snake, squeezing the life out of his victims? Or was the snake an honour? A sacred, decorative tomb to accompany them to the afterlife? With monsters like this, who knew? Maybe the weirdo just liked snakes.

"Our perp doesn't have a type," said Paula. "One male, one female. This one's possibly a good twenty years older than the first one. She turned to Pug. "Do we have an ID?"

"The doc says he's called Charles. Couldn't remember his surname, but if he lives on the island, it won't be difficult to find out."

There was some commotion behind them, high in the dunes. A woman with wide eyes and a thick woollen cardigan held a whining dog by its collar.

"Let me through. Let me through."

Local officers held the woman back behind the perimeter tape, spreading their arms to prevent her from making a quick run past them.

"I can't find my dad. I heard there was a body and I can't find him. His dog was wandering the streets. He's not answering his phone or his door. Please let me through."

Tennessee approached. "DS Daniel, ma'am. You say you can't find your father?"

"No. No." She was on the verge of hyperventilating. "Alice told me someone had been killed on the beach. But she didn't know who. I called Dad because I know he likes to walk up here in the mornings. When he didn't answer, I went round and found Fleabag running up and down the road making this awful whining noise."

Fleabag bucked left and right, trying to free herself.

"Can you describe your father for me?"

"Erm, yes. He's seventy-two, no seventy-three. Grey hair, almost white. About five-ten, slim build. He has a mole on his right cheek."

His heart sank; she'd described the victim perfectly. Tennessee didn't need to say anything; she could tell by the look on his face that the man in the sand was her father. The was a deep soulful moan before she buckled to her knees. She let go of the dog's collar and it ran towards the beach. When Tennessee tried to intervene, the dog lashed out, nipping his hand.

Tennessee had suffered his fair share of injuries before: concussion, a broken wrist, broken toes, and a surgeon had broken his nose in three places. But he'd never been bitten by a dog before. This was a different type of pain. He grunted, his head reeling as he watched blood pool from deep puncture wounds. Tennessee shook his hand and suppressed a swear word, then he pointed from Paula to the dog.

"I'm on it," she said. "Leave it to me."

Turning back to the woman, Tennessee got a grip of himself. Whatever pain he was feeling was nothing compared to what the victim's daughter was going through. He knelt in front of her and quietly asked, "What's your name?"

"Mona," she sniffed, "Mona Clydesdale."

Tennessee looked up to make sure that one of the local officers was paying attention. "Mona, I want a couple of officers to accompany you back home. They're going to ask you some questions about your father, okay?"

She nodded, great big tears rolling down her cheeks. "Can I see him?"

Tennessee dipped his chin to indicate yes. "But not just yet, Mona. We need to get as much evidence as we can so we can find out what happened to him."

As two local uniforms escorted Mona from the scene back towards the village, she could be heard mewling. "Why? Why would anyone hurt Dad?"

Why, indeed? Tennessee thought.

- CHAPTER 18 -

As TENNESSEE'S HAND WAS sanitised and patched up by the local doctor, a jobsworth was filling in an accident report with the attention to detail you'd expect from an airline pilot.

"It's just a scratch. You really don't need to do all that paperwork."

"Rules are rules, you know that, sir. Do you want to press charges?"

"You what?"

"It bit you." He was a broad man with red cheeks and unruly eyebrows. "The dog wasn't under control. You should press charges."

"Against who? The dog's owner is dead – possibly buried alive." He shook his head incredulously. "You want me to charge his grieving daughter? That'll look real good."

When the doctor was finished, Tennessee inspected his hand and admired the clean bandage.

It hurt like a son of a bitch, but he had no intention of showing it.

"I'm sure I know your face from somewhere," said the uniform. "You usually work with Cooper, don't you?"

"That's right."

"Yeah, we crossed paths back in the day. She was investigating a series of assaults in Highfields. She was quite the looker, had lovely long hair. I had a thing for her, truth be told. Not now. Not my type."

As if she'd give you the time of day, Jackass.

"Don't think I could date a woman who looked like a boy. Not right, is it? Where is she anyway? She's not sick again, is she? Getting paid the stay home? Man, that would be nice. I could do with some paid leave."

"You what?" Keaton, who was standing nearby, had obviously overheard. She approached with lightning speed and jabbed her finger in his chest. "You think it would be *nice* to stay home between bouts of radiotherapy?" She squinted at him; no fools would be suffered gladly today. "What in God's name do you think is *nice* about chemotherapy?"

He held his hands up in surrender. "Jeez, just making conversation."

"Well, make it somewhere else," Keaton said. "Leave."

He filed his accident report into a beige folder. "What?"

"Leave. You're dismissed. Get out for my sight before I strap you to the causeway and wait for the tide to come in."

He looked at Tennessee as if to say, "Are you going to let her talk to me like that?"

Tennessee looked back and forth between the uniform, with his angry face and puffed chest, and Keaton, whose steely eyes showed adamantine fury. "She's serious," he told him. "Now bugger off, or I'll help her do it."

IT WAS ACTION STATIONS. A lot had happened in the last hour despite Holy Island being such a remote location. Hong Evanstad and a team of SOCO's were combing the area for evidence; a family liaison officer from Berwick was with Mona Clydesdale; the victim was on his way to the morgue. It was a good start, made even better when DC Oliver Martin showed up with half a dozen extra-large pizzas. As far as Tennessee was concerned, that put Martin in his good books for at least a week. The boy could now do no wrong.

Police officers from Berwick had started interviewing the islanders. They needed to know if anyone saw or heard anything unusual early this morning. No doubt everyone in the village would be pointing their fingers at mainlanders. They would refuse to believe someone in their midst could be capable of murder. Still, there would be suspicions. People would talk over garden fences or huddled in pubs. They'd gossip about the newcomer who wasn't involved in island life, the woman who'd been here twenty years but always seems a bit off, and the teenager who once stole a bag of crisps from the village store. He was clearly a bad egg – only a matter of time before petty theft escalated to murder. They'd blame the parents.

Mona Clydesdale owned a cottage on Lewins Lane. It was late June but Mona had the heating on; it was stifling. Tennessee removed his coat almost as soon as he stepped over the threshold. He also took a moment to remove his shoes; the treads would be thick with sand and grass that he didn't want to drag into a grieving daughter's home. She had enough to deal with without his mucky feet. The downstairs of the house was decorated with terracotta floor tiles and light coloured wooden furniture. Most of the items were painted white or light grey but were sanded to give them a distressed shabby chic appearance. FLO Denise Oswald met Keaton and Tennessee at the door.

"I've offered to call a doctor," she told them after explaining Mona's mental state. "She said no, but I'll keep an eye on her."

"Does she live alone?" Tennessee asked.

"Husband and two kids. Husband's working in Berlin and won't be back until Friday evening. I've called his place of work and left a message for him to get in touch. I believe Mona's tried a few times as well. He'll get the news soon enough."

Tennessee nodded and played with the edge of his bandage.

"As for the kids, there's a boy and girl aged ten and eleven. They're at school on the mainland and would usually get the bus back in the afternoon. We've sent someone to bring them back early. We don't want the news to get out and for them to hear about it at school."

After the brief update, Denise headed to the kitchen to put the kettle on. Mona was sat at the dining table with her elbows propped on the wooden surface and her head resting in her hands. Her dark blonde hair fell forwards, covering her face like a veil. Tennessee took a seat opposite her.

"Have the officers already spoken to you about when you last saw your father?"

"Yes," she said, raising her head. "He was here last night. I just can't— I mean, how can he be gone? He was sat right there, where you're sitting, and now he's gone. It doesn't make any sense."

Tennessee swallowed. The chair suddenly felt uncomfortable; it was like wearing a dead man's shoes. He wondered if he should switch seats. If he was somehow disrespecting her father by being in that chair.

"He came for dinner every Tuesday and Thursday. I don't know what I'm going to do without him." She dabbed a tissue against red, watery eyes. "I know that sounds silly. I'm a grown woman. It's not like I need him to pick me up from school or tuck me in at night, but he was a big part of my life. It's a small community here, and I was used to seeing him a few times a week, if not every day. Duncan and Laura adore him."

"Your children?"

She nodded and crumpled the tissue in her fist. "He doted on them, spoilt them rotten. That's what grandparents are like, though. They forget all the rules they had with their own kids the moment

grandchildren are on the scene. I was allowed a bag
of sweets on the weekend for watching Saturday
night television, but I swear he is always... Sorry."
She sat open-mouthed, blinking at the window,
confused at having to switch the present tense for
the past. "He *was* always buying Duncan and Laura
goodies. Every day of the week. Laura has a real
sweet tooth, so he would buy her sugary things.
Sherbet's her favourite. Duncan's more into crisps.
His favourite thing in the world is a crisp sandwich
with loads of butter. I never make them right; he
always likes his grandad to make them."

Tennessee thought about Pat, his mother-in-law.
It could be awkward with her living with him and
Hayley, but he appreciated all the help she gave
their young family. Little Alfie adored his grandma; his baby's face always lit up when Pat sang to
him.

Somewhere in the house, a dog barked.

"Sorry. I've left her in the bedroom for now. She's
not usually so vocal. Is your hand okay?"

"Don't worry about that. Honestly, it's fine. Looks
worse than it is."

Feeling self-conscious, he moved his hand under
the table. Then Denise and Keaton returned with
tea in china cups. Keaton gave a sympathetic smile
that warmed her entire face. She really was a Jekyll
and Hyde. She could be a big cuddly bear if she
needed to be. Comforting and supportive. Or, she
could be a grizzly who made grown men run for
their lives.

"Can you tell me about your father?" Keaton asked. "What he was like? How did he spend his days?"

Mona cupped her tea and held it to her chest. She briefly smiled at a memory before the sadness overcame her once more. "His full name is Charles Tarquin Pennington. He hated his middle name. You know how if a child is naughty, you use their full name? If I was bad at school, I'd get the *Mona Lisa Pennington, get to your room* treatment. But I'd do the same to him. If I was in a mood, I'd call him Charlie Tarquin instead of Dad. Drove him crackers."

Keaton smiled and patted her hand. "Did he always live on the island?"

She shook her head. "He was born in Westerhope and met my mother when they were studying to become teachers. He worked in education right up until retirement."

"Which schools did he work in?" asked Tennessee, taking out his notepad. He would try to speak to some of Charles Pennington's colleagues to get an insight into his personality. Was he the sort to make enemies? Families tended to only see the best in each other, especially following a death.

Mona screwed her face up as she thought. "I can't remember all of them, but he enjoyed his time at King George's in Hebburn, and he spoke fondly about Fellgate Primary and Whitley Lodge."

Tennessee raised his head from the notepad. "I went there," he said. "Whitley Lodge." He sifted through his memories of his time there, wondering if the name rang a bell. He could remember

all his form teachers and was ninety-nine per cent
certain there'd been no Mr Pennington when he
was there.

"Was probably before your time."

"What subjects?"

"He was a Jack of all trades. You have to be
in primary school. He liked art the best, though,
especially the masters. He thought students who
weren't gifted in maths and English often shone
in art. He thought the arts were important. Not
everyone was made to sit spelling tests or do long
division."

"When did he move to the island?" Keaton asked.

"Would have been about ten years ago now.
Mum died when my two were still in nappies; she
got swine flu and pneumonia. She went into hospital one night and never came out. Dad moved
up here to be near us. I kind of insisted, really. I
wonder... If I'd never..."

Tennessee pulled his cup of tea towards himself. "You can't think that way, Mona. You're not to
blame."

She didn't look convinced. She shook her head
and looked out the back window. Beyond her stone
wall, sheep grazed the fields. Beyond that, the sea
cut a cold, dangerous barrier between them and
the mainland. Cars wouldn't be able to pass again
until the next low tide at three p.m.

"Did your father settle in quickly? Make many
friends?"

"He was lost for a while. Mum's passing had been
quick, and he withdrew into his own world. The
little ones were the only things to put a smile on

his face. He used to take them out in the stroller a few times a week. If they were crying and crying. You know when babies just cry for no reason?"

He nodded. Sometimes it didn't matter if Alfie was warm, fed, bathed, had a clean nappy; he could still scream the place down from time to time.

"Well, if they were like that, he'd take them out for fresh air. He swore by it. Said babies in Scandinavia are often left to sleep outside. He said the cold was calming, and you know what? It did the trick every time. They'd come back in sound asleep, their faces like serene angels. When he was out walking, that's when he'd get chatting with the other locals. He made friends that way. That's why I got him Fleabag. He said he didn't want a dog, but I knew the walks and fresh air were good for him, so when one of Finley's colleagues found themselves with an unexpected litter, I took one. I told him he'd be saving it from the shelter."

"It's an unusual name."

She laughed. "Her proper name is Welsh. We couldn't pronounce it, but it sounded a bit like Fleabag, so that's what we called her. We thought it was cute."

"Well, she is a very cute dog," said Tennessee.

"When she's not biting you?"

He shrugged. "She'd been through an ordeal. I know this is going to be quite a difficult question for you to hear, Mona. Did your father fall out with anyone recently? Can you think of anyone who would have reason to harm him?"

Mona shuddered and fell into a fresh wave of tears. Tennessee felt bad, but he'd be a fool not to ask the question.

"Not at all. Dad was well-liked. Yes, he was a bit of a loner when he first moved here, but he got to know the others and enjoyed drinking in The Ship and The Crown. He liked to have a pint and moan with Tom Richardson, Jeff Louis and old William Handleson."

Tennessee made a note. He was sure that the team conducting door to doors would speak to those men in due course. Still, he might go to see them himself and try to look a little deeper into Charles Pennington's life.

"I just don't know how I'm going to break the news to the children. They're going to be devastated. Absolutely devastated."

Denise pushed a plate of biscuits in front of Mona and gently put a hand on her shoulder. "I'll be here. If there's anything you need from me to make this easier for you, you just have to say."

Mona's phone was on the table. She turned it over so she could look at the screen. There were no missed calls or messages. "I just wish Finley was here."

"I'll try again," Denise assured her. "We'll get hold of him and bring him back home as soon as we can."

Tennessee got to his feet. The tiles felt cool through his black socks. "Did Charles ever mention someone called Eve Lynch?"

Mona's eyes moved from right to left as she thought. She was quiet for a moment before shaking her head. "I don't think so. Definitely not recently. Why? Is that the poor woman from Tynemouth?"

"I'm afraid so."

"No. I don't remember that name."

With time, investigators would go through Charles Pennington's belongings and check his phone contacts. If he had a laptop or computer, they would check those devices as well. There was a chance the killer had a thing for people walking alone on beaches in the wee hours. But more likely, there was a connection between Eve and Charles. Would there be more? Tennessee thought as he laced up his shoes. Was he dealing with a serial killer?

- CHAPTER 19 -

A LARGE GLASS OF tasteless rosé had gone to Cooper's head. Her stomach was empty; she had neither the energy nor the inclination to eat. The jukebox had been churning out music that reminded her of nineties caravan park holidays. She thought it couldn't get any worse when *Agadoo* started playing.

She'd been wrong.

The volume was turned up with *The Birdie Song* and again for *Wig Wam Bam.* Cooper had a headache. Still, she was pleased to see Benji's Bar full of smiling people. While she was down, she took comfort in the fact people were celebrating having known Benjamin Cooper. They were regaling each other with tales of fishing trips where they were always inches from capsizing, or the fish was the size of jaws.

"Mum?" Tina tugged at the sleeve of Cooper's cardigan. A couple of tanned ladies in their seventies, wearing skirts shorter than even Cooper would dare, bumped into her as they danced."

"You okay, T?"

She chewed on her lower lip. "You said I only had to stay as long as I felt comfortable, but I've been trying to leave for the past hour. Every time I get out of my seat, someone tells me that Grandad Ben would want me to stay."

Cooper took Tina by the hand and walked out to the patio area, where it was a little bit quieter but twice as smokey. "Grandad Ben wouldn't want you staying a second longer than you wanted to. If any of his friends are trying to guilt you into staying, it's because they're feeling helpless having suffered a loss. They're trying to regain some control by controlling their immediate surroundings. And unfortunately, that has included you. I'm sorry I left your side for that to happen."

Tina looked at the floor. "It's not your fault. I figure you're in the same boat. You don't exactly look happy to be here. Not that you should be happy..." She shuffled awkwardly. "You know what I mean."

"I know what you mean," said Cooper. She took a deep breath, then wrinkled her nose at the scent of cigarettes and acidic wine. "Where would you rather be? You fancy a walk along the beach?"

"If it's okay with you, I'd rather just go to bed. I want to give Josh a ring and go over some of my physics notes. I didn't really take in any of my revision from yesterday."

"I don't blame you. But don't give yourself a hard time if your studying is not going as well as it usually would. It's been a tough few days and you're out of your usual routine. Go up to bed and if anyone tries to stop you, use the self-defence moves I taught you. It'll teach them to think twice about grabbing a teenage girl when she's not suspecting it." She winked at Tina.

Tina grimaced. "I'm not punching anyone in the throat, Mum." She rolled her eyes and headed back inside the bar before scurrying through the back of the kitchen towards the alley that led to Julie and Ben's villa.

Cooper held her glass of rosé up to the light and inspected it. There was a slight cloudiness to it that she didn't like the look of. She put it on a table and pinched the bridge of her nose; her headache was fast becoming a migraine.

There was a lull in the music while the jukebox changed to the next track: *Oops Up Side Your Head*. A group of her parents' friends – buoyed by intoxication – sat on the floor, their legs wrapped around the person in front. In time to the music – sort of – they swayed from side to side, alternating between tapping the floor with their hands and clapping their hands above their head. Cooper's first thought was a question of cleanliness. When was the last time the floor had been disinfected?

Tiptoeing her way around the merriment, trying her best not to stand on anyone's hands, Cooper forced her way through to the bar where her mother was sipping some awful concoction the colour of de-icer.

"How are you doing, Mum?" She opened one of the fridges and got herself a bottle of water. She reached into her pocket, found a few euros and chucked them in the till.

"Erica. I know this is going to sound ridiculous, but your father would have loved today."

"You're right. That does sound ridiculous," Cooper said dryly.

"You know what I mean. He loved it when the bar was heaving like this. Everyone dancing. No one taking themselves too seriously."

Cooper gave half a smile.

"Darling, it's been such a serious day. You are allowed to smile. You are allowed to have fun."

The chilled water energised her. She swallowed down almost the entire bottle in one go; such was her thirst.

A man in a red and white checked shirt approached and asked for a double rum and Coke.

He had thin lips and a slight jaundice tint to his skin. His hair was shaggy and a light shade of grey, whereas his eyebrows were perfectly trimmed and jet black. Cooper was nearest the Bacardi, so she poured him a double measure, topped it up with the supermarket cola that was labelled as Coke and added lemon slices and ice. "That's seven euros sixty, please."

The man looked awkwardly from Cooper to Julie and back again. "Erm... It's an open bar. Isn't it?"

"Mum? I know you want everyone to have a good time. For Dad's wake to be a hit for whatever reason, but honestly, you can't have an open bar."

Julie looked upset. As if she was allowed a free pass to behave however she wanted today because she was grieving. And to a certain extent, she was.

Julie took the drink out of Cooper's hand and gave it to the man in the checked shirt. She turned her back to the bar so she could look at Cooper. "Your father would have approved."

"My father would want the bar to survive. He would want those kids, who have been working their arses off in the kitchen all day, to be paid for their work. For them to have job security."

"Listen to yourself. Talking to me like I'm a child."

Around them, what had been a busy kitchen had gone quiet. The staff who had been hurriedly washing dishes, refilling this that and the other, and bringing items out from storage to replenish the stocks in the fridge were suddenly still. Their ears had pricked up.

"Is this what every mother goes through? You get to a certain age and your daughter starts talking to you like you're the baby?"

"For goodness sake, Mum. That's not what's going on here. But if it makes you feel any better, Tina talks to me like that all the time."

Fresh tears emerged from Julie's eyes; she felt behind her back until she found her sunglasses, angrily forcing them back over her face.

"I haven't seen you in over a year and you swan in telling me how to grieve, how to run the business—"

"Erica," someone shouted from across the bar.

"In a minute," she shouted back. "I did not *swan in,* and I'm not telling you how to grieve, Mum. By all means, have a good time today, celebrate the memories, but you won't have a business if you keep giving away drinks. There must have been. .." She did some quick mental arithmetic. "Thousands of euros pissed away today. I think I'm the only one to put some money in the till."

As Cooper said it, she slapped her hand on the till and it opened with a jolt and a chime. She went to slam it back into position, only the drawer remained lodged in place. "Everything's falling apart, Mum." She tried to speak in gentle tones and get the message across in the nicest way possible. "This is your responsibility now. People's jobs depend on you."

A loud drunken voice from across the bar carried over *Blame It On The Boogie.* "Erica, sweetie."

"Not now." Whatever they wanted, they'd have to wait. She didn't want to play darts or pool, and she certainly didn't want to join in another choreographed dance.

Tears rolled from beneath Julie's shades. She grabbed a handful of flimsy serviettes and dabbed at her face, smudging her plum coloured lipstick. "I think I could do with a double Bacardi myself," she said with a sniffle. She marched across the kitchen, opened her purse and slammed a few euros in the till. "Happy?"

Not really.

"Erica." It was that voice again. She swallowed down all the emotions that were threatening to spill over into an angry yell and forced a polite response while her mother stomped about. "Yes? Can't it wait?"

"Sorry, sweetheart," said a woman with a round face, perfect teeth and a thick heavy fringe of chestnut hair. "But some geezer is looking for you." With her hands full with what looked like two cosmopolitans, she used her elbow to point across the busy room.

What now? Cooper thought to herself. She scanned beyond the pool table until her eyes settled on a tall but slim man. He had impeccable posture, salt and pepper stubble, and an air of confidence and intellect: Justin Atkinson.

She covered the distance in seconds, her heart swelling. "What are you doing here?"

"You sounded like you could use a hug."

She could. She really could.

- CHAPTER 20 -

IT HAD BEEN A tough day. Heck, it had been a tough few months, but as long as crime didn't stop for a break or a holiday, neither could CID.

The satisfaction they had felt after consuming a few slices of pizza much earlier in the day had quickly worn off and now Tennessee was itching for a good meal. He took long strides as he walked over to Keaton and Martin; they were chatting to a member of the public. He tilted his head towards one of the two pubs on the island: The Ship Inn. Keaton and Martin looked like Christmas had come early.

As Tennessee was driving, he could only have half a pint, but the others could relax and enjoy themselves. Heads of both staff and patrons turned and stared as the three detectives entered the bar. As was to be expected, there was a tense atmosphere in the room. People wondered how such a thing had happened in their safe, secluded community.

There was a reason there was no police station based on the island: bad things didn't happen here. Not since the Viking raids. The fear was written on all their faces. Some had moved here to get away from the cities and the crime associated with them. If they weren't safe here, where were they?

Keaton picked out an empty table in the corner. It was surrounded by three small stools covered in blue fabric. Tennessee went to the bar and bought himself a half, Keaton and Martin a pint each and a selection of meals. He knew the team well enough to guess what they'd want to eat. Fish and chips for Martin, mussels in white wine for Keaton, and with his vegan wife an hour and a half away, he ordered himself a beef and ale pie with extra gravy.

Martin took a gulp of lager and put his drink down with a thud. "Well, I think it's safe to say we're not going to get much sleep tonight. Do you think he was buried alive as well?"

Tennessee leant forward. He didn't want any of his neighbouring diners to overhear. "We won't know until we hear back from Margot. But she knows what to look for. Jesus..." He pushed his fingers through his blonde curls. "This is horrific. We need to find out what Eve Lynch and Charles Pennington had in common. The fact that the deaths occurred in such quick succession doesn't make me feel good at all. Not one bit."

"He's gonna kill again. Isn't he?"

Neither Tennessee nor Keaton answered. Martin shook his head and ran a finger through the condensation that formed on his glass. "Do we have any connection so far?"

"The only one I have is that Eve Lynch clearly liked art, her house was full of it, and Charles Pennington was a fan as well. He enjoyed art lessons when he was a teacher, and he named his daughter after the most famous painting of them all. But I can't work out why liking art would get someone killed?"

Martin was already halfway down his pint. It wasn't touching the sides. "Unless..."

"What are you thinking?"

"Could the killings be a distraction for robbery? If they both enjoyed art, perhaps they have expensive paintings that have gone missing while we're all too busy looking at the scenes he's created."

"You can check with Mona. She'll know if anything is missing from her father's house. But as for Eve, she didn't appear to have any family, and I don't think she knew her neighbours well enough to invite them in regularly. Still, it's a hypothesis worth following up on. I'll ask someone to speak to Avani Amin again. She seemed to know her better than most. Have you heard from HQ?"

Keaton shifted her weight on the barstool; it wasn't built for someone her size. Tennessee was a tall man, and his knees came a little higher than his hips as he sat, but he was nowhere near as uncomfortable as Keaton.

"I spoke to Whyte earlier," she said. "Saffron has her work cut out as statement reader; reports are coming in faster than she can process them. But she's doing a great job by all accounts. Plus, there's all the footage and photographs that were uploaded to the site. Anything of interest is being added to HOLMES2. Basically, it's business as usual. Except this is rather unusual, even for our standards."

Tennessee hadn't stopped, hadn't paused for breath. He hadn't really taken the time to think about if he was making the right decisions. "Would Cooper have done anything differently?" he asked.

"No," said Keaton and Martin at the same time.

They paused while their food arrived, pushing their stools back to try and create more space for the plates, cutlery and condiments. Martin didn't waste a second, picking up his knife and fork and diving straight into the battered cod.

"This looks piping hot," he said as a plume of steam erupted from the cooked fish. "You've known Cooper longer than I have, but I don't think she would have done anything differently. In fact, I think if she were here, she would have taken us for a pint as well."

Tennessee's mouth curled, but it was hardly a smile.

Keaton rolled her eyes while she dipped a chip into her white wine sauce. "For goodness sake, am I going to have to tell you to man up? You've done a brilliant job from the second that body was discovered on Saturday. You have this handled. So, stop doubting yourself."

"I can always rely on you to keep it real. But I just keep thinking maybe I should check in, give her a ring see what she—"

Keaton pointed her folk in Tennessee's face. "Don't even think about it. She's off duty. I'm going to say this once more because you're clearly having a moment: You, Detective Sergeant Jack Daniel, are doing a bloody fantastic job. It was only a matter of time before you flew solo and had to lead a major investigation. So it's come earlier than you thought? Embrace it. You've never been afraid of a challenge, so don't start now. You hear me?"

She stabbed her fork into a mussel, swished it around the thick, creamy sauce and popped it into her mouth. She eyed him as she chewed. She swallowed and repeated herself. "I said, do you hear me?"

He did. Sometimes in life, you just needed a pep talk, and there was no one better to deliver those than someone who had been thirty-one down at halftime, only to come out in the second and lead her team to victory.

- CHAPTER 21 -

AFTER MANY HOURS OF day drinking, the mourners had begun to turn in for the night. One by one, they picked up their belongings, cheerfully hugged Julie Cooper and slurred out words of drunken compassion. They swayed and staggered, holding onto the backs of chairs and edges of tables for stability. When only the last few remained, Cooper and Atkinson started to tidy up.

Cooper turned the jukebox down to its lowest setting. It was currently playing *Thunderstruck* by ACDC. At last, a song Ben Cooper would have approved of. Atkinson took a tower of empty pint glasses back to the kitchen and fetched some antibacterial spray and clean cloths. Together they wiped down the tables and filled a black bin liner with used serviettes and scraps of leftover food.

After recovering a stray pool ball that had rolled under one of the patio chairs, Cooper nipped upstairs to see Tina. She knocked gently, but when there was no answer, she pushed the door open ajar. Tina lay facedown under a pile of wavy hair. Her phone and numerous school books were strewn around her. Tina was either out for the count or faking it because she didn't want to be disturbed. If she was faking it, she was doing a good job. Cooper closed the bedroom curtains and switched the light off before quietly shutting the door behind her.

She was proud of Tina and how studying always seemed to ground her no matter what was going on in her life. Cooper would never understand how she managed to focus on her studies after some of the things that had gone on last year.

When she returned downstairs, she found the last few funeral guests huddled around a single table. Julie had pulled out her wedding album as well as a box of photos from their lives back on Tyneside. There was much pointing, laughing and reminiscing. Ben Cooper's old mullet from the eighties was a particular source of amusement.

Cooper placed a tentative hand on her mother's shoulder and gave it a squeeze. "Dishwasher's stacked. Is there anything else I can do?"

Julie must have softened since Cooper's last conversation with her. She placed her hand on her daughter's and looked up at her with an inebriated smile and squinty eyes. "No dear, you go and spend time with that handsome fella of yours."

"We're not together, Mum. We're just friends." Cooper's eyes flickered to Atkinson, and she knew that wasn't entirely the truth.

"Well, you can say that till the cows come home, but men don't fly two thousand miles for *just friends*. Besides, I saw the look on your face when he gave you that hug. I'd recognise that look anywhere."

Cooper didn't protest; she knew her mother wouldn't buy any of it. Instead, she bid goodnight to her drinking buddies, suggested her mother should have a glass of water or a coffee and went to meet Atkinson on the patio.

The sun was beginning to lower, and thanks to a breeze blowing up from the marina, the air had cooled. They had walked to the end of the street before Cooper turned back. "I should have brought a cardigan."

"You own a cardigan?" he asked suspiciously. It was a fair question; it wasn't her usual attire.

"It's strictly for holidays. When a leather jacket won't really cut it."

"Here," Atkinson pulled his long-sleeved t-shirt off. He was wearing a regular t-shirt underneath. "Put this on."

She gave the briefest of protests but quickly gave up the charade and gratefully took the item of clothing. It swamped her, but it did the job of keeping the night breeze off of her. Plus, it smelled of Atkinson. She liked it; there was something comforting about wearing a man's shirt.

"I came here when I was a little kid," said Cooper expanding her arms to gesture to the whole area. "It's what started Mum and Dad's dream of moving here. There was a little hole-in-the-wall place that sold ice creams. I was obsessed with them and needed at least two a day. It's still here, believe it or not, just at the end of the road. I always ordered a Mr Whippy with red sherbet sprinkles and a chocolate flake."

Atkinson put his arm over her shoulder and pulled her close to him. "We can talk about ice cream if you like, but if you'd rather talk about your father or the funeral..."

Cooper chuckled into his chest. "I would very much like to talk about ice cream," she said. "But failing that, I'd like to talk about current events. I haven't exactly been following the news today, but I heard something about a murder on Holy Island."

Atkinson's chest expanded and fell as he took a deep breath. She could feel the heat of his body through his t-shirt against her cheek.

"Same MO," he confirmed. "I didn't go to the scene; I was stuck at airport security. But I heard from Hong a couple of hours ago. It's appalling. What sort of person buries a fellow human alive?"

Though Cooper couldn't see him as her face was nestled in his t-shirt, she could feel him shaking his head. She pulled back and looked up at him. "Buried alive? You're joking?"

The idea filled her with absolute horror. It was the stuff nightmares were made of.

"I think I've spoken out of turn there. That hasn't been released to the public."

Cooper puffed up her cheeks before slowly exhaling. "I'm not surprised. And I'm not the public." She placed her hand on her heart. "But that's not the sort of thing people should read in the papers. They don't need to know monsters are real."

"Come on," said Atkinson, taking her hand in his. He walked further down the *calle*. "I know what you need."

"I can't face any more wine unless it's an exceptional sauvignon. I'm going to have a cracking migraine tomorrow."

Atkinson's stopped and a lent over a wooden counter built into a white building that looked out over the marina. "*Quiero dos* Mr Whippy *con* sherbet *rojo y un* flake *de chocolate, por favor.*"

A teenager with multi-coloured hair looked at him with disdain but quickly fulfilled the order. As they stepped away, Cooper gratefully took the cone of childhood memories. "That was some quality Spanglish *mi amigo guapo.*"

"What does that mean?"

"Never you mind."

They sat on the edge of the pier, their feet dangling over the side, and watched the sun's rapid descent towards the horizon. As darkness fell, she rested her head against Atkinson's shoulder, unable to break the contact between their bodies for even a moment. Her head was heavy with loss and guilt, but her heart was pleased to have quiet company. The water in the marina began to sparkle as restaurants and bars turned on fairy lights, and street lights buzzed back into life after resting all day.

"Are you sure I can't tempt you with some vino? According to Tripadvisor, the bar at my hotel has an excellent selection."

"You booked a hotel?"

"Of course. I didn't want to presume anything, and my sleeping on the beach days are well and truly over."

She slapped his chest playfully. "Double?"

"King. Sea view."

Her lips touched his. Two months – eight long weeks – of not being together erased in a second. "Then why," she mumbled into his lips, "are we sat here waiting for the mozzies to strike when we could be entwined in white sheets with a bottle chilling in the cooler?"

His hand found her waist as they kissed.

"How do you do it?" he asked.

"Do what?"

"Make me feel young again."

She got to her feet and dusted her dress and the long-sleeve t-shirt she'd borrowed. "One of my many talents. Come on. We only have eleven hours before my teenager notices I'm missing."

IT FELT LIKE HOURS had passed. The pub was warm, the barkeep friendly, and the grub satisfying. The three detectives managed to finish every last morsel of food on their plates. Still, the extra food in their bellies did nothing to alleviate their low moods; the task they were facing was monumental. Keaton and Martin ordered a couple more pints. And then a couple more. Tennessee didn't mind; they deserved a bit of relaxation time. Besides, if he needed a drink with a percentage mark, he could have it when he got home.

Keaton stood and stretched both her legs. Then she pulled her scapulars back, opening up her chest and letting out a rather impressive yawn. "April will be wondering where I am. We should probably hit the road."

The others agreed and got to their feet.

Keaton called shotgun and jumped in the front passenger seat. They fastened their seatbelts and drove back towards the causeway, chatting about Tennessee's choice of radio station and Martin's obvious infatuation with Saffron Boyd – which he vehemently denied.

It was late but still technically twilight. To their right, long grass jetted into a darkening blue sky; to their left, shorter marshy bits of grass poked out of the boggy land.

Tennessee slowed the car to a halt. Keaton rubbed her eyes and looked up from a game of Candy Crush. "What's the hold-up?"

Tennessee pointed ahead just as the last bit of suitable road was engulfed by the North Sea. Time and tide waited for no man, and nowhere was that more apparent than a tidal island. Every month the RNLI had to rescue at least one daft fool who'd tried to race the torrent and lost. Tennessee liked a good race but not one where losing could result in death. He wasn't going to be one of those fools.

"Balls," he said.

Martin put his hand to his forehead and took a deep breath. Keaton was more forceful, slapping herself with a facepalm movement.

"Balls," they echoed.
They were stuck for the night.

CHAPTER 22

"BUSTED."

The pep in Cooper's step faltered as she and Atkinson emerged from the resort hotel the following day. Sat on a sun lounger, with a face like thunder, was Tina.

Cooper had cherished every second of last night. She and Atkinson stayed up until the early hours, their limbs tangled beneath white sheets. Aside from the obvious, they'd spent time talking and catching up, hashing out the problems that had arisen towards the end of their relationship. Cooper didn't want to feel like she was anyone's property or a child that needed protecting. But the main issue in their relationship had come in the form of a big, burly man. Thanks to an iron-clad restraining order, he was no longer a problem.

It was a little after half seven and Cooper couldn't believe Tina was already awake and dressed. Unless it was a school day, she wouldn't emerge from her room until gone ten.

Cooper had used the power shower in Atkinson's room. However, she was still wearing her black dress from yesterday's funeral, and it had a funky aroma to it now. Atkinson had his running gear on and was ready to jog from Puerto Del Carmen to Puerto Calero via the cliff walk. There and back would take him about an hour at a gentle pace. He removed his arm from Cooper's shoulders and started jogging on the spot.

"As much as I'd love to watch your fifteen year old give you 'the talk' because you stayed out all night, I'm going running. I'll see you at lunch." He kissed her, gave Tina an awkward wave and headed out into the Canarian sunshine.

"MORNING, NOW BEFORE YOU say anything, I'm sorry. Wait—" Something suddenly occurred to Cooper. "How did you know I was here?"

"I logged into your Google account and used the *find my device* feature.

"Okay. One, how do you know what my password is? And two, isn't that a gross invasion of privacy?"

"Your password is *Metallicarocks87*. You don't need to be a genius to work it out – though I am. And no, you were kidnapped a few months ago. I think I have a right to be worried if you disappear."

Cooper exhaled and let her anger fizzle away. Tina might look like she was ready to throttle Cooper, with her arms folded and her forehead crumpled, but she was right. "I'm sorry I caused you to worry, T. Justin arrived after you'd gone to bed, and frankly, I needed a bit of a shoulder to cry on. I know you always approved of Justin, so be mad at me, don't give him a hard time, okay? I know I should have woken you before disappearing—"

Tina shoved her phone in Cooper's face. "Never mind that. This is more important."

Cooper blinked at the bright screen. She expected to see another murder scene, another attention-grabbing headline about an elderly person buried in sand. Instead, she was looking at an Instagram post by *Lana.Bellos365*. A heavily filtered photo showed a girl with sharp cheekbones and fake lashes next to a pale boy with light brown hair and braces over his teeth. She recognised the boy as Josh, Tina's boyfriend. She and Josh had been together for what seemed like forever now. She read the caption: *Studying with my new bestie at the Glass Tea House. Plenty of grey matter and blue skies.*

The glass tea house was a cafe in Northumberland Park, a landscaped area of greenery between North Shields and Tynemouth.

"What am I looking at, Tina?"

"Besties?" Tina practically screeched the word. "How can they be besties? They've known each other like five minutes."

"This is Lana from netball, right? Goal attack?"

"Yes, how did you know that?"

"You told me."

"And you remembered?"

"Of course I remembered." Cooper put her hands on her hips, insulted that her daughter thought she never listened to her. There was a deep rumbling from her belly and for the first time in days, she was actually hungry. "Do you fancy a full English?"

"No, mum." Tina's voice was sulky.

In the distance, Atkinson was picking up the pace, his long legs striding out in front of him as he rounded the marina.

"So, Josh is studying with someone else. That's not a problem, is it?"

"He's not just studying with someone else. He's studying with another girl."

"And you're jealous of Miss Long Lashes here? Come on, Tina. Josh adores you, and you know it."

"So why didn't he tell me? Why was it a secret? I asked him last night what he'd been up to all day. He told me he played football after school. He didn't say anything about going to the park to study with Lana."

The way Tina said *study* made it sound sordid. Jealousy never looked good on anyone. It didn't look good on Atkinson when he'd been insecure about Kenny. It didn't look good on Cooper when she'd been sick with envy about Veronica Rogers, and it didn't look good on Tina now.

"You can't stop each other from having friends. You said yourself you should have a wider social circle—"

"She's doing this on purpose. I'm out of the country for two seconds and... Urgh." She squirmed, her mouth pinching this way and that. "She knows how I feel about Josh. She knows that he and I are...." She picked up her biology textbook and slammed it on the floor. The hardback cover made a thudding noise as two hundred pages of GCSE science information met concrete.

Cooper adjusted her posture. She wanted a slice of toast, a change of clothes, and to check on her mother. Julie would be waking up to her fifth morning without Ben. The shock and denial would be wearing off soon, and she would be faced with pain and fear as well as the reality of now running a struggling business single-handedly. She'd also be facing a rather chronic hangover.

"Do you think you're overreacting ?" Cooper asked. "I mean, it's not like they're on a date. They're just studying."

Tina grunted and hurriedly started packing her things back into her satchel. "I knew you wouldn't understand."

Cooper wanted to understand, of course she did, but she also felt like there were more important issues at hand than puppy love. "So help me understand."

Tina scrunched her mouth into a terrible grimace. She looked like she wanted to scream, and for a moment, Cooper was worried she would. Shoving her hands in her pockets, Tina turned her back on Cooper, grumbling, "Forget it." She trudged off towards the sea, casting a final insult back at her mother. "And only old people listen to Metallica."

- CHAPTER 23 -

TENNESSEE SHIVERED AS HE knocked on the door to the morgue. He didn't know if it was the air-conditioning, the dead, or the woman who cared for them that made his skin ripple into goosebumps. It was probably a combination of all three.

Hayley had not been impressed that he hadn't come home last night. Although he called the second he knew he wasn't going to make it, he could tell by the tone of her voice that his apology was not getting him anywhere. When he returned home this morning for a shower and a change of clothes, his mother-in-law was especially unhappy about him being away with another woman. The fact Paula Keaton was not his type and that he was most definitely not Keaton's type was lost on her. He'd pick up a bottle of wine and one of those Indian meal deals with the veggie samosas that Hayley loved when he was finished today. That ought to get him back in the win column. If it didn't, he'd give Alfie his bath and read him a bedtime story. That was a guaranteed way of winning around the two ladies of the house.

"Ah, there you are, Jack." The top two buttons of Margot Swanson's lab coat were undone, and Tennessee was sure she'd had it altered to create a tighter fit around her waist. She held out her hand for Tennessee to shake, then she lifted her fingers in front of his face to display perfectly polished nails. "New shade. It's called Exotic Cranberry. You like?"

Tennessee didn't know what colour cranberries were, but Margot's nails were red with a hint of purple. They seemed a bit vampy, but he was pleased she kept them short for work. He imagined long talons would go straight through sterile gloves, then God knows what would end up stuck behind your nails. The thought of it made him queasy.

"Erm... Very nice," he said dryly, carefully manoeuvring his way around her.

Margot rested her hands on the side of a gurney. "Just terrible, don't you think?"

"Yeah. Think we're looking at a serial killer who's not afraid to—"

"Not that, sweetheart." Margot began to lay out her instruments. "I'm not talking about poor old Mr Pennington here. Didn't you see the news this morning?"

"Missed it. I was in a rush."

"Didn't listen during the commute?"

Tennessee shook his head, gulping when he saw the Enterotomes – special scissors used to cut through intestines. "Not today."

"A wee girl's been snatched. Poor angel. Her parents must be distraught. Can you imagine?"

Tennessee couldn't imagine. He wasn't a violent man by nature, but one thing guaranteed to get a reaction from him was a threat to his family or closest friends. If someone tried to take his little boy, it would be the last thing they ever did.

"Anyway, I just hope she turns up unharmed. Pretty thing she is as well." She stopped as if contemplating something, and Tennessee wondered if she was having the same dark thoughts he was. Margot didn't have children; that didn't mean she didn't have youngsters she cared about.

"Best crack on," she said, dragging herself back to the task at hand.

Margot donned her PPE, and something about the way she pulled on her nitrile gloves made Tennessee feel like he was about to have a cavity search. He swallowed and moved his back to the wall. Suitably attired, Margot unzipped a bodybag and picked up her dictaphone.

"Charles Pennington. DOB twenty-seven May 1941. Aged seventy-eight. Identification confirmed by next of kin. Height is five feet and nine inches. Weight is sixty-eight kilograms."

Margot carefully removed the deceased's clothing. She bagged individual items to be sent to the lab for examination. They would try to find DNA or other evidence that could identify the murderer.

"Commencing external examination. Extensive bruising to head. Blood in his hair. Jagged cut to left temple suggesting impact from a hard, sharp-edged object. The nose has been broken, as has the right cheekbone. Multiple pairs of oval bruises of approximately two centimetres in length and one and a half centimetres in width suggest beating by a closed fist. Estimate perpetrator's hands to be twelve centimetres across the full width of the knuckles."

"Was he beaten to death?" Tennessee was doing his best to watch the examination but knew he'd start turning his head away once the bone cutters came out.

"He was beaten, then he died," Margot said in a patronising tone. "But, my dear, if you want me to be more specific, you'll need to be patient. The manner of death was almost certainly homicide, but the cause and mechanism are yet to be determined. The blunt force trauma to the temple may well be the culprit, and at this gentleman's age, the shock and distress could have triggered heart failure. I won't know if he was still conscious when he was buried until I can examine the lungs."

"Any chance of a cup of tea?"

"In my sterile environment?" She raised an accusatory eyebrow. "Not likely. Besides, do I look like a tea lady to you?"

He shook his head. "I've never met a tea lady remotely like you."

"Well, if you want to take me to Costa afterwards, you need only ask."

146

Redirecting his attention to a poster warning of cross-contamination, Tennessee allowed Margot to continue.

"Distinguishing marks include a mole on the right cheek, an appendectomy scar, and a scar on the back of the right hand." She proceeded with the rest of the external examination, working her way from the head down to the toes. She took Charles Pennington's fingerprints and checked under his eyelids and inside his mouth. When she was finished, she picked up a scalpel. "If you're feeling fragile, now's the time to avert your eyes. Commencing internal examination— Hold up. What do we have here?"

Tennessee looked up. He'd been studying his shoes.

Margot placed her scalpel back on the bench and returned to Charles Pennington's hair. She parted his white hair with gloved fingers and removed a single strand of yellow. It wasn't until she bagged it and handed it to him that Tennessee realised what had caught her attention.

"Look familiar?" she asked.

"It looks like a fibre of the same fabric we found on Eve Lynch."

COOPER HELD FOUR TICKETS in her hand. She'd booked a sunset cruise for Tina, Julie, Atkinson and herself. The tickets were over thirty euros per person, but she thought her mother and daughter could use the distraction. Plus, she loved the idea of spending time on the water with Atkinson. She'd checked the reviews and it sounded like a lovely evening. There would be Champagne, canapés and a saxophonist. From what she'd read, they were almost guaranteed to see dolphins. That would cheer Tina up, she thought. Dolphins made everyone smile. Perhaps they could turn the trip into a private, family-only wake. No dodgy music or freeloaders dancing to *We No Speak Americano*. True, Atkinson wasn't family, but at least he'd be there for the right reasons.

Cooper hadn't seen Atkinson since that morning; he'd given her space while he dialled into a forensic conference in Dublin. Cooper used the time to sit Julie down and go through some numbers. Benji's was salvageable – just. They'd need to reduce staff numbers but only slightly. They could streamline the menu to reduce food waste and stop free pouring spirits. If someone asked for a single, they'd get a standardised single, not a treble. Julie would have to let the cleaning lady go and take on those responsibilities herself. She'd protested; the cleaner was an old friend by all accounts, but from what Cooper could tell, she hadn't exactly done a good job. It was money Julie didn't need to spend, and she'd do a better job herself. Cooper also planned on asking Tina to help out. She thought she could set up some social media for the bar. It had a Facebook page, but it hadn't been updated in months. She could set up Instagram, list the bar on Google and look into boosting some posts for greater exposure.

Folding the tickets into her purse, Cooper knocked on Tina's door. She hadn't seen her since that morning and assumed she was buried under a mound of revision.

When there was no answer, Cooper knocked again and pushed the door open. The room was empty. A pink Post-it note pressed to the cover of a hardback mathematics book read *Gone snorkelling. Back in three hours.*

Whilst Cooper loved the idea of Tina enjoying herself, getting some exercise and taking her mind off Josh, she wished she'd said what time she'd written the note. Three hours from when?

She was about to leave Tina's room when Cooper noticed a scribble in the margin of one of her many notebooks. Written in graphite, next to what looked like a tear stain, were the words *he said he loved me.*

Cooper sat down on the bed, her heart heavy. Love seemed like a pretty big emotion for a fifteen-year-old, but casting her mind back to her youth, all her feelings had seemed heightened as well. Fondness could be infatuation, joy could be ecstasy, and sadness was the deepest depression. Tina had always been the sensitive, mushy one in their little family, even if she hadn't always been able to express it. Still waters ran deep.

Cooper was beginning to see why Tina was so worked up. She'd been wrong to think of their relationship as puppy love. They were inseparable, and in fairness to Tina, her relationship with Josh had lasted longer than any of her own. The heat of protectiveness began to burn in her chest. He'd uttered the L-word for the first time, then hung out alone with another girl the moment Tina left the country. They'd just been studying, she reminded herself. Josh wouldn't cheat on Tina. Not shy, quiet, wouldn't-say-boo-to-a-goose Josh.

- CHAPTER 24 -

NINE A.M. FRIDAY MORNING and Tennessee was handing out copies of the autopsy report from Margot Swanson. Last night's vegan samosas had thawed Hayley's frosty feelings towards him, but he now had what was technically called 'a dicky tummy.' His lower abdomen cramped as he addressed the room. He'd better keep the morning briefing, well, brief.

"It's as we feared," he told them. "Another victim buried alive, suffocated in the sand. Margot's confirmed sand particles were found in the lungs of Charles Pennington, just like they were in Eve Lynch. Given the similarities in MO and the cause of death, I think it's safe to say we are dealing with the same killer. Other than that, I'm not sure what connects these victims. They're not that close in age, and speaking to Pennington's family, they don't think he knew the first victim. Both victims had appendectomy scars, but to be honest, I don't

151

think that's relevant; more of a coincidence than a connection." He turned to Saffron Boyd. "You said you might have something?"

Boyd got to her feet. Her hair was tied back in a loose bun, but a stray hair poked upwards like an antenna. "Yes, sir. Having looked at the victims' work history, they were both based in South Tyneside in the mid-eighties to mid-nineties. Pennington was at King George Primary School from eighty-six to ninety-seven, and Lynch worked for South Tyneside council until ninety-six."

"Do we know what Lynch did at the council? What department she was in?"

Boyd shook her head, more blonde hair falling free from the bun. She quickly pushed the stray strands back behind her ears. "All I know from her tax history is that she was being paid by South Tyneside Council. I'll try to dig further into it, but I'm swamped."

"Thanks. It's a good spot, Saffron. And just because Pennington's daughter didn't recognise Eve's name doesn't mean they didn't know each other. I mean, how many of us can name our parents' work colleagues? Whyte, how are the office team getting on?"

"Saffron's drowning in statements, gaffer. Everyone on that beach was a witness to the body being discovered, and yet, not a single one of them was a witness to the crime. I have no description of the perpetrator, and we can't narrow the timeframe down any further than we already have."

"Crap," said Tennessee.

"Exactly," echoed Whyte. "If you could get me a few more sets of eyes to help the statement reader and to speed up the rate we can view the footage, it would be most appreciated. I swear my eyes are starting to go square with all that screen time."

Tennessee turned to Keaton. "Can you have a word with Nixon? See if he'll give us a few more bodies. No pun intended."

Keaton laughed and cocked her head and his direction. "You're SIO. How come you're not asking?"

His stomach cramped again. "Because he's scared of you."

"True," she said with a smile. "I'll ask him this afternoon; he's at some committee bollocks this morning."

"Okay, cheers." That was a relief. Nixon made him nervous. "Which brings us to this." He pointed to two photographs on the murder board. "The fabric found in Eve Lynch's hand and a thread that was found on Charles Pennington. It looks to be the same material. We'll have it confirmed later today. Justin Atkinson's flying back today; he messaged earlier to say he'll double-check the results so we can be sure. Now, if this is the same material, it means one of two things. Either, our perpetrator is not forensically aware, because if he had half a brain cell, he would have disposed of the clothes as soon as he'd killed Eve Lynch. Or, he is forensically aware, but his need for ritual is greater than his need to dispose of his clothing. Between the clothes and the snake, these things are important to him."

"Like the tarot card killer?" Martin asked.

"Not in a hocus-pocus, closer to the devil type bollocks, but yeah, there's a process here." Tennessee's hand moved to his stomach. "Right. We all know where our priorities lie. Cooper's back on Monday; it would be nice to have at least one suspect to present to her. I don't think any of us want to look like we've been busy doing nothing this whole time. Martin, you're with me. We're heading back to Holy Island."

Martin got to his feet and handed his copy of the autopsy report to Keaton. "Have you checked the tide times, guv?"

"Erm... No, I didn't." Tennessee was beginning to sweat with pain. He edged to the door, calling back over his shoulder. "You check. I'll meet you at the car."

"How do people cope living here?" Martin asked. "No police, no supermarket, no doctor. They don't even have a Nando's. Their entire lives are dictated by the tides. If I fancy a pizza for tea, I just nip to ASDA. Can't do that here."

Tennessee hummed a non-committal answer. He was concentrating on the narrow country road that led to the causeway.

"What if you want a takeaway? Or want to go clubbing?" He pulled his phone from his pocket and accessed Google Maps. "Whoa. Say you went for a night out in the toon. You'd need to get a train to Berwick, then a bus to Holy Island. Takes over two hours, and I bet they don't run late at night. You'd have to get a hotel."

I think all the things you're listing as negatives are the very reasons people move here. No loud clubs, no mess from takeaways, no sirens—"

"Would you want to live here?"

"And have a five-hour commute every time I wanted to watch united at home? I don't think so. But I can see why others would."

As they crossed the causeway, Jack noticed how even though it had been a few days since it last rained, the land around them was damp and marshy, water pooling in puddles on either side of the road. A few hours ago, it hadn't been a road at all; it had been the sea.

They parked on Lewins Lane next to a rusty Vauxhall Astra that had been peppered in seagull poop. Tennessee knocked on Mona Clydesdale's door. It was Denise Oswald, the FLO, who answered.

"How are they?" he asked, referring to the second victim's family.

"As you'd expect." Denise's short brown hair was greasier than when they saw her last, and she had greenish shadows under her eyes. "They've kept the kids off school, understandably. Raven took them up to his farm to help with the sheep. It'll keep them out of trouble for a few hours. They've been crawling the walls stuck at home, and I think Mona's struggling to cope as it is without two hyperactive kids to deal with as well. They're obviously devastated and confused to hear about their grandfather. The girl, Laura, gave me a bit of a hard time when I couldn't answer her questions. The father came down on her like a tonne of bricks and sent her to her room, which probably didn't help."

"So Finley Clydesdale has returned from Berlin?"

"Yes, late last night. And it's probably nothing, but he was a bit shifty about why it took him so long to answer Mona's messages. If you ask me, he wasn't working in Berlin; he was off screwing someone else."

"That, or he's the one who killed his father-in-law," said Martin.

Denise pouted for a moment. "You might want to check the flight manifests and make sure he was on that flight."

Tennessee opened his notepad and wrote a reminder to himself to do just that. "Will do."

He and Martin followed Denise into the Clydesdales' living room, where they found Mona busy in the kitchen. Finley sat at the dining table, staring intently at a spreadsheet. He didn't look up.

Mona shuffled across the room to greet them. She was dressed in slippers and a dressing gown and looked like she hadn't got a moment's peace since finding out her father had been killed.

"Has there been any news?" she asked, wiping her hands on a tea towel and placing it on the kitchen bench."

Tennessee didn't want to lie or give a diplomatic answer, such as *enquiries are ongoing*. He shook his head. "I'm afraid not, but rest assured we'll be going through all the statements we took on Wednesday with a fine-tooth comb. We have a great team of forensic experts looking for physical evidence as well."

She looked to the floor, fighting back tears, then steadied herself against the door frame. Behind her, a beeping noise sounded from one of the appliances. The noise seemed to shake Mona. She went to the oven and turned it off. Opening the oven door, the entire downstairs of the house filled with warmth and the smell of freshly baked bread."

"That smells amazing," said Martin. "My mum likes baking bread. She tried to teach me, but I never quite got the hang of it. I'm too impatient. I never worked the dough enough."

"Oh, I really enjoy it," said Mona. "It's probably the only hobby I really have. I used to enjoy crafts and making jewellery. I never seem to have time these days, not with two children. I only made the loaf and the batch of rolls as some sort of distraction. I don't think it's working, though. I can't stop thinking about Dad. I just keep thinking how he must have been in the wrong place at the wrong time because there's no way someone would have wanted to hurt him."

Tennessee flashed a glance in Finley Clydesdale's direction but he didn't flinch.

"Mona, I was hoping you could accompany us to your father's house. If you're feeling up to it, that is."

"Of course." She removed a health looking loaf of brown bread topped with various seeds and placed it on a rack to cool. "I'll get myself dressed. Give me two minutes."

Mona rushed upstairs. After a moment of banging and clattering, she returned in a pair of mom jeans and a knitted sweater.

It was only a two-minute walk from the Clydesdales' home on Lewins Lane to Charles Pennington's place on Marygate.

"Before we go in, Mona, it's important to tell you that forensic investigators have been in the home. They're respectful and try to leave things as they found them, but I want to warn you in case anything seems out of place. Investigators have already taken your father's phone and tablet. Am I right in thinking he didn't have a laptop or desktop computer?"

"That's right. He had a book reader, though."

Tennessee and Martin waited while Mona undid the locks and showed them both into the house. The house hadn't sat empty since its owner's death with SOCOs having been in to do their thing. Still, the house had a chill to it, as if the very bricks and mortar knew that their owner had left.

"Can the e-reader be used to communicate digitally with anyone?"

"Oh, I don't think so. No," she said. "And even if it could, I doubt Dad would know how to do that. Whenever he wanted new books downloading, he had to bring it to my house and get me or the kids to do it."

Charles Pennington's home was a combination of floral wallpaper and highly polished pine. The house was a time warp with heavy fabric hanging from curtain poles and patterned tile surrounds on the fireplaces. It suited the old cottage.

"How is it I can help you?" asked Mona.

"I know it's a tough thing to think about," Denise said in a soft voice. "But DS Daniel needs to consider that your father might not have been in the wrong place at the wrong time. It would be irresponsible of him if he didn't. We need to understand your father's life, everyone who was in it or was once in it. We need to see if any of those people also link to the victim from Tynemouth."

Mona looked instantly heavier as if the thought of her father being specifically targeted weighed her down like an invisible cloak of chain mail.

"He kept lots of scrapbooks. Photos from the schools he worked in. Would those help?"

"They'd be a great help," Denise told her.

"They really would," echoed Tennessee.

Mona showed them to her father's dining room, where an old fashioned unit covered most of the wall. The base of the unit had a cupboard on each side and a set of draws through the middle. On the top layer was a display case for glassware or collectables.

"In here, I think." Mona opened one for the lower cupboards and bent to retrieve a few items. Her knees creaked as she straightened up.

"Are you okay, Mona?" Denise asked after Mona groaned and rubbed her knees. "Can I get you some paracetamol?"

"I don't think paracetamol cures ageing," she said. She placed a pile of leather-bound journals and photo albums on the table. "There are boxes of family photos as well if you think they'll help."

"Thanks. I think we have enough to get started with. Do you mind if we sit at your father's table?"

"Not at all."

Denise excused herself to go to the coffee shop and get them all hot drinks. Tennessee opened the first photo album; thirty smiling faces looked back at him. The first page was a class photograph of young children arranged in neat rows. A younger Charles sat in the front row on a chair while the front row of students sat crossed-legged on the floor. It seemed so stuffy and formal compared to the class photographs he'd seen colleagues bring into work to show off. These days they had sleek white backgrounds with kids posed in friendship groups, often with props from the fancy dress basket.

"This is Whitely Lodge," he said with a smile of nostalgia. "The uniform's changed, it's navy blue now, but the crest's the same." He flicked through a few more pictures from the same school until the uniforms changed to bottle green. "Do you know which school this is?"

Mona leant in and shook her head. "Sorry."

Martin performed a Google image search of King George Primary, Hebburn and showed Tennessee the screen. "Royal blue sweatshirts are what they wear now."

"What about thirty, forty years ago?"

"I'll phone the school. See if any staff were around then." He stood up and left.

For a few moments, Tennessee flicked through the albums, wondering if one of the angelic faces was responsible for burying two people alive.

"Grey."

Tennessee looked up from his daydreaming. Martin was back, phone in hand.

"School admin has been there forever. Before they changed to sweatshirts and polo shirts, the male students wore grey woollen V-neck sweaters with white shirts and red and grey ties. The girls wore white blouses with grey V-neck cardigans."

It didn't take long for Tennessee to find and select the class photos from King George's. There were eleven of them. Charles Pennington must have worked there for over a decade. Over three hundred and thirty former pupils.

"Could I take these, Mona?"

She looked hesitant but Tennessee didn't want to use his phone to take photos of photos. He'd prefer to scan the originals and enhance them where possible.

"We can have them back with you on Monday. I promise to take great care of them."

"Whatever helps the investigation, I suppose." She wrapped her arms around her middle and sighed before jumping, suddenly startled by a shriek from outside.

A skinny girl with dark blonde hair ran past the window, squealing at the top of her lungs and waving her arms above her head.

Two seconds later, a herd of panicked sheep thundered by.

"Oh, for crying out loud." Mona got to her feet and left the house, almost bumping into Denise and her tray of coffees.

"I assume that's her daughter?" asked Tennessee.

"Yip. That's Laura."

- CHAPTER 25 -

TENNESSEE TURNED LEFT OFF the A19. Two right turns later and he was in the car park of a MacDonald's restaurant. Oliver Martin was hungry and Tennessee never turned down the chance to eat fast food.

"I'll go in and get it," Tennessee said. The drive-thru would be quicker, but his stomach had been playing silly buggers for almost two hours and he was sick of clenching. There was no way he'd do what he needed to do in the home of a murder victim's daughter, and he'd never live it down if he stank out HQ. So the McDonald's at Silverlink would have to do.

Once he'd made his deposit at the porcelain bank, Tennessee ordered two Big Mac meals and hoped that was the end of the matter. Vegan food was bad for you. He swore it was.

"What took so long?" asked Martin.

"There was a queue," he lied. "Now fill your pie hole."

When they returned to the incident room, three new faces greeted him. All three were studiously scrolling through photographs taken after the Tynemouth murder. Eyes squinting, chins propped in hands as they clicked from one image to the next.

"You're a star," he told Keaton. She was updating the murder board and had blue ink smudged over her jaw. "I owe you one for sorting the extra help, that's for sure."

"One? You owe me like twenty-five. And how come your breath smells of Maccy D's? I could do with a portion of fries."

"I thought your body was a temple?"

"Hey, I don't care where I get my calories, as long as I get them."

Tennessee looked around the incident room and was pleased to see everyone getting on with their various tasks. Fingers fluttered over keyboards as HOLMES2 was updated and cross-referenced. The soundtrack to the office featured the rhythmic hum of photocopiers and printers. Phones rang, chairs scraped, feet shuffled.

"Don't get used to it," Keaton told him.

"Used to what?"

She swept a bulky arm in an arc to indicate the incident room in its entirety.

"All these people knuckling down on the case. I reckon we're going to lose some manpower to the Summer Holt investigation."

"That the missing girl?"

Keaton nodded. "Playing in her back garden one minute, gone the next. Her mum's Portia Holt, the romance writer."

The skin tightened around Tennessee's eyes. Even he'd heard of Portia Holt; Pat was a voracious reader of her novels. Her books could always be found on the coffee table in his living room: a bronzed Adonis, a swooning woman, the words *bestseller,* and *three million copies sold.* "Have they made a ransom demand?"

She pulled a face. "That's all I know. Fuller's SIO for now, but I doubt that'll last. They'll have some high profile negotiator come in if this is a hostage for ransom case."

Tennessee felt sick that people could be so cruel as to take a child to exploit their parents. Still, he'd seen worse. Much worse. "Has Whyte come up for breath yet?"

"Barely."

Keaton put the lid back on a dry marker and stored it in a drawer. Whyte, she told Tennessee, has been looking at door cam footage for the past three hours but had nipped out to interview someone. A Tynemouth resident had heard a suspicious noise at two a.m. on the morning of Eve Lynch's murder. Spirits were raised but quickly dashed when it turned out there was nothing more to the intel. The witness – if they could be called that – didn't see anything. Nor could he describe the noise in any more detail than "a dragging noise that lasted about five seconds."

"Never mind," Tennessee said with a sigh. He had somewhere else to be. "Fancy a drive out? I'm headed south of the water."

———

ARMED WITH ENHANCED COPIES of the photographs he'd taken from Charles Pennington's house, Tennessee and Keaton parked at King George's School. The school retained its red brick exterior from the turn of the century. A large glass atrium had been added to the front, increasing the square footage and allowing more light into the old building.

After being buzzed into the atrium, they were met by a lady with tight white curls and a stern expression.

"Yes? How can I help you?"

"Mrs Annabelle Jones? I'm DS Jack Daniel, this is DS Paula Keaton. You spoke to my colleague DC Martin earlier today. I wanted to thank you for the information you provided about the school uniform. It was useful. DC Martin mentioned that you'd worked here a long time?"

"Almost forty years," she said. "When Thatcher was the PM, and the radio was all Bucks Fizz and Culture Club. I miss music you can actually understand the lyrics to. These days it's all slang and nonsense."

Tennessee changed the subject. "I need to discuss a former member of staff. I don't know if you saw the news, but there was an incident on Holy Island in the early hours of Wednesday morning. I'm afraid a former member of staff has died in suspicious circumstances. You may remember him."

Her face scrunched up into several lines as if her skin were made of crêpe paper.

"You don't need to sugarcoat anything, DS Daniel. If *suspicious circumstances* means murder, then just say it. Who was it? You can say their name?"

"Charles Pennington."

Her eyes closed as if it took more effort to hold her lids open after the news.

"You knew him?"

"I remember Charles; he was a lovely man. Do you want to step into the office? The bell will sound soon, and then the world and his mother will be traipsing through here."

She showed them through to what must be command central. A bank of computers was monitored by admin assistants who fielded calls, counted dinner money, checked this and ticked that.

Presumably reading Tennessee's mind, she added. "It used to just be me in here. Well, not here exactly. I had a pokey little room with a hatch for dealing with parents. It's a storeroom now. Every year there's more paperwork. The number of students stays the same, but the admin seems to increase exponentially. Lots of it's done on computers now. I couldn't stand the darn things back then. I'm not too bad these days, though. I set up the year group Twitter accounts, and we have Spotify in the staff room. I've made some great playlists."

"Can you tell us about Mr Pennington?" Keaton asked. "What he was like? Was there anyone he didn't get on with?"

Annabelle Jones moved some papers and parked her rear on the edge of the desk. "He was a quiet man. Very polite. Old fashioned, even for those days. Always held the door. A *ladies first* sort of gentleman."

"So he was well-liked?

"He wasn't everyone's cup of tea. The more – how should I say this? – the more testosterone-fuelled amongst us thought he was a bit effeminate. Different times," she said by way of explanation. "But overall, yes, he was liked. He wasn't a pushover, but he wasn't as strict as some other teachers. I think that's why the children liked him; he didn't talk down to them."

"The men you referred to," started Keaton. "You wouldn't remember their names would you?"

"There were two of them. Bullies to the staff and bullies to the children. If you ask me, they bullied their wives too. Hmm, there was Mr Francis. He taught French. Made us all call him *Monsieur Francis*. Used to think he was so sophisticated. He'd jet off to the continent every Easter holiday. Then when the summer term started, he'd waffle on about this wine and that food. Laughed at me, actually laughed at me, because I'd never heard of whatever vineyard he was drooling over." Her eyes narrowed as she picked a small scab on the side of her thumb. "Prick," she added under her breath. "The other one taught PE and games. Oh, what was he called? Henry something. Petts. Henry Petts. The kids used to call him Sweaty Petty."

Annabelle let out a tiny chuckle, as did Keaton.

"He did have a certain aroma," she said with a tilt of her head and a raise of her eyebrow. "Big man he was. Not muscly like you, dear, just big. You'd think a PE teacher would spend a lot of time playing sport. Pretty sure the only time he ran was when he had to get to the bar before last orders. He had diabetes when he retired," she said, her eyes drifting upwards and to the side as she recalled the memory. "My niece has diabetes, but she was born with it. It's not the same."

Tennessee hoped Annabelle would have contact details for Pennington's former colleagues.

"*Monsieur Francis* died in a car accident. Silly sod was using his phone at the wheel. Idiot. And to think we talk about kids being addicted to their phones and driving too fast. You ask me, some of us elders are just as bad. At least no one else was hurt when he drove into that ditch. Do you know what he was doing with his phone?"

Annabelle leant closer to Tennessee.

"He was watching porn," she said in a whisper. "Now what people do in the privacy of their own homes is their own damn business, but *Mr Sophisticated* watching that filth while driving home to his family? It's disgusting, isn't it?"

"And dangerous," said Tennessee. "What about Mr Petts?"

"Oh, no idea. It's not like I wanted to keep in touch with him after he left here. I think he moved to the West End."

Tennessee decided to take a different tack. If they thought that Mr Petts was a credible lead, they'd be able to track him down one way or another.

"Could you take a look at these photographs?" He asked, spreading them out over the desk next to Annabelle. She hopped down from her perch, crossed her arms and pursed her lips as she perused the images of smartly dressed pupils sitting in neat rows around Charles Pennington.

"Oh my. Look at some of those haircuts."

"We'd like class registers for all the form groups Charles Pennington taught."

Annabelle picked up a photograph, gave a nostalgic smile and placed it back down. She looked up at Tennessee. "Charles worked here for ten years."

"We know. It will be a long list, but it would really help our investigation."

"I'm not sure I can tell you their names. Child protection and all that. Though I suppose none of them are children anymore, are they? But our records don't go that far back, I'm afraid. Sorry."

Tennessee sighed.

"Those computers can do amazing things but they're constantly running out of memory. I have to keep deleting old newsletters and the like to make more space on the hard drive. I keep saying we should use the cloud. I know we couldn't store sensitive information there, but the boring stuff we could. It would free up space."

"Paper records?" he asked hopefully.

She shook her head. "That was all moved to the council offices when we refitted the admin suite. They're on Westoe Road on South Shields."

Tennessee thanked Annabelle Jones for her time. He and Keaton stepped out from the school building into the bright June afternoon. "Looks like we're off to see the Sand-dancers."

Keaton rolled up her sleeve to check her watch. "It's ten to five on a Friday afternoon. I'd be surprised if anyone from the council is still there."

She was right. Most of the staff would be out the door by now. "Coffee?" he asked.

"I wouldn't say no."

They walked for a few minutes, crossing the Metro line and passing an Aldi, a Post Office and a social club. They reached a large cuboid building covered in panels the same rusty hue as the Angel of the North. At first glance they caused Tennessee to think of shipwrecks on white-sand beaches, but after sirens sounded in the distance, they reminded him of burnt-out Corsas.

Hebburn Central housed the local gym and swimming pool, as well as the library and a café. It was a modern building and had clearly cost a small fortune. Outside, trees and shrubs were arranged in a neat row in front of the entrance.

"In here," Tennessee said, nodding to the sliding doors. As soon as he set foot inside the building he was hit by the smell of the pool.

Keaton took a deep breath in. "I love the smell of swimming pools."

"Me too. Alfie's started swimming classes. I missed the first one but can't wait to take him. It's nuts how you can take babies swimming before they can even walk. Did you know all mammals can swim?"

Keaton pointed towards the café. "Not true," she said. "Porcupines can't swim."

"Seriously?"

"Seriously. Porcupines, rhinos and my April." She placed the photographs from King George's on the counter and ordered two cappuccinos. "The woman can cook for England and has the biggest heart in the world, but she swims like a brick."

Keaton paid by card and thanked the barista. She was handing one of the hot drinks to Tennessee when a wrinkled finger appeared over the pile of photographs and hovered over the chest of a cheeky-looking boy.

"Little Jimmy Webster."

The detectives turned to face a tiny woman with oversized glasses and pearl earrings. Despite the warm weather outside and the heat from the pool inside, she wore a fur coat.

"Right tinker he was."

"You know this boy?" Tennessee asked.

The woman cradled a pile of Mills and Boon books in one arm. She was either heading to or from the library.

"I know all those little boys. Might not remember all their names mind you. Memory's not what it was. I've lived here gone eighty years now. If someone lived on this estate and I didn't know them, they weren't worth knowing."

Keaton quickly bought the lady a tea and ushered her to a round table to join them.

After introducing themselves as Jack and Paula, they let the small woman sip her tea and tell them stories from her youth. She'd never heard of Charles Pennington or Eve Lynch, but she could name a good number of the children.

"Davey Smith," she said with a nod. "He was a wrong'un. Lovely parents, but they never disciplined him. Grew up not knowing the meaning of the word no. Got some poor lass pregnant at fifteen, said he'd get a job and support her, but by the time she went into labour he'd got some other girl pregnant. Course, he did a runner and didn't support either of them."

She moved her finger to a slim, blonde girl in the front row. "That's Donna Tucker. She still lives here. Has a little deli on the main road. She had the most gorgeous blonde hair, then she dyed it black when she was thirteen and started wearing thick eyeliner. Still does. Oh, I can't tell you what they used to call her."

"You can," Keaton said. "I'm not easily shocked."

She didn't need much persuasion. The woman flashed a wicked look from Tennessee to Keaton, tightened her fur coat, covered her mouth and whispered as if it were all one word, "Donna-Tucker-goth-cock-sucker."

Cappuccino sprayed over the table as Keaton snorted. She grabbed some serviettes to clean up after herself.

"See this boy here; he's Joe Joseph. He married this girl, Josefine Rudd, and she became Josefine Joseph. Can't make this stuff up."

173

Tennessee smiled, writing every name down as the lady talked.

"They had three kids: Jonny, Jenny and Jacky." She lowered her glasses and rolled her eyes at Keaton. "Mind you, that's not so ridiculous by today's standards, is it? They're all Dakotas, Armanis and Chardonnays."

By the time their tea-drinking friend had finished, it was gone half five and they had at least seventy names on a list. Keaton had added asterisks to any children who'd been called wrong'uns, toerags or little shits. It was time to TIE. They'd trace, interview and eliminate as many as they could. If they got lucky, someone would own up to knowing both victims. If they found who connected them, they'd be a step closer to discovering who killed Eve and Charles.

- CHAPTER 26 -

JULIE COOPER LOOKED SURPRISINGLY well put together. She'd ditched black mourning clothes in favour of a yellow dress. She'd washed and blow-dried her hair and coloured her lips in a garish shade of pink.

"Evening, Mum. You look nice." In contrast to her mother, Cooper wore flip-flops, denim shorts and a grey t-shirt; she had sweat patches under her armpits.

Julie kissed Cooper on the cheek and took a seat opposite her outside Benji's Bar. "Thank you, dear. Well, your father wouldn't want me to sit around crying all day, would he? I've decided to take a leaf out of Elizabeth Taylor's book. It's time to pour myself a drink, put some lipstick on and pull myself together."

Cooper lifted a chilled bottle of Dorada and toasted her mother. "Good for you."

Smoothing her dress over her knees, Julie said, "Thank you for the trip out last night. It was lovely to be on the water. I haven't seen dolphins in ages, and there's something about them that just makes you smile, don't you think? Happy, chirpy, energetic things. And..." She paused, an embarrassed look on her face. "Thank you for all your help this morning. I couldn't have done it without you."

"It must have been hard."

"It was, dear."

Cooper's morning had been spent chasing plumbers after the bar's hot water had gone kaput. She'd then driven Atkinson to the airport and returned to find her mum crying in a pile of Ben's clothes. *I can't stand seeing them in the wardrobe every morning,* she'd sobbed. Copper helped her sort the clothes into two piles. One was for the charity shop and one for the bin. It took hours. Naturally, Julie had a story to go with every item of clothing. *He wore this shirt on our day trip to Corralejo. I don't know why he kept these shorts; they're covered in turmeric stains.* Half the stories set off fresh waves of tears. It was uncomfortable to watch and Cooper felt helpless, unable to offer more than an ear and a tissue. Once finished, Cooper took bin liners full of her father's old clothes to a shop that raised money for the local animal shelter.

Cooper reached across the table and squeezed her mum's hand. "You're going to be just fine. You know that, don't you?"

Julie's lips spread into a broad smile, revealing a spot of pink lipstick on her front teeth. "One step at a time," she said. "Oh look, here's my favourite grandchild."

Tina, pink-faced and out of breath, approached the patio area outside of Benji's; her back hunched under the weight of a heavy backpack. When she removed it, it hit the floor with a tremendous thud. "I'm your only grandchild," she said, stretching her back by reaching her arms high above her head.

"How did today's revision go?" Cooper asked. "Sounds like you have half the British Library in there."

"It was okay. I'm struggling with chemistry."

"I find that hard to believe," Cooper said, sliding along the white wooden bench to make room for Tina.

Tina sat but only gave a shrug in response. She leant over to unzip her bag, rummaged about for a moment, then pulled out her mobile. "I set up Benji's Instagram account and added the first few photos."

She opened the app and showed Julie.

"Goodness, Tina. You've made us look so glamorous."

There was a sunny theme to all the images. Tina must have used the same filter on each one. Cooper especially liked a snap Tina had taken of a coaster with the logo for Benji's Bar printed on it. She'd stuck it the sand at a jaunty angle. Behind it, the brilliant blue of the sea contrasted the yellow card.

"I've written down the username and password for whoever you ask to run the account. They should use hashtag Benji's Bar in each post and encourage people who come to the bar to do the same. You can then search for posts that diners have made and repost them in your stories."

"Stories?" Julie looked confused.

"They're posts that only show up for twenty-four hours. It's up to you obviously, I mean, it's your bar, but I think you should ask Isabella to run the account."

Isabella was a young waitress who worked at Benji's. She was bilingual and a hit with the clientele.

"I've seen her personal account. It's good. You could ask her to run a promotion once a month for people to get a free drink, or bowl of chips, or whatever if they repost your content."

Julie still looked confused, but she also looked impressed. "Isabella it is then. Now don't be offended, you two, but you both look like you've been pulled through a hedge backwards. Get dressed. Glad rags on. I'm going to take the Cooper girls out to dinner. There's something we should celebrate."

Tina raked her hair back into a ponytail. For a moment, Cooper thought she would refuse and opt to spend the evening in her room studying or moping about over Josh. Instead, she nodded and said, "Okay, but can we not go to a seafood place. I've gone off fish."

"How can you go off—"

Cooper coughed to silence Julie, and to her amazement, it worked. "I'm all fished out as well, T. How about a good old burger and fries?"

She shrugged, which was good enough for Cooper, but she couldn't help wonder what had buoyed her mother's mood. Her father wasn't even cold yet.

"What are we celebrating?"

"Well, dears, I've been thinking."

"Uh oh."

"Stop it, darling. I've been thinking, and a change of scene would do me a world of good while I mourn your father. God bless his soul. The youngsters here are best placed to streamline the menu and bring our drink selection into the twenty-first century. They have it covered, and I trust them to look after the bar."

A sinking feeling built in the pit of Cooper's stomach.

"You work such long hours, Erica, and you'll need help with childcare—"

Oh no.

"I can be there for Tina when she gets in from school, and I can make sure there's food in the cupboards, that sort of thing."

Oh, God no.

Julie placed her hands on Tina's cheeks and squeezed. Tina scrunched up her face at the intrusion of her personal space but managed not to say anything.

"It's going to be such fun. Just us girls."

"Mum, what are you saying?" Cooper asked, fearing she already knew the answer. The sinking feeling intensified. She was on the Titanic, the iceberg emerged from the fog, a collision was inevitable.

Her mother practically jiggled in her seat with excitement. "I'm moving in, of course."

- CHAPTER 27 -

HE GLARED OUT THE window as the bus grumbled along Newcastle's Newgate Street. It had been a week since he killed for the first time. The rabbits that lived on the scrubland behind his childhood home didn't count.

Home?

He was supposed to call that place home, but it never felt that way. He never felt at home until he moved far away from the bad memories that haunted him here. He'd caught the rabbits using handmade traps after watching a survival show on television. Vince loved all that nonsense: Bear Grylls, Duel Survivor, Naked and Afraid. All you needed was some twigs, a length of string, and a couple of carrots. He stole the carrots from Kerys's kitchen and spent a morning snapping twigs from bushes and sticking them into soft ground as if making a miniature fence. The rows of twigs gradually narrowed towards each other, funnelling any leporine visitors towards the bait. He tied the string to a branch above the trap and formed the other end into a noose. He laid the loop over the carrots and secured it with a stick that acted as the trigger. The stick held the noose in place until disturbed, then the branch would straighten, and the noose would tighten.

His first few attempts at trapping had been unsuccessful: triggered but empty. When he finally caught a rabbit, he was beside himself. The noose tightened around the creature's leg; it was still alive. Rabbits had big teeth, and he was scared of being bitten. Sat in muddy jeans with torn knees, he flinched a few times before finally wrapping his little hands around the creature's neck.

He took a deep breath and squeezed.

He thought taking a life would make him feel mighty, god-like even. It wasn't as strong a feeling as that, but it did give him a sense of power. He was responsible for whether the rabbit lived or died, whether he set it free or choked the life out of it. It was the most power he'd experienced in his short existence. When the life drained out the rabbit, he placed it on the ground and stroked its fur. He expected it to look like it was sleeping, but it didn't. It didn't look at all like that. Its nose no longer twitched, its chest no longer rose and fell with each breath, and its eyes no longer blinked. It was a floppy sack of fur and bones. Lifeless.

He liked it.

The bus came to a stop. He pulled himself to his feet using a yellow handhold, made his way to the front of the vehicle and stepped out onto the street.

A man carrying a polystyrene box of takeaway food stopped to finish his last bite; it smelled like chips and gravy. A winning combination. The man crushed the container between his fat hands and chucked it towards a bin. He missed; the rubbish fell to the floor. A draft from the departing bus caused it to roll a couple of feet. He looked at the litterbug with disgust. Dirty bastard. People just expected everyone else to clean up their shit.

"You want to make something of it?" snarled the man, catching his look of repulsion.

He thought about whispering in the man's ear. *I'm the one all the newspapers are talking about. I'm the one the police can't find. I buried two people alive, and if you don't want to be next, you should pick up your fucking rubbish and put it in the damn bin.* But he didn't: he had bigger fish to fry. He shoved past, ignoring the man as he yelled after him, trying to pick a fight. He entered a glass building coloured with purple lights that moved in circular patterns. The lower floor housed bars and chain restaurants, but he made a beeline for the escalator and walked confidently into the casino.

It took a while to get served at the bar; the barman seemed to prioritise anyone in a short skirt or a low cut top. Eventually, he ordered a pint of Strongbow and took a seat at a slot machine. One-armed bandits held little interest for him, but there was a place to rest his drink, and the swivel seat meant he could people watch. Some patrons had clearly been out all day and were worse for wear; others were just getting started. Either way, they had no idea who he was or how close they stood to a serial killer. It gave him a thrill to call himself that: *a serial killer*. Soon the press and the police would start calling him that as well.

He took his time feeding pound coins into the bandit, thinking about how when he'd left Tyneside, he hadn't been old enough to smoke or drink, play the lottery or pay fucking taxes. A woman in a classy black dress smiled at him from across the room. Was it his build she was attracted to? He was a big man now, and though he never felt that much pride looking at his face in the mirror, he knew he wasn't ugly. He scrubbed up well. Or was she attracted to something else? Even the most depraved inmates on death row received fan mail and offers of marriage. Some women had a thing for murderers, a fetish of sorts. Perhaps the woman in the classy dress could tell. Could she sense it?

He slid another pound into the slot machine, listened to it drop, then the buttons lit up and a tinny jingle sounded. He grabbed the lever and pulled, watching the wheels spin. A blur of fruit, dollar signs, number sevens, and blue and red bars. The first wheel came to a rest on a pair of red cherries. The second wheel continued to whir, eventually stopping on another set of cherries. He held his breath; he'd never won on the bandits before.

More cherries. His luck was in.

Chime after chime after chime as golden pound coins rattled out of the machine. Forty-five quid; forty-five images of her majesty. The coins glittered hypnotically, and though the Queen looked to the side, she appeared to be judging him. He turned to flash a winner's smile at his admirer, but the woman in the classy dress had gone. Never mind. He didn't come here to score; he came here to make a choice.

He finished his drink, scooped the coins into his pockets and went to change them for notes. He couldn't be wandering around jingling like some bloody cat's toy.

Lighter, with two twenties and a fiver in his wallet, he bought another pint. He approached a row of roulette tables attended to by red-shirted croupiers. Around each table, five or six people clustered, mesmerised by the spinning wheel. At the furthest table, an almighty cheer erupted. There was much backslapping as a group of men in almost identical outfits celebrated a big win. Perhaps they were on a stag party and had some form of dress code. Maybe they just had no imagination.

He moved closer to the table, close enough to watch the wheel rotate and whip up a frenzy, not so close he'd have to make small talk with the other gamblers. Chips were placed on the board, with one man betting heavily on red twenty-five. Once the grid of numbers was speckled with chips, the dealer spun the wheel, causing the red and black numbers to blur as one. He threw in the ball; it whizzed against the wooden inlay, creating a noise that reminded him of a high-speed train rushing out of a tunnel.

Red or black? Red, like Vince's fat flushed cheeks? Or black, like Kerys's cold dark heart?

"No more bets."

His heart raced like the metal ball as he anticipated what was to come. Red, he'd kill Vince. Black, he'd kill Kerys. He told himself he didn't mind either way, but like a pregnant woman saying she didn't care if her baby was a boy or a girl as long as it was healthy, he knew it was a lie. Everyone had favourites; everyone had a preference. His preference was Kerys.

The ball slowed, and as it jumped between the grooved, numbered shallows, so his heart began to jump too.

He wanted to take Kerys out first; he wanted to take his time with her.

"Zero."

Green? He hadn't expected that. Nor had anyone else around the table. There were groans as the chips were swept up by the croupier before the next round of betting.

Green? Lucky fuckers. It seemed Vince and Kerys were safe – for now.

The ball screamed as it flew around the wheel once more.

"No more bets."

Red for Ronan. Black for Beth.

The ball bounced before it settled. The croupier called, "Red sixteen. Red sixteen."

His face spread into a grin so wide it was almost painful. He knew which snake was next.

- CHAPTER 28 -

THE DANIEL FAMILY HAD two rules: rule one, everyone had to help clean the house on Sundays; rule two, never wake the baby. Ever.

Jack 'Tennessee' Daniel was exploiting the second rule to get out of the first rule. While his wife and mother-in-law tip-toed about the house on Sunday morning, dusting, tidying and spraying every square inch with anti-bacterial spray, Tennessee was flat on his back watching a football game with baby Alfie sound asleep on his bare chest. Alfie was his pride and joy. Six months old and bright-eyed, with tiny hands and hair as soft as silk. Content and healthy; he was everything Tennessee could wish for in a son.

"Unload the dishwasher? You know I'd love to, but—" he gestured to the sleeping infant.

"Witchcraft," said Hayley with narrowed eyes. "It's the only explanation. Little darling never sleeps on demand for me."

"Shh," he teased. "Don't wake the bairn."

Hayley picked up a glass from the side table, its insides coated with a thin film of orange juice. "Another?"

"No thanks, but there's a beer in the fridge with my name on it."

She looked at her watch. "It's ten past eleven, Jack."

"Which means Wetherspoons has been open for three hours." He flashed a cheeky smile knowing his wife couldn't resist.

Hayley dusted the table then went to the fridge to fetch him a beer. He'd make it up to her later, much later, when the footie wasn't on. As his wife handed him a chilled can of IPA, he turned his focus back to the television. Zimbabwe was getting its arse kicked by the Democratic Republic of the Congo in the African Cup of Nations. Tennessee was more into the Premier League, but he had a bet on Zimbabwe – hence his interest. It was only a tenner. Still, he hadn't told Hayley. She didn't like him betting on sports.

Despite the financial motive, Tennessee struggled to concentrate: Cooper was due back tomorrow. He'd missed her. Work wasn't quite the same without her in the department. It hadn't been the same when she was off on the sick, it wasn't the same when she was recovering from being kidnapped, and it wasn't the same now. Yes, Tennessee had relished taking the lead, and though he didn't feel any further forward than when they'd begun the investigation, he still thought he was doing a good job.

A good job? That might be the IPA talking. He stroked Alfie's back and reassured himself he was, at the very least, doing a decent job. Nixon hadn't given him an earful yet, so that was something.

Zimbabwe started the second half two–nil down; it looked like he'd seen the last of that tenner. Within a few minutes, they substituted Chawapiwa for Mushekwi. A winger for a striker. A change of fortune, perhaps?

"Foul, ref," Tennessee hissed as loud as he dared with a sleeping infant on his chest.

The referee seemed to have heard. He swiftly delivered a yellow card to Mbemba of DR Congo and then another to Moke, the Congolese midfielder.

"This is more like it," he whispered to his son. "If he sends off half the team, Zimbabwe might stand a chance."

Alfie gurgled and turned his head to face away from the television just as the Zimbabwean goalkeeper committed a foul, awarding Congo a penalty.

"Oh f—"

Alfie stirred.

"Ducking bell."

Bakambu fired the ball into the back of the net. He ran to the left, beating his chest in triumph, his fist pounding into the blue and white fabric of his shirt. The Zimbabweans, in yellow with green trim, shook their heads and looked to the turf. Three–nil. This was almost as painful as being a Newcastle United fan. Back when they'd worn yellow and green, they'd been relegated to the second division. Hardly a surprise after they'd sold Gascoigne, Beardsley and Waddle.

"What a load of..."

When they'd worn yellow and green. It hit Tennessee like a brick. A brick that sang Phil Collins and Bobbi Brown songs.

Downing his beer, he handed Alfie to his confused wife.

"Excuse me, handsome, but you're either on baby duty or cleaning duty—"

Energised, with urgency seeping out of his pores, Tennessee kissed Hayley on the mouth to quieten her, then took off to their bedroom, bounding up the stairs two at a time. He yanked his phone from the charger and hit the third number on his speed dial.

"I knew I'd seen it before," he said when the line connected.

"It's my day off," grumbled Paula Keaton, her voice sleepy and gravelly. "Riley's out with friends, so April and I actually have some time alone for once in a blue moon."

"Your sex life can wait. This is important."

"Okay, I'll bite. What had you seen before?"

"The fabric. The fabric the first victim was holding. It matched the thread we found on the second, right?"

"Right." She said it as a long, drawn-out word as if urging him to get to the point.

"It's the 1988 Newcastle United away shirt."

Tennessee paced the room, phone glued to his ear. He expected the next words from Keaton's mouth to be full of praise.

"So?"

Not what he'd hoped for.

"So? So? It means we know what the fabric is. It's a 1988 Newcastle—"

"United away shirt. Yeah, you said. Even if you're right—"

"I am right."

She sighed. "Even if you're right, the murders took place in the northeast. Saying the killer has an NUFC shirt doesn't really narrow it down. Have you seen the toon on match days?"

Tennessee stopped pacing to look out the bay window at a large beech tree. "It's not any old footie shirt, though. A 1988 away shirt. How many clothes do you have from the eighties?"

"None. I was like five then."

Tennessee heard excitable commentary from the television downstairs: Congo had just scored for the fourth time.

"Exactly. Normal people don't hang on to clothes for over thirty years, let alone wear them. But this guy decides to wear it both times he murders someone? I'm telling you, Paula, the man we're looking for isn't just a fan. He's a fanatic."

- CHAPTER 29 -

DC OLIVER MARTIN WAS sick to the back teeth with interviews. He hung up the phone and blew a long raspberry; he was too tired for this nonsense. All his own fault, of course. No one forced him to stay up until three a.m. playing Call of Duty.

His last few hours had been spent painstakingly making his way through the list of names Keaton and Tennessee had pulled together. These days people rarely pick up their phones if they don't recognise the number for fear of scammers. Martin had lost track of how many messages he'd left asking people to call him back. But if they were anything like him, they'd rarely listen to their voicemails either. He sat up straighter and wiggled his shoulders, trying to ease an ache that had been brought on by a cheap gaming chair, dehydration, lack of sleep and a suit that didn't quite fit. It was his favourite suit, and he had saved for months to be able to afford it. Though it was a little tight across the back, he refused to stop wearing it.

He glanced down at the list again. Charles Pennington had worked at King George Primary for ten years. With thirty kids to a class, that was three hundred people they'd try to chase up. If they assumed the killer was male – because female serial killers were few and far between and almost always used poison as an MO – that left approximately one hundred and fifty. This was assuming they were barking up the right tree. Just because Eve Lynch worked in the area didn't mean South Tyneside was the connecting factor or that any of Charles Pennington's former students would have heard of her.

Martin rubbed the back of his neck. The murderer could be a former student, a colleague, or a former lover. Hell, he could be a Martian for all they knew.

A long rumble sounded from Martin's stomach; it was empty save for coffee and Red Bull. He checked his watch. It was early afternoon now and he was the only one foolish enough to be working on a Sunday. It wasn't like he had any chance of getting overtime. Not these days. Keaton and Tennessee would be with their loved ones, and Whyte would be doing something sporty, followed by a few pints. He didn't know what Boyd would be up to. Despite working with her since the start of the Blackburn case, Martin knew surprisingly little about her. He knew she was quiet and nervous and that she liked classic films. He remembered her saying she'd been to a double bill of Casablanca and The Big Sleep.

Martin took out his mobile and scrolled down until he found Saffron Boyd's name in his contacts list. His finger hovered over the call button. One lunchtime, the team had gone to the Cluny in the Ouseburn area of Newcastle, and Boyd had said they made an excellent Sunday lunch. When he'd asked if she liked Yorkshire puddings, she'd reminded him that she was, in fact, from Yorkshire and that not liking Yorkshire puddings was a sin punishable by death. Martin had laughed at that and spluttered Diet Coke across the table. Idiot.

He pressed call and felt his mouth go dry. Why was he so nervous? He was only going to ask if she'd eaten yet and if she wanted to get a roast dinner somewhere. She was new to the city and he wondered if she'd made friends outside of work yet.

Ring, ring.

What if she said no? He'd feel rejected, and seeing her again tomorrow morning would be awkward. But what if she said yes? Were relationships even allowed in the same department? Cooper had been involved with Fuller for a while back in the day, but they hardly ever worked together. He and Boyd were on the same team. He was overthinking this; it was only a Sunday lunch for crying out loud. As the phone continued to ring, he logged out of his computer and switched it off. When the screen turned to a black mirror, he used it to check his reflection. He looked okay for someone who'd had four hours of sleep.

193

He gulped as the call connected.

"Hey, it's Saffron. Leave a message."

It seemed the people in his trace, interview, eliminate list weren't the only ones not picking up today.

TINA'S NOSE TWITCHED AS she studied her chemistry textbook. She'd been on the same page for over half an hour. As no one – not even Tina – was that interested in endothermic reactions, Cooper suspected her daughter's mind was elsewhere. Tina wore earplugs to drown out the plane's engine and the general noise of the 737: the rattle of the drinks trolley, general chit-chat, a squeaky door to the toilet, and two teenagers who thought everything was hilarious. It was late. The plane would be somewhere over the Bay of Biscay now, and any windows with their blinds up showed nothing but darkness. Cooper looked at her daughter with sadness in her heart. Tina looked drained. Her skin was dry, her complexion dull, and her eyes were holding back an emotion that Cooper couldn't put her finger on. Uncertainty perhaps?

She nudged her and waited for Tina to remove one of her earplugs.

"Yeah?"

"Are you okay? You looked deep in thought."

The poor girl had been through a lot recently: a brush with death, her mother's kidnapping, a waste-of-space father on the wrong side of a restraining order, and her grandfather passing away. And now, to top it off, Julie had decided to move in without giving them much of a say in the matter. She could hardly begrudge her mother from wanting to spend time with her remaining family. Still, Cooper worried about how it would affect Tina. She was hoping to get her relationship with Justin Atkinson back on track and this might be one change too many for her daughter. Perhaps she and Atkinson should wait and put their feelings on hold for a few months.

Tina's nose twitched again. "I'm fine," she said.

The words were nothing more than an automatic answer. She wasn't fine. The slight twitch of her nose was a nervous tic, and Cooper had spotted it three times in ten minutes. She said she was fine because it was the easier answer and the answer she thought everyone wanted to hear. Tina put her earplug back in and turned her attention back to the book.

On Cooper's other side, Julie was fast asleep with a flimsy plastic cup of Jack and Coke in her hand. She let out a snore that could have drowned out the engine. Her arm jerked as she slept, almost spilling her drink.

Cooper looked around, feeling somewhat like a naughty teenager stealing from her parent's liquor cabinet, and started prising the cup from Julie's hand. Her mother's mouth opened again, but this time, instead of snoring, she murmured what sounded like, "Tonight, Matthew, I'm going to be Christina Aguilera."

Trying not to laugh, Cooper slipped the cup of dark liquid from Julie's grip and sat back in her chair. She was about to take a sip when she saw a steely-eyed flight attendant who had been watching her the whole time.

"What? I paid for it."

"I'd still consider it stealing."

"Stealing is charging seven quid for a single and a mixer."

The flight attendant folded her arms and moved towards the back of the plane where there was an unholy smell of soiled nappy. Fifteen years and Cooper could still recognise baby poop from fifty paces. She downed the drink, happy that her diaper changing days were behind her. She grimaced; the Jack tasted funny.

"IT'S FREEZING."

Julie rubbed her bare arms and gave an over the top shiver while they waited by the luggage belt. "I thought you said the weather had been nice?"

"It was nice," Cooper said dryly. "But it's one a.m. in Newcastle and you're wearing a dress smaller than a postage stamp."

"Are you giving me sass? Because I remember the outfits you used to go out in, young lady. I could tell Tina here a few stories about her mum that would make her blush."

Tina shuffled from one foot to the other. "I've heard them all." She turned to Cooper and yawned without covering her mouth. "How much longer?"

Cooper rolled her eyes. "The runway's less than a hundred yards from here. I could single-handedly get the luggage off the plane quicker than these—"

Before she could find a family-friendly insult, an orange light above the luggage belt began to flash and a siren wailed a low warning tone.

"Right on cue."

By some miracle, Cooper, Julie and Tina's bags all came out together and the three of them left via *nothing to declare*. Cooper was physically, mentally and emotionally exhausted. She was due back at work in – she did the maths in her head – just over seven hours. Trying to get up to speed tomorrow was going to be hell, and Cooper was going to have to do it after a night on the couch. The spare room wasn't set up for guests and she didn't want Tina to have to give up her bed. Julie could have Cooper's room tonight; she'd take the sofa.

A steady line of people returning from holidays filed out into the main terminal. The queue at the taxi rank was beginning to build and Cooper feared they'd be delayed even further. She pulled her wheelie case with one hand and used the other to wipe her sticky brow. It felt greasy and she thought she could feel the start of a pimple manifesting deep under her skin. Her hand ran back over her head where she felt the unfamiliar texture of soft hairs. Her hair usually felt bristly from being kept so short; she was clearly in need of a cut. Another job before work tomorrow: find the clippers.

Behind her, Cooper heard the squeaky wheel of Tina's case. "Urgh. Look at the queue. If you pass me your phone, I'll find us an Uber."

"We don't need an Uber," said Julie.

"Mum, I know you like to support *real taxi drivers*, whatever that means, but the queue is getting longer, and we're all tired, and— Oh." Cooper realised why they didn't need an Uber. Holding a bunch of flowers and a sign that read *Cooper Ladies* was a sleepy-looking Justin Atkinson.

Cooper fell into his warm embrace and felt as if she could fall asleep right there and then. "It's gone half one. What on Earth are you doing here?"

"Saving you a taxi fare, that's what. Ladies, your chariot awaits in the short stay car park." He tossed the keys to his Toyota at Tina, who caught them, called *shotgun*, and took off ahead with Julie.

Atkinson swapped the bunch of flowers for Cooper's case and held her hand as they made their way past the taxi rank to the parking lot. How could Cooper consider putting things back on hold when he'd made such grand gestures?

"I'll drop you off and leave you to it," he said, squeezing her hand. "I grabbed some milk, bread, butter and bacon. It's in a carrier bag in the footwell. I wanted to make sure you had things in for breakfast."

"Will you stay?" Cooper said it without hesitation.

"You're back at CID tomorrow. Don't you want to just get home and get to sleep?"

"Yes. But I want to sleep cuddled up to you." She stopped walking so she could pause and look him in the eyes. "I need to escape. Between Dad, and worrying about Mum and the bar, and Tina... I know it's selfish, and I should let you get back to your place, but please, let me sleep pressed up against you tonight."

Atkinson frowned. "Why is that selfish?"

"Because you've been nothing but supportive. I have all this family drama at the moment, and I'm heading into a major investigation tomorrow. I can't give you the time and energy you deserve. I feel like I'm using you."

Atkinson tilted his head to the side as he surveyed her. He stifled a yawn, ran his hand down her arm, then pulled her in for a quick kiss. "Use away."

- CHAPTER 30 -

COOPER PEELED HER BODY from Atkinson's. She moaned as she straightened up from the sofa, her bones feeling considerably older than her early-thirties skeleton should. Her body, she reminded herself, had been through more than most people her age. A baby when still in her teens, the loss of a friend, the grunt work of a newly-recruited police officer, cancer, chemo, kidnapping.

Yawning into her elbow, she debated waking Atkinson. He looked peaceful sprawled across the sofa with long limbs creeping out in all directions like the roots of a great, strong tree. She climbed the stairs, aching for a shower. Usually, there was just her and Tina in the mornings. With four people staying under Cooper's roof, she knew if she didn't get to the shower first, she might not get one at all.

Holidays and travelling were fun, when not associated with the death of a parent, but there was nothing like getting back to your own shower – or your own bed. Cooper twisted right and left under the running water, feeling the powerful setting massage her aching shoulders and tight back. She removed the showerhead from the bar and ran the spray up and down her legs. She covered herself in some sea salt and samphire scented shower gel before rinsing and stepping out of the shower to brush her teeth.

Feeling five years younger and ten years cleaner, Cooper snuck into her own room to choose an outfit for her return to Northumbria Police. She was nervous about heading back to HQ. This was a big case, and though she'd only been away a week, a lot had happened. Julie Cooper stirred slightly as Cooper selected a black suit and off-white silk blouse. She was more at home in jeans and boots, but she felt she needed to set a professional tone; the sheriff was back in town.

Heading back towards the stairs, and more importantly, back towards the kettle, Cooper heard a noise from Tina's room.

"It's not my fault?"

"What? So it's mine?"

"I didn't say that."

Though quiet and muffled, the second voice was definitely Josh. Cooper couldn't tell if he was in there with Tina or if his voice was coming through a phone or her laptop. How could he even get in? Wheelie bin to the flat roof of the kitchen extension, then through the bathroom window?

The voices stopped as if someone had hit the pause button and all sounds and movements were put on hold. She'd been rumbled. Cooper considered opening the door but asked herself how she would feel in that situation? She's never snuck anyone into her room overnight at that age – she preferred to be one sneaking out. If Tina and Josh were arguing about the girl in the Instagram photo, she should probably keep her nose of it, but she would need to speak to her daughter later. Another job to add to the list.

THE BLACK AND WHITE Warehouse was a hidden gem in Newcastle's Grainger Town. Tucked between a branch of Greggs and a barbershop, the unassuming entrance led to a tardis-like memorabilia store for all things Newcastle United related. Tennessee felt a pang of excitement as he took the stairs to the first-floor store. He hadn't been here since he was a boy. His dad had taken him before a Blackburn Rovers match; it must be almost twenty years ago. He picked out some trading cards, a keyring and a program signed by Peter Beardsley. Newcastle had gone on to win six-two with Shearer scoring early and trumpet-playing Solano netting two in two minutes. Afterwards, they'd gone to McDonald's and Tennessee wolfed down a strawberry milkshake and a mountain of McNuggets. Good times.

The store hadn't changed in all those years. Rows of programs, signed prints, Geordie keepsakes and souvenirs, as well as match-worn shirts and collector's items lined the walls and display cases.

The owner greeted Tennessee with an appraising look, an approving nod, and a deep voice. "Mornin'. Lovely day."

"It really is," Tennessee said, eyeing a vintage scarf. "Came here as a bairn. It's nice to see some parts of the city haven't succumbed to chain stores and franchise eateries."

"Tell me about it. Went to some celebrity chef's restaurant last weekend. As if Mr-cod-jelly-and-chips-ice-cream has ever set foot in the toon. Cost me a small fortune and I was still hungry when I left. Had to nip to KFC on the way home."

Tennessee laughed and squatted down to check out a signed football. "My other half wants to go there. Says they have a good vegan menu."

Behind the counter, the man pulled a face. "I'm a dinosaur. I know I should be open to new cuisines and all that jazz, but honestly, if it didn't moo, oink or cluck, I'm really not interested." Another customer entered the store and made a bee-line for a Kevin Kegan bobblehead. "Alreet, Dougie?"

"Nae bad, Lee. How ye daein?"

Tearing himself away from all things nostalgic, Tennessee remembered he was there for work. "I wanted to ask about the 1988 away shirt."

"A classic. Don't have any in, I'm afraid, but I know how to track one down. It'll set ya back about a hundred and seventy quid minimum."

"I'm not looking to buy one." Tennessee pulled out his warrant card. "It's actually to do with... It's a long story. Do you sell many?"

Lee, the store owner, folded his hairy forearms and stared at the ceiling. After a few seconds, he exhaled and shook his head, his lips turned downwards at the corners. "Can't say I do. One a year at the most."

"When was the last time you sold one?"

His head tilted one way and the next as he thought, much like the Keegan bobblehead. "Christmas time, I suppose."

The other customer approached the counter, cash in hand, ready to buy two postcards depicting the Tyne bridges. He was a big man with the posture of a shy old lady: head bowed, shoulders folding in on themselves. "Aye, the eighty-eight was nae a real fan favourite; they finished last n were relegated to the second division."

Tennessee rolled his eyes. "And then they came so close to getting promoted the next season."

"Only to be gubbed to it by, of all teams, Sunderland." He shook his head at the memory. "Now the burgundy n navy ninety-six away shirt, that was a stunner."

"My dad bought one," said Tennessee, reminiscing. "My mum went ballistic with him 'cos they needed the money to fix the car. Didn't we finish second that season?"

"Aye. Thanks to Ferdinand, Hislop, and Ginola. Good times."

They were good times. Tennessee, just a small boy at the time, could still remember the beer garden where he'd played on the tyre swing while his parents sipped lager in the sunshine when the news broke: Newcastle had signed Alan Shearer for a record-breaking nine million. The place went nuts, beers were on the house, grown men cried. England might not have been able to bring football home in 1996, but Keegan brought Shearer home, and the toon had never seemed sunnier.

"Say I did want to buy an eighty-eight shirt," Tennessee mused. "Where would I start, other than here?"

"eBay," said Lee and Dougie together.

Lee laughed. "There's actually a super fan meet up happening soon. Kind of like a swap meet for footie fans. There's usually a fair amount of vintage gear."

He nodded. Though he didn't actually need a shirt, Tennessee did need to be amongst superfans if his theory was correct.

"I'll be there buying some stuff for the shop," Lee continued. "Dougie?"

"Aye, I have my ticket."

Tennessee smiled as Lee wrote down the details for him: the twelfth, at the five-a-side centre in Gosforth Park. It was promising.

"Thanks for this," he said, holding up the piece of paper with Lee's scrawled notes.

"Nee bother. We're a dying breed, though. Most of this is done online these days. eBay, Facebook Marketplace and the like. I got this garden gnome on eBay a few years ago. Bargain at twenty quid. It's part of a set, you see, so if I can find the right buyer, I'll easy get hundred, hundred and fifty quid for it."

A vibration in Tennessee's trouser pocket told him he'd received a text message. He squinted at the screen, the brightness was set to full and it hurt his eyes. It was Cooper; she was back.

- CHAPTER 31 -

COOPER FELT DRAINED, BUT she mustered all the strength and confidence she could and strode towards HQ with her head high and her shoulders back. Whilst she'd had every right to burst into tears on Longsands beach, she was embarrassed. It seemed so long ago now.

When she'd joined the force, it had still been an old boys' club. Emotions, other than anger, were frowned upon. They were something to be buried and pushed down until you reached breaking point. Thankfully things had changed, and mental health was a much bigger talking point than in days gone by. Posters adorned walls, helplines had been set up, and independent charities such as Police Care UK launched to support serving and retired officers. Still, she couldn't help but feel shame that so many of her colleagues, along with fire and rescue, had seen her fall apart so publicly.

She tried to put it from her mind, focusing on the perfect blue sky, the smell of shrubs and the pleasant feeling of a breeze brushing her cheek. She approached the entrance to HQ just as Chief Superintendent Howard Nixon was leaving. They almost collided as he pushed through the rotating doors with the aura of an ill-tempered boar.

Cooper leapt out of his way, fearing she would be steam-rolled. "Sorry, sir. Didn't see you there."

Nixon's face mellowed at once. "Cooper. You're back."

"Yes, sir."

"Right." He shaded his eyes from the sun. "Must dash, but yeah, good to have you back, Erica."

Cooper's eyes narrowed, and she watched askance as Nixon unlocked his car using a key fob and walked towards it. *Good to have you back?* Who was that, and what had they done with Howard Nixon?

It didn't take long to reach the incident room. Once inside, Cooper was met by the smell of garlic breath and strong coffee. The department was quiet, save for two faces that Cooper didn't recognise. One was swearing at the printer, the other typed furiously as she updated HOMES2. DS Elliott Whyte came out of a meeting room balancing a stack of papers in his arms so high it almost blocked his vision. He dropped the files on a table and let out a sigh as they collapsed from their neat pile into a scattered mess.

"Balls."

Cooper coughed.

"Ma'am!" He stood up straight and smoothed his shirt. "You're back."

"Well observed."

He squirmed. "I— I'm pleased. You've been missed. Not that Jack hasn't done a great job, he has."

"Are those for me?" she nodded at the clutter of paper on the table.

"Yes. I was told to assemble everything on the case so far."

It was a lot. "This is everything?"

"Actually, that's about a third. I couldn't carry it all at once."

Oh, joy.

"Boss?" Whyte's dark, heavy brows came together and he began to study a hair on the back of his middle knuckle.

"Yes?"

"I lost my dad last year. I know what you're going through. If you want to talk, that is."

Cooper softened. He was trying.

She lowered her chin. "I'll keep that in mind. Now, looks like I have a lot of reading ahead of me." Her eyes darted back and forth over the various files, loose pieces of paper and sheets stapled together. She planned on spending a good few hours self-briefing and getting herself back up to speed. It wasn't just the burials in Tynemouth and on Holy Island she had to contend with. As a DCI, she needed to be abreast of all of CID's comings and goings. A lot could change in a week.

"Anything I can do to help?"

"Coffee. And not the vending machine rubbish. She handed him a Starbucks loyalty card. Would you?"

As Whyte left searching for rich, dark energy, Cooper selected a file and made herself comfortable. He returned just as she'd opened the autopsy reports. Caffeine and aspirated sand: fun. After thirty minutes on Margot's findings and results from Atkinson's lab, Cooper booted up her computer and trawled through the other events of the week: a rape in East Boldon, an armed robbery in Low Fell and a domestic murder not far from Rothbury. All reported, solved and charged within the week. Good going, CID. Ongoing cases included a little girl going missing from her back garden. Fuller was taking the lead and was treating it as an abduction. There was also racist graffiti sprayed on the home of an Iranian family in Bedlington, the suspected poisoning of a horse due to run in the Northumberland Plate and a series of smash and grabs in the West End. Interesting, but not enough to take her away from the double murder. She picked up another file and began to sift through statements that had been marked as worthy of following up.

By lunchtime – and another Starbucks run later – most of the team had gathered in CID. Tennessee had rolled up with a bumper bag of burgers from the Fat Hippo, and they were all tucking in with the enthusiasm of a pack of wolves after a kill.

"Martin, talk to me."

Oliver Martin gulped down his American style burger with pickles and mustard and wiped his mouth on the back of his hand. "So far, the only connection we have between the victims is South Tyneside. They both worked there in the late eighties, early nineties. We have a list of students who were under Charles Pennington's tuition back then. I'm working my way through it."

"And?" asked Cooper with a mouthful of minced beef.

"And it's proving a massive pain in the arse, to be honest, boss. But I know it needs doing, so I'm cracking on the best I can. Loads have moved out of the area, half the women on the list could have changed names by now, and at least a third of the ones I actually track down are suspicious of the police and don't want to talk at all."

"I found something in Eve Lynch's bank statements," said Boyd. She had her dark blonde hair tied back in a bun. She looked business-like, but at the same time, her forehead had been pulled back so tight that she looked like she'd had a facelift. "A lottery win. Not a life-changing fortune, well it would be a fortune to me, but not by lottery win standards."

"How much?"

"Thirty-five grand."

Cooper whistled. "When was this?"

"Four years ago. She hasn't done anything wild with it. A few hundred on clothes here, a nice meal there. Most of it's in an ISA."

"Very sensible." She bobbed her head side to side and wondered if the amount was enough to make her a target. "Who stands to inherit her money?"

"We don't know yet," said Boyd. "No will, no dependents."

"What about Pennington? Was he rich?"

"Not especially," added Whyte. "We're still waiting on his bank statements. I'll tell them to get a wiggle on."

"Good."

Heavy footsteps and the door opened so hard it banged off the wall behind it. Keaton stopped in her tracks. "You got burgers? Why didn't you text me?" She looked like she hadn't been invited to a party.

"I did," said Tennessee.

Keaton checked her phone, called it garbage, and sat down to unwrap a burger from its grease-proof paper packaging. She slapped a hand on Cooper's shoulder and sent a wink in her direction. "Glad you're back, Coop."

"Am I really that bad a guv?" joked Tennessee.

"You're a great guv, but now Coop is back, I can return her bloody seagull. That thing is driving me and April nuts."

Cooper smiled. "There's a crate of beer in my car for you."

"I need it. Do you know how many times a day that thing poops?"

"I do. Anyway, where've you been? Saw you got called out to a homicide in Cowgate?"

Keaton shovelled a handful of chips into her mouth and shook her head. "You won't believe this. Definite contender for the Piece of Piss award at this year's Christmas party."

Everyone, suspecting Keaton had quite the tale to tell, leant forward in anticipation.

AT THE SAME TIME, thirty miles away, Ronan Turnbull looked out his front window on Collingwood Drive in Hexham. On the south bank of the Tyne, Hexham was a town famous for its history in the leather industry and an impressive abbey. Strategically important, it had been fought over in the border wars and the War of the Roses.

Wyndon Water wove its way behind Collingwood Drive. If the wind blew in the right direction, Ronan could hear the stream babble; he found it relaxing. Ronan Turnbull's home was a detached homage to upper-middle-class England. A well-kept lawn, double garage and recently renovated kitchen and bathroom. Ronan applied the same discipline to housekeeping that he did during his time in the forces, and before that, his time in the ring.

A white van slowed, stopping only for a moment before its reverse lamp illuminated. A beeping sound signalled a backwards manoeuvre. A ninety-degree turn and the van's rear tyres began to edge up Ronan's drive. A bit rude. If the driver needed to turn, he should do it in the road, not on his drive. He watched, beady-eyed from the living room window, hoping the driver didn't veer onto his lawn. He'd only just mowed it.

The reverse lamp dimmed, the engine disengaged, and a man in high-viz jumped from the driver's door, clipboard in hand. Another lost delivery driver needing directions.

Opening the front door, Ronan waited for the usual *'scuse me mate, looking for number forty-two.*

The voice was muffled, as if he didn't want to open his mouth to speak. "Mornin', got a delivery for you."

"I didn't order owt."

High-viz checked his clipboard. "Three hundred kilos of kiln-dried sand for thirty-five Collingwood Avenue."

"Must be a typo."

"Says here it's for a Ronan Turnbull."

"Aye, that's me, but I didn't order any sand." Was this bloke slow or something? How many times did he have to say it?

High-viz shrugged and opened the back doors to the van, revealing twelve twenty-five kilo bags of sand stacked on top of each other like a floppy Tower of Pisa.

"Good name that, Turnbull. Proper local name." Still, he spoke quietly, the words filtering out of the corner of his mouth where he dared part his lips. "Wait. You the one who was in the paper? Getting knighted by her Majesty?"

Ronan felt his cheeks warm. "It's a British Empire Medal, not a knighthood, but yes, that's me." He knew, being British, he should shrug it off and act coy. No one liked a bragger, but the medal was a big deal, and he was proud to have been awarded one.

The Lord-Lieutenant of Northumberland presented him his medal on behalf of the Queen. Later this year, he would be invited to a garden party at Buckingham Palace to hobnob with the other BEM awardees.

High-viz bowed his head. "Yeah, it was in the Mail. Services to amateur boxing and the children of Northumberland. Amazing work. Amazing."

"Thanks, mate," said Ronan. He was used to the locals giving him pats on the back for his achievement, but not randoms. He was enjoying his fifteen minutes of fame. "But I'm still not signing for that. I didn't order it. Does it say who placed the order?"

Surveying the delivery note, High-viz said, "Hmm, let's see. A Mr T. Wiggy." He stepped forwards and turned the clipboard to face him.

"I don't know anyone by that name," he replied, searching his brain for some explanation.

"Sure ya do," High-viz said. He lifted his eyes, a look that troubled Ronan. "T. Wiggy? It's Twiggy, ya bastard."

Without warning, the man drove his forehead onto the bridge of Ronan's nose. The headbutt caused his nose to shatter, spraying scarlet over the man's fluorescent yellow jacket.

Ronan staggered backwards, momentarily stunned by the assault. He'd been trained for sudden attacks, but since leaving the forces, he'd ceased being as vigilant as he once had. He slipped, clattering onto his back. The man filled the doorway for a moment, his silhouette blocking out the sunlight of the fine July day.

"Twiggy's back, Ronan."

B BASKERVILLE

He stepped over the threshold and closed the door behind him.

- CHAPTER 32 -

COOPER WAS UNUSUALLY TIRED considering her day had primarily been spent sitting on her backside. She had to remind herself that she'd suffered a loss and was also fatigued by the journey home from the Canaries. Yes, Lanzarote was in the same time-zone as the UK, but travelling still took it out of a person. Cooper rubbed her eyes as she took the key out of the ignition and checked the rearview mirror. Atkinson was pulling up behind her. He had a bag of vegetables and what looked like a leg of lamb in a carrier bag. Angel. She was halfway out of the car when she remembered to put the handbrake on. Her brain was fried after a long day of catching up on everything that had gone on in her absence. Granted, she hadn't been out and about chasing leads or conducting interviews, but she'd had more screen time today than she'd had in a long time.

"I just want to make sure you all eat," Atkinson said. "I can take my portion home and be out of your hair."

Cooper rubbed her palms over her fresh buzzcut and laughed. "Stay. I'd like to catch up. Even with the mother and daughter in tow."

"Three generations of Cooper ladies under one roof. Is Tynemouth ready for that?"

"Tynemouth might be, but I'm not."

On the dining table, Cooper found a note from Julie saying she'd popped to the off licence to buy a bottle of wine to reward herself after a day of tidying the spare room. Unable to keep curiosity at bay, Cooper climbed the stairs while Atkinson turned the oven on. Not only was the spare room – more accurately the junk room – now clean and tidy, the day bed seemed to have been replaced with a John Lewis double. Cooper had questions. How had she got one delivered so fast? And how long was she planning on staying? If Julie was only going to be there a few weeks to a month – as had been agreed – then why was the day bed disassembled and propped against the hallway wall?

At least the room smelled of furniture polish instead of fusty spare bedding and old towels. Speaking of old bedding, the sheets appeared to be new, and was that a matching lampshade? It seemed to Cooper that Julie wasn't just visiting while she grieved – she'd moved in.

By the time Julie returned, the lamb was seasoned, diced and browning in the pot. She had not one bottle of wine but two. The first was opened immediately so Julie could have a glass while watching the news. Cooper declined.

"I'm home." Tina's voice carried from the entranceway. "Sorry, I'm late. Had to check in with some teachers."

"Everything okay? No one causing problems because I took you out during term time?"

Tina shook her head. "Actually, everything was fine. I wanted to make sure I'd covered all the right topics and revision notes while I was away."

"And?" Cooper asked, watching Atkinson turn the meat.

"I'm ahead. Think Mr Glidson is annoyed I'm ahead of schedule."

"Ignore him. He's insecure because you're brighter than he is."

"Mum!"

Cooper waved Tina's shock away. "You know it's true. Just don't repeat it at school," she said with a grin.

While Atkinson turned his attention to the vegetables, chopping with OCD levels of precision, Cooper lowered her voice to address Tina again. "Did I hear Josh in your room this morning?"

Tina froze. "No."

"It was definitely his voice, T. And it sounded like you were arguing."

"It was a video call. Whatsapp. I'll use headphones in future."

Cooper took a step forward, but Tina was already busying herself, emptying her school bag and shifting awkwardly from one foot to the other. "I'm not having a go, sweetheart. I was just worried after what you said in Lanzarote about him being out with that other girl."

Tina shook her head rather violently, a cue she was getting worked up but didn't want to say anything. "No. That was— that was nothing. I was just being sensitive."

"You sure?"

Tina gave one definitive nod and made to leave the room.

"Well, if you do decide to sneak a boy into your room, leave it until after your GCSEs, okay?" Both Atkinson and Tina turned to see if she was joking. She winked and waited for Tina to make a cheeky remark, but instead, her face clouded.

"When can I get Steven back?"

Cooper sighed. Tina wasn't in the mood for joking. "Tonight. Paula's bringing him over in an hour."

While Tina disappeared to the depths of her room and Julie sat engrossed in a news story about the missing child, Summer Holt, Cooper helped with dinner by making the dumplings. She combined flour with suet and salt in a large mixing bowl, stripped the leaves from a sprig of rosemary, chopped them and stirred them in. She inhaled, appreciating the aromatic smell of fresh herbs. After adding water, she moulded them into balls and placed them in the fridge to chill.

"I don't envy you," said Atkinson. "Raising a teenager."

"What are you talking about? You have two."

Atkinson blinked and put a wooden spoon on the benchtop. "Had two. They've flown the nest, living their own lives. I hardly hear from them. The only time they call is when they need money."

Feeling bad, Cooper wrapped her arms around him. She couldn't imagine a time without Tina, but that day was approaching, and fast.

"It's a hard tightrope to walk," he continued. "Disciplining teenagers, that is. Too strict, and they'll resent you and do the things you disapprove of anyway, just via sneakier means. That was always my mistake. But too lenient, and they take advantage when you slip over the boundary from parent to friend."

Cooper squeezed him. "Friend? I don't know if Tina's ever looked at me like a friend. I'm more like a landlord who doesn't charge rent and cooks all the meals?"

A tilted head and a crooked smile. "Cooks?"

"You know what I mean. A landlord who doesn't charge rent and who buys all the meals."

THE AIR WAS STILL and muggy in Hexham. He'd waited until after midnight for the sky to darken and the streets to empty. Still, he'd need to move quickly. He was exposed here. He drove the van just over a mile, through Causey Hill to Market Place. Market Place was the town's beating heart every second Saturday when the Farmer's Market would be in full swing. The abbey stood proud in the square, the east face marked by three long stained-glass windows running vertically up its ancient walls. One of the earliest seats of Christianity in England, the church had been desecrated by Viking raids and Scottish strikes. Both William Wallace and Robert the Bruce attacked the church, destroying books, shrines and important relics. The priory was set alight, and traces of molten lead from the roof could still be found on the abbey floor. It was a beautiful spot, and he relished the idea of it being befouled once again.

He squeezed the van between two bollards, quietly mounting the paved area around the abbey. Ronan, gagged and groggy, blinked at him when he opened the rear doors. He removed his high-viz vest and tossed it into the back of the van, though what he wore underneath was just as conspicuous. He sweated under the synthetic fibres, lifting the yellow and green fabric from his middle to wipe his forehead and cheeks. The smell of the material made him grimace. He hadn't washed it since the first time he'd done this.

Taking a length of duct tape, he added another layer of soundproofing to Ronan's gob. He'd always been a foghorn, bellowing orders like he ruled all of Tyneside. Though he was concussed and barely conscious, he couldn't take the risk of Ronan's shouts waking the neighbours.

Grabbing him by his broken leg, he heaved, dragging him from the van. Ronan's eyes contracted with pain, but only the slightest high-pitched squeak escaped the duct tape. He dragged Ronan to the foot of the abbey and stared down at him. He must have worked it out by now? He must have seen the papers and read the headlines. The bags of sand? It was his turn now. He collected the first two bags from the van; fifty kilos was no weight to him now. Ronan's eyes were sad and defeated, his whimpers more and more desperate as he failed to verbalise his pleas for life.

Funny, he'd pleaded and begged for Ronan to stop all those years ago.

Ronan didn't stop. Nor would he.

He bit through the corner of the plastic, allowing the sand to pour over shattered limbs. Previously, he'd had to pile the sand up, pushing it into position. This way, he could watch the sand pour from above, like an hourglass showing the trickle of time as he counted down to Ronan's death.

Another bag. Another.

He'd leave Ronan's head for last. Allow his anxiety to reach its peak. This snake wouldn't slither anywhere ever again.

- CHAPTER 33 -

COOPER WAS PLEASED TO sleep in her own bed last night. With Julie in the spare room, she'd been able to move from the couch to upstairs where she belonged. Unfortunately, she'd had the bed to herself. Atkinson had gone home after dinner, which was understandable; they still didn't know exactly where they were in their relationship. Were they officially back together? They hadn't discussed it, hadn't gone on a date yet.

Julie made a simple breakfast of scrambled eggs on toast and handed Tina a packed lunch, even though Tina told her she preferred the canteen. Steven was back and he'd grown in the short time they'd been away. Cooper was sure he'd become louder too. He made himself at home in a cardboard box in the corner of the kitchen, much to Julie's distaste.

"Disgusting thing to have in a kitchen. Must have a hundred diseases."

"He's NOT disgusting."

"They are, Tina. They eat rotten meat, they fish through bins—"

"Mum!" Cooper snapped before Tina lost it. "Steven is fed the finest North Sea cod. He eats better than a lot of humans, and as he's lived indoors since he was a hatchling, I hardly think he could be riddled with plague."

Tina's lips twisted as if she had a mouth full of bees. She threw her lunch into her bag and headed for the door, slamming it in her wake.

Cooper left for work in a quieter, less violent fashion. She hoped upon her return that no new furniture or furnishings adorned the other rooms of the house and that Steven was as they had left him: in one piece and very much alive.

COOPER PULLED UP AT HQ with plenty of time to spare before the morning briefing. Saffron Boyd was the first to arrive.

"Both Pennington and Lynch had lottery wins, boss." She sat across from Cooper and nervously pulled out her evidence. "Lynch won thirty-five grand four years ago, as I mentioned, but Pennington also had a win. His was back in ninety-seven. Forty grand."

The doors opened as Tennessee, Martin and Whyte arrived. Whyte was finishing the last of a cereal bar while Tennessee had a definite smell of bacon about him. Martin sat next to Boyd, flashing a bashful grin before turning his attention to Cooper.

"Morning, Coop."

"Boyd here has confirmed both victims as National Lottery winners. Might be a coincidence, but thirty-five grand and forty grand aren't amounts to be sniffed at."

Boyd pushed the bank statements to the centre of the table as Keaton joined them. "Current accounts show both victims as not being especially wealthy. Pennington's balance hovers at around two grand, and Lynch's at about five hundred. Pennington's money is in his house. Property on Holy Island isn't cheap. As for Eve, she put ten grand in an ISA and has made the rest last."

Cooper bobbed her head from side to side and noticed she had orange juice on her shirt. She moved her hand to cover it. "We don't know who will inherit Eve Lynch's money. What about Pennington?"

"His daughter," answered Boyd.

"And therefore her husband and kids," Cooper added.

Tennessee straightened up. "I can't get past the fact our killer wore the same shirt both times."

"The 1988 away shirt? I saw it in the file. Good spot."

He rubbed his chin. "I think he's a superfan. That or the shirt holds some other significance."

"You don't think...." Martin's eyes darted from left to right then he shook his head. "Never mind."

"Say it," Boyd urged.

"You don't think he's some mad Newcastle United fanatic, killing lottery winners to raise cash for a new striker? I mean, we finished in the bottom half of the table last season."

Whyte swallowed a laugh. "That's a bit bat-shit-crazy. No offence, mate."

Cooper shot him a look. "This whole case is bat-shit-crazy. There are no bad ideas, Martin. You know that."

"In that case," said Tennessee, "there's a superfan event on the twelfth in Gosforth. I know we can't sit on our backsides until then, but I'd like to check it out."

Cooper glanced at the calendar. "Fine. It's up to you how you spend your Saturday's. But, for now, let's focus on the connection. Did you get anywhere with the TIE list?" she asked Martin and Keaton. "Anyone you got a bad vibe from?"

Keaton opened her notepad. "A few shifties, yeah. Let's see. Davey Smith, Jason Beaumont, Jake Hale—"

A shadow appeared over the table, and collectively their eyes lifted to an ashen-faced Howard Nixon. The superintendent was out of breath, his skin shiny. He pierced Cooper with an electric look. "We have another one."

———

THERE WAS TRAFFIC CHAOS on the approach to Hexham. The section of Beaumont street that looped around the eastern side of the abbey had been closed to civilian traffic. The roadblocks caused tailbacks all over the small town as residents tried to start their commutes or open their businesses for another day of daytrippers visiting the old market town.

Cooper arrived with Tennessee, Keaton and Martin. Whyte and Boyd waited at HQ, updating HOLMES2 and checking any new postings to the website receiving photos and videos from the day of the triathlon. Following Tennessee's hunch, they kept their eyes peeled for vintage football shirts.

Around the abbey, screens were set up and police tape held back gawkers as well as a pushy reporter from the Hexham Courant. The other people of Hexham went about their day, opening shop shutters, getting their morning papers or a spot of breakfast on their way to work. A gaggle of middle-schoolers trudged through the streets in bottle green uniforms adorned with golden crests.

"The usual, boss?" Keaton asked as she heaved herself out of the backseat of Cooper's car.

She nodded. "Yes, please. Check in with the local bobbies and find out the CCTV situation."

Cooper and Tennessee made a beeline for the crime scene manager, signed in, and began to don PPE to preserve the forensic integrity of the site. Once through the cordon, she tried to pick Atkinson out of the colony of bunny suits.

"See anyone Atkinson-shaped?"

Tennessee raised a brow. "You know his shape better than I do."

"Cheeky."

A mound of sand, similar to the crime scene photographs from Longsands and Holy Island, stood beneath lengthy stained-glass windows. Dull from the outside, they were undoubtedly impressive when viewed from inside the abbey. The mound had been partially demolished to reveal the victim's head and torso so a doctor could confirm death. The remaining pile was formed into the familiar coils of a great serpent. This was less detailed than the previous two, though it was still undeniably from the same artist. The tail wrapped around the lower coils, and a diamond-shaped head rested on the top. Two round eyes with vertical slits marked his eyes.

"Erica." Atkinson moved towards them with long, determined strides. "Jack. How are you?"

Tennessee shrugged. "Well, I lost my SIO status to some DCI I've never heard of." He smirked in Cooper's direction.

"Behave. And you haven't lost anything. We're working together on this." She turned to Atkinson. "What can you tell us?"

"So far, not a huge deal. Local police have already made an ID. He's a bit of a local celebrity by all accounts. But in terms of forensic evidence, I've identified the tyre tracks. Run of the mill Michelin Aglin CrossClimates. Width, two-one-five. Ratio, seventy. Fairly standard van tyres."

"Any identifying featured?"

"There's a tear in the tread on the rear left tyre."

Cooper nodded in appreciation. If the killer had to transport his victim as well as the sand, it was likely he'd need a large vehicle such as a commercial van. This information could help them track down the killer, but it would also help build a case against him if they matched the defect on the tyre tread.

"I'll have to confirm it in the lab, but I'm almost certain this is kiln-dried sand. Not regular sand from a beach. More likely, it comes from a DIY store. The nature of the sand is why the sculpture isn't as defined as the previous two; it would be more difficult to mould. They've likely added moisture to form the more intricate parts, such as the head. I can't be sure, but I'd hazard a guess at a spray bottle."

"Okay," Cooper said. "Anything else for now."

"He put up a fight. He's been badly beaten. Countless defensive wounds to his arms." Empathy coated Atkinson's face with sorrow. "Good news – if you can call any of this good – is that I'm confident we'll have DNA evidence."

Spirits lifted, Cooper asked her next question with nothing more than a tilt of her head.

"I'll put a rush on it."

"Appreciated. We're going to go find Keaton. I'll see you later?"

He nodded and Cooper's spirits lifted further.

———

Paula Keaton shook hands with a uniformed officer then weaved her way through bumper-to-bumper cars to reconvene with Cooper as she stripped out of her forensic suit.

"Any luck?" Cooper asked her. "Atkinson said the victim's a local celebrity."

Keaton nodded. A slight breeze was coming from the east; it blew some strands of her hair free from her ponytail. They wafted above her head for a moment before she tucked them behind her ears and folded her thick arms. "Ronan Turnbull. Forty-five. Local man who lived on Collingwood Drive. That's just over a mile that way." She spun around and pointed south-west. "He's ex-army, did a couple of tours before moving here in 2016 and opening a boxing gym. Might not have been in his prime anymore, but his physique caught the attention of the yummy mummies. His gym was in the local paper every time one of his athletes won a medal, plus they did a load of charity work. Free self-defence classes for the elderly, that sort of thing. Oh, and he was named in the Queen's Birthday Honours."

"Do we know anything of his life before he moved to Hexham?"

"Monkton."

"Monkton? The same Monkton that's next to Hebburn?"

Keaton could picture a map of South Tyneside in her head. Hebburn was about two, maybe two and a half, miles away from Monkton. "The same." She moved aside and let two chefs carrying crates of fresh vegetables pass by. "It's the South Tyneside connection again."

"Does anyone on your list live over this way?" Cooper asked.

"Yeah, two of them." Keaton pulled out her notepad. "May Ratcliff lives in Corbridge, and Joanne Worthington lives just off the B6305."

Out of the corner of her eye, Keaton saw Martin galloping across the square to meet them. He looked like a child running to his mother; it made her want to pat his head and clean his cheeks with a hanky.

Martin took a dramatic breath. "Residents Association," he said with a pet lip and an eye roll.

"What about it?"

"They think security cameras are an eyesore. Think they look unsightly in a historic place such as this."

"You're kidding?" Cooper asked. She propped her fists on her hips and looked about, anger written on her forehead in two deep frown lines as she searched doorways and rooftops for cameras.

"I wish I was," he said. "I've got a jewellers, an art gallery, a betting shop and a wine merchant, oh and a designer clothes store. All have great internal cameras; not one has external cameras."

"Okay, looks like we're doing this the old fashioned way," Cooper said. "Paula, get a team together to speak to the locals. We need a van in the area late last night or early this morning. Martin, inform the victim's family then speak to his neighbours. I want you two to piece together Ronan Turnbull's movements yesterday. Where had he been? Who did he see? Who saw him last? And how in God's name did a big man like that end up buried outside a church? Jack, you and I will visit May Ratcliff and Joanne Worthington."

- CHAPTER 34 -

COOPER RUBBED HER EYES. "Are you seeing what I'm seeing?"

Tennessee shaded his eyes from the sun and turned to face the field. They'd pulled up at a farmhouse on a country road leaving Hexham.

"You're not hallucinating. I see them too."

"They're bloody massive."

The field was a faded green, dehydrated from an unusually warm summer. One summer storm and the countryside would be lush again, but Northumberland's grassy hills remained muted for now. Scattered throughout the field, long-necked and freshly shorn llamas turned their heads to eyeball the two detectives. Their ears pivoted like satellite dishes, listening for the sounds of threats but hearing only passing cars.

"Tina couldn't say the word llama when she was little. Used to call them leemoos."

"Cute."

Cooper paused to smile and appreciate the memory of when Tina was so small, she could carry her for hours either held tightly to her chest or propped on a hip. These days, Tina could probably give Cooper a piggyback, but not the other way around.

"Well, we can't stand here gawping at the animals all day. We have work to do." Cooper began to walk up the lane towards the white farmhouse.

Behind her, she heard Tennessee ask, "Do you think we can pet them? I know they spit, but it wouldn't be the first time I've been spat at doing this job."

Cooper gave him a *behave-yourself* stare and knocked on the door. "Mrs Worthington?" she asked when the door opened.

"It's Ms, actually. Can I help you?"

After brief introductions, Joanne Worthington grabbed a bag of chopped carrots, apples and sweet potato. She pulled on her boots and invited Cooper and Tennessee to walk and talk while she fed the livestock. As soon as they'd entered the paddock, the llamas started to approach. A smallish one with honey-brown fur was the first to arrive. Her teeth chomped through chunks of apple with a satisfying crunching noise.

"I was a bit rude to the other detective when he called," Joanne said without prompting. "The vet was over. We'd just had to put one of the older members of the herd down. We'd had her for over thirteen years, and I was— I was in no mood for anything other than a good cry and a bucket of chocolate."

"I'm sorry to hear that," Cooper said. "I don't think DC Martin will have taken it personally."

Joanne sighed and handed out carrot chunks to two much larger llamas that had neared. The taller of the two was easily twenty centimetres taller than Cooper. She didn't want to admit it, but she felt intimidated.

"In answer to his question, yes, I was taught by Mr Pennington back in the day. I heard what happened to him. Hard not to. It's all the newspapers cover at the moment. Is it true that it happened in Hexham last night? Another sand snake?"

"There was an incident in Hexham," Cooper said before taking a step back. Another three llamas had joined them.

"I heard it was Ronan Turnbull. Oh, don't worry about Cher and Beyonce. As long as I keep feeding them, they're happy. I hope it's not true. Ronan's a nice man. Easy on the eye."

"Going back to Mr Pennington. What can you tell me about him?"

Joanne pulled a confused face. "Not much. He taught me in primary school. Year five, I think. To be honest, I barely remember him; he was straight-laced, boring but not too strict. I remember he taught us how the moon goes around the Earth and the Earth goes around the sun. He had us out on the school field running circles around each other. It was hilarious. My friend Natalie was the sun and she had to spin around on the spot while I ran in a huge circle around her. Meanwhile, James – was it James? It was James or Ryan, one of the twins – he was the moon and had to run rings around me while I was running around Natalie. We all got so dizzy we had to go the medical room to sit down with buckets between our knees."

She paused and handed some more carrots to Beyonce. "That was the main thing I remember of my time with Mr Pennington. Old Penny, we'd call him. I remember that class because it was funny and we all laughed so hard. But most of the time, we were just in the classroom, staring at the blackboard and counting down the minutes to hometime."

"Did any of your classmates particularly dislike Mr Pennington?"

"Not especially. There were trouble makers, of course, but no, no one talked about him more than any of the other teachers."

"Do you recognise the name Eve Lynch?"

She shook her head. "Only from the papers. Gosh, I hope this third one isn't Ronan. It's a bit weird knowing two of the victims."

As she said it, the implication that she was a connecting factor dawned on Joanne. She shivered despite the heat of the day. Whether Joanne was worried her link to two of the victims made her look like a suspect or made her a potential target, Cooper didn't know.

"Is there anything else?" Joanne asked as the rest of the herd arrived and Cooper found herself surrounded by giant fluffy creatures that had no respect for her personal space.

"I have a question," Tennessee said. "What does llama meat taste like?"

"We breed them for their wool, DS Daniel. But..." she paused and took one of the apple segments for herself. She chewed and swallowed. "Beefy lamb."

DS PAULA KEATON LOVED cases such as this. She knew that sounded awful, and she wished she lived in a world where murder and assault didn't occur, but as long as she did, and as long as serial killers weren't relegated to the world of nightmares and horror films, at least she got to be the one to hunt them down.

Collingwood Drive looked much like any wealthy street in upper-middle-class commuter estates. Four bedroom detached homes with long drives and well-maintained lawns. Double garages, rockeries, herb gardens and birdbaths. And yet, while the houses were expensive, the cars were cheap. An old Polo here, a two-door Cl there. Antique Fiestas and a bashed-up Suzuki.

A crippling mortgage in exchange for good schools and a low crime rate? Keaton wasn't falling into that trap. She and April had their eye on somewhere cheap. Their plan was to be mortgage-free as soon as possible. Even her younger brother, Riley, who had moved in with Keaton after their father had raised his fists to him, was contributing to their deposit thanks to his part-time job at Tesco.

Both inside and out of Ronan Turnbull's home, scene of crime officers moved with care. They photographed and documented everything, planted flags and took samples. This was a job where every movement was conducted with deliberate precision. No one wanted a case such as this to be compromised by contaminated evidence. To prevent a dangerous criminal from walking free, they couldn't slip up in their collection methods or chain of custody.

Keaton wondered what sort of man they were after. She didn't mean to be misandristic, but even a woman of her stature and athleticism would struggle to overpower a man like Ronan Turnbull. The first two victims? Yes, easily. They were older, weaker and weighed less. But Ronan's death involved overpowering and beating an ex-military high-level boxer, moving his body and shifting all that sand. She let her brain mull it over for a minute or two while sipping from a bottle of Evian. No, this wasn't your typical one-punch murder down the Bigg Market after some gobshite tried to nick your taxi.

She screwed the lid back on the plastic bottle and called Cooper to update her.

"Boss. How's it going?"

"Well, you just missed a llama take a bite out of Jack. Serves him right for asking what llama meat tastes like."

That wasn't how Keaton expected their conversation to begin but she was happy to roll with it. "That's effing priceless. You know he was bit by a dog on Holy Island?"

"Same hand," Cooper said, and Keaton could hear she was suppressing a laugh. "Do you have news?"

"Yeah. The SOCOs are working their arses off over here. Hong's running the show while Atkinson works the burial site. It's a bit of a mess. Looks like Ronan put up quite a fight, as you'd expect. I haven't been inside as we're low on bunny suits, but Hong tells me there are broken vases and photo frames, other signs of a struggle too. Also, there's plenty of blood spatter. They don't think it all belongs to the victim either."

"Excellent. Some viable DNA from the killer will make our lives a lot easier. Anything else?"

"Yip. They've got a tyre print that matches the one at the abbey. We have a few grains of sand on the driveway and a footprint in the hall."

"Have you talked to the neighbours yet?"

"Some of them," Keaton confirmed. "So far, no one can recall seeing Ronan yesterday. But that's not surprising. Most people would have been at work during the day. When they got home, they would have just done the usual: dinner, catch up with the kids, watch television."

"No mention of a van?"

"Sadly not. We need the local retired busy body who keeps tabs on all the neighbours' comings and goings. Every street has one. Mine has two. I'll find them. Just give me time."

COOPER ENDED THE CALL. The news that they were likely to have DNA from the guilty party was excellent. She just hoped the DNA would match someone in the database. Atkinson would get the results to her the second they came through. It wasn't preferential treatment. A case such as this was high stakes, and Cooper knew that Nixon would fork out whatever money was needed to rush lab results.

Corbridge was only four miles east of Hexham. Another Northumbrian market town that suffered in the border wars. At night, livestock had to be rounded up from the fields and ushered into the town. Cattle raids were common, so watchmen had to stand at either end of the town, protecting it from its northern neighbours.

Cooper parked outside of May Ratcliff's home on St. Helen's Street. The old sash windows had seen better days, its white paint peeling away to reveal coats of teal and navy beneath. The front garden was suffering equally; potted herbs and flowers were desperate for a drink of water. There was no answer, but after only a few minutes of asking around, Tennessee had tracked May to an independent coffee house on a tight lane marked with double yellow lines. Cooper slowed to allow Tennessee to jump out while she went in search of parking. Corbridge was busy with a coachful of daytrippers from Edinburgh. She had to drive at a snail's pace through the crowds until she found a space outside the local butchers. She struggled to fit the BMW into the tiny bay but managed it on the third attempt.

Some smug bastard in a Land Rover chortled to himself as he watched her manoeuvre. "That car a bit big for you, luv?"

Cooper swallowed her annoyance, switched the engine off and made her way to the machine to pay for parking. As she fed a couple of pound coins into the ticket machine, she spotted the Land Rover as it came to a stop at the next junction; its right brake light wasn't working.

WHEN COOPER ENTERED MAY'S Tea Rooms, she found Tennessee at a corner table with two milky teas and a slice of billionaire's shortbread. Three wrappers littered the table cloth, telling her Tennessee had ordered four of the caramel treats but had scoffed three of them while he waited.

"Tea? It's probably lukewarm now, but I can order another one. Did you have trouble finding a space?"

"Something like that," she answered, grinning to herself as she thought of the look on the laughing man's face when she pressed her ID against the driver's window and reprimanded him for his broken brake light. He'd fumbled and stuttered his way through the usual *I'm on my way to the mechanic's right now, honest*. The golf clubs on his back seat suggested another story.

"May Ratcliff's the lady behind the till," said Tennessee, his eyes on the shortbread. "She said she'd speak to us as soon as the work experience girl is back from her break."

A bell tinkled above the door, and a sour-faced girl in her early teens dragged her feet behind the counter and donned an apron.

"She's not normally like that," May said to Cooper as she dusted her hands on her apron and took a seat next to Tennessee. "The news has upset her."

"Did she know the victim?" Cooper asked. Northumbria Police hadn't released Ronan Turnbull's name to the press. Still, news could spread like wildfire in small communities such as these. With SOCOs at Ronan's house, it wouldn't have taken the locals long to ID the victim for themselves.

May shook her head and propped her elbows on the wooden table. "No, she didn't know Ronan. I did. Knew him from way back when. Nah, young Sophie's a bit, well, she's a bit triggered. Her dad was murdered when she was little, and her mum moved the rest of the family up here from Birmingham to have a quieter – safer – life in the country. When I was opening up, I saw her texting her brother about not being safe anywhere. Poor thing."

Cooper agreed. She hadn't lost her father in the same way as the young woman serving tea and cake to impatient customers. Still, she did wonder how long it would be until the words *heart attack* no longer knocked the wind out of her.

"Hopefully, work will keep her mind off things," Cooper said. "So, you knew Ronan?"

"And Charles Pennington," she said, sharing a pointed look with Cooper. "But that's why you're here, isn't it? It can't be a coincidence, can it? I mean, I'm no detective, but the primary school teacher and the big kid from the boxing gym we all went to after class... It's got to be someone I knew." She shuddered from top to bottom just as Joanne Worthington had done. "Gives me the collywobbles thinking about it."

"Some of your class would go boxing after school?" Cooper asked, pen in hand.

May nodded. "A fair few. Mostly the lads. I was the only girl. It was ninety-one, ninety-two perhaps. Not exactly the dark ages, but still, boys went to Cubs, girls went to Brownies, boys played football, girls played netball. Just the way it was most of the time."

"What was the name of the boxing gym?"

"Hebburn Boxing Club, or something like that. Boxing Gym? Boxing Academy? I don't know. It closed down donkey's years ago. Pretty Boy Fisher used to train there. So did a few other big names. Think the bloke who ran it was called Frankie something. There wasn't much else to do after school, so we'd go over to the gym and do an hour or so on the heavy bags. Ronan was a few years older than us. Let's see, I was ten, so he must've been sixteen or seventeen. He was the national champion in his age and weight. Moved like lightning. He took a few of the youngsters under his wing and gave them extra training, one-on-ones. Didn't matter if they were big or small, strong or weak, if he saw potential, he'd give up his time to coach them. Really kind seeing as he must have a tonne on himself, what with training for the nationals, training to get into the army and doing his A-levels."

Cooper took a sip of her tea – it was cold – and slid her shortbread over to a grateful Tennessee. "Sounds like a lot of people would have looked up to him?"

May's head tilted from left to right and back again. "I didn't make the grade. Never got picked to be in his special little gang. He did give me his old gloves when he found out I couldn't afford a pair and that I'd been hitting the bag bare-knuckle. Some of the lads thought he was up himself, but I think they were just jealous. I mean, if someone punches you in the face enough, you're bound to start disliking them eventually."

May removed her elbows from the table and slid her arms over her lap. She looked out the window, where life continued as usual despite the horrific news from Hexham that morning. Her face saddened, and she turned to check on her work experience girl.

"I know you're busy, May. We appreciate you taking a moment to speak with us. Could I ask you to write down all the names of the children from King George Primary who also attended the boxing gym? You don't need to do it this instant. Here's my email address," Cooper said, handing May a white card. "By this evening or tomorrow morning would be great."

May got to her feet. "I don't know why I'm suddenly so down. It's not like we were close." She swallowed and fussed with her apron strings. "But we'd nod hello if we passed in the street or saw each other at the supermarket. It's odd thinking that will never happen again, you know?"

"I know," Cooper replied. She gave May a nod goodbye and placed her hand on her arm for a moment. "Look after yourself. And the girl."

- CHAPTER 35 -

AFTER SPENDING ALL OF Monday and half of Tuesday in a forensic suit, complete with mask, gloves and boots, Justin Atkinson seized the first opportunity he could to venture somewhere without PPE. He waited for the printer at the back of the lab to finish ejecting the documents he was waiting for, then left in search of the one person who could put a smile on his tired face.

The air conditioning at Northumbria Police HQ was under central command, preventing air-con wars between the male and female police officers. Justin felt the cool breeze of chemically enhanced air as he exited HQ's rotating doors into the lobby. Compared to the sticky warmth outside, it was a blessed relief. Naturally, that'd meant it was about two and a half degrees too cold for Cooper.

ID presented, and after a quick phone call to CID, Atkinson was shown to the incident room.

"I have the results," he said, printout held aloft above his head.

Cooper was bent over a desk studying a Filofax style planner. She snapped it shut and pushed it into her handbag before flashing a surprised look at him. "You could have just emailed me. You didn't have come all the way out to the shark tank."

He sat on the edge of the table, close enough to be flirty, not so close he'd threaten Cooper's professionalism. "And miss the chance to see you?"

Cooper gave him the look he was after: playful and coquettish. Though behind her eyes, he could see all was not as it should be. The diary? It was early July now, which meant Cooper was due some more tests at the Northern Centre for Cancer Care. She hadn't mentioned it to him, and he hoped between her father's passing and the pressure she'd no doubt be under from Nixon that she wasn't keeping things to herself again. Perhaps she'd talk to Tina? He hoped so.

"Well?" Cooper pressed. She looked at him with hopeful eyes. "Tell me you have a match."

Keaton, Martin and Whyte had all subtly positioned themselves within hearing distance.

Cooper shook her head at them. "Quit lurking about and get over here. DNA results are in."

It wasn't just Keaton, Martin and Whyte's eyes that fell upon Atkinson. Suddenly he was the sole focus of the incident room. Fingers stopped typing, heads turned, and mouths closed. How did Cooper do it? Be the centre of attention like this at every meeting? This was no place for introverts.

He cleared his throat. "We ran the DNA samples from Roman Turnbull's house, and I'm afraid there's no match in the PNC."

The air in the room changed as everyone sighed together. From the far corner, someone growled, "Bugger it."

"But..." The eyes turned again, and Atkinson noticed Cooper's head tilt slightly as if she could guess what was coming. "I can confirm the sample belongs to a white male—"

A sarcastic voice uttered, "That's sorted then, lads. We've ruled out eight per cent of the men in the region. Should be a piece of piss now."

Cooper raised her eyebrows at Keaton, who in turn picked up a paper cup and hurled it in the man's direction. It hit his chest then bounced to the floor, leaving a trail of residual cola over his crotch. "Pipe down, Pinky. Brain's speaking," Keaton said, holding up another paper cup to show she wouldn't hesitate in repeating her actions.

Atkinson stood up and smoothed the creases from his trousers. "Yes. Right. As I said, the DNA indicates a white male. We also ran a familial DNA test and got two matches."

Cooper pressed her palms together. "Now we're talking."

"The first match is Natalie Beaumont, born in seventy-eight and arrested in twenty-twelve. The second match is for an unsolved rape in twenty-eleven."

COOPER MOVED TO THE front of the room and wrote the name Natalie Beaumont on the murder wall. "Get me what you can on her," she told the room. "You have five minutes."

Around her, computers were fired up as everyone logged in to a series of databases. Within seconds, they had her address.

"Arrested in twenty-twelve," Whyte repeated, his eyes scanning back and forth as he read the PNC. "Bloody hell. She's on a no-fly list."

That piqued Cooper's interest. "Blimey. You don't see one of those every day. Email me the document." She pinched her nose, wondering what Natalie Beaumont had got herself into. *Isis? Far-right extremism? Far-left?* "Anything else?" she asked the room.

Keaton's pen was aloft. "I know that name: Beaumont. It came up earlier when I was collating lists of everyone Charles Pennington taught. Not a Natalie Beaumont, but a Jason and a Kerry."

The net was tightening; adrenaline danced inside Cooper. She'd let herself be distracted by her own domestic situation, but now she felt how thirsty her brain was for information. She surveyed the room, looking for Tennessee.

"Alfie has a fever," Keaton explained. "It was his second swimming class last night, and Tennessee thinks he picked something up from one of the other toddlers. He said his mother-in-law has a cold, and Hayley, well she..." her voice trailed away.

Cooper mouthed, "Depression?"

Keaton nodded, a sad look on her face.

"Okay. Well, grab your things. You're with me," Cooper said, zipping her handbag closed and pulling the strap over her shoulder. "Address?" she called over to Martin.

"Warkworth."

Cooper sighed. Warkworth was almost an hour away. She gave Atkinson a fleeting hug, releasing him quickly. "Dinner tonight? Mum said she'd cook."

ATKINSON WAS PLEASANTLY SURPRISED that Cooper had moved in for a hug with so many colleagues around. He'd been less pleased by how she'd flinched and pulled away so fast. He caught the look of pain she tried to disguise. She was sore and low on energy. He wasn't a religious man, but as soon as Atkinson was back in the fresh air, he looked to the sky and asked for Cooper's next check-up to show she was still in the clear.

THE PEBBLE-DASHED SEMI-DETACHED HOME on Morwick Road looked odd to Cooper. Its garden was neat with precision trimmed privet hedges but the home only had one upstairs window facing the road. Rather than resembling a face with two upstairs windows as eyes, this house, along with others on the road, looked more like a cyclops.

Turning to look in the opposite direction, Cooper saw the houses would have a distant but unobstructed view of medieval Warkworth Castle.

Cooper had chosen Keaton over Martin, Whyte or Boyd as she thought she might need some muscle. But while Keaton drove, Cooper read the email Whyte had sent her. It turned out Natalie Beaumont was on British Airways' internal no-fly list rather than the government one. Realising Natalie Beaumont was unlikely to be part of a terrorist cell, she called during their drive to make sure she was home.

Keaton parked behind a purple car adorned with stickers advertising Nat's Cleaning Co. When she and Cooper knocked, the door was opened immediately.

"Natalie? I'm DCI Cooper. I called from the car."

Natalie nodded and ushered them into her living room. She was in her early forties, and though short in stature, she had a strong build. She'd pulled her hair back into a tight bun which accentuated her pointy chin, and she wore black leggings with a purple t-shirt emblazoned with the same company logo as her car.

"You said you needed to talk to me about my family?"

Keaton nodded as she took a seat. "Your DNA was entered into the system following the incident in twenty-twelve."

"I'm so bloody embarrassed about that," she said, her cheeks blooming with red blotches. "Too much sun and alcohol. It wasn't even my fault." She sat and propped her elbows on her knees and peeked at Cooper and Keaton through her fingers. "Hen party in Ibiza. We had a great time, but some of the girls were getting lippy on the flight back. Freya was the worst, talking like she owned the whole damn plane. It turned into a right palaver. Families started arguing with us, then the flight attendants joined in. Then we started fighting amongst ourselves because me and Caz were telling the others to shut up and stop causing a scene. Anyway, we were all arrested on landing." She peeled her face from her hands and slumped back into her armchair. "It was Freya's hen do, and half of us were so mad at her we didn't go to the wedding."

"The reason we're here, Natalie, is because a DNA sample found at a crime scene closely matches yours."

She looked nervous. "What does that mean? Closely matches?"

"The sample belongs to a male relative of yours. We need to find your father and any brothers or male cousins as quickly as possible so we can eliminate them from the investigation."

"Right," Natalie said bluntly. She sucked her lips into her mouth and lowered her brows half an inch. "You know I was adopted?"

Cooper shook her head.

"Right," Natalie said again. She glanced at the kitchen. "This requires tea and biscuits." She pushed herself to her feet with shaking hands. "I don't really talk about my parents. Give me— Give me five minutes."

She returned in no time with quaint china teacups filled with weak tea and handed Keaton a packet of custard creams.

"I'll start at the beginning, I suppose. My birth parents were Beth and James Beaumont. We lived on Buchanan Street."

"In Hebburn?" Keaton asked, tearing open the packet.

Natalie nodded. "Yeah. There were nine of us kids. Three girls, six boys."

At times, Cooper felt like she had her hands full with just Tina. She couldn't imagine another eight children in the house. "Nine? That's a big family."

"It got bigger." Natalie stood, reached over to Keaton, took a biscuit, and sat back down. She dipped it in her tea and let the excess liquid drip back into the cup before taking a bite. "James got lung cancer. It was terrible. I don't remember all that much because I was about nine when I left, but I remember the coughing and how weak and helpless he looked at times. It was a long illness, and us kids were – well, we were neglected before he died – but we were really neglected afterwards." Natalie dipped her head towards Cooper's notepad and pen. "There was me, Kerry and Grace. Then the boys were Jason, Kevin, Robert, Tyrone, Shane and Marcus."

Cooper jotted the names down. "Any middle names?"

"Yeah. Robert was Robert Phillip, and Tyrone's middle name was Douglas. Do you need the girl's middle names?"

Cooper shook her head.

"After James died, Beth spiralled. She started doing meth. I didn't know that at the time, but I worked it out when I got older. And because all she cared about was drugs and her new boyfriends, we hardly got anything to eat. So, we were taken into care. The lot of us. Us girls were lucky, though. Really lucky. First, we got to stay together. Second, we hit the jackpot with the couple who fostered us. They ended up adopting us girls. We were all old enough to know they weren't our real Mum and Dad, but we called them that all the same." She paused. "But you're here to talk about the boys." She dipped what remained of her biscuit. "The boys were split up; I mean, no one could take on six boys at once. Marcus and Jason stayed local, and we all kept going to the same school to begin with, which was nice. It felt like we still had some sort of normality."

"King George's?" asked Cooper.

"That's right. At first, we'd get letters from the others, but they stopped after a while. I guess they were getting on with their own lives. New families, new schools. I don't know. I think they got bounced about a fair bit between foster parents. Kevin and Robert could be a handful. When I got older, my parents – adoptive parents – wanted to move. Dad got a job in Newcastle, so we moved to Kenton and went to school there. I lost touch with Marcus and Jason after that." She exhaled forcefully, looking into her teacup for answers. "You don't— What crime did you say this was to do with?"

"I didn't," Cooper said.

Keaton steered the conversation back to Natalie's male relatives. "You said the family got bigger?"

"Yeah. Bloody Beth Beaumont. Have you heard of baby addiction? Basically, she was addicted to newborn babies. She liked the attention she got when she was pregnant, and she got this intense feeling of dependence from caring for infants. The second us kids became toddlers, she'd lose interest and want a new baby. It's a form of compulsion. An obsession."

Natalie placed her cup on a side table and got to her feet. The muscles in her face had tightened as she dredged up memories from her childhood.

"She had more kids after we were all sent to foster care. Six, I heard. All of them taken into care too. It's ridiculous. Why didn't someone stop her? Or – I don't know – it's not like we can force sterilisation on someone, but still, someone should have stopped her. At least fifteen kids. All neglected, all put into care." She went to shove her hands into pockets but realised she was wearing leggings. "I was mad at her for so long. I guess I still am. You can hear it in my voice, can't you?"

"Take a deep breath," Cooper urged, fearing Natalie might be on the verge of a panic attack.

"So, male relatives... Yes, there were my six full brothers. Plus, another two half brothers, from what I heard. James, my dad, had a brother and a sister, but the sister died before we were born, and his brother lived in Australia. That seemed so exotic when we were little. Australia! The other side of the world. We rarely ventured outside of South Tyneside. And Beth? It's hard to remember. I went to a birthday party for an Uncle Mark. He had three boys called Liam, Ed and – sorry, I can't remember the other one, he was just a baby."

"That's okay, Natalie. You've been a great help." Cooper stood up.

"Fifteen," Natalie repeated, pacing quickly now. "At least fifteen kids that she had no intention of caring for beyond infancy. We weren't dolls, for Christ's sake. We were just kids!" She picked up her china teacup and hurled it at the furthest wall.

- CHAPTER 36 -

COOPER CONSIDERED LEAZES TERRACE one of the most beautiful streets in the north. Or, it would be if a great big football stadium hadn't been built right behind it. Four storeys of classical architecture and pristine gardens protected by wrought iron fences. It was a lovely place. So close to the city centre and yet so tranquil amongst Leazes Park, the lake and tennis courts.

Cooper finished a phone call and signalled to Keaton to stop arguing with a traffic warden and just pay for parking.

"That was Whyte. He's already rounded up two of the cousins and an uncle."

"Bloody hell, that was fast," Keaton said. "I'm gonna have to start calling him the Great Whyte Shark if he keeps that up."

"Before you choose a nickname for him, I'll just let you know, one of the cousins lives on Berwick Park Road."

"That's literally over the road from HQ."

"Took him sixty seconds to walk there."

After speaking to Natalie Beaumont, Cooper had phoned Nixon. He'd given her the go-ahead to round up and take DNA samples from as many of her male relatives as they could. It would be expensive, but it would be worth it if it led them to the killer. After a fifty-minute drive south through Northumberland and back into Tyne and Wear, Cooper was now looking for Kevin Beaumont. They'd found his address easily enough, and as a close relative of Natalie's, there was a reasonable chance this was their man.

Despite the pleasant serenity of her surroundings, Cooper's stomach felt tight. She was well aware of the potential dangers and was secretly relieved that Nixon had ordered them to hang back until backup arrived. With backup ready to go and positioned at the front and rear of the house, Cooper approached Kevin Beaumont's home. She opened the iron gate and climbed the stately stairs. An NUFC mug was visible through the window, and a black and white striped cushion adorned one of the armchairs.

The door was opened by a slight woman who breastfed an infant under a shawl. Upon seeing the police on her doorstep, she moaned. "Oh, not again."

"Again?" Cooper asked.

"The cars. Some little toerag has been keying the cars on the street and nicking their aerials." She leant forward, supporting the weight of the baby, and looked up and down the street. "They haven't done mine, have they? Red Mini Cooper?"

Cooper shook her head. "Not that I'm aware. We're actually here to speak to Kevin."

"Oh. Is everything okay?" She looked confused, eyes narrowed slightly, head pulled back, giving herself an extra chin.

"We think he can help us with a case we're investigating," Cooper told her. "Are you Mrs Beaumont?"

She shook her head. "Not yet. Two kids but still no ring. I'm Elsa. I'd invite you in to wait, but I don't know how long he'll be."

Keaton subtly waved her hand to allow their backup to back off a little. She leant against the black railing. "I take it Kevin's a football fan, living this close to St James'?"

Elsa laughed. "Just a bit. Been a season ticket holder for as long as I've known him. We could have got a biggish house with a garden further out in the suburbs, but oh no, he had to be as close to possible to the hallowed ground."

Cooper's thoughts turned to Tennessee. *I think he's a superfan.*

"I'm a rugby girl myself. Copthall stadium is my hallowed ground," Keaton told her, allowing her casual chatting to put the woman more at ease. "Don't suppose you know where Kevin is, do you? We think he might have witnessed something earlier this week."

Elsa hesitated. "He went for a few pints with his brother."

"Where?" Cooper asked, excited that she might get two Beaumont boys for the price of one.

"I don't know. But if I had to hazard a guess, I'd say The Strawberry."

THE STRAWBERRY PUB WAS within spitting distance of St James' Park. On match days, the place was packed wall-to-wall with the black and white army. The venue's unusual name was due to its history. Once upon a time, the area was a large strawberry patch. Nuns from St Bartholomew's would tend the gardens, and the proceeds from their strawberry wine helped fund the nunnery. Outside, it was a magnolia building adorned with a giant logo for Newcastle Brown Ale. Inside, it was much like any traditional pub, apart from the drawings of football players on the wall and a sign reading *Nee Mackems* that hung from the bar. It was now late afternoon, and despite it being a school night, the pub was beginning to fill up with patrons wanting a mid-week escape in the form of Guinness or Brown Ale.

Cooper hoped to get home at a reasonable hour. Tina had netball training after school so would be home just before six. If Cooper could meet two Beaumont brothers and be home in time to spend time with her family, it would be a successful day.

The officers who had arrived as backup were instructed to give Cooper and Keaton space. They were to lurk at a distance, covering exits in case either Beaumont made a dash for it.

It didn't take long for Cooper to find who she was looking for. Usually, she'd enquire with the bar staff to see if they recognised the name or face of the person they were after, but that wouldn't be required this time. Two men were sat at a table on the roof terrace; one looked like a bald Natalie Beaumont. They shared the same hazel eyes, pointed chin and slightly rounded shoulders. He sat back in his chair, one hand behind his head with his elbow aiming skywards. His other hand clutched a pint of lager. The other man's posture was less relaxed. He cupped his drink with both palms and slumped forwards as if trying to make himself smaller. Unlike his drinking partner, he had a full head of chestnut hair.

"Kevin Beaumont?"

It was the bald one who looked up. "Who's asking?"

Cooper and Keaton identified themselves.

"And you are?" Cooper asked the other man.

"Jason."

"Jason Beaumont?" Cooper asked.

"Aye. Why?"

Both men slurred their words, but while Kevin seemed as relaxed as he had when they'd walked in, Jason was avoiding eye contact and tapping his foot against the terrace floor.

"We need to speak with you both urgently. Would you mind accompanying us to the station for a chat?"

"Yeah, I'd mind," said Kevin. "I'm enjoying a quiet pint with my brother."

"Sir, DNA from a series of violent crimes shows a familial match to your sister Natalie, whose DNA we have on record. The easiest and quickest way to eliminate yourself from the investigation is to provide us with a DNA sample. I can assure you, if it isn't a match, the sample will be destroyed."

"A series of violent crimes?" echoed Kevin, sitting up straighter and peering at Cooper with questioning eyes. "Oh, bloody hell. It's not what I think it is, is it?" He looked at his brother. "Drink up, Jason. We'd best get this sorted." He lifted his glass and poured three-quarters of a pint down his throat.

"I'm not going." Jason's voice was quiet.

"Jason." He bent over the table to whisper. "It's those bloody sandcastle killings. Fuck's sake. We go to the station, spit in a tube, tell them where we were when those folk got hurt, then you get to go home again. Right?" He looked to Cooper.

"Exactly. And I hate to put it so bluntly, Jason, but you either do it the way your brother described, or we arrest you. I know that sounds harsh, but if you've nothing to hide, you'll want your name scratched off our list as soon as possible."

"NO." Jason Beaumont shot to his feet. "I'm not going nowhere."

"Jas—"

But before Kevin could calm his brother, three uniformed officers were upon him.

As Jason was tackled to the floor, handcuffed and escorted to a waiting police car, Kevin picked up his brother's Carling and downed it in one.

- CHAPTER 37 -

OLIVER MARTIN'S HEAD CRANED above a computer screen. "Coop?" His neck appeared to grow three inches as he tried to get Cooper's attention. It was early evening now, and she hadn't long returned to HQ.

"I managed to find the uncle in Australia. Name's Leslie Beaumont. He has two sons, one of whom lives in Perth and the other..." He checked his notepad. "The other is called Greg and lives just up the road in Edinburgh."

Cooper paused by his desk, holding a set of manila folders to her chest. "Did you just say *whom*?"

Martin straightened his tie. "Why, yes I did. Anyway, Edinburgh's not that far away. Two and a half hours commute from Tynemouth or Hexham. Only ninety minutes from Holy Island. It's an outside chance, but I thought it would still be worth tracking this Greg down. I've just got off the blower with Police Scotland. Morningside said they'd get alibis and DNA."

"Good work. Like you said, it's an outside chance, but let's hope they can get a sample to our lab by tomorrow night. Have you seen Whyte? Boyd?"

Martin took a sip from an almost empty bottle of Lucozade. "Not since Whyte brought Liam Beaumont in."

"Did he hold any of them?"

"No, boss. They were cooperative as far as I heard. Swabs are already at the lab. But I think he's hit a brick wall tracking down any more Beaumonts."

"All right," said Cooper. "Looks like it's just you, me and Keaton for now. Fancy interviewing Kevin Beaumont while I tackle Jason?"

He glanced at her through the corner of his eye. "Me?"

"No, Ant and Dec's secret love child." She gently punched his shoulder. "Yes, you. You're not the rookie anymore, Martin. Keaton will be there. She'll take the lead, but if you have questions, don't be afraid to ask. He's in interview suite three. They were pretty sozzled, so we've given them time to sober up a little and plied them with coffee. Kevin seems the chattier of the two; his solicitor is with him and happy for the interview to go ahead."

Martin got to his feet. "Right. Thanks, boss." He puffed his chest and headed for the double doors.

INTERVIEW SUITE THREE WAS as soulless as it sounded. At only three and a half metres long and two meters wide, it was basically a shoebox with furniture. The walls had been painted off-white many years ago, but they now resembled a mosaic of black streaks and smudges from years of chairs and shoes scuffing against them. Carpet tiles in green-blue didn't line up correctly with their neighbours, which was a nightmare for any officer with OCD. On the wall, a white air-con unit doubled as a heater. Unfortunately, it only had two settings: ice box or sauna. Of course, that could work to a detective's advantage if they wanted to make a suspect sweat. Literally.

Martin nodded to Keaton, Kevin Beaumont and his solicitor as he entered the room. The atmosphere was pretty relaxed as the three of them discussed the new series of Love Island. At least that was what Kevin was discussing; Keaton nodded along as if she actually watched the show.

As Martin took his seat, Kevin – bald as a coot and rosy-cheeked – said, "Okay, let's get on with this, shall we? You have my saliva. I suppose you'll want to know where I was when those poor sods were killed?"

"We'll get to that," said Keaton.

"Yeah," Martin added. "We thought we'd just have a chat for a bit first. Your sister said you had a tough time as kids. All taken into care?"

"That's right. We're the offspring of Meth Beth. Hebburn legend that she was. I wonder how many sprogs she pushed out in the end. She must be mid-sixties now."

Martin had checked earlier and found Beth Beaumont was still alive and well, aged sixty-four.

"I was the eldest, followed by Robert. I was sixteen when our dad died, so I wasn't in the foster system for long. Managed to get an apprenticeship at a garage and got out of care and into my own place as fast as I could. Robert found it harder. He was maybe fourteen or fifteen and hated his new school. Bastards bullied him something rotten. I had to meet him after school and sort a few lads out. Wait—" He stopped himself and glanced at his lawyer. "That's not incriminating, is it?"

The lawyer shook his head. "No one's interested in school gate scuffles from the eighties. Right?"

"Right," Keaton confirmed.

"But you really think those murders on the news are connected to my family?" he asked. His chest seemed to cave slightly as he spoke. The weight of the situation kicking in.

"We know they are," Keaton said. "Tell us about your other brothers. Where are they?"

"Jesus." Kevin Beaumont wiped a hand over his face, then looked at it, his palm glistening, his fingers shaking.

"Do you need a break?" Martin asked. Time was of the essence, but he couldn't risk evidence being thrown out because interviewees were too intoxicated or stressed to give accurate statements.

"Just a few minutes," he said, tugging at his collar. "And some fresh air."

ACROSS THE HALL, IN interview suite four, Cooper felt her time would be better spent banging her head against a wall.

"Where were you on Saturday the twenty-second of June?"

"I dunno. Was ages ago."

Jason Beaumont spoke into the table. Eyes down, head bowed, his greasy chestnut hair flopping over his face. He'd refused his right to counsel and was being as uncooperative as possible.

"Okay, let's try an easier one. Where were you on Monday?"

"Lot's of places."

Cooper ground her teeth. "Where were you between ten p.m. on Monday evening and five a.m on Tuesday morning?"

"Probably in bed."

"Probably?"

"Yeah. Probably. It means *almost certainly, as far as one can tell, in all likelihood*—"

"Thank you for the definition, Jason." Cooper remained steely faced, but inside she wanted to throw her cup of water over his oleaginous head.

"In your own bed? On Northcote Street, Arthur's Hill?"

"Probably."

"Well, I'm going to assume you mean your own bed. I'm going to go out on a limb and guess you didn't get lucky on Monday night and charm your way into some lady's boudoir. I know, risky bet, given your delightful conversation skills."

He raised his head briefly to shoot her a cold stare.

"So, back to Saturday the twenty-second. Think harder."

He shrugged.

"Jason, you are under arrest. This is a triple murder investigation. This is serious shit, and if you don't start talking—"

"You'll what? Arrest me for murder? You already did that."

"I didn't have to. You could have come with us voluntarily. You forced my hand. Now, give me an alibi I can check, or you can start making yourself comfortable in the cells."

"If you think I'm dobbing in one of my brothers after we were failed over and over by our mother, by the state, by our foster families... You've got another thing coming. My lips are sealed. I'll wait my twenty-four hours and be on my merry way."

Cooper stood up. Jason Beaumont wasn't the only one who could waste time. "Actually, you'll be staying until the DNA results come back. No matter how long that takes. Now, if you excuse me, I'm going to call the lab and ask them to take their time."

A SLOW COUNT TO ten and a deep breath or two later, Cooper entered interview suite three. Martin stood to offer his seat to the DCI, but she shook her head and told them to continue. She grabbed a spare chair and took a seat in the corner, allowing Martin and Keaton to carry on with their chat. If they'd already built a rapport or got into a good rhythm, there was no point in disrupting it.

"You were saying Jason and Marcus were housed together?" Keaton asked, turning back to Kevin Beaumont.

"Aye. They didn't like it; foster dad was an arsehole. At least they got to see the girls at school. I lost touch with Marcus, so did Jason. Heard he's livin' in the Canaries now."

Mention of the Canaries hit Cooper like a cannonball to the solar plexus. She coughed involuntarily and tried to clear the flavour of bile that stung the back of her throat. It was Kevin, their interviewee, who handed her a plastic cup of water.

"Thanks." She thought of her mother, how the new widow had been home alone all day without even a text from her daughter. Cooper typed out a quick message to see how she was doing and if she needed anything bringing in from the shops on her way home.

"What about Shane? Or Tyrone?" Martin pressed.

He shook his head. "Can't really help you there. Shane was the youngest. There was like twelve years between us. Youngest of James's kids, I mean."

Martin nodded to show he understood.

"I got letters to begin with. But they were just kid stuff. Talking about his favourite trading cards. Funny how they've come back into fashion, isn't it? I was busy with my new job, meeting lasses, actually having some money for the first time. I wasn't interested in cartoons and toys, and I guess

I stopped replying. I regret that now. It shouldn't have mattered what he wrote to me about; I should have written back. Bit shitty of me. As for Tyrone, he was the third-youngest and would've been six or seven when we all left home." He shrugged again. "Sorry, nee idea about him or Shane. To be honest, we don't really talk about the others, me and Jason. We go for a few pints every couple of weeks and keep it light-hearted. Superficial stuff like what's on the telly."

"And if Newcastle are playing four at the back?" Martin asked.

"Aye. Just usual bloke talk."

"Did you or your brothers have Newcastle shirts when you were little?"

"Pfft. You're joking, aren't ya? We could barely afford school uniforms. Think my hand-me-downs made it as far as Tyrone before the school changed from jumpers to sweatshirts. If we were lucky, we'd get a few quid each to go to the church jumble sale and see what new threads we could get. Was never anything special like a football strip."

"No second-hand ones?"

"Not that I remember. Why?"

Martin opened a folder and showed Kevin a picture of a 1988 Newcastle away shirt.

"Does this shirt mean anything to you?"

"It's an old toon shirt. Eighties?"

Martin nodded. "You don't recognise it?"

"I recognise it, yeah, but if you're asking if me or my brothers had one, I'd seriously doubt it. Dad? Yeah, maybe. But... Look, I'm forty-seven. Forty-eight next week. I left home over thirty years ago." He turned his palms to the ceiling. "Sorry, I can't be more help."

IT WAS HALF FIVE when Cooper got home. She'd decided to send Kevin Beaumont home, given his cooperative nature and the fact he had an alibi for the time of the murders. His alibi was his wife, so it wasn't the strongest of alibis, but it was an alibi nonetheless. Jason, meanwhile, was grumbling about the quality of the mattress in his cell.

Cooper dropped her bag by her front door and followed her nose to the kitchen where her mother was stressing over a cod loin that hadn't been properly pin-boned. She plonked a bottle of sauvignon on the counter, the glass bottle chiming against her countertops.

"White, as requested."

Julie examined the label with curious eyes, popped it in the fridge, glanced over to Steven's corner and tutted. "Urgh. He's done it again."

"It's just poop, Mum. It's in a box, on the floor. I promise it won't ruin dinner."

Unappeased, Julie opened the kitchen door and hollered towards the staircase. "Tina! That thing needs cleaning again."

Cooper winced. *That thing* was not the sort of expression that would help Julie bond with her granddaughter.

"It's just a little seagull poop, Mum. You love telling that story about how I defecated all over the new cream carpet when I was a baby. You tell everyone who'll listen about how you and Dad saw the funny side."

"It's different when it's your own little one's, you know that. Bet you thought Tina's poop smelled of roses."

Cooper had thought no such thing. "Steven is Tina's little one. So I don't want to hear any snide remarks about him over dinner. Okay?"

Tina stormed into the kitchen armed with a replacement sheet of newspaper and some anti-bac wipes for the floor around Steven's box. Cooper dropped to her knees to help clean.

"You're home early," said Cooper.

"So are you," was the reply.

Fair enough. Cooper's job didn't always lend itself to the nine-to-five lifestyle, and over the years, Tina had to get used to early starts or late dinners.

"Was netball cancelled?"

"Nope."

"Why did you miss training then?"

Tina didn't answer. She scrunched up the old newspaper and took it straight to the outdoor bin. A wise move, as Julie would have had something to say if it went in the kitchen bin.

"Is this about Lana?" Cooper pressed when Tina returned. "Because you shouldn't let any boy troubles you're having get in the way of your hobbies. Especially one you love as much as netball."

Steven flapped his wings and hovered a foot above the tiles for a good seven seconds.

"Boy troubles?" Tina's face was coated in disgust. She curled her upper lip and wrinkled her nose.

"You think I'd skip training because Lana fancies Josh? Thought you knew me better than that."

It was a mean thing to say, and though Cooper knew Tina's anger wasn't really directed at her, it stung all the same. No matter how hard she tried, she'd never truly understood everything that made Tina, Tina.

"I survived a season with Shelly Smith and her mates. I can survive a season with Lana. I'm wing attack. It's not my job to make friends; it's my job to get the ball to the shooters."

"And give wing defence a cheeky elbow when the refs not looking?"

Tina smiled, the muscles in her forehead and jaw relaxing. "It's only a foul if you get caught."

Steven squawked and hovered once more. He'd be ready for release any day now. His wings were powerful enough to make audible swooshing noises as he beat them through the humid air of the kitchen.

"That's my girl. How about you invite Josh to dinner on Friday? Your Nan hasn't met him yet."

Tina huffed and walked away. Cooper took that as a yes. She settled onto the sofa to enjoy a moment of quiet and decompress after what had been one hell of a long day. She watched whatever was on the television but didn't take in a word of it, barely registering who was even on screen. She could have happily drifted off if it weren't for the doorbell chiming and Julie rushing to invite Atkinson in. Cooper checked her watch. She'd been zoned out for fifteen minutes but felt as if she'd only just sat down. Ignoring the lost time, she pushed to her feet to give her tall, handsome sort-of-boyfriend a hug.

- CHAPTER 38 -

JUSTIN ATKINSON ENJOYED JULIE'S miso cod with broccoli and edamame. With such great ingredients available locally, it was hard to go wrong. And having lived on an island for a decade and a half, Atkinson imagined Julie knew a thing or two about seafood.

There was some drama after Tina barely touched the fish. She ate the rest of the meal, but it wasn't enough for Julie who called her fussy and started a story with *in my day...* Thankfully the rest of the evening passed without incident.

Despite his full belly, a nagging feeling still grumbled in his stomach. Cooper wasn't the same recently. He could sense something was off, like a dog honing in on an unfamiliar scent during its perimeter check. Something wasn't right, and it caused his otherwise highly logical mind to spiral.

If she was sick—

If he lost her—

If Tina lost her—

Unable to talk to Cooper in private before dinner, he waited until Tina had excused herself and Julie had nodded off in front of the television.

"Fancy a walk?" he asked. "We could go down to King Edward's bay?"

Cooper finished loading the dishwasher, topped up the rinse aid and popped a tablet in the drawer. She closed the dishwasher and turned to him. "Sounds good. It looks like a lovely evening out there." She glanced at her phone. "It's still nineteen degrees if you can believe that. "She grabbed her bag, fished out her keys and pushed them into her pocket. "Let's stay up the top though, I don't think I have the energy to handle all those stairs down to the sand." Then she smiled. "Well, I probably have the energy to get down all those stairs. It's the coming back up that's the problem."

Putting his arm around her, Atkinson guided her down the tail end of Front Street, turning left to walk along the seafront. He held her close with her arm tight around his waist, her fingers finding their way under his t-shirt to touch the bare flesh of his hip.

As they rounded East Street, King Edward's bay came into view. Steep cliffs on either side protected the cove from wind, and hungry diners tucked into lobster and langoustine dishes at Riley's Fish Shack. Deck chairs surrounded fire pits and wispy plumes of smoke dissipated into the warm salty air.

"You're quiet," Cooper observed.

"That's because I'm worried about you." Atkinson stopped in his tracks and turned to face Cooper. He rested his arms on her shoulders, his hands cupping the back of her head. Though still completely captivating and beautiful, the spark he was so used to had left her eyes.

"You're sweet," she said, "but you don't need to worry about me. I'm still finding it hard knowing that Dad's gone. The permanence of it. It's weird to think I can't just call him or send a text, that I'm not going to warn him about sharing fake news on Facebook or laugh at his dad-jokes ever again."

She took a deep breath and looked at the sea. Waves rolled in, shades of peacock green that faded to denim blue as they retreated.

"It's awful, but I'm done crying. For now, at least."

"It's not just that," Atkinson said. He paused, fumbling over the words in his mind before speaking them aloud. He wanted to be supportive and thoughtful; he didn't want to come across as nagging, overbearing or worst of all, a worrywart.

"You have more tests coming up soon. Another mammogram and, weren't they going to run a BDX? I know you like to go about things in your own way," he angled his head and gave her a knowing look, "but if you're concerned about them, I just want you to know that I'm here, and it's okay to feel anxious. It's natural."

She pulled away, and he hoped he hadn't done the wrong thing in broaching the subject.

"You're right. I'm a bit preoccupied, but I'm not particularly worried about the results."

"I'm glad. Though I can't help but notice how tired you've been."

They pressed into the railing allowing a couple on an evening bike ride to pass by safely.

"It's just this case," Cooper said once the cyclists had passed. Below them, on the beach, two seagulls fought over some discarded mackerel bones, their squawks carrying up to the cliff tops. "I think these homicides are revenge killings. I don't know what happened to the man we're looking for, but to kill three people in the way he did— To bury them alive..." She shook her head and followed one of the seagulls as it flew over the cliffs towards Tynemouth Priory, soaring through the old ruins before disappearing down the other side. "I just can't get over how depraved people can be. It's like they're another species sometimes. So yeah, I'm not that worried about the tests. I've been through them before. If they're clear, great, and if they're not, then I'll deal with it like I dealt with it last time."

"We'll deal with it," Atkinson corrected her.

"If I'm honest, I'm more concerned about having a panic attack. After what happened..." She swallowed and looked away again.

"That's completely understandable, but I'll be with you. And if you don't think I'm enough muscle, we can bring in reinforcements; Paula comes to mind. Or, you could check out a taser. Fifty thousand volts should keep any nutters away."

Cooper laughed and put her hand in his. "I wish. You know they don't just let us take those things home with us whenever we want? Now come on, let's see if the ice cream place is still open."

———————

THE SKIN AROUND HOWARD Nixon's eyes crinkled as he spoke into a microphone on Thursday morning. Around him, the air flickered with camera flashes, his low voice occasionally drowned out by the clunk-clunk of shutter noises. Cooper watched Nixon out the corner of her eye before turning her gaze back to the journalists, photographers and cameramen gathered before them. The press conference had been arranged to update the media with information regarding the third victim. They'd also appeal once more for witnesses to the events on Holy Island.

The usual faces were there: Vince Shepherd, a rotund man from the Evening Chronicle; Megan Mercado, a glamazon from ITV; and Dennis Moore, who always reminded Cooper of an arthritic greyhound. There were also several faces she didn't recognise. This was a big case, and it had attracted a great deal of media interest. There were bound to be representatives from national newspapers, the broadsheets, tabloids, internet news sites, and broadcasting companies in the room. The red BBC logo was printed on the side of a Panasonic video camera. No doubt footage from today would be replayed and analysed on the six o'clock news.

Blair Potts, a member of the press office, whose large teeth made her appear slightly horse-like, pointed to a raised hand in the third row.

"Abu Hassan, BBC Look North. Why wasn't the Holy Island causeway closed when Mr Pennington's body was discovered?"

Cooper cleared her throat and leant forward to bring her mouth closer to the microphone. "The causeway had been open for five hours before the victim was discovered. We had no reason to believe the person responsible would have remained on the island. Detectives and local police decided to keep the causeway open, allowing residents to go to school and work on the mainland. That being said, random checks were conducted on vehicles leaving Lindisfarne until eleven a.m. when the causeway closed again."

Hassan seemed satisfied with the answer. He nodded politely and returned to his seat.

Cooper and Nixon turned their attention to the next reporter to be acknowledged by Potts: a wheelchair user with a gaunt face and black hair styled in micro braids.

"Eliza Wilson, News Guardian. Are reports of an arrest accurate?"

"I can confirm a man in his forties is helping us with our inquiries. I can't give further details at this time."

Eliza thrust her recording device forwards. "Do you believe this man to be the killer? And how did he select his victims?"

Journos. "As I said, I can't give further details at this time."

Jason Beaumont may be in custody, and he may be an uncooperative, moody little swine. But that didn't mean he was necessarily responsible for a triple murder. Cooper had no intention of naming him in the press until the DNA tests came back and she knew for sure.

Cooper sat up taller and faced the nearest television camera. "I'd like to reiterate the need for witnesses to come forward if they saw a white van in the area of Collingwood Street, Hexham on Monday the first of July. We'd also like to hear from any stores that sold a large quantity of kiln-dried sand in the last week, especially if these sales were to the public rather than trade accounts."

Vince Shepherd stood up when Potts pointed in his direction.

"Final question," Potts told the room.

Shepherd ran a hand over a bushy beard of dark auburn. "Vince Shepard, Evening Chronicle. Do you believe the suspect in the sandcastle killings is responsible for the disappearance of Summer Holt?"

Cooper was about to tell Shepherd they had no reason to believe that when Nixon cut her off. "A press conference regarding Summer is scheduled for Monday."

"Does that mean you don't anticipate finding her before then? Has a ransom demand been made? Do you think she's alive?"

Shepherd threw his questions out one after the other like verbal hand-grenades. Nixon got to his feet and gathered his things. He signalled to Potts that she'd have to deal with any reporters who didn't get the message: this conference was over. Cooper followed his lead, slinging a bag strap over her shoulder before leaving the room under a barrage of camera flashes.

COOPER RETURNED TO THE incident room after a quick loo break and a trip to the canteen for some elevenses. She found Tennessee examining the murder wall, his eyes flicking from one crime scene photo to the next.

"Hey, Jack. How's the little one?"

"His temperature's come back down now," he said, taking a step to the left to peer at a printout of the yellow and green NUFC away shirt. "Between Alfie crying all day, Hayley crying all day and Pat coughing her lungs up all day, I have a serious headache."

"You should take a day for yourself, Jack. I know you don't begrudge looking after your family, but if you need some time away from the office to see to your own mental health, you know you can arrange it."

"You, me, Paula, Oliver, Saffron, Elliot." He counted the team on his fingers. "Since when were any of us good at looking after ourselves?"

Cooper pouted. "Other than Paula, you might have a point. That woman lives in the gym."

Tennessee led Cooper to the desk he was working at and fired up the computer. "It's how she works out her demons. I heard her dad was getting remarried and didn't want his lesbian daughter or gay son to come to the ceremony. She says she's not bothered and doesn't want him in her life, but you know, it's got to sting."

Cooper felt sick. "What a bellend. She's better off without him."

"My thoughts exactly," said Tennessee, using one finger to enter his password. "Anyhoo, as we're having problems locating some of the Beaumonts, I ran their names through the Gazette. You said Natalie and the other Beaumont sisters were adopted, so I thought—"

"That if some of the boys had been, they might have taken their adoptive surnames? Good idea."

The screen turned white as Tennessee opened a document. Robert Phillip Beaumont had dropped his first name and now went by Phillip Hall. Marcus James Beaumont had changed his name to Marcus James Newton."

"Brilliant," Cooper told him. "Update the murder wall, run the names through the PNC and pay a visit to Local Intel. See if the LIO has anything on the Beaumonts."

"On it." Tennessee logged out. "What do you want for lunch? I'm having a cheeky Nando's delivery if you want one?"

In need of some vitamins, she ordered a salad bowl and turned on her own computer. A stream of beeps indicated she had mail; the DNA results were back.

"Well, well, well," Cooper murmured to herself. "A perfect match."

Across the room, Whyte and Boyd looked up from their files.

She read the results twice to be sure, pausing to yawn and rub her itchy eyes. Greg Beaumont from the Morningside area of Edinburgh was in the clear. As was Liam Beaumont of Berwick Park Road.

Another cousin: negative.

Another uncle: negative.

She continued to read, sighing at the news that she'd have to release Jason Beaumont. His DNA confirmed he was not the one who'd left blood spatter all over Ronan Turnbull's Hexham home. She picked up her phone and dialled the custody sergeant to update her and authorise Jason's release. It was a shame. She'd really hoped Jason had been their man.

Hanging up, Cooper stared at the line of red capital letters.

POSITIVE.

Chatty, relaxed, happy-go-lucky Kevin Beaumont.

Not a match for what had been dubbed the sandcastle killings.

A match for the unsolved rape in 2011.

- CHAPTER 39 -

ON THURSDAY AFTERNOON, KEVIN Beaumont was arrested for the 2011 rape of a homeless woman in Middlesbrough. By Thursday evening Cleveland Police were interviewing him at their facilities on Bridge Street West. Cooper felt for his girlfriend and his children. Had she known? Surely not. Still, women had stood by their rapist boyfriends or husbands before, and as strange as it seemed, Cooper had once allowed a dangerous man back into her life and the life of her daughter. She hadn't known what Kenny was doing at the time, but she had been warned. The humiliation of it still haunted Cooper in those dark moments when sleep evaded her and she felt alone.

THE NEXT MORNING, SEVENTY-TWO hours since the discovery of Ronan Turnbull's beaten and broken body, Cooper ate breakfast by herself. Julie was still in bed; Tina had left early to join a before-school study group. She trailed her finger over the rim of an empty teacup, creating a smudge of the beige lipstick she was wearing. The porcelain was smooth and cool, and it felt pleasant against her balmy skin. She pulled her finger away and examined the warm shade pooled in the valleys between bifurcation ridges and whorls. She pressed the pad of her finger onto a sheet of kitchen towel, leaving her fingerprint and briefly feeling like someone on the other side of the thin blue line. The cup of lemongrass tea tasted light and refreshing, like a freshly cut lawn; the perfect start to the day. Until she remembered the speciality tea had been one of many small gifts from Tina's father. She stood, retrieved the rest of the box of pyramid teabags from the cupboard, and hurled them into the kitchen bin.

The drive to HQ passed in a daze. After a night of fitful sleep, Cooper barely registered the blatant road rage occurring in the outside lane. She parked, entered the building, bought a bottle of mineral water from the canteen and made her way to the incident room. She entered her ID and password into a computer and searched the database for further information on the crime.

On the sixteenth of November 2011, Kevin Beaumont beat and raped Nadine Ramsay, a homeless woman, in a poorly lit alley only a stone's throw from Middlesbrough train station. Cooper pulled up a map; the headquarters for Cleveland Police was just around the corner. A commuter found her the morning after and phoned for an ambulance. Her internal injuries kept her in hospital for two nights before she was sent home.

Not that she had one.

Wiping a clammy hand over her forehead, Cooper's heart broke. Nadine Ramsay overdosed a month later. She'd taken a lethal dose of methadone, and now she'd never know that justice would finally be served and her attacker would be held accountable.

"You okay?"

Cooper looked up to see Whyte staring at her from behind a Betty Boop mug.

"You look like you're about to throw up. No offence."

Cooper felt like she might be. Poor woman. "None taken. I'm fine."

She couldn't get over how that bastard, Kevin Beaumont, seemed so happy to hand over his DNA and eliminate himself from the murder investigation. He'd had been cooperative and polite. Had he forgotten what he'd done all those years ago? Did he think because he'd targeted a homeless woman that no one would believe her? That her claims would go unheard or unrecorded? That his violation of her wouldn't matter?

It did matter.

She mattered.

WITHIN TWENTY MINUTES, MOST of the team had arrived for the morning briefing. Frustrated at not having DNA samples from all the Beaumont men yet, they were at least happy to have removed a rapist from society.

Cooper led a round of applause for Elliot Whyte and Saffron Boyd for making the arrest. Whyte looked taken aback at the rare compliment. He took his seat next to Paula Keaton and greeted her with a fist bump. His eagle-like nose was tinged green across the bridge. Apparently, Kevin Beaumont hadn't taken kindly to being arrested in front of his children. According to Boyd, Whyte had slapped handcuffs on him while saying, "If you don't want your kids to see you arrested for rape, don't be a fucking rapist."

Cooper couldn't have put it better herself.

"Right. Are we all here?" Cooper scanned the room doing a mental register of who should be in attendance. She held up a file and allowed a smug grin to form on her lips. Not too smug; it's wasn't like they'd made an arrest in the sandcastle case. "We got the warrant for the care files on the six Beaumont boys. You'll never guess who their social worker was?"

Keaton was the first to speak. "My money's on Eve Lynch."

"Bingo. Whilst the council were predictably unhelpful in telling us her role at STC, we now have the connection. One of the Beaumont's is on a blast from the past killing spree. We've ruled out Jason and Kevin, so we need to turn our attention to Robert, Marcus, Tyrone and Shane. Tennessee?"

288

Tennessee stood up and blew his nose. The whites of his eyes were bloodshot and he sounded bunged up as he spoke. Pointing to the list of names on the murder wall, he addressed the room. "Robert now uses his middle name and his adoptive surname. He is Phillip Hall. And Marcus Beaumont is Marcus Newton. I've found no formal change of name for Shane or Tyrone, but that doesn't mean they're not using nicknames or pseudonyms."

Tennessee returned to his seat and sniffled. Cooper would send him home if his symptoms worsened. She needed him well-rested and didn't want him coughing all over the incident room.

"Given the news about Eve Lynch, I think we can safely move any cousins and uncles to the back of the queue. Martin, I want you to confirm Marcus Newton is in the Canaries and hasn't flown home recently. If that's the case, eliminate him. Speak with the Policía Nacional and have them meet with him to see if he knows anything."

Martin made some notes and agreed.

"We now have two main avenues. First, track down Phillip, Tyrone and Shane. One of them has killed their social worker, their former teacher and someone they used to box with. Phillip will be forty-five now, the same age as the third victim, Ronan Turnbull. Perhaps they were rivals? Tyrone and Shane were younger; they should be thirty-eight and thirty-five, respectively. That makes them too young to be sparring partners or opponents for Ronan."

Tennessee sneezed, then added, "May Ratcliffe, the woman with the café in Corbridge? She told us Ronan would take younger kids under his wing for private tuition. Perhaps..."

"Perhaps he coached Shane or Tyrone," Cooper finished for him. "But why—"

"Why kill him?" Keaton asked no one in particular. "I've met some dodgy coaches in my time. Maybe Lieutenant Colonel Golden Gloves was a bit of a bully?"

"Or a pervert?" said Martin.

"Or both?" Boyd suggested.

Whyte leant forward and propped his elbows on his knees. "If I was abused as a child, I'd want revenge." He rubbed his sore nose. "Then again, if I had been, I wouldn't be who I am now. I might not have the confidence to report it or to track the person down and deal with it myself."

Cooper agreed, and there was a moment of silence while some in the room were taciturn, feeling dour but thankful for the safe and nurturing homes they grew up in. Others thought about the trusted adults who had let them down.

"If he thinks these people wronged him all those years ago, why hold on to it until now?" Tennessee asked.

Keaton unfolded her thick thighs and refolded them with the opposite leg on top. "Something must have made him snap."

"It's the little things that push a person over the edge." Saffron Boyd's mouth was pinched to the side as she looked through Cooper to the murder wall behind her. "There's huge trauma, that's for certain. He felt abandoned by his mother, lost his father, was taken into care, and separated from his brothers and sisters. But as a child, there'd be so much more on top of that. Not having the right clothes to fit in. Not getting the same toys everyone else did at Christmas. Birthdays going unacknowledged. The trophies won and lost, a compliment or a snide remark, the drawings prized and stuck to the fridge and the ones scrunched up and put in the bin."

It was hard to reconcile that the unfortunate little boy Boyd had just described and the monster who buried people alive were the same person. One had become the other, and it was the monster they had to stop before he killed again.

"First avenue – find the men on our shortlist. Second – work out who is at risk." Cooper closed her file. "The mother, Beth Beaumont, is presumably a target. Go through these files and find out everyone who fostered the boys, no matter how short a time period they were in their care. He might have a grudge against them. I want the mother under surveillance. Paula, can you take care of that?"

Keaton tipped her head. "I'll arrange some plain clothes to keep an eye out."

As the team got to their feet they made moaning and groaning noises. Backs were straightened, and knees were massaged. They needed a boost.

"One more thing," Cooper said. "We started with a suspect field of tens of thousands: a white male with a football shirt. We've narrowed the field to three, which means we're doing brilliant-ly. *You're* doing brilliantly. Now let's finish this."

- CHAPTER 40 -

TRUE TO HER WORD, Keaton had sent a car to keep an eye on Beth Beaumont. Northcutt had already updated her to say the sixty-four-year-old had a gentleman caller. When Keaton expressed concern, they assured her that Beth seemed to be on intimate terms with him. There was no way it was one of her many sons; at least they sincerely hoped he wasn't.

Cooper thanked Keaton for the update and was now looking for Martin or Tennessee in the hope they could give her some good news. Last she heard, Shane Beaumont had disappeared and Tyrone Douglas Beaumont was a ghost. There'd been no record of him since 1999. But just because the computer hadn't spilled any new beans on their suspects didn't mean they were at a dead end. The fact they were elusive meant the team were on to something. One of them was likely the murderer; the other two might have gone to ground because, like their brother Kevin, they had something else to hide. Why come forward to rule yourself out of a murder if it got you banged up regardless? If they'd heard about Kevin and were in a similar situation, they wouldn't repeat his error and would be keeping their heads down.

Right on cue, Tennessee entered holding a file and a can of RedBull. "I've managed to speak to eight separate people who fostered Shane Beaumont over the years."

"Christ, they really were bounced around, weren't they?"

"Just a bit." Tennessee sat and opened the can of energy drink. The fizzing noise filled the otherwise quiet room. "I told them all that someone they fostered in the nineties was wanted in connection with a violent crime. I didn't give specifics, but once their names hit the press, they'll put two and two together."

"You told them to be vigilant?"

"Lock the doors and all that jazz. Told them to dial 999 if they're contacted by anyone they used to foster. Same advice if anyone tries to gain access to their home or if they suspect they're being followed. Gave them my mobile too."

He popped two ibuprofen and took a swig from the can.

"Make a start on Phillip and Tyrone's foster parents. Make sure to ask if they've seen anyone they fostered a long time ago or even just thought they recognised someone. Maybe we get lucky and they've spotted one of the brothers."

"If we have a sighting, I'll get a car out to them straight away, and I won't be far behind ready to interview them."

Cooper slipped her boots off for a moment to rub her feet. She had to update Nixon before the end of the day and couldn't face that with aching feet and a caffeine deficiency.

⸻

ON HER WAY TO Nixon's office late in the afternoon, Cooper spied DI Neil Fuller bent over a drinking fountain. Once upon a time she thought he was rather fetching; now she couldn't help but see all his rodent-like features. He straightened up and wiped his furry mouth on the back of his little rat hands. It didn't help that his fingernails were currently a touch on the long side, and he smelled like something the cat would drag in. Somewhere between a garbage dump and rotten fish. A hint of feral dog too. She couldn't blame him. He was working a case almost as challenging and upsetting as she was. Had he slept at all this week?

A missing five-year-old made every parent with a shred of empathy pray for her safe return. They'd also thank the heavens it was someone else's child and not their own. Cooper understood that sentiment; she'd come close to losing her own daughter once. As much as she wanted Summer Holt to be found unharmed, she was grateful it wasn't Tina.

"Neil. How are you holding up?"

He couldn't speak. He pressed his back to the wall, his mouth opening and his hands moving as if he wanted to spill every stress, frustration and dark thought, only he couldn't. Then the tears came.

The first responders to a child abduction were often haunted by the experience for years after the fact. There would be no happy ending, regardless of the outcome. If Summer turned up dead, Fuller would consider it a professional failure. He would question every move he made until his dying day, turning to either counselling or a vodka bottle. If Summer was found, she, her parents and Fuller would have to go on knowing what her abductor had done to her. They'd smile and be thankful; they'd say the right things to the press and treasure each day their family was together.

But they'd always know.

Little girls weren't kidnapped because their captors wanted to take them to tea parties and petting zoos. They were taken because—

Cooper swallowed. Her case was awful, but she was dealing with adults. It was always different when children were involved. Still, there was a third outcome, possibly the worst one: Summer could never be found at all. Every year new appeals and aged photographs guessing how Summer would look at age six, eight, ten, fifteen. Each press release showing the withering faces of two parents who lost their reason for being. A couple who couldn't let go, or move on, forever stuck in perpetual purgatory.

Yes, it was always different when children were involved.

Fuller's tears slowed. "I don't know what to do."

She moved to take his hand, but he pulled it from her reach.

"How do I tell them not to worry, that it'll be fine?"

"You don't," Cooper said. "You can't make that promise. You can only promise to do your best, that every force in the goddamned country will do their best."

He bent over the fountain again, this time splashing the cool water over his reddening face.

"Are you eating?" she asked.

He raised an eyebrow and scanned Cooper's skinny frame. "Are you?"

A fair point, but Cooper was eating again following her father's passing. It wasn't just herself who required her to be fuelled and nourished; her family, her colleagues, the public, they all needed her to take care of herself.

She moved to the other side of the corridor and placed a flimsy cup in the coffee dispenser. It wasn't as good as the coffee in the canteen, and it wasn't a patch on the nearest Starbucks, but it did the job. Shiny, black and bitter, it was the shared activity of all the people who drank it, from Africa to Europe to the Americas. A beverage that connected the tired and anxious the world over.

"Here," she said, handing Fuller the cup before taking another one to fill for herself. "Take half an hour. Drink that and get some fruit."

He shrugged his shoulders just as his phone began to chirp. "Fuller. Yeah. I'm on my way." He ended the call and wiped his eyes, readying himself. "A possible sighting."

"Sounds positive."

"We've had a million possible sightings, Erica. Each one a false alarm."

Hopes raised. Hopes destroyed.

He walked away, leaving drips of coffee like a trail of brown bread crumbs. Cooper took a moment before following the trail. Hansel and Gretel escaped the witch and made it back home. Perhaps Summer Holt could do the same.

As she knocked on Nixon's door, Cooper vowed to mention Fuller to him. The man needed help. She couldn't take his caseload, but something needed to budge. He was shouldering a missing child and returning each night to an empty home. If Nixon didn't do something, she feared Fuller would be found at the end of a rope.

- CHAPTER 41 -

THE FEAST BEGAN AT seven p.m. on the dot. Cooper arranged for a delivery of tapas from Allard's restaurant. Flatbreads, black pudding bonbons, belly pork and spiced meatballs covered every square inch of the dining table. The five diners – six if you counted the seagull – tucked in with gusto.

"Blooming heck." Julie removed her cardigan, took a sip of wine and soda and began to fan herself with a napkin. Evidently, the spiced meatballs were a touch too *picante* for her tastes. Cooper thought they were relatively mild.

When the last of the bonbons disappeared and the drinks had been topped up, the group – sans seagull – moved to the living room. Tina and Josh sat side by side on the sofa, fingers interlaced but posture stiff. Julie took the other end of the couch, leaving Cooper and Atkinson in armchairs at opposite ends of the room. He felt far away, yet the house felt busy and cluttered. Five pairs of shoes by the door, five mobile phones strewn on various side tables, five drinks on coasters, five sets of body heat adding to the July warmth.

Five minds, each preoccupied.

"Has everyone had enough to eat?" Cooper asked, breaking the silence.

"Yes, Ms Cooper. It was delicious." Josh rummaged in his jeans pocket and produced a crumpled twenty-pound note. "Dad said I have to contribute."

"Don't be silly. Use it to go to the cinema or something."

"No, Dad said I had to—"

"And if Reg asks, I'll tell him you did. You two should go and do something fun. You've studied so hard recently."

Tina and Josh shared a smile, but it was a half-arsed one. Despite what Tina had told her and their best efforts at acting like nothing was up, Cooper saw straight through them. They'd been arguing about something again.

"Actually," Tina said. "I thought we could all do something together on Sunday."

"Oh?"

"Steven." As Tina said his name, five heads collectively angled their ears towards the kitchen door. A *swoosh swoosh* noise told them he was flapping his wings again. Feathered semaphore flags spelling out that he wasn't a baby anymore. "It's time."

"Really? Our feathered baby is ready to fly the nest?"

"I think so," Tina began, her face flushing with pride before she was cut off by her grandmother.

"It's about time."

Both Tina and Cooper flashed death stares at her.

"Oh please, he's been making a mess all over my kitchen."

"It's Mum's kitchen," snapped Tina, her voice high-pitched and abrasive. "And he's been here longer than you have."

It looked like Tina's fingernails were digging into Josh's knuckles. Wisely, he kept quiet while Tina set her face in a formidable expression, lips thin and eyes burning.

"Are you going to let your daughter speak to me like that?"

Cooper pinched her nose and looked at Atkinson. Silently, she tried to convey an apology. He sent a warm smile back in her direction and mouthed, "Families."

"It is my kitchen, Steven has been here longer than you have, and I did warn you about insulting him."

Julie looked horrified. "I should have turned him into a feather duster. You know in Lanzarote they're considered vermin?"

"You're not in Lanzarote!" Tina stood, not letting go of Josh's hand, forcing him to stand as well. She closed her eyes and took a deep breath, keeping her temper at bay. "Josh and I will be releasing Steven on Low Lights beach on Sunday afternoon. We'll say goodbye, then get takeaway from The Waterfront. Justin, you are very welcome to join us."

"I wouldn't miss it," Atkinson said.

"Grandma, you are not invited." Tina stomped from the room, dragging Josh with her.

THE CASINO SMELLED OF new money and cheap perfume. The sound of slot machines spewing pound coins like heavy rain on a tin roof. He sat in front of one, his eyes squinting against the glare of the lights and a blinding neon sign that blinked between yellow and green. He inserted a coin and pressed the button. Wheels span, numbers blurred, bells chimed.

His mind was filled with images of his attack on Ronan Turnbull. The deception felt cunning, rolling up to his front door like that. The fight itself was thrilling. Years of pent up resentment and fears fuelled every punch into his face. As for finishing him off in front of somewhere so sacred—The God-botherers must have had a meltdown. But that feeling of intense excitement hadn't lasted long, and he felt no freer now than when he formulated his plan a few weeks ago.

Killing Ronan hadn't killed the nightmares.

The wheels slowed, settling on a red seven, a bell, and a watermelon. He'd lost. Not that it mattered.

His heart thudded as a thin woman with protruding collar bones sauntered past. The red dress hung from angular shoulders, the fabric clinging to the curves of her fake tits and her lower back. Her skin was tanned, and a stripe of silver at her hairline betrayed her age. He wasn't attracted to her. In fact, she enraged him.

She looked just like Beth: sixties, skinny, colouring her hair and skin, spending more time on her nails than her children.

Spending more money on drugs than on food for the bairns.

He ground his teeth until a dull ache pulsated in his temples.

She wasn't Beth.

But she could be.

She could be a warm-up, a dress rehearsal.

Behind him, a fight broke out at the entrance. Security had refused entry to a group of men dressed as Borat. They were young, out of shape, and their green mankinis were not appropriate clothing for fighting. After the third penis had fallen out, they made a hasty retreat, tucking their privates back behind the vivid fabric of their costumes. The door supervisors laughed, then moved aside for two stylish couples on a double date.

When he turned, he'd lost his Beth substitute. He stood, craning his neck over the casino's clientele. There she was, her red dress weaving between the green poker tables.

Red and green should never be seen.

He tore his eyes from her and made his way to a space at the roulette table. Three down, three to go. Red, he'd take Kerys; black, he'd go after Beth. This was no game of Russian roulette; there wasn't a one in six chance of death. This was his game. He called it Northern Roulette, and someone would definitely die.

- CHAPTER 42 -

COOPER'S EYES WERE BARELY able to open, and the weight of her quilt felt like a warm cocoon. It was Sunday morning, and the faintest rose blush glowed through her bedroom curtains, telling her it wasn't quite dawn. She checked her watch. It was four twenty-six in the morning.

"Someone better had died," she grumbled into her phone.

"Ma'am, there's a sandcastle shaped like a snake on Sandhaven beach."

Cooper didn't recognise the voice and didn't want to shoot the messenger. She flexed her jaw, peeling her tongue from the roof of her mouth. She was dehydrated.

"Right. On my way."

"Local police have been dispatched from South Shields. They want to know if they should preserve the scene or—"

"He buries them alive. Screw preserving the scene. Tell them to dig the victim out and if they're still warm, begin CPR."

"Ma'am."

A beep signalled that the call had ended. Cooper looked to the other side of the bed where Atkinson slept soundly on his front.

She watched his back rise and fall with peaceful breathes before nudging him. "Wake up. You're going to get a call any second now."

He blinked at her with a confused expression, his eyes looking smaller without his glasses. "Are you the oracle?"

He sat and stretched while Cooper began to dress. She had half her clothes on when Atkinson's phone began to vibrate.

COOPER PARKED NEAR THE Sand Dancer pub and trotted through the car park to access the beach. The water was calm: no breaking waves, no wind, no mist, no sea frets. The shallows shone like a mirror, reflecting the purples and burnt oranges in the sky above. The sand near the water's edge was formed into parallel ripples, like miniature mountains and valleys. Cooper saw the birds first. Fifty or so sandpipers wading along the shoreline looking for insects or small crabs. Their stick legs and long, thin beaks perfectly suited to the task. Tynemouth Priory loomed on the other side of the mouth of the river. The aureate glow of the morning shone through holes in the old ruins. For a moment, it looked as if someone had left the lights on.

When Cooper's feet hit the soft sand, she was glad she chose boots over heels. She powerwalked towards the scene. An inner and outer perimeter had already been set up, and several men and women from South Shields Police stood in pairs, their heads bowed in conversation.

As she approached the crime scene manager, she wondered what, or rather who, she would find. Who had been targeted this time? She knew Beth Beaumont was under surveillance, and they'd warned as many of the Beaumont children's foster carers as they could to be vigilant. Another few steps and she saw the mound of sand more clearly. She could see deep gouge marks where the first responders had carved their way through the sand to get to the victim.

"Cooper," she said, introducing herself in breathless tones, her legs sapped of energy from the loose sand.

The crime scene manager checked her ID and waved her through. Cooper braced herself but stopped when she saw an officer removing the perimeter tape.

"What's going on?" she asked the crime scene manager.

"False alarm." He pointed to a squat woman. She had rosy cheeks and a black bob with two thick streaks of grey at the front. "Sergeant Chakrabarti can tell you more, ma'am."

She rubbed the back of her neck and approached the woman, who stood with perfect posture and an air of confidence despite her short stature.

"Sergeant Chakrabarti? I'm DCI Erica Cooper. Please call me Cooper. I've already heard too many ma'ams for this time of the morning."

Chakrabarti nodded but didn't smile. "Certainly. As long as you call me Sita."

"What's this about a false alarm, Sita?"

Sita rolled her big eyes. "No body." She scrolled through her phone and brought up an image of the sandcastle. "As you can see, it was a large mound of sand, shaped like a coiled serpent. But when our team began to dig, we quickly realised there was no one in there."

"It's similar," Cooper said, looking at the image and at then at the mound of sand behind Sita. "But it's not quite right. The markings aren't the same, and the tail is definitely different to what we've seen previously."

"Time wasters?" asked Sita.

"Little shits is what I'd call them."

Sita's mouth finally formed a smile. "The guys are upset at being called out at this hour on a Sunday."

"They're not alone." Cooper stifled a yawn. "You'll follow this up? See if you can track down the jokers?"

Sita nodded slowly. "Oh yes. And when I find them, I will let them think we believe they're responsible for the triple murder."

A woman after her own heart. "Give them hell," Cooper said before turning and making her way back to her car. She could be home before the clock struck six. She sent a text to Atkinson, letting him know that firstly, he didn't need to bother bringing his team out, and secondly, she was going back to bed.

SEVEN HOURS LATER, COOPER was at a different beach, under very different circumstances. She parked in Low Lights car park, near an ice cream van receiving a parking ticket from a ruthless traffic warden.

"Bit harsh," said Josh from the back seat. "Kids are watching. That's like giving Santa's sleigh a parking ticket."

Tina carefully exited the vehicle. She cradled a large cardboard box against her chest, supporting its weight in both arms.

Low Lights was a small beach inside the mouth of the river. At the water's edge there was a thin strip of sand popular with babies and small dogs. Behind it lay a short but steep embankment of rocks, and behind that, a promenade connecting North Shields fish quay with Tynemouth village. They followed the promenade to the end of the beach where they could reach the sand without clambering down the rocks. Nearby, two young boys were making shell-shaped sandcastles out of plastic moulds. Such an innocent activity, and yet it made Cooper feel on edge and a little queasy.

"Do you want to say a few words?" Cooper asked.

Tina pulled a face. "He doesn't speak English. That would be weird."

"You raised a baby seagull in our kitchen," Cooper reminded her. "That was weird."

"Weird, but brilliant." Atkinson laid a plaid picnic blanket down for them to sit on. "We're going to see the power of nature in action. Steven's never been around other gulls, but he's going to know that he is one of them."

"Do you think he'll be able to catch his own food?" Tina asked him, her face showing concern.

"Oh, undoubtedly. His instincts will kick in straight away. We had a house cat when my boys were young. It had never left the house and had every meal served to it in its red plastic bowl, and yet when a mouse got in one day, the cat pounced on it without hesitation. It just knew deep down that his job was to catch it and kill it. Steven will be the same."

Tina considered his words for a moment, then said, "You're right. Okay, let's do this. Good luck, Steven."

She opened the box lid and carefully lifted the feathered one out. Josh snapped photos on his phone as she placed him on the sand. Instantly, Steven's great wings began to flap, and he took off towards the old wooden staithes that projected into the mouth of the river like a neglected garden fence.

"Look at him go," Josh gasped.

"See, I told you he'd know his kind." Atkinson patted Tina on the back as Steven landed on one of the thick wooden posts jutting out of the water.

A fluttering in the water beyond the staithes caused the gulls to scream in surround sound. Their voices high and frantic as a whole flock of them dove towards the deep indigo waves. One emerged with a small fish in its yellow and red beak. The others circled him, dipping and diving, vying for the right to steal the prize. The squabble was violent, filled with bites, pulled feathers and pained squawks. It would be disturbing to someone not accustomed to Tyneside gulls.

"Any idea which one Steven is? I've lost him," Atkinson said.

"Me too," said Josh.

Tina's arm stretched beyond the staithes to a patch of green grass. "He's over there. While that lot were squabbling over that tiny fish, he's managed to knick that man's battered haddock."

They laughed as they watched an apoplectic man chase after an ecstatic herring gull.

"Speaking of battered fish." Atkinson wiggled his long legs before standing. "I'll go and join the queue at The Waterfront. Three lots of haddock and chips, and a chip butty for Tina?"

With Atkinson gone to collect their lunch, Cooper looked at her daughter with pride. "You did a good thing, T. Without you, there's no way Steven would have survived."

Tina didn't look up. She was fiddling with a loose thread on the blanket; that didn't mean she wasn't listening.

"I'm serious, Tina. You really cared for him. He relied on you for everything, and now he's back in the wild. You'll make a great mother one day."

Tina's body stiffened and she looked at Cooper with horror. "Urgh, Mum!"

- CHAPTER 43 -

SIX BEACHES, SIX SANDCASTLES, zero victims.

Either the killer was playing with them, or he'd inspired others to play with them.

"Sad little twats," Keaton grumbled as she returned to HQ on Monday afternoon. She stomped her boots on the heavy-duty doormat and left a dusting of sand behind. "They'll wish they were the ones buried alive if I get my hands on the time-wasting terrors."

Terrors. The word gave Cooper an idea. "Nip to the press room and have them release a statement, Paula. Don't use the word terrorism as such. But say something like *instilling terror in the civilian population* or *terrorising local residents*. That sort of thing."

Keaton laughed. "Love it. The journos will take the leap from terrorising to terrorism to get clickbait. Then the limp-dicked morons who are pulling this bollocks will see what deep shit they could actually be in?"

"Exactly. Should be enough of a scare to get them to pack it in."

Keaton left in one direction, and Cooper followed a different corridor toward the incident room. She was no sooner through the door, powering up a computer and making herself comfortable when Nixon's anaemic and wrinkled face appeared at the door.

"Cooper. A word. My office."

"Sir."

Reluctantly, she got to her feet and trailed behind the superintendent with filial submission, like a child knowing they were about to be scolded for not doing their homework.

"Good luck," mouthed Tennessee as she passed him.

She entered Nixon's office and was about to shut the door when he told her to leave it open. Great. He wanted the whole department to hear him give her a bollocking.

"You've been chasing ghosts all weekend, Cooper."

"Yes, sir. Hoaxes. But we need to—"

"I don't want to hear another word about false alarms."

"Yes, sir. Neither do I, which is why DS Keaton is going to scare the life out of the culprits with a press release. The lifeguard stations up and down the coast have agreed to extend their hours to try and catch them in the act. And, we have someone in tech scouring social media. I don't think anyone

313

would go to this much trouble and not brag about it to their mates."

He frowned. His beady eyes instilling a terror of their own. "I don't want any more resources going on these copycat cases."

"We have to check every single one of them, sir. Hoax or not. Would you rather someone suffocated when we could have got to them in time? We'd be crucified."

Nixon didn't look like he was breathing. He was holding his breath until ready to explode. He picked up a fountain pen between his fore and middle finger, wiggling it in a see-saw motion. The nib smacked into an open notepad sending tiny splatters of ink in all directions. It reminded Cooper of blood spatter, only blue.

"Perhaps we need someone with more experience?" he finally said through gritted teeth. "Someone to oversee things."

Cooper seethed at her superior. She could taste acid, and whilst she would be grateful for any help offered, she was not going to let someone step on her or Tennessee's toes when they'd come so far in such a short space of time.

"I've barely been back a week. And in that short time, we've already taken this case from having seemingly no connection between the victims to narrowing our suspects to a single family. And with all due respect—"

The pitch in Cooper's voice betrayed the fact she wasn't feeling respectful at all.

"There is no one with more experience. There might be older detectives, there might be longer serving detectives, but not one of them has the experience I have."

Nixon's eyes flicked to the open door. He clearly hadn't expected to be answered back in such a fashion, but Cooper couldn't help herself. Something inside her was making her fight her corner.

"The Tarot Card Killer, the Blackburns, the Hansons," she said, counting them on her fingers as she listed the criminals now removed from the streets of Tyneside, Wearside and Northumberland. "Extortionists, kidnappers, people smugglers, arsonists, drug dealers—"

"You've made your point, Cooper." Nixon examined his hand; it was covered in blue ink. "You may go."

But Cooper wasn't done. Whatever was driving her mood, she couldn't subdue it. She had to get one last point across. She moved to the doorway, seeing at least four or five officers in the corridor who had been eavesdropping on their conversation. She turned back to Nixon and added to her list. "Rapists, thieves, murderers, and bent coppers. Let's not forget the bent coppers."

DESPITE ALL HER BRAVADO forty-eight hours ago, Cooper was banging her head against a brick wall by Wednesday. They were stuck. They had gone over everything they had so far with a fine-toothed comb and come up empty-handed. Whyte lost his mind checking and double-checking footage submitted to the website they'd set up; Martin could recite the social work files for the Beaumont children by heart; Keaton had driven up to Lindisfarne accessing CCTV cameras on both sides of the causeway; and Tennessee returned to Hexham, where he went over the statements from the only two people to have spotted the white van used to transport Ronan Turnbull to the abbey.

Word had got out about what Cooper said to Nixon, and she'd received nods of support and pats on the back all of yesterday. Now she felt like a fraud. Martin hadn't even been able to rule out Marcus Newton, the second youngest of the Beaumont children. The Policía National reported that Newton's home was empty and his neighbours hadn't seen him in a few weeks. They were waiting to see if his name was on any flight manifests for aircraft entering the UK.

With everyone busy twiddling their thumbs, Cooper excused herself to nip to a branch of Marks and Spencer at Silverlink retail park. She bought a basket of fresh vegetables, including carrots, asparagus and purple broccoli. In the next aisle, she grabbed a tub of mini Swiss rolls and rocky road bites. She hoped she could have a bit of a girls' night with her mother and daughter; there was a new Netflix series everyone in the station seemed to be gossiping about and if she didn't binge-watch it soon, she'd hear all the spoilers. A few items from the feminine healthcare aisle went in the basket, as did a bottle of multivitamins and some new bath oil. Cooper avoided the chilled and frozen sections knowing her shopping would have to sit in HQ until she could leave for the night. Still, she grabbed some dried fruit and nuts from beside the checkout to graze on during the short drive back to the station.

With shopping in hand, Cooper nipped to the loos as soon as she entered HQ. She sat, did her business and waited for a few minutes thinking about the months and years ahead. Questions whirred in her brain about how long her mother would want to live with them, whether Tina would be moving out in two years, and if she and Atkinson were in it for the long haul. Would they get to a point where they would live together full time? Would they ever be ready for that? And then there was work. Whilst she loved her job and got a thrill from seeing a case through to prosecution, she also knew that there were few promotion possibilities. She was already DCI, and though she was grateful to have come this far, especially at this age, any new chapters in her life were likely to come from her personal life rather than from her professional one.

She stood and zipped up her trousers before exiting the cubital to wash her hands. She was surprised to see tears in her eyes when she looked in the mirror. All these thoughts and questions, all these worries, hadn't come from nowhere. Still, she was surprised to see them written so clearly on her face.

Another toilet flushed and Saffron Boyd emerged from the cubicle.

"Ma'am," she said, washing her own hands. "Are you... Are you okay?"

317

Cooper sniffed and splashed some cold water on her face. "I'm fine, Saffron. Ignore me."

She took a paper towel from the dispenser and dried her face.

"Is it your father?" Boyd asked. "You must miss him."

Cooper nodded, though in truth, none of the messy thoughts she'd had concerned Ben. "Yes, I do miss him." But with a quick change of subject, Cooper was back in work mode. "Have we located Phillip Hall?"

TENNESSEE SCRATCHED HIS EAR as he stared at the murder wall. He was over the worst of his cold. His nose had stopped running and he no longer felt like his brain was pulling away from the inside of his skull every time he bent over. He still looked like death warmed up and had a tickly cough to contend with, but he was grateful to be the least ill member of the Daniel household. Alfie had a doctor's appointment later in the day – which Pat would take him to – and Hayley's friend had promised to pop in and cheer her up with some office gossip. Tennessee knew that in the darkest depths of his wife's PND, no amount of office gossip, good humour or kind deeds would help. Still, her heart was in the right place, and he knew his wife would appreciate some adult company from outside the family.

He looked on the bright side; she was improving. The good days outweighed the bad now, and though the bad days made him feel like a rug had been pulled out from under him, he was confident they'd get through it.

The murder wall was mocking him. The faces of those killed told him to hurry up, that he'd never make DI if he couldn't find their killer. The scrawled names of their suspects danced before his eyes, teasing him: Shane, Marcus, Tyrone and Robert, aka Phillip. He sighed, feeling he should know more. He was missing something. Shane and Tyrone were ghosts, as if no record of them existed beyond their young adult lives. Marcus may or may not be living on an island off the Moroccan coast, and Phillip's home in Seghill looked to be recently abandoned. A team had been sent to speak to him over the weekend, but they found the house secure and his car gone.

Tennessee pursed his lips as he thought.

"Your face will stay like that if the wind changes," Boyd said with a slight smirk. She held a printout from the computer in her hand.

"What's that?" Tennessee asked.

Boyd handed him the sheet of paper. "The answer to our prayers," she said. "Potentially, at least. ANPR clocked Phillip Hall's car entering the Tyne Tunnel northbound."

- CHAPTER 44 -

PHILLIP HALL WAS NOT a happy bunny. "Is someone going to tell me what the hell this is about?" he bellowed. "Murder? You've got to be shitting me?"

The man was a mess; dirty, bedraggled, and stinking of BO. There was mud under his fingernails, and the ends of his trousers were soaked through. His shoes were so grubby they had requested he remove them and leave them at the front doors. Having saved the interview room from having mud dragged all over it, they had unfortunately added the stench of sweaty feet to the smell of unwashed armpits.

Tennessee folded his arms and looked at the man. Thanks to a warrant, he knew him to be a Newcastle United season ticket holder. "We've been looking for you," he said.

"So everyone keeps saying. And as I keep telling them, I've been effin' camping."

"Camping or hiding?" Cooper asked. She sat beside Tennessee but didn't seem as calm and collected as usual. In fact, she'd suggested Tennessee take the lead. He was happy to do so, but he was suspicious of her motive and couldn't help but notice she was fidgeting.

Cooper wasn't the only one who couldn't sit still. Hall was a burly man, and despite his constant swearing, he looked troubled as he sat across the table from them. He rubbed his face with his hands, trying to rid himself of dirt. It didn't work. Every now and then he'd stop and scratch furiously at his scalp, like a dog attacking an itch behind its ear.

Hall raised his hands, exposing his grimy palms. "Camping," he repeated. He picked at something wedged beneath one of his nails. It was a tiny sliver of wood. "Sometimes I like to get away from things."

"You haven't just been camping," Tennessee said. "You've been completely off-grid. Your mobile phone has been switched off, you left no instructions with your neighbours to water your plants or keep an eye on your property, and until an hour ago, you kept your car off every main road in the northeast."

"That's not a crime," Phillip told them. His brow furrowed into deep crevices and he pointed a muddy, chewed fingernail in Tennessee's direction. "I've been in the North York Moors. There's no point having my phone on if I'm never going to get a signal anyway. My neighbours would probably rob me blind if I told the thieving bastards I

321

was gannin' out of town for a few days. And as for the roads, I've never liked driving on motorways or dual carriageways. Not since I broke six bones in a pile-up."

Tennessee leant towards him, both hands on the table. He watched as Hall recoiled and then shuffled backwards in his chair.

"Look, I wasn't hiding, all right?" He scratched his head again. "I just wanted to go somewhere for a few days and be by myself. You know, look at fields and trees, not buildings. Drink out of a river instead of a can of crap lager. You know, be somewhere where the little things that piss ya off about modern living don't get to ya. No phones, no emails, no bloody annoying junk mail through the door. And if that makes me a damn criminal, well...."

Tennessee considered the man. He was agitated, but he was also pissed off. "If you don't like motorways and dual carriageways, why were you driving through the Tyne Tunnel?"

"Because if I wanted to get north of the water again, it was that or the Tyne Bridge. The toon is a fuckin' nightmare with bus lanes and one-way streets, so I chose the tunnel."

The Tyne Tunnel was notoriously overpriced. No one Tennessee knew would choose the tunnel over the bridge unless they were in a hurry or it saved them a significant amount of time. He paused, quite comfortable in the silence, and took a sip of warm water with honey and lemon. *Unless they were in a hurry, it saved them time, or they were in the area anyway,* he thought.

The cup warmed his hands. He held it for a moment longer before stating, "You were in the vicinity of your mother's house."

Hall narrowed his eyes, confused. "You what?"

"The entrance to the Tyne Tunnel isn't too far from your mum, Beth Beaumont's, house."

His face reddened. Even through the muck, the colouring in his cheeks was clear to see. "Listen, just because she pushed me out her lady parts don't make that bitch my mother. The television did a better job of raising us kids than she ever did. And how was I supposed to know she was still living 'roond there? Haven't spoken to that cow since the day they made us pack our bags and leave to go to some stranger's house."

Hall certainly hated his mother. The vein pulsing in the side of his temple was a testament to that.

"Okay, here's the deal. You, or a close relative, murdered three people." He opened a brown folder. "If you're guilty, the cheek swab we took earlier will confirm it, so there's really no point in lying to us. Is there anything you'd like to tell us, Phillip?"

Hall was statue-still for a moment. "First it's murder, now it's three murders? Bloody hell. I told you, I've been—" He swallowed and rubbed a big hand over his jaw. "Wait. Is it Beth? Has Mam been killed? Is that why you're gannin' on about her house?"

Tennessee slid three photographs over the table. Images from the morgue of Eve Lynch, Charles Pennington and Ronan Turnbull. The pictures were deeply unpleasant to look at.

Hall grimaced and looked away. With his eyes still averted, he placed a shaking finger on the photo to his left. "I recognise her. She was my social worker."

"Did you kill her?"

"God, no."

"Did you like her?"

Hall squirmed, moving his weight over to one butt cheek. "I guess. She was younger than most socials we dealt with. Somehow that made her seem nicer. She was kind but a bit useless really."

"I need you to look at the other two photographs again, Phillip."

Hall pulled his eyes back to the desk as if it were a monumental effort. He looked back and forth at the two faces and shook his head. "No. I don't know them."

"That's a lie," Tennessee said. "This is Charles Pennington. He taught you at King George's Primary from eighty-three to eighty-four."

The man shrugged. "I guess he looks vaguely familiar. Pennington was all right as far as teachers went. Bit of a fuddy-duddy. I'd have no reason to kill him, though."

Cooper lifted her head. "So, you did it just for fun?"

"No. That's not what I said. You're putting words in my mouth." He turned to Tennessee. "She's putting words in my mouth."

The two detectives gave each other a wry smile as Hall agonised.

"How long is this DNA test going to take anyway? I want to get out of here."

"Depends," said Tennessee.
"Depends on what?"
"How nice we are to the lab technicians."

TENNESSEE WAS DOING A good job as far as Cooper was concerned, but the room felt stifling. She wanted to push the pace and get either a confession or some good intel out of Hall before she passed out. The air felt thick in the interview suite; she tugged at the open collar of her shirt and told herself it was just Hall's body odour.

"Okay, Phillip," she said, pulling her chair in so her knee brushed against that of her interviewee. She felt him flinch away. "If you want to get out of here before the lab results come back, you need to give me something solid. Where were you on the evening of Friday the twenty-first and the morning of Saturday the twenty-second of June?"

"I was camping," he said through gritted teeth. "In the North York Moors."

Cooper didn't appreciate his tone but she persisted nonetheless. She tapped the image of Charles Pennington. "And the twenty-fifth and twenty-sixth of June?"

"North. York. Moors."

"This is Ronan Turnbull," Cooper said. She tugged at her collar again. The room was hot and stuffy, and the inside of her shirt was coated in a thin film of perspiration. Hopefully she wasn't giving off a smell like Hall's. "He was a boxer. Trained at a gym not far from where you grew up. He's the same age as you."

"So?"

"Did you train with him?"

"I didn't box."

"Are you sure?"

"Think I'd remember getting punched by this bloke." He glanced at the photograph. "He looks as if Tyson Fury had a baby with Brad Pitt, then the baby was thrown down a flight of stairs."

Cooper straightened, wanting to slap him. His disrespect for the dead and the way he could make such a flippant remark about throwing an infant down some stairs irked her.

"He wasn't your rival? Didn't beat you to a regional final?"

"No."

"And where were you on the first and second of J—"

"I'll give you a clue. It starts with N and ends in 'orth York Moors."

Cooper slapped the table with both palms. The resulting sound made both Hall and Tennessee jump.

"I don't want to be here any more than you do, Phillip. So if you don't want to sit in the cells all day waiting for your results to rule you out, you're going to need to be more specific. Did you stop for petrol, or buy food when you were there? Nip into any local pubs?"

He rubbed his head; a flake of dandruff floated down to his moss-coloured jacket. "No."

"Did you use a credit card for anything? Or go anywhere where you'd likely be picked up on CCTV?"

"No. Fuck." He looked to the ceiling. "I passed some other hikers, but no, I didn't stop and talk to anyone. I slept in my tent and kept off the beaten path. This is what I get for liking nature?"

TENNESSEE GOT TO HIS feet and paced the room, his footsteps matching the tick-tock of a plastic clock hanging from the wall. He was aware of Phillip Hall tracking his every movement.

"I'm covered in muck." Hall held up his hands, rotating them forwards and backwards to display the coating of soil and grime on either side of his arms. "You must believe me. I was hiking. Had nee idea any of this nonsense was gannin' on with my family."

"See, I like hiking, too," Tennessee said. "And here's my problem. While you do look and smell like someone who's been sleeping in a sticky tent for a couple of weeks, I have one question. Why no insect bites?"

"DEET," he answered quickly.

"You don't smell of DEET," Cooper said.

"She's right. You don't smell of DEET in the slightest. So, until we can prove you were in the moors, or the DNA comes back negative, I'm going to keep asking questions. When was the last time you talked to your brothers?"

For another thirty minutes, Tennessee tried and failed to get anything useful from Phillip Hall. He claimed to not know where Marcus was, or if his brother was even in the country. He didn't know if Shane or Tyrone were still using their birth names or if, like him, they had adopted new monikers.

"Could your brother, Shane Beaumont, be going by another name?"

"I really don't know. We didn't keep in touch."

"What about Tyrone?"

He shook his head. "I don't know. They're strangers to me. I don't know if I'd even recognise them if they walked past me."

Having grown up as an only child, Tennessee couldn't relate. He'd always wanted a brother or sister and was quietly envious of Keaton's relationship with her brother. He thought of Alfie, his young son, and how he wished for more children. Then he thought of Hayley, and his heart seemed to lower in his chest. What if she reacted to future births the way she had with Alfie? He couldn't ask that of her.

While the young father briefly disappeared into his thoughts, Hall was still talking.

"...Last time we were all properly together was the day before Dad died. We weren't allowed to go to the funeral. *No place for children*, they told us. Dad must have known it was coming because he called us into his bedroom one by one to talk and give us gifts."

Hall's voice caught in his throat. The first time he'd shown any emotion other than anger or self-preservation.

"It was like some fucked up version of Christmas. We didn't have much money, and it wasn't like Dad could get to the shops the state his lungs were in. So he gave us the stuff he treasured. He gave me a compass he'd had since he was in the Scouts. I kept it for years. Lost it in Snowdonia the summer before I turned thirty."

He sighed and propped an elbow on the table so he could rest his face in his hand. "I was such a little shit at the time. I thanked Dad, of course, but I was actually kind of pissed off. I wasn't into hiking then; I am now, but not back then. I snuck into wor Kelly's room one day to see what she got. I found this old collector's coin in her pyjama drawer and I got so jealous because I thought maybe it was worth something. Then I found out Tyrone got Dad's new footie shirt—"

Tennessee stopped pacing. It felt as if all the moisture had been sucked out of the room. The slow withdrawal out to sea before the tsunami rolled in. He dove into a file, and with a shaking hand, slapped a picture on the table.

"Aye, that's the one. Bloody swamped him."

- CHAPTER 45 -

ALL HELL BROKE LOOSE.

James Beaumont had given his sixth child, Tyrone Beaumont, a football shirt as a parting gift before his death in 1988. Cooper pictured the seven-year-old being called in to see his dying father, the fear and sadness he must have felt. It was lung cancer that killed James. Young Tyrone would have heard a cough that never let up, rattling in his breath as fluid built in James's chest and throat. He'd have seen his father waste away no matter how much he ate, witnessed a man in constant pain when the illness spread to his bones. He'd have been scared about how life would change once his father was gone. But being from a poor household, Tyrone may have been thrilled to receive the football shirt, only to have guilt punch him in the gut over the circumstances that brought it to him.

Cooper couldn't spend too long thinking of the scared, helpless Tyrone, for the same distinctive yellow and green away shirt had been connected to all three murders. There was the scrap of fabric in Eve Lynch's hand, the fibre on Charles Pennington's body, and Atkinson had confirmed another thread was found in Ronan Turnbull's home. She wanted every person connected with Tyrone Beaumont brought in to help with their inquiries, and she wanted it done yesterday.

"All the siblings, even the half ones. Any relatives in the northeast, anyone who fostered him or anyone who was fostered with him. Former employers, anyone we can connect with him."

"And if they can't come in to speak to us today?" Whyte asked.

"Then we go to them," Cooper told him. She wrapped an arm around her stomach as she looked out the window. It was a lovely day: a blue sky, mottled with fluffy clouds and white contrails, people making the most of the warm weather in shorts or skirts, sleeveless tops and shades. But Tyrone was out there somewhere, planning another kill, no doubt. They had a police presence at Beth Beaumont's house but didn't know who else he may be after.

"I want to know the last time they saw him. I want to know what name he's using, what was said, any rumours they heard."

Whyte signalled to Boyd to follow him, and they left to organise the mass gathering of local Beaumonts.

"Paula," Cooper called. "Get on the phone and speak to anyone who's not in the area, especially foster parents and siblings. Even if we've spoken to them before, they might have thought of something else. Keep prodding."

Keaton scribbled down a list of names and picked up the handset of the nearest phone.

"Tyrone seemed to drop off the face of the planet after 1999," continued Cooper. "Last we know, he was working in a caravan park near Berwick. After that, we have nothing. I know we're going back a while but see if we can find someone who worked with him. They might know where he went next."

"Berwick's on the Scottish border. Should I check in with the cousin in Edinburgh?"

"Good call. Do it."

Cooper turned from Keaton, allowing her to get on with the task at hand. She was pleased to see everyone starting their various jobs; teams were formed, phone calls were made, and records searched. She approached Tennessee; he was hunched over a computer, typing furiously. He coughed into his elbow, opened a menthol sweet and popped it in his mouth. Angrily, he scrunched the wrapper in his fist, using it as a miniature stress ball.

"No Tyrone Beaumont, no Tyrone Douglas Beaumont, no Ty Beaumont, nothing. No record in the PNC or the database. DVLA has nothing, nor does National Insurance."

Cooper sat next to him. She pouted before suggesting, "Perhaps Beaumont became Beau?"

His index fingers jabbed at the keyboard as he leant back in his seat, balancing on the two back legs. "Nope. I'll try Ty Beau."

"My mum used to do that," Cooper said with a snort. "Tae Bo, that is."

"Mine too. She accidentally kicked the sofa and broke a toe." He leant further back. Another cough sweet and more jabbing at the keys. "He might have used his middle name. Robert Phillip became Phillip. Maybe Tyrone Douglas became... Nah, it's another dead end. No Douglas Beaumonts look like good matches."

"Try Doug."

Tennessee started crunching his teeth against the outer layer of the hard sweet. The cool medicinal smell of peppermint wafted up to Cooper's nostrils.

"Douglas, Doug, Dougie," he repeated in a whisper. "Come out, come out wherever you are."

Tennessee gasped; his body shuddered as the seat toppled backwards, his back hitting the floor with a thud.

Cooper was about to laugh when she saw the silent, wide-eyed, open-mouthed look on her colleague's face.

Tennessee was choking.

Pulling him to his feet, Cooper slapped her hand on his back three times. It was no use; the sweet was lodged deep in his throat.

No, no, no. Their training meant Cooper stayed calm on the surface. Her face was all business as she asked him to bend over the desk while she slapped the middle of his spine again and again. Internally, she panicked. She couldn't lose Jack. Not Jack. Her friend and colleague, Hayley's rock and Alfie's world.

He was going blue.

His legs started to shake.

The phone in Keaton's hand clattered to the floor as she leapt to her feet and wrapped her arms around Tennessee's middle. She formed her left hand into a fist and placed it just below the ribs. She wrapped her right hand around the left and pulled with all her might, lifting the tall man off his feet.

Nothing.

"Try again." Cooper couldn't keep her cool any longer. Tears rushed to her eyes as Tennessee's body went limp. She'd never felt so useless.

Nothing.

"Again, Paula."

There was a pop, and the cough sweet flew in a great arc across the incident room. Keaton released Tennessee, and he fell to his knees. He gulped in a lungful of air, then another, and another. His breath came in audible whoops as oxygen rushed into his body.

Cooper rubbed his back as he knelt; he'd scared the crap out of her. By the looks of Keaton, he'd done the same to her. She was ghostly white, pacing by the window, her hand clamped to her mouth as tears streamed down her face. In all their years working together, Cooper had never once seen Keaton cry.

Tennessee grabbed the edge of the desk with one hand, his other pointed up at the screen. It pointed to his last search.

When his voice came, it was raspy and sounded painful. "Dougie Beaumont," he wheezed. "I met the bastard."

- CHAPTER 46 -

GRAINGER TOWN, THE HISTORIC heart of Newcastle, smelled of breakfast food and smoke. There'd been a basement fire earlier that morning; Tennessee read about it during his morning scroll through the latest news. There were few shoppers and tourists at this time of the morning; instead, the streets were filled with wait staff, store assistants and delivery drivers. It was eight a. m. and Grainger Town was beginning to wake from her slumber. Pigeons fought over crumbs, shutters were raised, and every few minutes, the stairs around Grey's Monument spewed commuters from the Metro station that lay beneath it.

The Black and White Warehouse was still closed. The plain entrance showed no signs of life, and there was no movement in the windows upstairs. A laminated card warned *smile you're on camera*. Tennessee rested his back against the door and finished the black coffee he'd picked up from a

B BASKERVILLE

food truck. He used his free hand to massage the sides of his torso. His ribs ached from the life-saving manoeuvre Keaton used yesterday. He decided not to tell Hayley what had happened at work the previous day. He hated keeping secrets from his wife, but she had her own battles and fears to deal with. She fretted enough about the dangerous nature of his job, she didn't need to worry about his inability to distinguish his oesophagus from his windpipe as well. Moments later, a hairy man dressed in jeans and a black vest emerged from the Metro station. He swung a set of keys in his hands and hummed a nineties dance hit that Tennessee couldn't remember the name of.

"We open at nine," he said, shooing Tennessee out of the way so he could open the first of the locks.

"Lee Forbes." Tennessee held his ID up for inspection. "DS Daniel. We spoke last Monday."

Lee scowled. "Yeah, I remember you."

Tennessee could sense the man's annoyance. "Mind if I come in and ask you some questions?"

"Do I have a choice?"

Gone was the jovial man Tennessee had met at the start of the month. "Not really."

He followed Lee up the darkened stairwell to the memorabilia store. The place seemed different in the dark. Spooky. The bobbleheads appeared to be staring at him, and the bookshelves filled with programs and biographies looked as if they could topple over and crush him at any moment. His brush with death was getting to him.

Tennessee waited for Lee to disable the alarm, switch on the lights and start brewing a pot of tea before beginning his questioning.

Lee mellowed once he had a mug of tea in his hands. Tennessee couldn't blame him; the mug was adorned with the image of Andy Cole. With sixty-eight goals in eighty-four matches, Cole gave most Newcastle fans a warm fuzzy feeling.

"Sorry if I'm a grumpy bastard. I like my routine in the morning. I get antsy when it's disrupted. Plus, I'm sure the missus is sleeping with our window cleaner. That doesn't help."

"There was another man here when I visited last. Scottish accent, big bloke, strong build, knew a lot about—"

"Dougie? What about him?"

"I need to find him. Do you know where he lives?"

Lee shook his head.

"A full name or contact number?"

"He's just a customer. A new customer, mind you. Said he grew up here but moved to Scotland in his teens, hence the accent. Said he'd just moved back at the start of the summer. Speaking of which..."

Lee moved to the front of the store to open some windows.

"Gets hotter than Satan's nutsack in here without the window open."

"When was he last in?"

Lee thought for a second. "He's been in since your visit. Just the once, I think. Bought one of these." He held up his Andy Cole mug. "Says he's mad keen on the Toon. That his dad was a big fan, but he died when he was a bairn."

Tennessee's suspicions were correct. It was too much of a coincidence. Tyrone Douglas Beaumont was now Dougie.

"Did he pay with a credit or debit card?"

"Always cash."

Balls. Tennessee picked up a souvenir football and passed it back and forth between his hands. "What day was this?"

"Friday morning. Lunchtime at the latest."

"Do you have a till receipt showing the exact time?"

Lee looked down. "Erm..."

"You don't record cash purchases, do you?"

"Some might slip through the net."

Tennessee shook his head in disgust; there was no denying his anger. He'd paid tax since his first day of work, and he was happy to do so. Contributing to the greater good to pay for services like the NHS and education was only fair if everyone paid their share.

"Do you want me to pass on a message if he comes in again?" Lee asked, his voice sheepish.

"No. If he comes in again, you pretend like this conversation never took place. He's a dangerous man. Do you understand?"

Lee looked taken aback. "He's built like a brick shithouse, pardon my French, but I don't think he's dangerous."

"You think wrong. If he comes in, you call me straight away." He handed Lee a card with his details on it. "You can pretend you're calling the missus, ordering a pizza, I don't care, but you call straight away. Got it."

A reluctant nod.

Tennessee glanced up at a black bubble fixed to the ceiling. "Tell me that camera works."

"Usually does."

"I want any footage you have of Dougie. Send it to me today at the email address on the card."

Lee looked like he was about to complain. As if he was about to tell him he could have the footage, but he'd have to sift through it himself. He opened his mouth, a surly look on his face, but Tennessee spoke first.

"By the end of today, or I'm calling Revenue and Customs."

TENNESSEE STEPPED BACK OUT into the bright morning. The street was busier now, the sunshine painting Grainger Town a soft yellow. Across from the Black and White Warehouse, an elderly man in a flat cap sold flowers from a stall. Despite the remnants of his cold, he could make out the sweet smell of honeysuckle. He bought Hayley a bouquet of multi-coloured tulips and Pat a white and blue mix that reminded him of a summer meadow.

Buying flowers for his mother-in-law? That ought to earn him some Brownie points.

Tennessee dodged a Ford Focus that had almost driven the wrong way up a one-way street and called Cooper. He waited, listening while she excused herself from an interview with one of Dougie's foster parents.

"The good news is, the man I saw was definitely Tyrone Beaumont. He's going by Dougie now. The bad news is, I've no idea where he's staying or what surname he uses."

The Ford edged its way back into the main road. A series of car horns indicated the annoyance of other drivers while they waited.

"Okay, so we're no closer, but at least we've confirmed Tyrone and this Dougie are one and the same."

"The store owner's going to send me any footage he has by the end of the day. Hopefully, there's a good still we can use. I don't want to rely on my memory for making an e-fit."

"I've managed to get Vince Rivers to come in. He and his wife fostered Tyrone, Dougie, whatever we're calling him for a couple of years."

"What's your take?" Tennessee asked.

"He's going to a lot of effort to paint himself as a saint. Other than that, he says he hasn't seen or heard from him since he ran away from home when he was fifteen."

"Kids don't run away for no reason."

"I don't know about that," said Cooper. "I once worked a case where a girl ran away because her parents bought her supermarket-brand hair straighteners instead of the GHDs she'd wanted."

Tennessee snorted and brought the bouquet of tulips to his nose to take a whiff. "Glad I didn't have a girl."

Over the phone, Tennessee could hear the sound of coins dropping into a vending machine. Cooper was grabbing a snack.

"What's your next play?" she asked. "Any idea where he'd be now?"

"Not a clue, but I'm about to start a walkabout for local cameras. I know he was here Friday morning and the Monday before that. It might take me all day, but I'm going to trace his movements. Hopefully, I can follow him back to his lair."

Cooper told him that would be amazing and asked if he'd need any help. He asked for as many pairs of eyes as the department could spare. His wish was granted.

"The family and foster families aren't giving me anything new," Cooper told him. "If we can't find where he's staying..."

"I have a plan B." Tennessee watched as the man in the Ford exited his vehicle to yell at one of the drivers tooting his horn. A topless man with sunburnt shoulders jumped out from behind the wheel. Fingers were jabbed in faces.

"Jack?"

"Yeah, just a sec. I might need to diffuse a road rage situation."

Sunburnt man threw a punch at Ford Focus. It missed. Ford Focus kicked out, hitting Sunburnt in the groin. He yelped and fell to the floor.

"And now it's assault."

Tennessee laid the flowers on a bench and hoped they'd still be there in ten minutes. As he sprinted towards the fight, he noticed more people jumping from their cars.

"Plan B," he panted into his phone while running, "is that I know where he'll be on Saturday."

- CHAPTER 47 -

HE WAITED IN THE van, eyes down, pretending to do a crossword. Still, he was hyper-aware of the comings and goings in the street. South of the Tyne, the town of Ryton was expanding with clusters of new-builds popping up on its outskirts. This street was spanking new; half of it was still under construction. There was a smell of asphalt, freshly laid concrete, new siding and newly-opened tins of paint. The scent took him back to when he worked in construction. Working off-the-books and cash-in-hand with the other runaways and illegals. It was hard work – back-breaking – he respected those who worked up a sweat to put food on the table. He didn't respect the couple who lived in the four-bed detached house he was staking out.

Vince Rivers and his wife, Kerys. He remembered the little lady as a two-faced bitch: a happy, caring woman when she was out and about, a miserable cow at home. You could get more love out of a stone. Vince was a man of little emotion. The only time he cracked a smile was when his team scored. They'd done well for themselves, judging by the size of the house. It was amazing what you could afford if you squirrelled away all the money you were paid for fostering. Sure, they had a roof over their heads, food in their bellies, and clothes on their backs, but that was a bare minimum. Those were legal requirements. Beyond that, not a penny was spent on them.

Ryton was only fifteen miles from the place he'd stayed in Hebburn, but it was a different world. Here, no one knew Vince or Kerys. They'd started over as wealthy, decent people. He'd missed his chance earlier. Vince left the house, leaving Kerys to sunbathe in the back garden. It would have been the perfect opportunity if it weren't for two bairns playing in next door's garden. He wasn't too worried about young witnesses, but he didn't think innocents should have to see such things. He'd decided to wait, and wait he did. Five hours of waiting to be precise.

Kerys was in the kitchen, head peering into the fridge as she decided on her next beverage. She looked frailer than he remembered; she walked with a limp, sported orange peel skin on the backs of her things and groaned when she had to bend her knees.

Vince was upstairs. He looked agitated when he'd returned home, but whatever was bugging him was soon forgotten. He'd just opened the bathroom window and was whistling to himself, not a care in the world. He wondered if Vince would still be whistling if he knew his wife was about to be murdered. Perhaps he would.

Now.

He slipped out of the van and gently closed the door. He approached the house with all the confidence of someone who lived there. No one would question him; the children had gone back indoors, and the rest of the homes were unoccupied. A tall wooden gate marked the entrance to an alleyway between the two houses. He reached over, feeling for the catch; it was easy enough to open. He closed the gate behind him, careful not to make a sound. His heart rate picked up, his palms began to sweat.

Five.

He entered the back garden, saw Kerys's sun lounger and empty wine glass. A bottle of tanning oil lay on its side on the dry grass; a copy of *Take A Break* was open, its pages fanning back and forth in the light breeze.

Four.

He approached the bi-fold doors that opened into the modern kitchen. Kerys struggled with a corkscrew, cursing and muttering about screwtops in the same whiny voice he remembered.

Three.

He picked up a ceramic plant pot. Basil, he guessed, judging by the smell. It weighed about three and a half kilos. Perfect.

Two.

He stepped silently into the kitchen. Kerys, her back to him, stretched onto her tiptoes to reach for clean glasses. He stepped further in, his feet silent on her white, polished tiles. This was a modern kitchen, built for a modern house. A sharp-cornered kitchen island and high-gloss cabinets; everything was clean and precise. He smiled, knowing he was about to make a right mess.

He lifted the plant pot. She turned around.

One.

COOPER EXAMINED A MAP on Friday afternoon. A large aerial view of Newcastle was pinned to the wall in the incident room. Dougie Beaumont's movements from this time last week were marked using tiny red stickers. Their man liked to walk. CCTV had found him walking west on Blackett Street in the centre of Newcastle. He was picked up by several cameras around the Old Eldon Square area, where he opted not to take a bus or use the Metro. He then moved up Gallowgate and onto Barrack Road. Once passed St. James' Park, there were fewer cameras. Dougie had wandered into greener pastures, but Tennessee had been a determined man. Over many hours, he'd tracked the man in black. He kept his head down as he marched towards his destination, never once stopping to speak to anyone or check directions. Here the trail seemed to vanish until footage emerged of their suspect passing a branch of Aldi on Ponteland Road. The journey had taken him over an hour, and the pavement outside Aldi was the last location they had for Dougie.

Running her finger along the line of red dots, Cooper wondered where Dougie was headed. Where was he sleeping? The nearest hotel was an airport Travel Lodge, another thirty-minute walk north. She pursed her lips as she thought. She didn't know of any B&Bs in the Cowgate or Kenton area, but there were many rental properties. He could have rented a room somewhere. Or an Airbnb.

Cooper's legs were tired from standing in front of the map. She took a seat and rubbed her knees. Christ, she felt older than she should. She still had many years with a three at the start of her age, and she wasn't ready to be the sort who made moaning noises every time they stood up or who huffed and puffed every time they climbed a flight of stairs. Not yet.

She leant sideways and retrieved her handbag from the floor. Rummaging in the bottom of it, she found her phone and planner. The screen of the phone showed a couple of messages. Julie was annoyed that Cooper would be home late; Tina asked if she could get a takeaway instead of helping her grandmother cook. She ran her thumb over the glass front and felt another crack; she'd need to replace it soon, or splurge on an upgrade. She typed quick replies to her mother and daughter that she wouldn't be too late and that they should go out to eat. It would be her treat as long as they chose a restaurant and booked a table.

The planner was functional. A plain blue cover with coffee stains. Inside, a week-to-page layout showed Cooper's appointments and reminders.

Shopping lists were scrawled between meetings, and small doodles of flowers and hearts made her smile. She must be in a good place with Atkinson if she was drawing hearts in her diary like an adolescent. She flicked the pages back a few weeks before jumping forward to the next week. She had tests at the Northern Centre for Cancer Care scheduled for Monday. Written there in red ink, the words made her nervous. Still, it was important that she attend; she needed to be checked over. Dr McDermott had concerns; he'd requested a mammogram, a bone density test, and some other examinations. She'd arranged a few hours off for that morning and was pleased Atkinson had agreed to go with her. She didn't know if she'd be able to keep the panic attacks at bay without him.

She closed the planner and took a sip of water from a bottle. There was a team out in Cowgate with a photo of Dougie Beaumont. They'd been instructed to spread out from his last known location, going door-to-door in the hopes someone would recognise the triple murderer. The rest of the team were still talking to all the connections they could find for Dougie, aka Tyrone. They'd reassemble soon. Unless they caught Dougie in the next few hours, they were going ahead with plan B.

THE RIVERS' UNCONSCIOUS BODIES looked like oversized ragdolls on the kitchen floor, all floppy and lifeless. They could wake up at any moment, and whilst they were older and not as intimidating as he'd once found them, Vince was still a big man. He didn't want another black eye; the one Ronan Turnbull had given him still hurt. Taking two cable ties from his back pocket, he bound Vince and Kerys's hands together. Next, he stuffed their mouths with tea towels. He walked through a utility room and took a door into the Rivers' garage. The space was relatively empty. Some shelving lined one wall, each shelf filled with boxes from their recent move. He'd always travelled light and kept as few possessions as he could get away with. Having all this junk would drive him mad. He opened the garage doors, jogged across the street, started the van and reversed it into the dark, square space.

It took next to no effort to move Kerys; she weighed six stone soaking wet. He dropped her on the mattress he kept in the back then went back for Vince. He squatted, slipped his hands under Vince's armpits, took a deep breath then began to pull. It was a good thing he trained deadlifts; otherwise, his back would be in agony tomorrow. Still, lifting him into the van was a chore. After three attempts, he gave up.

He returned to the back garden and collected the sun lounger. He folded the legs in and used the main body of it as a ramp, laying one end on the ground and the other inside the van. A grunting noise made him turn.

Vince was awake. Wild-eyed and desperate, he was on his knees trying to shuffle out of the garage.

He smiled at the pitiful escape attempt, cracked his knuckles and formed a fist. "Not so fast, big boy."

Vince's eyes plead with him. The irony. He used to be the one making that face.

"The bad news is that you've got a long night ahead of ya. The good news is it's the last one you'll ever have."

- CHAPTER 48 -

SATURDAY THE TWELFTH OF June, and tribalism was in full effect at Gosforth Park. An area of lush greenery, the park was home to wild deer, rabbits and other species. It was also home to two golf courses, a five-a-side centre, a hotel, a pub, and Newcastle Racecourse.

"Who schedules a football meet up sale the same day as the Northumberland Plate?" Keaton asked. She stood outside her car, having found the inside of it had turned into a sauna the second she killed the engine.

Around them, people arrived for both events. The Northumberland Plate was the premier fixture in northeastern horse racing. Run on the flat over two miles, the race attracted the nations top jockeys. It also drew the region's well-to-do race fans. Designer suits and shiny shoes, fitted summer dresses and oversized hats, the Northumberland

Plate was an excuse to flaunt both your wealth and your figure.

"They didn't," said Cooper, stretching her arms above her head and feeling the warmth of the sun on her face. "The Plate was delayed a week after that horse was poisoned."

"Oh yeah. I saw that on the news. Arsenic, wasn't it?" Keaton asked. "Did they catch who did it?"

Cooper shook her head. "Not yet. My money's on a rival jockey or someone with a lot of money on the outcome."

"Who's the new favourite?"

Cooper scrunched her face up as she tried to remember. "Rocket Queen."

A coach pulled up in front of them. Thirty race goers alighted, already in a state of giddy inebriation. A woman in a bright green dress with a hat wider than your average sombrero almost blinded the man walking behind her when she stopped suddenly and he walked into the brim. Seconds later, another coach arrived; this one housed those who wanted to trade collector's cards, buy programs from classic matches and have their Newcastle shirts signed for a tenner by former players who needed the cash.

The horsey folk sneered at the football fans. On any given day, they'd likely be mates in the same pubs, cheering for the same team. Today they were separate tribes. The horses softened their accents, the footballs hardened theirs. They formed small groups, eyeing the other with disdain. The posh folk curling their lips at the commoners; the working folk jeering at the trust funds in silly hats. Like a clan marching into enemy territory, the football fans adopted confident postures and walked in formation.

"This place is a tinderbox," said Cooper. She checked her watch, wondering where the armed unit was. They were hoping to catch a dangerous serial killer and didn't want any of the public getting hurt in the process. The task force was equipped with tasers, but a little muscle in the form of firearms wouldn't go amiss.

Tennessee came running over from his vehicle. He was dressed in an NUFC shirt, ready to blend in. "Coop, major incident at the Metrocentre. Possible terrorist attack. Two men with machetes—"

"Armed response?"

"Diverted to deal with it."

"Bloody hell. So, we're not getting any?"

"There's a standard unit of armed officers here working the races. More of a deterrent than anything. There are fifty thousand people attending today, and that's not counting the memorabilia swap and the golf. Nixon says we can liaise with the security detail, bring them up to speed on our operation."

Cooper swore. "Talk about the right hand not knowing what the left hand is doing. Paula?"

"I'm on it, boss."

Keaton left to find out who was in charge and give them the good news: a serial killer might be amongst them. Her feet kicked up plumes of dust as she walked over the scorched ground.

ELLIOTT WHYTE TUGGED AT the Newcastle shirt he'd been forced to wear.

"Stop fidgeting," Saffron Boyd warned him. She pulled her light-brown, dark-blonde hair into a ponytail. A bead of sweat formed in the Cupid's bow of her lips.

"It just feels so unnatural."

"Would you prefer to walk in wearing a Sunderland shirt? You'd be pulled limb from limb."

She made a fair point.

A trailer to their right opened, and a magnificent bay horse with a blaze of white on his nose was led towards the racecourse.

Boyd pouted at the impressive beast. "I hate horse racing. The horse does all the work, and the jockey gets all the credit. It's just running for lazy people."

Whyte raised his dark eyebrows at her. "What about cycling?"

"Also running for lazy people."

"Rowing?"

"Swimming for lazy people."

"Golf?"

She paused. "Hiking for drunks."

He laughed. It was good to see Boyd start to relax around him. She was funny when she wasn't a nervous wreck.

"Whyte." It was Cooper's voice coming from behind him. "It's time."

THE TEAM GATHERED AROUND Cooper, looking as casual as they could. From what she could tell, the public had barely registered them; they were all too busy having a good time.

"No one has seen Dougie Beaumont arrive. We've had eyes on all the coaches, and so far, no one has matched his description. He might not be coming, he might arrive later, or he might have slipped past us. Either way, we need to get bodies inside to check."

Feet shuffled in anticipation. Cooper took a slow breath to steady her stress levels and noticed others were doing the same.

"Tennessee, Whyte and Martin. As discussed last night, you're going in with Ngannou, O'Malley, Grant and Bailey."

The task force nodded.

"Play it safe. Your safety's as important as anyone else's. I don't want any of you getting hurt."

She meant it. While everyone knew she was closest to Tennessee, there was no way she'd be able to forgive herself if her plan got one of the team maimed or killed. Cooper inserted an earpiece, and others followed her lead. They tested their mics, and those not going inside the five-a-side centre spread out to cover the exits.

Keaton opened her arms and pulled Martin into her. She slapped him on the back twice and told him to be careful. Despite her constant teasing of the young man, Cooper knew she thought of him as family.

At one side of the building, Cooper took her position outside a fire exit. She wiped her forehead with the back of her arm. It was unbearably hot, and the humidity made her feel like she was trying to breathe underwater. Her mouth was dry with fear; she licked her lips, but her tongue was rough. She was dehydrated.

"Go ahead," she spoke into her mic. "If you see Beaumont, hang back until you can separate him from the crowd."

A band started playing somewhere in the racecourse. It troubled Cooper, but at least it covered the sound of her heartbeat thumping in her ears. A gust of wind blew dust and dried dirt into her face, along with the smell of hotdogs and horseshit.

She managed to say, "Good luck," into the mic before vomiting over a disabled parking bay.

FANATICS AT A MEMORABILIA swap, like kids in a candy store. A din of voices, some rough with age, some younger and higher in pitch; the older voices just as excitable as the younger ones. The room mingled as one; chatting and laughing filled the air. Nods of recognition for established friendships and handshakes to seal new ones. A Manchester United joke here, a Chelsea joke there. And whilst no one would dream of insulting Newcastle United, its owner was fair game.

"Wish he'd hurry up and sell," huffed a man with thick blond ringlets.

"He doesn't care about the club. Only thing he cares about is money." The man's friend moved out of the way as fast-flowing streams of people tried to be in too many places at once; they crossed one another's paths, occasionally colliding as they jostled for position.

Tennessee, Whyte and Martin moved from stall to stall, pretending to look at the merchandise. They were actually looking at the sellers and fellow visitors. Every time his eyes fell on a larger man, Tennessee's breath caught in his throat. He wasn't a claustrophobic person, but he felt on edge. There were too many people, too many variables.

Then there he was.

"Eyes on," he whispered into the mic hidden in his collar.

Tyrone, Douglas, Dougie. Whatever he wanted to call himself. Dougie Effin' Beaumont was hunched over, his posture passive and submissive, palms turned outwards in a gesture of openness. Despite the hustle and bustle, Tennessee could pick up his voice. A slight Scottish accent, presumably acquired during his years of exile, spoken softly with rising inflexions to put others at ease.

A wolf in sheep's clothing.

A wolf in yellow and green.

"I've lost you," crackled Whyte's voice in his ear.

"Cake stall."

A towering, five-tiered cake gave off the smell of marzipan and icing sugar. It resembled a glamorous wedding cake, only it was for those married to the beautiful game. A crowd gathered as a woman in chef whites prepared to cut the first slice, and a man in an apron gathered pound coins.

A pound per slice? Tennessee would be tempted if he wasn't acutely aware of what one of the customers had done to five people in the last few weeks.

Early that morning, the bodies of Vince and Kerys Rivers were removed from a snake-shaped sand sculpture on Seaburn beach in Sunderland. The snake looked much the same as the others, only this time the serpent was bicephalous – two-headed. The sandy tomb was discovered by a group of lads on their way home after a boozy all-nighter. They may have been intoxicated, but they had the sense to dive in, pull the bodies free and begin CPR. Sadly, they were too late.

The blade of the chef's knife was clean and sharp. It pierced the first tier, cutting smoothly through the black and white striped frosting. The first slice was placed on a paper napkin and handed to a young girl whose hair was styled into pigtails. She grinned and took an enormous bite.

Tennessee took a step forward. "It's too busy," he warned. "We need to wait for him to go to the bathroom or the bar. Or to at least move to the edge of the room."

"Copy."

Dougie waited his turn; a patient adult while all the children were served first. The woman in chef whites smiled at him and handed over a large slice of cake. The frosting was designed to look like hundreds of tiny footballs; the inside was the sort of dark gooey chocolate that could solve any of the world's problems. Dougie turned, cake in hand, then his eyes fell on Tennessee.

"I've been made."

- CHAPTER 49 -

As IF IN SLOW motion, the slice of cake tumbled to the floor. Chocolate exploding over the feet of anyone nearby.

"STOP! POLICE!"

Dougie spun around. He wrestled the knife from the chef and pointed the blade towards Tennessee. Gone was the bad posture and warm face. The act fell away to reveal the monster within, chest puffed and eyes filled with fury. Those nearby fell backwards or backed away. Screams echoed in Tennessee's ears, but it was not his own safety he thought of as he stared at the pointed weapon: it was Hayley's. His family needed him.

"PUT THE WEAPON DOWN!" Whyte bellowed over and over, edging forward, his taser pointed at Dougie.

"It's over, Dougie." Tennessee's voice was loud but calm. "Put the knife down. You're surrounded."

Dougie lunged forward, his free hand grasping someone nearby. It was the young girl; she still had chocolate around the corners of her mouth. He pulled her head to his chest, wrapping a thick arm around her neck.

She cried for her dad, scrunching her eyes closed, petrified with fear.

Her father ran to her, only to be pulled back by O'Malley, a short but confident man from the task force. "No. Wait," O'Malley commanded.

The girl was only nine years old, ten at the most. Dougie held her tightly as he edged to his left, using her as a human shield. He moved slowly, one step at a time, knowing he was safe as long as the girl stood between him and the tasers. At a side door, he stopped to flash an evil grin at Tennessee. When Dougie winked at him, his blood turned to ice. Then he was gone.

"FIRE EXIT," he yelled into the mic. "Coop, he's coming your way. Suspect is armed. Suspect has a hostage."

HE POWERED THROUGH THE fire exit, his feet skidding on loose gravel when he saw Cooper and the others. The fire exit opened into a parking area. The parking bays were filled; Cooper stood between an Insignia and an Escort. Behind them, a high green fence separated the racecourse from other areas of the park.

"Stay back. I'll kill her. I mean it." He waved the knife at Cooper then placed it against the girl's neck.

She was a tiny thing, with long strawberry-blonde pigtails and nails painted baby pink. Tears flowed, and her breath came in short, panicked gasps.

Cooper held up her hands to show they were empty. She couldn't risk him harming the child. In her periphery, she saw Paula Keaton motion for an officer with a taser to hold fire until he had a clear shot.

"Dougie. Let the girl go and we can talk."

He shook his head.

"It's over, Dougie. It's time to put the knife down. Let the girl go. She has nothing to do with this."

Cooper saw his Adam's apple lift and fall as he swallowed. He glanced down and moved the knife an inch from the girl's neck.

"I'm not ready for it to be over," he said. He looked over his shoulder. Tennessee stood in the doorway. Behind him, Whyte held a nervous crowd at bay.

"Because you haven't finished your list?" Cooper asked.

His eyes met hers.

"She's not on your list, Dougie. She's an innocent little girl, not one of your snakes."

He made a sound between a laugh and a sob, and his face crumpled for a moment.

Cooper felt the atmosphere shift. She glanced at the doorway and saw Whyte restraining a desperate man, white with fear. The girl's father was distraught. In her ear, she heard Keaton communicating with armed response. One male, one female, both armed with Heckler & Koch G36s, were at the edge of the parking area. They kept their distance but had their weapons trained on Dougie.

Dougie pivoted right and left, his eyes searching for an escape route. He pulled the girl's head closer to his chest as he checked over his shoulder to make sure Tennessee wasn't sneaking up on him. As he turned back, the girl's hand flew to her cheek, blood ran down her young face, and she cried out in pain.

"Dougie, she's hurt. Come on, this isn't the way. You don't want to do this."

"Don't I?"

"I know you don't," Cooper said. "You want to finish your list, not start a new one."

"You're right," he growled. He took a step forward and spotted the G36s.

There was a flash of white as the knife soared through the air. The blade nicked Cooper's thigh. Blood teamed through the thick material of her trousers. The pain was like fire, burning her entire leg. She clamped a hand over the wound and looked up to see Dougie pushing the girl to the side.

Startled, the officer's taser fired. Spiralled wires erupted from the yellow plastic barrel. The darts connected with the girl; her body convulsed violently, her mouth open in shock but unable to scream.

"Stop!"

Dougie sprinted forward and leapt towards the parked cars. Like a leopard climbing a tree, he effortlessly vaulted onto the bonnet of a Mitsubishi Warrior. Another long-legged bound and he was on the pick-up's roof.

A high-pitched pop preceded the sound of cracking glass as a single gunshot fired through the truck's windscreen. A spider web spread across the screen before it exploded, sending bright shards of glass shattering in all directions.

The sound reverberated off the wall of the building. Cooper ducked behind the Insignia to shield herself as tiny shards of glass rained down upon her. Her leg throbbed, the blossom of scarlet growing bigger with each second. She looked up in time to see Dougie clear the fence. He was gone.

- CHAPTER 50 -

THERE WAS A THUD as Dougie landed two-footed on the roof of a Citroen. His feet slipped from beneath him, and he rolled to the ground, grunting. Keaton gave chase, a look of steely determination contorting her features. She and an armed officer took the same route, jumping effortlessly onto the parked cars, then pulling themselves over the green fencing to enter the racecourse.

Cooper grimaced with each step. She and Tennessee took a longer route into the racecourse – one that didn't require stunts better suited to a Tom Cruise movie.

"Tend to the girl," she shouted back at Whyte and Martin. "Get an ambulance. Evacuate the main stand."

If the racecourse was busy before, it was packed now. A red carpet led to a VIP area that bustled with important-looking people. It was a bubble of wealth and glamour. White fences were adorned with white roses; crisp white sheets covered the tables. Empty seats surrounded equally empty Champagne flutes and pint glasses. The VIPs stood, eyes on the track, waving their betting slips and bouncing with excitement. Cheers of encouragement went up from some as they supported their favourite horses; others wailed deep, desperate sobs as they realised they'd gambled far too much. Stomaches bloated with expensive food and fine wine, they had arrived as well-dressed ladies and gents, but had devolved into manic chimps. They were all teeth; preening, flexing and asserting dominance over one another via the strength of their vocal cords or the size of their wallets.

As Dougie knocked over the first table, he was met with shouts of annoyance. The shouts turned to screams as the race fans spotted armed response coming their way, assault rifles pointed.

"Hold fire," Cooper shouted into her mic as she ran. "It's too crowded." But even as she said the words, she saw Dougie grab a pint glass and shatter the rim, forming a razor-sharp weapon.

She kept her eyes glued on Dougie, fearful they might lose him in the crowd. As he zig-zagged through the guests, they made like rats in a bin: screeching, fleeing, doing anything to get out of his way. Chairs fell or were thrown, drinks spilt, tables upended. People ahead saw the chaos and ducked behind their tables. As if the cheap plastic could protect them from Dougie, his weapon, or the G36s that followed.

A man, his shirt stained with beer, stood his ground. Brave or stupid, he lowered his weight, ready to tackle their fleeing suspect. Dougie stole a quick glance over his shoulder; Keaton was gaining on him. His arm moved in a great arc, smashing the bottom end of the glass into the man's head. He dropped like a sack of spuds. Keaton, unfazed, jumped over the man as he held his head and writhed on the ground.

Dougie reached another fence; this one only came to his waist. He slowed.

Armed response had a better view now, but still, panicked people ran across their path. "Freeze. Put the weapon down, or we'll shoot."

"Don't," growled Cooper as Dougie rolled under the fence.

A child had already been hurt. They couldn't risk another member of the public being injured, or a horse for that matter. What a PR nightmare that would be.

A speaker crackled. "And it's number four, Rocket Queen by a neck. Swift Blossom gaining."

Another fence easily vaulted. He was going to get away, cross the racecourse and disappear into the woods. Who knew how long he'd hide, waiting for his chance to tick one more name off his list.

The armed officer, lean and dark, brought the G36 to his shoulder and squeezed the trigger. The bullet glanced off Dougie's arm.

Hundreds of heads ducked as one as the guests lowered themselves to the floor. Screams rang out, covering the sounds of hooves on the all-weather track.

"...and it's neck and neck. Rocket Queen and Swift Blossom."

Keaton was almost there. Cooper didn't stand a chance of catching them; her leg was leaking blood, her head felt woozy. The track blurred before her, stripes of green and brown smudging each time she blinked. Still, she could see the danger.

Keaton was within arm's reach. Her strong legs thundered; she was ready to strike.

Cooper skidded to a halt. Dust mushroomed around her as she grabbed the white, waist-high fence. Fear coursed through her as she saw the future. "STOP!" she yelled, but it was useless over the noise of everything happening around her.

Tennessee slid in behind Cooper. Unable to stop himself, he catapulted over the fence. On all fours, he looked up at the racecourse. His mouth formed a perfect oval of horror before he found the strength to echo Cooper. "Stop! Paula, stop!"

DS Paula Keaton froze just as Swift Blossom tore across her path. Her arm jerked backwards violently, and she rolled, gripping her bicep as her arm hung limply beside her. She cursed through the pain of a dislocated shoulder, grinding her teeth while her legs went into spasm.

DS Paula Keaton stopped in time. Dougie Beaumont did not.

Nor did the seventeen other horses running in the Northumberland Plate.

As THE FINAL HORSE crossed the line, a broken body remained on the track. Trampled by beasts weighing five hundred kilos apiece, Dougie Beaumont was crumpled and unmoving.

"Victory for Rocket Queen. Rocket Queen by a head."

- CHAPTER 51 -

THE FIRST THING HE noticed was the smell – sweet and sterile. With his eyes closed, he parted his lips and moved his tongue around his arid mouth. Thirst was the overriding sensation. He opened his eyes; the room was too bright for him, so he clamped them shut again, wrinkling the skin around his orbitals. That's when the pain kicked in.

He felt as if someone had dropped a twenty-kilo dumbbell on his head. His nose throbbed, his jaw ached. The sheets felt like ice on his chest; his shoulders, elbows and wrists raged. He couldn't breathe through his nose, but it itched like a hundred spiders were crawling over it. Trying to scratch the itch was impossible. His arm refused to move, his fingers finding nothing but the rough texture of a plaster cast.

Blinking, he tried to become accustomed to the light. He was in a hospital bed, both arms cocooned in white plaster. Spokes held his arms at right angles. He wanted to get out of there. Hormones flooding his veins told him to leave, to get out. If he could swing his legs to the side of the bed, he might be able to stand.

He grunted, but neither leg moved.

His face felt hot with pain, his arms cramped, and his chest stung with every breath. Yet his legs felt nothing. The realisation caused him to yell. He yelled long and loud until a young woman in purple scrubs entered the room and plunged a needle into his hip.

He sighed, then the darkness came.

COOPER GOT THE CALL that she'd be able to speak to Dougie Beaumont early on Sunday morning. She had plans to go to Alnwick with Atkinson; they'd wanted to visit the castle and gardens, but it would have to wait. She sent a text to apologise and suggested an early lunch after tomorrow's hospital appointment instead. They had both booked Monday morning off work and Cooper thought it might be a good time to speak to him privately. She wanted to discuss their relationship but didn't fancy doing it with Julie or Tina earwigging in the next room.

She washed quickly but took her time changing the dressing on her thigh. She'd needed a couple of stitches and a pint of blood, but she was otherwise all right. She'd have a nasty scar, but that was

371

nothing new. If she didn't like it, she'd cover it with another tattoo.

Checking her reflection in the bathroom mirror, Cooper saw her hair was looking fluffy and could do with a tidy; she'd tackle that later. She had enough to think about without fixating on the length of her hair.

Downstairs, she found Julie at the kitchen table reading the Sunday papers and drinking strong coffee.

"That smells like it could power a jet engine."

Julie looked up. "Morning, dear. I hope you don't mind, but I got up early and made a start on the laundry."

Cooper did mind. She'd never liked people going through her things, no matter how innocent their intentions.

Her mother didn't wait for Cooper to answer. "You know, if you do a load each day, you'll be able to keep on top of it."

"I do keep on top of it."

"Hardly, the basket was overflowing, and the bathroom needs a deep clean. When was the last time you cleaned under the freezer?"

Cooper poured herself a small coffee.

"I've never cleaned under the freezer."

Julie looked at her with a horror-struck expression.

"Oh, please," said Cooper. She grimaced then poured the coffee down the drain. "I work full time. More than full time, actually, given it's Sunday morning and I'm off to interview a serial killer, but don't let that stop you from having a dig."

Julie's face creased. She lifted the paper, hiding behind it. "I'm not—"

"Yes, you are. When was the last time you cleaned under the freezer at Benji's? Have you even called to see how they're getting on? Or checked the social media accounts Tina set up for you?"

Julie turned a page, letting the noise of paper brushing over the kitchen table cover the sound of her sniffles. Cooper felt guilty; she hadn't meant to make her mother cry. Julie must miss Ben terribly, and anything to do with the bar would be an awful reminder that he was no longer with her. If Julie wanted to help with the housework, Cooper should be grateful. She *was* grateful; she just didn't want help if it came with a side dish of digs about her home keeping skills. Since returning from her father's funeral, Cooper had worked a major investigation. She'd seen one colleague almost choke to death and another nearly crushed in a stampede. She'd tried to get through to a teenager who no longer wanted to communicate with her, and she'd tried to rebuild the relationship she'd effectively ruined in the springtime. During all of this, she'd made room in her home for her grieving mother.

No wonder she was drained. There was the dark cloud of tomorrow's tests hanging over her, possible bad news, medical complications and big decisions.

Letting the air out of her lungs, Cooper opened her mouth to apologise, but Julie beat her to it.

"I'm sorry, dear. You're right. I just— I just want to make myself useful, so you don't..." Her voice caught in her throat. "I'm not ready to go back to the bar, and I thought if I made myself useful you wouldn't..."

"Hoy you out?"

"Something like that."

Cooper was exasperated. What did she take her for? "You don't have to make yourself useful, Mum. And I'm not going to ask you to leave."

Yes, she wanted her home back and for things to return to normal, but Cooper was hardly going to pack her mother's suitcase and put her on the next flight to Lanzarote.

"You can stay as long as you need," she said, but she knew her tone of voice didn't match her words. "I've got to go."

THE HEAT AND HUMIDITY of the past few weeks finally tipped the barometer from fair to stormy. The first flash of lightning lit up the sky as Cooper drove into the centre of Newcastle. The rain poured down in sheets; the sky was dark and looked more like night than day. The BMW's windscreen wipers turned on automatically, immediately finding the quickest setting. At the junction near the Great North Museum, a man comforted his terrified dog as it cowered from the sudden booms coming from the sky. Pedestrians in summer clothes dived under bus shelters, and servers at local cafés hurried to move outside diners indoors before their food was ruined.

Cooper followed Claremont Road and turned left onto Queen Victoria Road. By some miracle, she found a spot in the car park nearest the main entrance of the Royal Victoria Infirmary. The RVI was a hospital that opened its doors as early as 1752 and now operated as a seven-hundred-bed teaching hospital for Newcastle University. Pulling an umbrella from the glove box, Cooper stepped out into a puddle. Warm water seeped through her socks and shoes. The rain was falling faster than the drains could siphon it away. Despite the brolly, water whipped against her face and she was forced to bow her head as she ran towards shelter. In the short time she'd been exposed to the weather, she been completely soaked through. Cooper lowered the umbrella and shook it violently, spraying water in all directions.

Behind Cooper, a knock on a glass panel caught her attention. She turned to see a perfectly dry Tennessee waiting for her.

"Almond croissant or chocolate twist?" he asked once Cooper negotiated the revolving door and wiped her soggy shoes on the mat.

"Almond croissant. How come you don't look like you've been dipped in the Tyne head first?"

"Hayley dropped me off. She has an appointment with her therapist."

Cooper bit into the pastry and flicked crumbs from her shirt. "Does it help?"

He shrugged. "Can't do any harm. She hasn't been in a while, so I gave her a nudge. I'm hoping we won't be here all day; Alfie's feeling better so I want to take him to the pool. Plus, Pat said she'd watch him tonight so me and Hayley can go to the cinema."

Cooper smiled but said nothing. A drop of water weaved its way down her forehead to her nose. She shook her head like a wet dog and looked around the foyer. The area had filled up as anyone due to leave waited for a lull in the weather.

"You spoken to anyone yet?" she asked.

"A Dr Lane briefed me. Douglas Beaumont is awake and in pain. Well, above the waist he is. He's paralysed from L1 down, whatever that means."

"It's the top of the lumbar vertebrae. 'Bout here." She poked Tennessee in his lower back, causing him to jump.

"He has fractures to his jaw, nose, orbital, collar bone, both arms, six of these things." He pointed to the back of his hand.

"Metatarsals."

"Right. Erm, what else? His ribs, his hip, both legs. Thigh on the right, and shin on the left—"

Cooper cut him off. "Basically, he's broken his entire body?"

"Then there's the internal injuries. How's your leg, by the way?"

They finished their pastries and threw the servi- ettes in the bin.

"Could be worse," Cooper said with a snort.

"A lawyer's with him, and the doc will be keeping an eye on him. We have to stop the interview if he shows any sign of distress."

Cooper rolled her eyes. The rules were there for a reason, but had Dougie stopped when his victims were distressed? No, he'd beat them then buried them alive.

- CHAPTER 52 -

UPSTAIRS, COOPER TUGGED AT the neckline of her shirt. Hospitals put her on edge, and though logic told her she wasn't in any danger, she found herself standing closer to Tennessee.

A stocky man with big ears and a small mouth extended a hand. "DCI Cooper? I'm Dr Lane. I'm sure DS Daniel has told you about Mr Beaumont's injuries. He's lucky to be alive."

His words echoed in Cooper's head. *Lucky to be alive.* If only his victims could say the same.

"I know you have a job to do, but I'm sure you can appreciate I do as well. If Mr Beaumont shows any signs of anxiety or discomfort, I'm afraid I'll have to call an end to the visit. He needs as much rest as possible at this time."

Cooper shook the doctor's hand and nodded.

Outside the door to Douglas Beaumont's room, an officer sat on a plastic chair with a bored expression on his face. Slapping a hand on his shoulder,

Cooper sent him home – the man he was guarding was hardly a flight risk.

Inside the hospital room, the first person Cooper noticed was the lawyer. He'd taken the only seat and wore an ill-fitting suit, his striped tie askew. They nodded in greeting, then Cooper turned to the bed.

Whatever she had imagined Dougie's injuries to look like, she hadn't expected this. The man lay motionless in the centre of the bed, propped up on pillows. Blankets covered his lower body, but the thin fabric couldn't hide the casts and braces strapped to both legs. His face was visibly swollen, both eyes were almost entirely closed, and his jaw was held in place by a strap of material.

In defiance of his injuries, Dougie smiled at the detectives.

The expression made Cooper shudder. "How can you smile? You're going to jail for the rest of your life. Even without a confession, we have ample evidence, including DNA. You will be convicted, Dougie, or should I call you Tyrone?"

"Dougie," he said through clamped teeth. "I haven't been Tyrone since the day I left for Scotland. And I'm smilin' because I did what I set out tae dae."

"No, you didn't. Beth Beaumont is alive and well."

Dougie blinked. "She's a meth head. I wouldn't say she was well in the slightest. Besides, someone will finish what I've started."

A chill ran through Cooper, and she glanced at Tennessee. "What do you mean?"

"A story like mine is bound tae be telt. There'll be books. Hell, there'll likely be a movie. Hollywood loves a revenge story; John Wick grossed eighty million."

"You want to be famous?"

"Infamous. And no, not really. I just wanted justice. But the world loves people like me; I outsmarted your lot for weeks. One by one, I tracked doon and murdered those who made my childhood unbearable. You only caught me through my own arrogance, nae through skill. If I hadn't been so cocky when I met your young man there – if I never telt ya I was going to that memorabilia swap, you'd still be twiddling ya thumbs."

"We had your DNA."

"But nee one to compare it tae." He turned to the doctor. "Drink, please."

The doctor poked a straw through the wires holding Dougie's jaw in place so he could take a drink of orange juice.

Cooper shoved her hands in her pockets; they were still wet. "Why did you kill those people? Charles Pennington had a daughter, two grandchildren. Vince and Kerys took in hundreds of children over the years."

"Should we start at the beginning?" Dougie asked.

The lawyer coughed, and though he couldn't move his body, Dougie silenced him with a stare.

"I told ya, I don't need no Poundland Robert Kardashian." His fingers twitched as he turned back to Cooper. "You ken about my mum?"

"The baby addiction? Yes."

"Imagine being someone's entire world. Feeling nowt but love, warmth and safety, then being tossed aside like ya were worse than nothin'. Once she gave birth to Marcus, I was forgotten. I became an inanimate object, gathering dust and taking up space. Then Shane came along and I may as well have been invisible. The older kids may as well have been dead."

Cooper felt for him, but this man was a murderer. Other people had terrible childhoods and awful parents; they didn't go on to become serial killers.

"Then Dad died."

"And he gave you the football shirt," Tennessee said.

He nodded. "Aye. I was seven when Dad passed, and for five of those years, Mum acted like I didnae exist. Dad was my only real parent, and he was deathly ill. That shirt swamped me. I was a scrawny wee thing. A right runt. But it felt like a security blanket, ye ken? I loved that shirt."

"It's currently in an evidence locker," Cooper told him. "They had to cut you out of it. It'll never be in your possession again."

It was a cruel remark. But not as cruel as burying someone alive.

Dougie was quiet for a moment before continuing. "I moved around a bit after that; one home tae the next until Vince and Kerys offered a long-term placement. I'd have been better back home with Mum. She might not have known I existed, but she never lifted a hand to me. Vince was quick tae anger. He hated backchat, hated being woken up on the weekend, hated shoes in the house. You ken he had a favourite belt for hitting us? One time I left the iron on face doon and it burnt the ironing table. You ken what he did? He dragged me, kicking and screaming, to Hebburn cemetery after dark and strapped me to an obelisk. Bastard whipped me black and blue and left me for the ghosties to get. I'd wet myself twice by the time he came back for me." His voice slipped away before he changed the subject. "And Kerys was like the evil stepmother in Cinderella. Us foster kids were basically her wee little slaves. If we wanted to eat breakfast, we had tae dae the dusting; if we wanted lunch, we had tae dae the hoovering."

"You killed Kerys because she made you help with the housework?"

"I killed that bitch because she starved me. I'd have happily helped with chores, but it wasnae about that; it was about control, about having power over us. She knew Vince hit us kids when he was drunk or tired, but she never said a word. Just like Pennington. Every day I went to school looking thinner and sadder than the day before. I would roll up my sleeves when bringing my work to his desk, made sure my bruises were on display. He never once asked me about them. He caught me eating out of the bin one day and didn't say a damn thing. He was scared of Vince just like everyone else was. And rather than be an adult and protect me, he protected himself."

The doctor stood and leant towards Dougie. "Do you want to take a break? Leave it for today?"

Dougie shushed him. "Do you know why they sent us to the boxing gym?"

Cooper shook her head. "Exercise?"

He scoffed. "They sent us because it was dirt cheap, and they could have us out of the house for a few hours twice a week. They sent us tae get pummelled because they wanted peace and quiet."

"And that's where you met Ronan?"

"Everyone else made fun of me for being the smallest. They called me Twiggy; I was an easy round of sparring for them. But Ronan, he was one of the big kids – about seventeen – he was kind, gave me pointers, offered to give me some private tuition. Can you see where I'm going?"

She could. "He groomed you."

"The things he did." Dougie showed no emotion as he told his story. His eyes didn't well up; there was no fire in his gaze. His face remained neutral as if he were talking about a show he'd watched on television. A coping mechanism, perhaps. Imagining it happened to someone else and not him. "And I won't be the only one. Drink, please." He took another slurp through closed teeth. "Do some digging. You'll find the others."

"Eve Lynch was your social worker. You killed her. Why?"

"Why do you think? Same reason Pennington made the list. She knew, and she did nowt. Actually, she did worse than nowt. She'd come to the foster home now and again, but I couldnae say owt in front of Vince, not without getting a hiding. She was supposed to come every six weeks but she didnae. Looking back, I know she was young, overworked and underpaid. The department was understaffed, and those who did the work could hardly keep track of the kids on their files. Some cases were shelved for years."

Cooper was confused. He seemed to empathise with Eve Lynch's position and yet killed her anyway.

"By the time I was thirteen, I'd basically become Ronan's toy. Every Monday and Thursday, I was his tae dae whatever he wanted tae. Then one day, I saw Lynch in Asda. Vince and Kerys weren't around, so I knew it was my chance. She didnae even recognise me. I felt like my heart had just been trampled on, but I tried to explain what was going on. I couldnae tell her the worst of it, but she got the idea. I thought this is it, she's going to save me, but then I told her Ronan's name."

Dougie blinked a couple of times. Cooper could see the ends of his fingers twitching in their casts.

"Of course, Mr Golden Gloves was the toast of the town. The son of a businessman, tipped to box in the Commonwealth Games and ready to join the army as an officer. Do you ken what she said? She accused me of trying tae derail a promising young man's career by spreading nasty rumours. How many teenage boys do you know who would make up something like that, DCI Cooper?"

"I don't know any." Cooper felt hot, and her damp clothes stuck to her body. She was sickened.

"I ran away as soon as I could. I went with another boy from Vince's house; he had a cousin over the border who could give us work, cash-in-hand. I lied, telt them I was sixteen, took the first work they offered and never looked back. I moved to Berwick for a bit, but they wanted proper ID and National

384

Insurance and all that shit. I didnae stay long; I couldnae stand folk using my real name when I'd started calling myself Dougie. After I went north again, I felt like I had some control over my life for the first time. I rebuilt myself from scratch. All the manual labour and decent grub, it wasn't long until I didnae even look like Tyrone anymore."

Cooper moved closer to the window and wrenched it open. It only opened a few centimetres, but it was enough to provide her with some fresh air.

"What changed?" she asked. "Like you said, you had a new life. Why come back?"

"I had tae work every day of my life tae try and forget the things that happened to me. Moved further and further north until I got a job at a hotel on Skye. I was still running, hoping the further north I went, the smaller the memories would seem. It worked until I saw his name in the paper: Ronan Turnbull. It was when the Birthday Honours were announced. There was even a picture of him with his arms around some kids from his club. I was almost sick. He was supposed to go to the palace for some garden party, but there was no way I could let that happen. I wasnae Twiggy anymore. I wasnae the scrawny wee boy he used over and over. Ronan Turnbull was not going to meet the bloody Queen of England and live the rest of his life as a hero."

"I really think we should call it a day," Dr Lane announced.

"And I really think you should pipe down," Dougie fired back. "I'm opening up here. It feels cathartic, ye ken?"

Dougie was finally showing some emotion. His voice was tense, and though he couldn't open his mouth, he bared his teeth as he recounted the tale. "I couldnae sleep that night. I went to bed and made a list. Six snakes who only looked out for themselves. I took out five. I'll take that. I don't give a shite if it puts me in prison; it was the right thing tae dae. It was justice. Besides, what can the other prisoners do tae me that hasnae already be done? Losing the use of my legs might be a blessing in disguise. The lawyer tells me I'll get a bottom bunk and access to a special bathroom. No communal showers for me, DCI Cooper. And I'll be assigned a pusher, someone to roll my wheels about for me."

Cooper took in a deep lungful of humid air. "You don't regret any of it, do you? It didn't have to be this way. You could have spoken out. People are coming forward now about past crimes: the film and music industry, the Scouts, the church. It doesn't matter how long ago the abuse took place; it will be investigated these days."

"Aye. *He said, she said*. Nowt would have happened."

"That's not true, Dougie. They didn't have to die. You didn't have the right to make that decision. If you'd come forward and reported what happened, they would have been disciplined or punished in some way."

Even as she said the words, she knew it wasn't true. Lynch and Pennington's crimes were crimes of inaction, and they were both long retired from their previous careers. Even if hearings took place, it wasn't as if they could be struck off from teaching or working in social care. There was a case to be made against Vince and Kerys Rivers, but they'd need others to come forward before they could go to trial. Ronan Turnbull was likely the only one to be arrested and charged. Unfortunately, Cooper knew less than six per cent of reported rapes resulted in a conviction for the perpetrator.

Dougie fixed her with a steely stare. As if reading her mind, he said, "Not a damn thing was done back then and not a damn thing would be done now. No one was going to punish them. Not the way I did. I was a lost boy, neglected by the system, but I'll inspire other lost boys, you'll see. My legacy will live on, and other snakes will be hunted down. You're right; the world is changing. Victims are believed, but only if they have the strength tae say something, tae stand in court and make themselves vulnerable all over again while the world watches. I've shown those who cannae speak out that they can lash out instead. That there's another way to get justice. Everyone who abused a bairn, everyone who knew and did nowt, I want those snakes to hear my story and live in fear. They should go tae bed every night terrified that one of their victims will return. Because, thanks tae me, they will."

- CHAPTER 53 -

THOUGH IT WAS DAYLIGHT, Justin Atkinson switched on the lights in Cooper's bathroom so the extractor fan would kick in. His post-run shower had filled the room with billowy plumes of steam. He'd run a little faster than usual today and his muscles felt heavy. He really needed a cool bath with Epsom salts, but today wasn't about him and his needs: it was about Cooper.

Cooper hadn't given him all the details after her meeting with Douglas Beaumont, but she had told him she feared he'd spark copycats. Copycat killings might be rare, but they weren't the stuff of thrillers or urban legends either; they were real. Some copied fictional crimes. Luka Magnotta was inspired by American Psycho; Thierry Jaradin stabbed a young girl while dressed as Ghostface; John Warnock Hinckley Jr. tried to assassinate Ronald Regan partly due to his obsession with Taxi Driver. But some copied real crimes, especially where media coverage gave notoriety to the perpetrators. Dunblane inspired Port Arthur; Jack the Ripper inspired Derek Brown; Eddie Seda sent cryptic notes to the media just as the Zodiac Killer had. Worst of all, as far as Atkinson was concerned, was the Columbine effect. Sixty-three shootings were alleged to be inspired by the events of April twentieth, 1999. Over two hundred and seventy deaths and almost four-hundred and fifty wounded.

Atkinson hoped Beaumont's actions would spur people to talk about child protection and pursue justice for past crimes. Still, he hoped no one took the law into their own hands the way Dougie had. Most of all, he hoped for a world where neither of those things was necessary, a world where no child suffered abuse or neglect.

He could dream, couldn't he?

Taking a squeegee, Atkinson wiped down the shower screen before drying himself on a teal-coloured towel. He liked Cooper's bathroom. Her place had better water pressure than his, and the room always smelled of something floral. A smart grey suit hung from the hook on the back of the bathroom door. Once dry, he dressed and checked his reflection in the mirror. He was overdressed for taking Cooper to her check-up, but they planned on having lunch after. He'd booked a table at a new Pan-Asian restaurant that had opened in Jesmond. It had good reviews, and he was looking forward to some Sichuan sirloin.

In the afternoon, Atkinson had a conference to attend. Of course, if there were any problems, if the doctors found anything or if Cooper had a panic attack, he would drop the conference in a heartbeat. He was nervous; that's why he'd run so fast that morning. Unfortunately, there was no out-running anxiety.

He returned his Garmin to his wrist then fiddled with a box that housed his favourite cufflinks. They were silver and square, designed to look like two elements from the periodic table. The left had a small number four and the letters Be to represent beryllium. The right showed the number sixty-eight and an Er for erbium. The cuffs were a birthday gift from his sons, and he was ashamed to say it had taken him three years to notice that if he held them together they spelt *beer*.

Atkinson secured erbium into the buttonhole, but he was a butterfingers when nervous and beryllium slipped from his grip. The little square of silver tinkled as it hit the porcelain sink then bounced towards the floor, landing in the bathroom bin.

This is what happens if you don't put your glasses on first, he thought. He knelt down to rifle through the bin. A slither of white caught his attention. He would have left it well alone, but he was a scientist, and curiosity was in his nature. It was hidden well, wrapped in loo roll, then stuffed inside an empty toothpaste box. He would have never noticed it if he hadn't gone looking for the cufflink. *Oh, there you are*. He grabbed the cufflink and put it in his pocket before turning back to the bin. He pulled the white plastic from the paper and turned it over in his hands.

It was a pregnancy test.
It was positive.

COOPER STARED AT HER wardrobe and frowned. She opted for trousers that weren't too snug and a blouse that was easy to take off and put on again multiple times. It was unusual to have follow-up tests nine months after radio and chemotherapy. The usual aftercare involved tests at three and six months, followed by yearly check-ups. Dr McDermott wanted to keep a close eye on Cooper given how young she was when diagnosed and how intense her occupation was. He was a shrewd man, and though Cooper had never said anything, he knew she didn't always take the best care of herself.

On today's agenda were a physical exam, a mammogram, an appointment with a dietician, and a bone mineral assessment. The bone densitometry DXA was a low dose x-ray that diagnosed or assessed a person's risk of osteoporosis. It had been unavailable at her last check-up, but Cooper knew she wouldn't be going ahead with it today either.

There was a thud as the front door closed in its frame.

It was too early for Tina to be leaving for her last week of school, and Julie was still in bed. She hadn't told her mum about today's tests; she knew she'd insist on coming with her and Cooper really only wanted one person there – Atkinson. She opened her bedroom door and looked down the hallway to the bathroom. The bathroom was empty, a few wisps of steam still floating up to the extractor fan, distorting the straight lines between the teal metro tiles on the feature wall. Odd. He knew they'd be leaving straight after breakfast.

Where could he have run off to?

ONCE AGAIN, ATKINSON WAS running. He ran through the streets of Tynemouth in one of his best suits and his most expensive pair of shoes. He must look like a banker late for work or an accountant running from the taxman.

He stopped at a corner to take a deep breath and stretch his calves. Cooper was pregnant. He couldn't believe it. When they'd first got together, she'd explained how her chemotherapy treatment had caused her periods to cease. That they'd come back in time, but she'd be unable to take hormonal contraception. She told him she planned on getting a coil fitted, but with her and Atkinson breaking up in the spring, she mustn't have bothered.

He placed one foot in front of the other and started running, picking up the pace until he was almost sprinting. It all made sense – the tiredness, the tenderness. She'd flinched at his touch a few times, but it wasn't the return of the dreaded C word; it was sensitivity caused by increased blood flow and lactiferous duct growth. *Lactiferous duct growth?* He shook his head as he ran, a slight sweat beginning on his brow and under his arms. Always the bloody scientist.

His boys – the twins – were grown now. They were at Edinburgh University having the time of their lives and doing more carousing than study-ing. While Ellis was failing his undergraduate in infectious diseases, Rowan was spectacularly fail-ing his economics course. You'd think majoring in economics would have taught him not to squan-der the twenty-eight grand he was investing in the course – not counting rent and living expenses – but no, Rowan was a law unto himself.

Atkinson wondered if he was ready, or able, to go through it all again. All the sleepless nights, scraped knees, PTA meetings, school runs, packed lunches, Saturday morning football.

Was he ready for this? Did he want to do this?

COOPER RUMMAGED IN THE back of the fridge and found some yoghurt that hadn't gone bad yet. She paired it with some oats, honey and half a rapidly browning banana. If the dietician asked, she could at least make it sound like she'd had a nutritious breakfast and wasn't surviving on a diet of Star-bucks, pastries and adrenaline.

She sat at the table and thumbed through a leaflet advertising a marine biology summer camp held at the university-run lab at Cullercoats Bay. It might be something Tina would be interested in. She could do with a hobby that didn't involve

Lana or being glued to Josh's side; the pair were still being off with each other as far as Cooper could tell. She'd talk to Tina later; marine biology camp would be right up her street and would fill the void left by Steven the seagull.

The kettle boiled just as Atkinson came bursting through the door. He was a sight. His suit crinkled around the elbow and knee joints, his brow was dripping wet, and his glasses were crooked. Scuff marks painted chalky lines across freshly-polished black shoes, he sounded like he'd just run a marathon, and his face was drained of colour.

"What the hell happened to you?" she said, laughing. "You know we're leaving in…" She checked her watch. "… like five minutes?"

He nodded, breathless. Then from behind his back, he brandished a ginormous bouquet of peach roses, chrysanthemums and snapdragons.

"For you," he said, one hand on the kitchen counter while he composed himself.

Cooper put the leaflet down and took the flowers. "They're beautiful," she said. "But shouldn't we celebrate after we get the all-clear?"

He took her hand. "You're pregnant."

Her mouth fell open. How could he possibly know? She planned on telling him today anyway. That's why she'd insisted they book somewhere for lunch, just the two of them, so they could talk. She was caught off guard having to have the conversation now.

"Erm. Yes. Yes, I am." She touched her stomach, thinking of the tiny life growing inside her. "Is that okay?"

"Okay? It's flipping amazing!" Atkinson scooped her up in his arms and spun around. "I thought you were sick." He put her back down and kissed her lips; she took in his sweet-smelling aftershave. "Why didn't you tell me?"

"I was worried. We've only just got back together, and I wasn't sure at first. I mean, it's very, very early days."

"I guess we weren't as careful as we could have been."

Cooper sighed. "I took a few things for granted when I shouldn't have. It's my fault; I should have—"

"Hey, hey, none of that *it's my fault* nonsense." He had a great big dumb grin on his face. He looked like an excited Labrador. "I'm thrilled. Are you?"

An equally silly grin spread over Cooper's face. She had a billion concerns and questions. She was fretting about her health, her job, her daughter and her mother. But yes, she was happy.

She was really, truly happy.

"I am. But, how did you know?" She cast her eyes downward and examined her waist. "I can't possibly be showing yet."

"I found the test. You hid it pretty well. I mean, you are a CID detective. You would know how to cover your tracks after dealing with so many criminals." He finally sorted his glasses out so they weren't lopsided and lifted his palms defensively. "I wasn't snooping. I dropped a cufflink in the bin." He glanced at his sleeves where only one cuff was secured by a cufflink. "Oh, it must still be in my pocket. Guess I got distracted."

Cooper frowned. "But I took the test at work. I came out of the toilets and bumped straight into one of the new DCs. I was a mess. My face was flushed and I looked completely unprofessional—"

She thought back to sitting in the cubicle, coming out with tears in her eyes and Saffron Boyd assuming she'd been upset about her father's passing.

"No," Atkinson said. "It was upstairs in the bathroom bin." He pointed to the ceiling. "It was wrapped in loo roll and stuffed in a toothpaste box."

There was a pause while they both stared at each other. Then the sound of footsteps padding into the kitchen caused them to turn their heads towards the door.

Tina didn't look up as she dropped her textbook-laden school bag onto a chair and filled the toaster with four thick slices of brown bread. When she turned to look at Cooper and Atkinson, they both wore the same expression: heads tilted left, mouths open like confused goldfish.

"What? I'm famished."

"Sit down, Tina," Cooper said. She pulled a seat away from the kitchen table, its legs squeaking against the tiled floor.

Cooper's mind raced. She was unable to comprehend what was happening. It didn't make sense; Tina was on the pill. She had put up a very convincing argument about taking contraception earlier in the year. But whilst Tina was disciplined to military levels with some activities, she could be scatterbrained and unfocused in others. If she'd missed a pill or two— Cooper's mind whizzed back to the flight - turbulence, a rude air steward, and Tina throwing up.

If she and Josh had— Oh, no.

Their awkwardness, their hushed conversations, Tina's sudden dislike of seafood.

Cooper was worried about becoming a mother again. Was she really about to become a grand-mother?

DCI Cooper will return

- Message from the Author -

Dear reader,

If you've enjoyed hanging out with Cooper and Tennessee (or even if you haven't!), please consider writing a review on Amazon or Goodreads.

You can find out the latest news and behind the scenes information, and sign up for my newsletter at betsybaskerville.com.

If you'd like to connect with me online, I can be found on Facebook (B Baskerville - Author).

Speaking of dogs, I'd like to thank those of you who entered the competition to have your dog featured in Northern Roulette. It was a tough choice, and I wish I could have written more dogs into the plot to accommodate all the entries. In the end, it was Fflei - AKA - Fleabag, whom I could picture accompanying Charles Pennington on walks around Holy Island on chilly, blustery mornings.

Thank you to the lovely Amanda and Jane for reading an early draft of Northern Roulette and for being such great friends to me in the dojo. You ladies are two of the nicest face-punchers I've ever met!

Thanks also need to go to Mama and Papa Baskerville, who drove me and a very squirmy pooch to Lindisfarne to take the photo for the cover of Northern Roulette. If you'd like to read more about how I created the cover, please visit my website.

Speaking of the cover, do you recognise the tall, mysterious man walking towards Lindisfarne Castle? That's my partner - Rob. Is he portraying Tennessee, the handsome detective who's always there when Cooper needs him? Or is he our strong, obsessive perpetrator, making his way to Cove's Haven to enact retribution? You decide.

- ABOUT THE AUTHOR -

Born and raised in Newcastle upon Tyne, Betsy often refers to herself as *an author by day and a ninja by night*. If she's not writing, she can be found working up a sweat in the dojo.

Aside from kicking things, Betsy loves walking her Welsh terrier, sailing, eating absurd amounts of food, watching UFC and reading crime fiction.

As well as the DCI Cooper series, she has written stand-alone novels The Only Weapon In The Room and Dead In The Water.

Milton Keynes UK
Ingram Content Group UK Ltd.
UKHW020335130924
1618UKWH00004B/117